An Author's Love

Jai Baker

Table of Contents

Chapter One

Kate peered at the blue-and-white stick. Brown eyes, anxious with worry, were now bright with surprise as she gazed at the window on the blue and white bar—PREGNANT.

Kate had been sick for days, but since September, she surmised she was coming down with the flu until her co-worker brought sushi for lunch, making her stomach heave queasily, that Kate dashed for the restroom. Shaken, she left work early to stop at the local pharmacy. Walking down the aisle, Kate stopped where they sold birth control and condoms, and… she noticed the home pregnancy kits on neat shelves. Her stomach twisted as she scanned the wide variety of test kits. Kate forced herself to choose one.

And now, in the bathroom of her apartment within the bed-and-breakfast inn, she called home for the last few months, facing a life-changing event. She stepped out of the bathroom into the small hallway, her eyes distant, dreamy, as she stopped in her tiny kitchen.

I'm… Kate looked down at herself at the elegant white blouse she still wore from work; her flat stomach seemed to have given her grief just hours before. For not having an appetite this morning, now empty, its grumblings had a whole new meaning. She was with child.

Her breathing was the only sound in the still room as Kate placed a hand on her abdomen with wonder and curiosity. Warmth filled her chest, coursing her body down to her toes, bringing life into them as her mind repeated the sentence. She gazed out the window at the afternoon sky and smiled.

"I have to tell, Nolan."

Nolan Roth stared outward to the grand expanse of his backyard with a smile as he admired the evergreen forest surrounding his three-story mansion. The day was perfect, as if taken from a scene from a classic book, despite the summer. Because, in five hours, he would see her. His smile lifted as he thought of Kate after being away for a business trip: signing deals and shaking hands with clients whom he called partners in the world of commerce.

Nolan climbed the ladder, starting small with an idea. He grew with his blood, sweat, and tears until he became the state's first and youngest self-made millionaire.

But to the folks of Forest-Bend, he was just Nolan. Kind, helpful, friendly, and generous. Who adopted him when the city life grew too confining, and he needed a place where Nolan wasn't revered.

He pushed away his black bangs, his mind still on the woman who had brought a smile to his face since he met her six months ago. It had been a typical day. The Easter holiday passed, and the promise of spring was right around the corner.

When he saw her.

Nolan had run errands in town, talking merrily to a few friends; Kate struggled to lift a large box into the back of her minivan: a new face amongst so much old. He hurried to help her. He remembered her surprised face when she saw him, her brown eyes widening with gratitude as together they lifted the heavy box into her trunk.

He could see Kate's shy smile to this day.

"Th-thank you."

Nolan nodded, smiling, getting a good look at the pretty woman with long black hair and eyes that sparkled in the sun. "It's a lot for you to take on by yourself."

"I don't mind," Kate replies. "I want to make an impression on my boss."

He nodded. "I have never seen you before."

"I just moved here three days ago and, Oh! — I'm sorry!" She outstretched her right hand. "I'm Kate."

Nolan smiles as he lifted his hand. "I'm Nolan. Nice to meet you, Kate."

Nolan walked down the hall, thinking of the plans for the evening with Kate. The doorbell rang.

That's strange. Kate isn't supposed to be here until eight. He pondered this, not that he minded seeing her. He hurried downstairs, and his heart lifted. Excitement had Nolan flinging open the door. His throat went dry. His heartbeat fluttered with anticipation and turned to shock. He stepped back. "*Camille!*"

॰

Kate drove quietly down a winding road, focusing on what was before her. Her mind was a whirl of emotions about the day's events, making her feel apprehensive about telling Nolan of her recent discovery: she, Kate, was with child.

How would Nolan react to this? They had only known each other for half a year: six months spent with whispered conversations under the stars of their dreams, her hopes, and his accomplishments. The business he started on his own and the stories she worked on, hoping to become a published author. Kate talked to Nolan daily ever since she got his number.

3

It wasn't until a month into their friendship did Nolan asked Kate out to dinner. Nervous at first, Kate hesitated on his offer; she was unsure if she should accept. It wasn't until she walked through the town's stores that she saw a beautiful red dress displayed in a boutique. Kate called Nolan, her stomach full of butterflies as she tells him, 'Yes.'

Butterflies were in her stomach when Kate turned into the driveway of a white mansion, darkening against the setting sun—breathing in deeply to calm the nerves and surprise igniting within her.

When Nolan said he had a surprise for me. Kate thought. *I didn't expect it would be his giant mansion.* Kate half-smile, half grimaced as her nerves made her stomach twist. She killed the engine, placing a hand upon her stomach and, looked warily at the house.

What other secrets are you hiding from me? She thought wryly, remembering when he had surprised her with an invitation to his home. Kate had assumed he lived in the city since his job was located. Kate checked her reflection in the rear-view mirror, brushing her hair to look neat before unbuckling her seat belt and opening the door to a warm September evening. Crickets chirped as Kate walked on gravel, her shoes crunching on stone as her eyes traveled to the large door. She rang the bell. A loud trill echoed from within.

Kate's eyes wandered from the manicured bushes to the large fountain that burbled happily. She couldn't help but smile at Nolan's guile when the front door revealed a middle-aged woman.

"Yes, may I help you?" she asks.

"Good evening, ma'am," Kate says. "I'm sorry to bother you, but I'm here to see Nolan."

"Nolan?"

"Yes. Nolan invited me to come here. I—this is where Nolan lives?" Kate started to feel nervous that she was in the wrong house.

"No, this is Allen Roth's house." Said a woman, Kate realized was a maid, who eyed her up and down. "Who are you?"

"Oh, I'm sorry." Kate lifted a hand. "I'm Kate Alma." The woman didn't shake her hand; instead, she said.

"What is your business here?" Kate blinked at the maid's accusatory tone; she stammered.

"N-Nolan invited me to his home yesterday," Kate lowered her hand, placing it in her middle. "I... I have something important to tell him." The maid nodded once, then opened the door fully.

"Please come in," she says respectfully. Kate obeyed with a "Thank you" before gaping at the ample space. It was as big as the bed-and-breakfast she was staying in. Kate stared in awe at the large staircase that led to who knew where.

"This way, please." Kate started, waking up from her ogling.

"Yes, of course." Kate followed the maid down a great hall until coming to a stop at a large sliding door. The maid pushed it to the side, revealing to Kate a beautiful parlor with two matching maroon sofas that she sat down to the maid's instruction.

"I will get, Mr. Roth." She says before leaving the room. Kate stared in awe at the room, amazed by Nolan's taste in fine arts and brands.

He never strikes me as tasteful. Kate thought, looking down at her palms. *I thought I knew Nolan, but he still surprises me.* She smiled wistfully, thinking of her child. *I hope he will like the surprise I have for him.* The sound of fast footsteps made

Kate look up, rising to her feet, quickly hiding her concern with a smile as the door slid apart, revealing a breathless Nolan.

"Nolan." She breathes. Nolan didn't respond as he entered. He turned his back on her to slide the door behind him with his hands. When he turned, his eyes were wide with emotion Kate had never seen before.

"What are you doing here?!" Kate blinked, taking a step forward.

"You invited me to your home, remember?" Kate spoke. She was surprised to hear the accusation in his voice.

"You invited me for movie night and—"

"Kate," Nolan spoke in a low voice. "You have to leave." Kate started in surprise.

"L-Leave? B-but—"

"You can't be here, Kate." Nolan took a deliberate step, his face hard. "You should have never come!" Kate looked at him, shocked, hurt.

"You invited me, Nolan." She says. "If you didn't want me to come, you should have called and canceled our date—"

"Shh!" Nolan stepped forward, grasping both her arms.

"N-Nolan!"

"You can't be here, Kate!" he spoke, voice fierce, but his face looked scared.

"I-I had to see you!" Kate gasps, looking at him fearfully. "N-Nolan, what's wrong? Y-you're scaring me!"

"Why did you come here?" he demands.

"I needed to tell you something important." Kate gasps. "N-Nolan! Y-You're hurting me!" Nolan let go, stepping back as if Kate was made of acid. Lifting a hand, he pushed back his hair. Kate noticed he was trembling.

6

"Nolan?" she breathes. Nolan groaned; letting go of his hair, he laid his hand on his face. Kate took a hesitant step forward. "Nolan, wh-what's wrong?" Nolan didn't respond; he just looked at her with one eye that looked wild. "Please tell me what's wrong?" As she looked at Nolan, Kate felt tears in her eyes. "If something is wrong, let me help you. I… If something happened, you could have called me. I wouldn't be upset, but… something happened today, and I couldn't wait to tell you."

"What is it?" Kate saw Nolan; his hand pulled from his face as he stared at her; the look he gave her made her look down sheepishly.

"I'm pregnant," Kate whispered.

Silence filled the room with sudden cold.

"Y-You're what…?" Kate looked up slowly, her expression somber.

"*I'm pregnant.*" She repeated. Nolan didn't answer, just stared at Kate.

"I… I just found out today," Kate spoke. "I hadn't been feeling well this past week, and I…" she shrugged halfheartedly. "I was going to tell you, I…" she trailed off.

"*Kate.*" Nolan breathes. Kate placed a hand on her middle.

"I'm sorry," Kate whispered. "I… I'll leave."

"Nolan!" Kate started at the unfamiliar voice. She saw Nolan stiffen just as the door slid open, revealing a tall woman with creamy pale skin, blond hair, and green eyes, carrying a baby with her same complexion and… the woman looked at Kate, first seeing this stranger in her lovely abode. Her face frowned.

"Who are you?" she demands. Kate had no answer. Her eyes were wide as she stared at the beautiful woman. Nolan looked down, unable to look at Kate, who turned to look at him, stunned.

"Nolan." She whispers.

"Nolan!" the woman spoke just as the baby lifted her tiny arms and cooed. Pain crossed her features, her throat tightened, her body heavy, and her heart... Kate ran out of the room, leaving a slight breeze past Nolan and... *His wife.*

Chapter Two

"SHE'S PREGNANT!" Camille screeched. Nolan nodded dumbly. Camille stood over him where he sat on the parlor sofa, where for the past hour, Nolan told her about what he had been doing while she was away. She glared at him, her arms crossed over her gold sequin blouse. "So, while I was away with our child, you decided to make another!"

"That's not what I was doing," Nolan mumbles.

"Oh," her voice was snarky. "So, you decided to take up a mistress, have your way with her until I get back because you were bored!"

"It's not like that!" Nolan glared at her. "she wasn't a woman I was having fun with; she… she's…" he trailed off.

"She's what? A mistress? A home wrecker?" Camille's face twisted into a sneer. "A slut."

"Don't call her that!" Nolan was on his feet, his eyes blazing. "She is none of those things, Kate's…" he didn't continue.

"There you go again, saying but never finishing. Keeping secrets."

"This isn't what I wanted, Camille," Nolan spoke shortly. "I didn't think. I didn't know she could get…." Nolan trailed off, knowing how foolish he sounded.

"Get pregnant!" Camille finished with a sneer. "So, how did you think that happened? You trip naked and fell on top of her?"

"That's not what I meant." He murmurs, looking away.

"What then?" he didn't answer. "What? Don't tell me it was an early mid-life crisis?! You were bored with your old wife." He looked at her.

"You know that's not it at all." He stepped forward. "Camille, you know how much I care about you. You're my wife, the mother of my child. I would do nothing to hurt you." He lifted his hand to touch Camille's shoulder, but she pulled away angrily.

"If that's true, then why did you do it?"

"I…" Nolan paused.

Kate smiled. Her long lashes fluttered as she looked at him tenderly, her head tilting up as her lips pressed warm and soft against his.

"I don't know," Nolan confesses. "I can't give you a definite answer; she was just so… Nice. I guess I wanted to be with someone who was—

"Naïve?"

"No. Someone who could take charge."

"You mean to tell me that a 5'4, 110lb woman controlled you to have sex with her?" Nolan looked away.

"You're putting words in my mouth, Camille." He grumbled.

"So, she seduced you?" she asks. Nolan looked at her.

"No. I did." Camille stared at him for a long time. Nolan looked down. He let out a breath.

"I want to work this out, Camille." He breathes. "I want our marriage to work out. When we never fought when Esme was born. I want us to be a family."

"But you said it yourself," Camille spoke. "Before I left, you said we were never a family. We were only together because we were 'conforming' that there would never be a nuclear family." Nolan winced.

"You're right." He looked at her. "I did say that. My words were cruel, and they cost me my child and you. I didn't realize how much I wanted a family until you left with Esme. My world was empty. I wanted you back. I…"

Kate took his hand, looking at him with sleepy eyes under the moonlight. "I love you."

Nolan stepped forward, lifting his hand; he placed it on her shoulder. This time, Camille didn't flinch.

"I love you, Camille," Nolan spoke. "I want us to be a family. I want to be a father to Esme. I want to be a good husband to you. If you let me."

Camille stared at him for a long time, her green eyes distrustful but full of yearning. Nolan saw she still wanted him.

"Would you do anything for me?" she spoke, voice low, impassive.

"Yes, of course. Whatever it is. Counseling. Keeping tabs on me, anything!"

"That's not what I mean, Nolan." She pulled back, letting his hand fall. "I need to know I can trust you. What you say tonight holds value. Whatever happens in the weeks to come. You won't betray me."

"I swear, Camille," Nolan replies. Something twisted in his stomach, and for an instant, he wondered why that was, but he continued.

"You and Esme are my main priority."

Camille smiles but didn't touch her eyes.

"I know you will."

Chapter Three

Kate leaned over the toilet and retched. Her stomach heaved, emptying the contents that were her morning meal. Kate raised her head weakly as she stared at the pink bathroom. Morning sickness was in full swing for the new mother as Kate lifted a hand and pulled down the toilet level, washing away the bile.

The sound was strangely soothing as she rose to her feet shakily before going to the sink. Kate washed her mouth, swishing water before spitting out acidic bile. Her eyes trailed up to see her reflection, shocked by her appearance. Had it been only three days ago she was packing away returned books to their proper shelves? She had been unwell all day, but her mind was still giddy at the prospect of seeing… Kate's hand fell to her stomach. She looked down; a sad smile crept at the corner of her lips.

Nolan.

What am I going to do? She thought as she stepped out of the bathroom, her mind numb with weariness and… he was not the man she thought he was. Kate closed her eyes, which stung painfully as she stood in the narrow hallway.

A knock made Kate jump, breaking her trance. Letting go of her middle, she walked toward the door and opened it.

"Mrs. Roth!" Kate gasps. Camille stood on the other side of the door, her face expressionless. Still, her eyes shone as she took in Kate's disheveled appearance. "U-Um, what are you doing here?!" Kate's voice was meek as she stared at the powerful woman.

"May I come in?" Camille spoke coolly.

"Y-yes, of course." Kate opened the door, moving to the side to let Camille enter. Kate could not help noticing the sneer on her face as she looked around, taking in the small kitchen where she stood. Kate closed the door and walked forward.

"M-may I help you?" Kate asks. Camille looked at her before smirking.

"You look like you had a rough morning." She says, not kindly. Kate looked down at herself; her gray shirt was wrinkled and wet with water. Kate raised her head.

"I'm fine," she replies calmly. "It's nothing I can't handle."

"Yes. Nothing beats carrying the child of an ex-lover who is married." Kate winced, looking down. Shame and betrayal warmed her sallow cheeks.

"Yes," Kate spoke. She lifted her head to face Camille, face ashen. "Mrs. Roth, I'm so sorry for what happened. I never knew that Nolan, Mr. Roth, was married to you. I believed he was—" Camille lifted a hand, and Kate fell silent.

"You seem to know a lot about my husband."

"No, ma'am, far from it I—"

"You call him, Nolan," Camille replies, her expression darkening. "But you didn't know his first name was Allen." This surprised Kate; seeing her expression, Camille smiled smugly.

"What else did he tell you? Did he tell you of his daughter, Esme? His pride and joy? Did he tell you he flew around the world while you were just a high schooler?"

She stepped forward, voice growing languid. "Did Allen tell you he is the richest man in the state? Forbes ranked him: top ten multimillionaires in the U.S?" Kate stared at her for a long time, shocked by her words.

13

She looked down.

"No," Kate replies quietly. "he never said that to me. All he told me was that he was a successful businessman. He told me of his hopes, dreams, and fears…" She let out a shaky breath. "His love."

A pause.

"He really fooled you." Kate looked up to see a cruel smile on Camille's lovely face.

"Excuse me?"

"Nolan is good at convincing people. It is why he is so liked. This town treats him the way he does because he can do it. He has this town in the palm of his hands and why he could string you along with his quote-unquote: 'Dreams, his fears.'" Camille adds snidely. Kate felt she was smacked in the face.

"I know what he told me. Nol-Allen, would never li—

"He lied. He was single." Kate froze.

"*He did*," she agrees. "And no amount of remorse can express how truly sorry I am for hurting you and your family, especially your child." As she said this, she placed a hand on her belly. "No amount of apologizing can undo what I've done, but I am sorry, I truly am. I want to move past this. Just me and my child."

"Funny you should bring up children," Camille spoke as if Kate didn't voice her regret and shame. "You see, we can't let this get out that you're pregnant with Nolan's child. This is a very provincial town, and gossip carries fast." As Camille said this, she went into her Louis Vuitton purse.

"I won't tell anyone, Mrs. Roth. This secret I wish to keep—"

14

"That's good. We both agree on something. Other than the fact you're a home wrecker." Kate gaped at her, shocked. "That's why I'm here. My husband takes pride in fine things, as do I. We don't want this mishap blotting our happy home, that is why…" Camille laid a thick white envelope on the counter and slid it to Kate.

"What's this?" Kate asks, picking it up with suspicion. Camille smiled without humor.

"That, my dear, is 17,000 dollars. Call it recompense. For the pain; you've been through."

"Pain?" Kate looked up, stunned by the money, even as confusion crossed her face. "I'm not in pain, Mrs. Roth. I feel—

"But you will be. After the abortion."

Kate froze.

"Y-you want me to what?" Camille looked at her.

"Well, you must know? You can't have his child. He already has one. Allen doesn't need stress with a mistress, much less a bastard." Camille prattled on, but it fell on deaf ears as the two words fell like stones in a hollow well. Kate stared at the rich, powerful beauty, no… She was powerful, but Kate didn't see her as beautiful. In her eyes, she was ugly…

"It's for the best," Camille continues. "no one would know you're pregnant. It's still early." She eyed Kate's middle. "Besides, everyone wins. Allen gets his family, I get my husband, and you can do whatever you do at your book job." Her face turned condescending.

"You want me to kill it?" Kate's voice was low. Camille looked at her as if she was a foolish child.

"Oh, they don't feel a thing at this stage."

15

"But I will!" Kate looked at her face, contorted with passion. "I will feel every moment."

"That's what the money is for. It won't be easy, but you'll move on."

"You call my baby a mishap!" Kate screamed. She stepped forward angrily. "You think having his child is a blot on your empire! It's all about you, about Nolan's reputation." She glared at the woman with revulsion.

"I don't know what Nolan told you about me, and I don't care. But my baby," she clasped her middle. "My child won't be killed for your wants, Camille. I won't do the procedure."

Camille stared at the woman like a fly on the wall.

Bothersome…Insignificant.

"You mean to tell me you'll have his child?" she says, testing the words. Her hands clenched into a fist.

"Nolan doesn't want this baby. Neither do you," Kate's eyes narrowed, fists clenched. "But it's not for you both to decide. *It's mine.*"

"You would hurt my marriage for a fling." Camille's face twisted into something ugly. "A so-called make-believe romance that you two shared your secrets, hopes, and *dreams.*" Camille stepped forward.

"You are as pathetic as you are naïve," she spoke menacingly. "Because *I know* Nolan's dreams, his desires, his *love.*" She hisses the word love. "*And it's not you.*" Kate glared at her.

"Get out!" she commands. "I want you out! Take your money. I won't be a part of your wicked ways." She shoved the money at her. Camille stepped back with a cruel smile.

"So be it then." Camille lifted her fist…

And punched herself in the face!

Kate gaped at the woman, who hit her face, dropping the envelope. Camille stepped back as she punched, slapped, and…

"What are you doing!?"

"Help!" Camille screamed. "Please, someone get her off me!" she scratched her arm and slapped her face. Kate, stunned by this, leaped forward for Camille.

"Stop this!" Kate screamed. "Wh-why are you—!"

"AAAAAHHHH" Camille cries.

BOOM!

Kate turned at the sound of wood breaking! She gasped when she saw the Forest-Bend sheriffs step forward. Seeing the commotion, she was knocked back before Kate could pull away or explain herself. Kate felt her body shoved roughly to the corner, her arms pulled back, and she cried out with pain and shock. Voices echoed around her as Kate turned her head to see an officer go over to Camille, demanding what happened. Camille responded in broken accents; to Kate's shock, she saw her sobbing, pointing a trembling finger at…

"She attacked me!" Kate's world crumbled as she stared at what was happening around her, hearing the false statements of assault and the cruel, untrue words brought to her ears. Kate would have collapsed to her knees, but the brute strength of the officer holding her down wouldn't let her. Kate felt something cold and heavy on her wrist. She heard the click as it tightened her wrist. She knew what was happening.

"No!" she screamed. "You can't do this! She's lying! I didn't—!"

"You have the right to remain silent! Anything you say can…" the sheriff read out her rights. Still, it fell on deaf ears as she was carried out of her

17

room, protesting her innocence while being led down the hall to onlookers who heard the commotion. They now looked at the woman being carried away in sobs, protesting in broken accents.

"I'm pregnant!"

Kate was led outside to even more onlookers and bed-and-breakfast patrons. She saw with blurry eyes people, some of whom she once called friends, looked at her with shock while others started whispering amongst themselves. The door to the cruiser opened, and she pleaded to the unsympathetic officers one last time, but to no avail.

"Duck your head." Ordered the officer. Kate obeyed. She felt her body bend to fit comfortably into the cramped back. Kate lowered her head when the door was closed. She didn't look up when the officers entered the driver's side and started the car, nor did she look up when she felt the car's movement as it drove away from the inn.

಄

Kate threw up in her jail cell toilet as soon as she was brought inside. Her stomach heaved empty, causing her to dry heave so terribly with tremors that officers had to come in with a doctor to calm her. Kate was later given a pregnancy test and answered questions about her medical history. She responded with weary responses, her mind still unable to process that she was in prison for a crime she never committed.

The doctor came back soon after and confirmed she was pregnant. When they ask who the father was, Kate begs to use the phone, stating: "It was an emergency!" It took hours, but she was given her phone call. Kate dialed the number she memorized in her head once she entered the jail. Her one salvation to all of this.

"Hello?" Kate's eyes welled up with tears when she heard his voice.

"N-Nolan!" she gasps.

"K-Kate!"

"N-Nolan! Y-you have to help me!" There was a long pause; she could hear noises in the background. "Wh-where are you? Nolan!? Are you there?"

"I'm here!" His voice lowered; it was no longer surprising but a slow boil. "I'm at the hospital."

"Hospital?! B-but wh—" Kate remembered. "Oh, no."

"What do you want, Kate?" he demands. Kate was surprised by the sharpness in his voice. "Can you hear I don't have time for this? I shouldn't be talking to you after what you've done!!" Kate was stricken.

"Nolan," she spoke. "you have to believe me! I did nothing to your wife. Please, it's a misunder—she came to the inn and…"

"I know. Camille told me everything." Nolan's voice grew hard. "She also said how you punched her in the face when she offere—"

"I didn't punch her!" Kate screamed. "I don't know what she told you, but you have to believe me. I didn't do this! She said things about me an—"

"So, you hit her?! It's because of you, Camille needs stitches on her arm and—

"I didn't hurt her!" she screamed.

"Then who did!?"

"She did! Camille did this to her—"

"Don't you dare say that about my wife!" Nolan growled. "She would never do this to herself!"

"But she did, Nolan!" Kate sobs. "I know you don't believe me, but you know me! I would never harm anyone without meaning to!"

19

"But you did. You hurt my wife to get me!" Nolan snarls. "Just as I want to make things right with my family, you come attack the most important thing to me." Kate froze. Her eyes welled up with the words he once said about her as they lay in bed. Just two warm bodies alone, except for the millions of stars. Kate felt her heart shatter, even as her love for Nolan crumbled in her chest.

"Nolan, please," she breathes. "I know you hate me. I'm sorry for what happened, but I need you... your child needs you. I need help; they put me in jail. I don't have the money to make bail. I... I need you." A pause. Kate waited with bated breaths, listening to Nolan's breathing.

"Stay out of my life, Kate." he spoke, his voice hard, curt. "you are never to call this number again. If you so much as come near my family or me, I'll have you jailed." Kate, desperate, pleads.

"Nolan, please don't do this! I love you!"

"Goodbye, Kate." He says.

"Nolan!"

Nolan hung up.

Kate screamed into the dead phone as tears spilled down her cheeks. Officers came to find Kate on the floor. They pulled Kate out of the hallway to her struggles until she was led back to her cell, where Kate collapsed in broken sobs onto the lumpy bed.

Chapter Four

Kate spent four days in the Forest-Bend jail. She ate little and slept just the same; her body felt weak with strain; the memory of the phone call rang in her mind of Nolan's cruel words, his choice to believe his wife only to throw her away like an old rag doll. A small part of her mind tried to think that Nolan would help her clear her name. But it was overtaken by the grief and betrayal for what he had done to her. Kate looked up when she heard metal pull back. She stared glassy-eyed as the sheriff looked at her face professional as he spoke.

"*You're free to go!*" Kate blinked slowly as the words sank in.

"*I…*" she croaked, voice hoarse with disuse. "*I'm free?*" she could not believe it, even in her ears. She rose from her bed involuntarily to stare at the cop with a wary expression. He nodded.

"You've stayed here long enough." He says, nodding at the cell. "Time to return to society."

"B-But how?" Kate was too glad to be free of her prison, but she was still distrustful.

"What about bail?" she asks, stepping forward. "Wh-wasn't a $3000 bail on—"

"Someone paid your bail." Kate blinked; she was out of the cell, and the officer shut the door behind her. The bang made her cringe at the sound. The sheriff gestured to her before walking the hall. Kate followed warily, but her mind was full of questions.

"Paid?" she spoke. "By whom?" Kate didn't make many friends in the town, much fewer close friends who would be so generous.

"It was Mr. Roth." Kate stopped in her tracks. The officer stopped to turn to look at her.

"M-Mr. Roth!" Kate gasps, her eyes widening. The officer scowled but nodded.

"He came and paid for your bail." Kate stared at him, shocked.

"B-But what about…" her mind raced with a hundred questions. "Are they going to press charges? What about the doctor? Does he have my test result? Is Nolan here?" The sheriff looked annoyed as she asked so many questions.

"Look, lady, I'm just here to take you to the front desk." He says. "If you want answers, ask them." She nodded sadly, but hope rose within her for the first time in days.

Kate's hope quickly extinguished when she got the answer to her questions.

Kate's lab results returned negative, relieved that the child she carried was healthy, but the worse news came afterward. Kate's face fell when she learned Nolan had come last night and paid for her bail, but crestfallen she didn't get to see him. Knowing, he was so close. It didn't help that although she was free, the Roth's had summoned a restraining order against Kate. Stating that she was a danger to Nolan's wife and child.

Heartache crushed Kate, not even when the sheriff announced Camille would not press charges. The female officers gave Kate her phone and clothes in a gray bag with a frown before she stepped outside the town; staring wearily at the empty overcast morning, before taking a breath, she walked out into the gray dawn.

 formula

Thunder loomed as streetcars honked. Rain pelted like pebbles on thin, dirty glass. Kate didn't notice the storm. The walls and roof protected her from the elements of nature. But not from the cruelty of mankind. Kate stared. Glassy eyes bloodshot from the hours of tears that pooled down her exhausted face. Sad, brown irises replaced once bright with inspiration and fantasy were full of pain and grief as she sat alone in her new room, staring at sheeting rain through the grubby low-end motel just outside the town she once called home.

Kate immediately raced to the bed-and-breakfast inn. Harsh whispers and glares greeted her from the patrons, who witnessed her shame upon entering. She went to her room to find the door blocked off. When she inquired about it; returning with flush cheeks downstairs to the guests' jeers; the owner eyeing her with disdain and anger, replies "**Were in back!**" When Kate demanded why, for she still paid for the room, the old matron's owner retorted.

"*You've caused a great commotion, scaring away our guests!*" Kate stunned and hurt when the owner added. "*We don't want service from someone who causes violence on good people!*" Kate walked to the back of the inn, where she found her stuff in large black industrial bags. She breathed with silent relief, seeing her notebooks and folders still intact. They didn't steal her prized items in their haste. They didn't care about her belongings. Kate was disgraced even worse when she left the inn; not wanting to be blamed and kicked out or sent back to jail. Kate thanked the owner, but the woman retorted scornfully.

"Your thanks are not welcome here. You are never to step forth in my inn again!" Kate left with a heavy heart with her few belongings and the laughter of the patrons behind her back.

Kate didn't fair better.

Her phone died at the prison, causing her to purchase a new charger. As it charged, she received more devastating news when she heard a message that she was fired from the library after news traveled about the incident. Kate drove to the library and met with cold stares from her coworkers and glares from her boss, who led Kate to the back; displeasure on her face as she told Kate, adding that she was not to apply for a job with the library.

"You're welcome to visit. But don't stay too long, or you will disrupt our readers." Heat rose in Kate's cheeks, but she nodded wordlessly before leaving with her check.

Kate watched the world go by in front of her. Seeing the passing cars not blocked by parked cars. Her eyes roamed dully to the large sign of the motel that illuminated outside; she looked down at her bags that she had picked at; doing inventory, making sure everything accounted for: She hadn't brought many things from New York, just clothes, shoes, writing supplies, and her treasures that were safe and sound in her safe box.

The owners tossed everything in their hurry; taking only her portable charger and laptop. Thank goodness she saved her documents on her flash-drive inside the box next to Kate's thigh. Kate lowered her head, wrapping an arm around herself despite the unseasonable weather. She felt cold in the warm room.

What am I going to do? She thought. The days' weight lay across her like a heavy blanket. Everything and everyone she knew was against her: she had no job, no home, no friends, or family; it was her, and… Kate's hand landed on her flat stomach. *Three weeks.* She was three weeks into the first trimester. Nothing had changed in her outward appearance, but Kate knew deep down…

Something was happening.

Kate felt a moment of comfort. Yes, she was alone, an outcast to society; by the townsfolk, she thought her companions.

But despite her loneliness, Kate wasn't alone. Her child needed her; her child, who didn't ask for this, would undergo isolation and scrutiny with narrowed eyes and whispered sneers about her conception.

"She will be an outcast," Kate murmured. "*Just like me.*" She thought back to what Camille says about rebuilding her family; of Nolan's reputation being ruined if the town found out about Kate and their…

Kate shuddered at the word.

"No," she whispers. Once upon a time, Kate believed she would raise her child with her beloved, hold his hand, lean down, and kiss her with his gentle passion. His love.

"*Naïve fantasies.*"

Kate stiffened but clasped her hand protectively on the flat of her stomach.

"*I promise*," Kate spoke. "*I **swear**. That you will have a good life." She looked up at the sheeting rain. "Even if I have to work with you on my back for months. I will give you the best life this world offers." Kate smiles. "This town is beautiful. It's home to me now, even if no one accepts me." She frowned, even as her eyes stung with tears.

"Even if they don't accept me. I will do whatever it takes to give you a normal life, a happy childhood." Tears spilled onto her cheek, down to her hand. Kate cried, cleansing her body of grief and heartache: she was on her own. No one would be there to counsel or give her advice; she had no one to laugh with or lovers to kiss. It was only Kate.

Kate lifted the safe box onto her lap, lifting the top. She smiled sadly at the items. Her gaze lastly traveled to an old gold watch that winked in the lamp's light. Kate gazed sadly at it.

"I'm sorry, daddy." She breathes. "I know how much this watch meant to you, but… I have a family to raise now." She pressed the gold piece to her forehead, closing her eyes; resolve sparked within Kate for the first time in days.

"*I know what I have to do.*"

Chapter Five

Wood groaned as Kate pushed the heavy door. Dust and cobwebs fell as she heaved, glancing down to see debris had been blocking the door until she could finally step inside with a long-sounding *creak*! Sunlight entered behind Kate as she stepped into the dusty, gray room. To her surprise, she saw on her left a table on its side; brown kitchen cabinets stood along with the counter, and the sink was still intact, albeit covered in grime.

She looked away from the kitchen to look at what she assumed was the living room that too was messy. Dust covered the small coffee table as Kate stepped forward, kicking up dust on the hardwood; she walked to a sheet-covered sofa which she pulled back, revealing a perfectly intact black leather sofa.

"At least the sofa is all right." She muses. A cough made her turn to see the Realtor. His face scrunched in a grimace.

"Sorry," Kate spoke; she glanced around the room. "You say this is the cheapest home in town." The man nodded.

"It's the best we have. It's a twenty-minute drive to downtown and eight minutes to the town." Kate nodded slowly. "It's going to take much work. The last tenants had moved out quickly, so no one bothered to pack their furniture." He nodded at the living room.

"This place has hot and cold water but no heat, so you'll have to use an electric heater or the fireplace." He nodded at the mantle. She turned to see a small brick fireplace with one signatory log; covered in ash.

"It's cute." She says, smiling weakly. The man grunted. Kate looked at him.

"Thank you," she says sincerely. "This cabin will work nicely." The Realtor grunted again.

After touring the bathroom and mini laundry room, Kate was led to the two bedrooms in the back. She gasped, only to cover her mouth when she entered the main bedroom. Opening the window, she thanked the Realtor after signing the contract; the man left with a dissatisfied grunt and a mutter. She was relieved when the man was gone. It was evident that he was not pleased helping someone like her. News *did* travel fast in this town. Camille was right about that. Kate frowned as she stood in the hall, hearing the Realtor's truck pull away, leaving her alone in the dusty red brick cabin.

It's not much. Kate thought sadly, she turned standing in the hall to peer at the two doors; the one on the left, the Realtor says, was the 'master' bedroom, but the room was more medium; enough for a bed and chest of drawers. Kate sat on the small bed left by the previous owners' dust flew up, making her cough. She eyed the room wistfully.

It was not the bed-and-breakfast, but… Kate looked down at her middle. "It's home now." She whispers. Kate pressed her hand to her belly. "*Our home.* We're on our own now. All we have is each other." She clasped her stomach firmly.

"I will do everything to ensure you are comfortable," Kate vowed.

CB

The final act of summer's warmth ended with the curtain of autumn that fell gently upon the stage of nature. Tree branches swayed in the brisk air as their emerald hands absorbed the last gliding rays, transforming their open palms into splashes of scarlet, apricot, and gold, applauding the season's end.

Kate looked up with a sigh, her breath hot in the mask that protected her mouth and nose. She had finally done it. After weeks of careful planning, scrubbing, brushing, mopping, sweeping, dusting, and polishing, her task was complete.

Kate was the proud owner of the newly cleaned cabin in the forest. She sat up after wiping the floor with wood polish; the scent of artificial lemons burned her nostrils despite the mask. She turned her head slowly, looking at the improvement of the second bedroom; at the moment was empty except for her cleaning supplies, courtesy of her new job. Kate's eyes roamed the interior of the windows: clean of grime, the floor polished to perfection. Only the dingy white wall remained.

But not for long. Kate thought, pushing herself to her feet; she puffed, wobbling slightly. Her hands went involuntarily to her lower back, pushing up her swelling belly. Kate spent her whole morning cleaning; after a light breakfast of cold cereal she stood proudly at her finished home, spic and span. To Kate, the spare room held great significance; it was where her baby would sleep. She smiled as she laid a hand on her belly, hidden by denim overalls.

"Everything is coming perfectly." She breathes, walking out of the room, and pulling off the mask; she took in clean air as Kate walked to the living room and sat on the clean leather chair with an exhausted sigh. She yawned. "What a day." She saw her phone and picked it up, pressing the center button to reveal it was 12:45 pm.

It's still early. Kate thought. *Maybe I can get to work on painting the spare room, and…* her thoughts trailed away when she looked down at the date that came once a year: November 28.

Thanksgiving.

Kate laid her head on the sofa cushion, staring at the date warily as the realization hit her like a sad bell.

No stores will be opened today. Kate thought wistfully. *Especially, the hardware store.*

Kate closed her eyes. Her hand spasmed on the phone before it fell on the carpet; she didn't pick it up as her hand curled into a fist. Her eyes stung, and her breaths increased, thinking about her memories of past thanksgivings: once full of joy and warmth; of smells hot from the oven as her mother pulled out the turkey to her father, who laughed, cutting the bird, giving Kate her favorite piece.

She remembered her plate piled high with food; she didn't think she could eat another bite. Yet, when dessert came, Kate seemed to have enough room for a slice: whether it was sweet potato pie, apple pie, or her favorite, chocolate cake. Kate's memories blurred, shifting to the present, not in her childhood home with her loving parents laughing and singing, being with peers who talked and smiled at her: no, she was alone. Her only company was a sofa, her smartphone, and her imagination.

Her imagination started working, weaving ideas into writing outlines as she saw characters.

Kate imagined the pretend family sitting around a large dining table. A beautiful woman with long black hair, her face shining, beamed, as she placed a large turkey on the center of an overflowing table. Kate's mouth began to water as she pictured cornbread brushed with honey butter, hot buttermilk biscuits, baked mac & cheese, a bowl of mashed potatoes with gravy, candied yams, and cranberry sauce before setting with the piece de resistance: the stuffed turkey, large, glistening, and delicious.

Kate's stomach growled, but she didn't notice as the image changed, seeing the woman turn her head to look at dark chocolate skin: his hair, loose and accessible to his eyes, a dark gray, danced as he looked at her lovingly. Kate opened her eyes with a gasp; she sat up from the sofa, her chest pounding wildly as she laid a hand on it. She picked up her phone and saw it read: 3:33 pm. Time ticked unbeknownst to her as she dreamed. To her surprise, her mouth felt dry. She needed something to drink.

Pushing herself up with an effort, Kate rose from the sofa and staggered to the kitchen. The smell of artificial lemon made her sick as she walked to the counter, where she picked up a glass and filled the cup with water from her water mug. Kate took a deep sip of the sweet lukewarm water. She breathed, coughing, after pulling her lips from the cup's rim. Kate looked up wearily, her eyes full of sadness. Despair loomed over her: teasing what could have been and what was now.

He must be having dinner now. She thought.

Nolan. Served the most refined meals made by the most expensive chefs. Nolan, smiling lovingly at his wife, took the hand he kissed, only to look down at a coo as their baby daughter beamed at her parents.

The perfect family.

Kate's throat bobbed as she laid a hand on her baby bump. *Once upon a time...* she smiled sadly, eyes welling up, but she forced them down.

There will be time to cry tonight.

Kate turned to the table.

"Time to get back to work." She spoke.

CB

The sound of laughter and the clinking of champagne flutes filled the air of the grand hall. Festive brown, black, and rich gold decorated the party. Over a hundred guests chatted merrily with affluent guests, dressed formally in elegant dresses and clean suits and ties as they partook in the chef's Thanksgiving-themed meals, served on silver platters by uniformed servers.

Nolan took it in with a frown. Watching his guests: Camille's wealthy girlfriends and his partners, Camille's suggestion, mingled. Nolan sat for three hours with, new clientele he was to meet in the days to come out of state, his reaction to the latest sports team winning, and his acceptance of the many invitations with his affluent colleagues.

But despite Nolan's silver tongue and prize-winning smile... *he was bored.*

His guest had eaten their fill of the heartiest dishes created by his hired chef, who made delicious meals that Nolan loved; hiding his wife's disdain for her meals made by '*common locals*' with compliments to his cook.

The dinner went perfectly, as Camille planned, and now everyone lazed: drunk on wine, turkey, and five kinds of pies.

Nolan glanced to his right, where he saw the nanny sitting across the room where his six-month-old daughter interacted with other babies and toddlers of their guests. He smiled gently as he saw Esme shake a ball that tingled with the sound of the bell.

I missed her so much. He thought. *I thought I would never see her again, but...* He trailed off. Picking up his goblet from a server, he took a drink of his cranberry punch.

I won't be separated from Esme again. He vowed. *Especially after Camille...* Nolan stopped and grimaced. A peel of laughter made him look up to see Camille with her girlfriends: she was in the middle, like her rich friends, with so many shades. Yet, same minded.

Nolan watched as his wife laughed, slapping playfully on the arm of her best friend, Janey, who lifted her head and, seeing him, smiled. Nolan smiled, nodding courteously, but he felt hot. The hall, though vast, was feeling too close for comfort. Nolan rose from his chair where his empty plate, once holding a large slice of Dutch apple pie, before pushing back the large curtain that revealed a dark but expansive backyard that he slipped out from behind the patio screen.

Backyard lights lit up when he breathed in the crisp November air. Nolan's chest felt hot, and his chest beat raced slightly. He heard music playing in the hall and the guest's cheerful excitement, but he didn't turn. He wanted to be alone.

Nolan took in the peace that silence gave in the night: owls hooted as crickets chirped in the distance. A slight chill blew from the west, cooling his dark skin and sweat that dew on his forehead. Nolan looked down at himself.

"That's why." He murmurs aloud, looking at his tie. He started loosening it as he lifted the right hand that held his drink, still annoyed why Camille insisted on making the dinner formal or why she had to invite so many people. He just wanted to spend thanksgiving with just the two of them, Camille, *Esme...*

Nolan swallowed hard on the last of his cocktail. He lowered his hand from the loosened tie staring at his chest, where his heart twinged. He lowered the cup, holding the stem of the glass. He heard ice fall to the ground, but Nolan didn't care as he thought of her.

Kate.

33

It had been so long since he thought of her name. Thought of the woman who entered his monotonous life under glittering gold and pearly smiles. Kate, a woman of humble beginnings, leaving the busy streets of New York to live in a small town to start a new quiet life as an enchantress of the written word.

How is she? He thought softly.

He hadn't seen Kate since the night she came to his home to discover a secret that damaged her honor and her reputation in the town.

Was she all right after...?

He paid her bail. Persuading, Camille after her attack by his mistress would show the townspeople how forgiving and brave, she was after facing terror from a woman... who wouldn't hurt a fly.

He didn't want to believe it, but... when he rushed into the hospital, seeing Camille's arms bruised; her face *scratched.*

He raised his head to the tall pines that loomed over him.

What is she doing right now? He thought softly.

"Nolan?" Nolan half turned, startled, thinking it was his wife, but he relaxed when he saw who it was.

"Janey." He spoke

"What are you doing out here alone?"

"I just... Needed some air." He mumbles. Janey raised an eyebrow.

"It's so dark."

"I don't mind." He shrugged. "Does Camille need me?" He grimaced, hoping she didn't want him for some asinine demand or complaint.

"No." Janey smiles. "I saw you go behind the curtain when you didn't come out...." She took a step forward. "I wanted to see how you were doing."

34

"That's kind of you. But I'm…" He trailed off.

"You didn't look all right." She says. Taking another step forward. "You look unhappy. Is everything all right?"

"I'm fine." Nolan lied. He tried to hide his sadness with a smile. "Thanks for checking on me, Janey."

"You looked distracted before I came out here."

"I was just thinking."

"It must have been serious," Janey noted. Walking over to a table covered in a protective fabric where she sat down easily.

"No, it was—" Nolan stopped and shook his head. "I'm fine."

He could tell Janey had been drinking heavily, so he stepped back, looking away casually.

"Janey, I—"

"You can't deny that you and Camille had quite a few marital spats."

"Yes. But we're working it out." He spoke calmly. "We've been going to a marriage counselor. And so far, I've been working hard to repair the tear."

"Yes." She stepped forward. "Although some say you should have let that tear continue."

"Who has been saying that?" Janey shrugged.

"Just whoever." She replies easily. "You know." She placed a hand on Nolan's chest. "A lot of folks in town said they used to see you with the woman. Kate, was it?" Nolan didn't move.

"Seems odd that a girl like her caught her eye on you. She's so lowly. She's doesn't even have connections to network you to potential investors. She's just some plain librarian. *Nothing special*."

"What's this have to do with me?" he murmurs.

"Rumors say that she came to you already pregnant," Janey spoke silkily. "She just wasn't showing. Camille says she had a boyfriend before meeting you." She shook her head. "These poor people: always trying to take from the rich so they can never work a job. She wanted to ride on the backs of hardworking people." Nolan gaped at her.

"Kate didn't—"

"*Shhh*! It's over, Nolan. You don't have to worry about some nobody from a big city." She stepped closer, and her hand slid to his shoulder and neck.

"Janey, I—" he started.

"It's not too late to have your needs quench." She smiles seductively. "If you wanted to cheat on Camille… You should have come to me." Janey kissed him. Nolan froze as he felt her lips on his, tasting alcohol that reeked her breath… He pulled back.

"J-Janey! Wh-what…? Why?" He stopped, lifting a hand to wipe his lips, stunned by the kiss.

"I know you want me, Nolan." She purrs. "Ever since you came to this town. I saw you. You weren't happy with Camille."

"No. This is wrong, Janey! I don't—I like you, but not in that way. You're my wife's friend. I don't—" he stopped. "Janey, I'm not interested. I'm trying to repair my relationship with my wife and child. You can't jeopardize that. I love Camille."

"No, you don't." He stared at her. "You wouldn't let that girl seduce you if you wanted out." He didn't answer. Janey smiled, taking his hand, and placing it on her breast.

"I want you, Nolan." She spoke. She drew closer to him. "Be with me. You want me. Leave Camille." She lifted her head, ready to kiss him again.

36

"Love me." She breathes. Nolan didn't answer as Janey raised her lips for another.

Nolan pushed her back, making her gasp.

"You're unbelievable. You think I would leave my wife and child; after all we've been through." He spoke, voice growing with anger. "You would come and tear my marriage apart."

"Your marriage has already torn apart!" Janey yells. "I see how you look at Camille. She's—"

"She's my wife and mother to my daughter," Nolan says. "I won't let you ruin me for your delusions."

"Oh, you won't sleep with me, but you would sleep with some poor girl!" Nolan, who had turned around, froze.

"Kate is not some poor girl."

"Then what is she!? Don't tell me you actually cared for that stupid bookish girl. She must have had something that she wrapped you around her little finger, that slut—"

"Enough, Janey!" Nolan spun around even as his chest pang at Kate. "Get out of my house! I never want to see you again!!" Janey laughs snidely.

"You don't order me! I'm Camille's best friend. I'm always here. Now that I think about it." She grinned wickedly. "Camille wouldn't be too pleased if she found out that her husband tried to seduce her best friend."

Nolan froze. She grinned. Triumphed.

"I win."

"*Guess again.*"

Nolan's back went rigid.

He turned his head to see Camille standing out the open patio window; her green sequin dress glimmered under the bright lights as she stared, not at her husband but… Janey.

"C-Camille." Nolan breathes.

"Camille!" Janey stepped back. "I—"she glanced at Nolan, who watched his wife with shock. "I don't know what came over, Nolan—!" Nolan woke from his stunned trance after seeing his wife; now, he looked at Janey, who stared at her best friend, eyes shining, her face askew as she blubbered. He turned to his wife.

"*Camille*." He breathes.

"So, this is how you will hurt me," Camille spoke. "After three years of friendship, after all, I've been through, you would betray me!

"Camille, it's not what you think!" Janey started. "Nolan, he tried to— "

"**Save it**!" She stepped forward. "How could you do this to me!?" Janey stepped back, surprised.

"You would take advantage of my husband after he's suffered enough from that snake!" Nolan started, his eyes growing wide as Camille hisses the last word with disgust.

"After all she's done to me! The days I spent after that whore assaulted me— you will hurt my husband. HURT ME!"

Janey stopped talking.

"Camille, I—" Camille stopped in front of Nolan, who didn't move.

"So, this was your plan. You pretend to be my friend only to prey on my husband when we have a marital spat. Do you think you can slink your way so you can sleep with him!?" she screamed. Janey stepped back; fear crossing her face.

38

"Camille, that's not true! You're my best friend. How could I ever think of taking your husband?" She smiles sweetly.

"So, I didn't see you seducing, Nolan?" Camille asks. Janey froze. He felt Camille's hot hand slip into his cold one. "And here I was looking for my dear husband only to see my best friend threaten him," Camille feigned shock. "Clearly, I'm the dumb one. I didn't see or hear you use your body to get what you want—*I'm stupid*!"

"N-no, Camille! Of course not! You're not—"

"Then you admit it?"

"I—"Janey hesitated.

"Then I'm sure Nolan can tell me his side of the story, I mean—" She looked at him—"By the way he sounded, Nolan wasn't interested in talking to you." Nolan's face hardened as he squared his shoulders.

"I wasn't."

Janey froze. She looked at Camille, pleading.

"Camille, please." She started. "I'm sorry, I didn't mean to—"

"Lies!!" Camille hisses. The scar on her face crinkled as her lips curled. "After all I've done for you. I thought you were my friend, but you used me to get close to Nolan!"

Camille squeezed his hand. Hard.

"*He is mine*!" She spoke, voice unrecognizable to Janey's ears, but familiar to Nolan's. "Nolan is my husband and father to our precious daughter!"

"Y-you can't!" Janey stepped back. "It's your word against mine!"

"Oh, really," Camille let go of Nolan's hand and walked to the sliding door that was half open before stretching a hand inside. Nolan heard humming as he turned to see the blinds' part revealing the party hall and his guests who stood watching, glaring at Janey with derision.

Janey stepped back.

"No."

Janey collapsed to the ground.

"Get out of my house!"

"Ca-Camille pl-please!"

"Consider this friendship over." Camille came forward. "You are no longer part of my friends."

"No!" Janey looked at her hands clasped as *real* tears trailed down her olive cheeks. "Camille, please, I'm so sorry!" She looked at Nolan, seeing his impassive face.

"You are no longer welcome in my house." He spoke.

"Nolan, pl-please! I-I thought you felt the same for me. I—"

"You thought wrong, Janey. I won't leave my wife. And I won't have someone in my presence who tried to blame me for something I didn't do."

Janey flinched. She lifted her hands, beseeching.

"Pl-please don't. You love me— *I love you!*" She pleads. Nolan froze. His eyes widened as he heard Kate over his phone line, pleading her innocence. His gray irises flickered... Camille laughed, making him look at her as she smiled; that didn't touch her eyes.

"I'll make you pay for coming between my husband and me, you backstabbing slut!" Camille hisses. "Now get out, or I'll call the Sheriff!"

Janey looked at the faces that stared at her angrily before looking at Nolan one last time. With a sob, she rose quickly to her feet, pushing past Nolan and Camille, shoving the guest out of the way as she fled.

Nolan buried his face in his hands as he sat alone in his office. Below him, he could hear the last of his guests leave, saying goodnight while others chatted, laughing. He didn't have to guess what it was about. The whole town will know by dawn. Nolan felt his throat tighten as he heard footsteps, followed by a closed door.

"Everyone's gone?" he asks. He didn't look up to know his wife had entered.

"Yes." She spoke. Camille stepped forward, stretching.

"Chantel just put Esme to bed." He spoke, looking up. "I checked on her before coming here."

"Good."

"You can check how she is."

"I'll check on her later," Camille says loftily. Nolan frowned. "Why didn't you come back down?"

"I needed some space after…" he trailed off. "Did you know everyone would be at the window?" Camille shrugged as she moved languidly.

"It seemed odd that Janey didn't come back," Camille replies. "She told me she was going to use the powder room, but…" she smirked. "When Nicole said she went outside because you had texted Janey, asking to speak to her." Nolan's eyes widened as heat surged through him for Janey's guile.

"But I know you don't have her phone number." Camille continues.

"Because I know you don't interact with the girls and me unless you're with Esme." She stopped at his desk.

"You wouldn't hurt me after all I've been through."

"I wouldn't do that to you, Camille," Nolan spoke, voice firm. "I want to rebuild our marriage."

"Oh, I know." She walked around the desk as Nolan faced her. "Especially after all the lengths I've done to protect our family." Nolan stretched his hand to his wife.

"I know." He looked at her cheek, seeing the three-inch scar. "You were trying to help me. I didn't know, Ka..." he swallowed. "What lengths she would go to harm you." She took his hand and leaned into him.

"Kate has done things," Camille spoke silkily. "But *hurting* me isn't one of them."

Pain crossed Nolan's chest. He didn't move. *He couldn't.*

Camille kissed him.

Chapter Six

Kate looked up at the sound of barking outside her home. Turning from her dishes, she washed silently; she peered out the window to see a dog running from the woods, barking loud and deep. Before Kate could question it, the dog ran to her front door. It wasn't long before she heard a frantic scratching on the wooden frame. Kate walked to the door and opened it slowly to peer down at the large dog. The dog's paws pushed her back. Afraid, Kate stepped back; her hands fell instinctively on her baby bump as the dog entered her home looking at Kate with large chocolate brown eyes. It barked, walking forward; claws clicking on polished wood for… Kate squealed, jumping back, frightened, regretting opening the door. Was it going to attack? The dog stopped and then barked more urgently, wagging its bushy tail.

Is something wrong? She thought. Kate had seen German shepherds through movies and TV but never this close, much less in this town. Kate gulped.

I have to stay calm. Kate thought, her legs trembling; the German shepherd turned in a circle before sitting right in front of her waiting, watching her calmly. Kate hesitated a moment before holding her breath and extended her hand, palm down to the dog, remembering seeing people do this on TV; the dog got back to its feet. Kate froze, but her hand was still as the dog stepped forward just by her hand, giving it a nudge with its snout; it sniffed her hand, its tail wagging as it snuffled before bumping her hand on his nose and laid its head underneath her hand. Kate felt the fur under her palm, letting out a relieved exhale before petting the creature's head, still careful of its giant canines.

"H-Hello." She spoke meekly; the dog stared at her, welcoming her caresses as she stroked under its neck: it was then she noticed it was wearing a large black collar with a gold tag. Curious, she kneeled and read the name.

"Pilot." Kate looked at the dog. A smile started to form on her lips. "Hello, Pilot." She says kindly. The dog wagged its tail. "How did you get here? Are you lost?" The dog bumped her hand, wanting more petting. "Where are your owners?" At that moment, Pilot seemed to remember why it was here. The dog pulled back and started barking, turning for the door before stopping. It looked at Kate with bright, intelligent eyes as she rose to lay a hand on her stomach.

I think he wants me to follow him—Kate thought. The dog waited for her. Kate hesitated. *If I follow him, he could take me to the problem.* Kate glanced out the window before going for her coat hook where her red fleece poncho hung and putting it on. She followed the dog.

ಌ

The dog led the way through the woods over a cloudy midday. Kate followed the dog as he trotted, its paws crunching on the green earth. *Where is he taking me?* She wondered. Just as she was ready to turn back, she heard a voice call, "Pilot!" Kate saw a middle-aged woman with short silver hair leaning against a large rock. The dog, Pilot, ran to the woman with a bark, snuffling. The woman patted his side before he pulled back and ran to a stock-still Kate, who gasped when she saw her.

"Are you all right!?" The woman looked at her with surprise.

"Oh, my, I didn't see you there, dearie." The woman spoke in a clear, soft voice. Kate hurried to her, her face full of worry.

"A-Are you all right, ma'am?!" she cries, seeing the poor woman's state.

"I seemed to have sprained my ankle." The woman spoke.

"Oh, no! C-can you stand or walk?" Kate winced at the last question. The woman smiled.

"I was walking and tripped on a hidden tree root."

"Oh no, I'm sorry." The woman beamed.

"No need to apologize. It is the woods, and anything can happen." Kate looked at her anxiously. "My dear, I'm fine. It's a good thing Pilot girl called you here."

"Pilot... Girl?" Kate echoed. She looked at the dog with newfound eyes as she, not he, rested on the grass by her owner. "Oh." She says. "I thought your dog was a boy," the woman laughs.

"You're not the only one who said that." Kate smiles weakly.

"Let me help you, ma'am. Can you stand?"

"I can try." Kate helped the woman get to her feet, using the rock for support. The woman braced against it, letting out a puff of air.

"Let me bring my car. You're in no condition to walk." But the woman shook her head.

"The trees would get in the way. I saw your car on the way here, and by the size of the trees, it would scratch your car pretty badly." Kate winced.

"Maybe I should call 911?"

"Pfft! No need: this is nothing." The woman gestured to her left leg. "we don't need an ambulance for a minor sprain. I can walk." Kate looked at her, unconvinced.

"A-Are you sure? We are far from my home, at least fifteen minutes."

"That's not a problem. I don't mind the walk, although..." the woman grimaced, looking down. Kate eyed the woods, seeing trees, rocks, and a

45

small brook that Kate had never seen before. Finally, she noticed a long thick branch; walking over to it, she picked it up from the floor before handing it to the woman.

"Here." Kate says, "you can use this as a cane while we walk. You lean on it and me as we walk to my house. I have a first aid kit inside." The woman nodded as Pilot barked.

"I never got your name, ma'am," Kate spoke as they walked.

"Oh, I'm sorry, my dear, it's Emily." Kate smiles.

"I'm Kate." She replies. "It's nice to meet you."

Kate poured a steaming mug of tea into a decorative teacup. The warm smell of Cinnamon Apple wafted into the small kitchen. Emily smiled at Kate where she sat, her left leg propped up by a chair.

During the past hour, Kate was busy. Once they entered the cabin, twenty-five minutes later, Emily or miss Watson had to rest every few minutes as they trekked to civilization. Upon entering, Kate sat the old matron on the kitchen chair, taking off her boots: the two women winced when they saw a giant purple swelling on Emily's left ankle. Kate immediately got to work. Grabbing her first aid kit, she pulled out an instant cold pack and stretched tan bandages; Kate wrapped the ice pack in cloth before wrapping it carefully on Emily's foot. Once finished,

Kate offered to make tea for the older woman's trouble. Kate placed a sandwich beside Emily, who thanked her before taking a bite. Kate smiled before bending down and putting a few slices of deli ham and a bowl of water on the floor beside Pilot, who sat beside her owner.

"This is delicious." Said Emily. Kate thanked her as she rose to her feet, wincing a little. Kate let out a breath, gripping the side of the table as she did.

"Are you all right, dear?" Kate nodded, then huffed, placing a hand on her middle.

"I'm fine, just a cramp," Kate assured her.

It looks like my bending days are ending. Kate thought with a sigh, hiding her awareness with a smile she said:

"I'm glad you like it, miss Watson."

"Oh please, Emily is fine." Kate nodded. "You have a lovely home."

"Thank you." Said Kate, going to her seat where her sandwich sat.

"It must have been costly when you bought the place."

"Actually, it was affordable," Kate replies. "When I bought the cabin, inside was in terrible shape but with some cleaning." She half shrugged, gesturing to the house.

"You did this all on your own?!" Emily gasps.

"Mm-hmm, and pregnant nonetheless."

"Pregnant! Oh my gosh! Congratulations!" Kate smiles. "You did this all alone with a baby. Amazing." Kate chuckles weakly.

"It wasn't so bad. I just did the cleaning and painting." She says modestly.

"It must have taken weeks to complete."

"Not really," Kate explains it to Emily. It soon didn't take long for them to discuss their occupation and life.

"You're a pastry chef!" Kate gasps. Emily nodded and told her career as a chef, traveling abroad to learn everything about culinary.

"Your life sounds amazing, Emily." Kate breathes.

"It was." Emily sighs. "But my days of cooking are over."

"Oh, don't say that. You can always teach the next generation of bakers." Emily laughs.

"As you will influence the world with your best-selling novel." Kate laughs. "have you had any luck with the agents? I had friends who wrote books before, and they say it's a difficult process."

"It is," Kate says dryly.

"Have you published anything?"

"Just some short stories to magazines and novellas."

"Hey, better than nothing." Kate smiles, nodding.

"I wish I could cook like you. All your baked goods sound wonderful." She says.

"You can. It's just practice."

"I watch many YouTube videos on cooking and baking. It's an important skill."

"It is. You do not know how I tell people and my son that cooking is a basic life skill. You need it to survive. Not everyone is going to have private chefs. In my son's case, the town's bar and diner." Kate laughs, feeling free for the first time in so many months.

"I agree. I hope to be as good as you, Emily."

"Aw shucks don't say that" Emily says modestly. "You cook to suit your needs. Be unique, as long as it's edible." She giggles. "I can give you some cookbooks I've bought and recorded over the years.

"That would be lovely. I'm always willing to learn." Kate replies before changing the subject.

"Pilot is such a strange name for a girl dog," Kate noted. "What made you choose that?"

"Oh, I got it from my favorite book, Jane Eyre."

"I've heard of Jane Eyre." Pilot walked over to Kate and put her head on Kate's lap. "I'm afraid I haven't read it yet. I've been busy reading so many other books, and then there's work." Kate sighs.

"You look tired, dear. Are you getting enough sleep?" Kate shook her head, petting Pilot.

"I have too much work to rest." Emily tutted.

"That's not good." She reproached kindly. "You have to rest. You have a baby inside you, and if you break down…" she saw Kate shudder.

"I just want my baby to have a home to come to."

"How many months are you?" Kate hesitated before breathing.

"Three months."

"Ooh, and you helped carry me here, saying nothing." Kate nodded wordlessly. Pilot wagged her tail, nuzzling Kate.

"What about the father? Is he here to help?" Kate winced.

"No," she whispers. "We broke up."

"Does he know? Oh, I'm sorry, I shouldn't pry."

"No, it's alright." Kate took in a breath before letting it out shakily. "He knows, but… he doesn't want the baby."

"So, you're alone." It wasn't a question. Kate nodded. "I'm so sorry, child."

"It's alright. I know this wasn't going to be easy. Sometimes, I wish things were different, but…." Kate looked away, sniffling.

"I'm sorry, child. Everything will work out." Kate's eyes stung, but she looked at the woman who treated her so kindly, who didn't look at her as if she was what everyone says she was.

"Thank you."

HONK! HONK!

Kate and Emily looked up as they heard crunching leaves, as she sensed the heavy presence of a truck. Kate peered out the window and saw a large Ford truck approaching the front of the house. A tall man with long brown hair came out of the door. Kate walked to the door and opened it just as the man was about to knock. Surprise crossed his face when he saw Kate before his eyes narrowed.

"**Where is she**!?" he demands. Kate's greeting got stuck in her throat. Instead of answering, she opened the door fully and gestured for him to enter, his face brightening when he saw Emily.

"Mom!" he cries. Kate closed the door, turning to see the man go to his mother, leaning down to hug her, peppering her with questions.

"I'm fine, son," Emily says.

"You shouldn't have gone alone into the woods, mom." He scolds. "You could have waited for me."

"And miss out on this beautiful day? Heck no!" Pilot barks as she walked over to her.

"Pilot girl!" He beamed, stroking her head. "How bad is your leg?" the son eyed his mother's foot seeing the bandage.

"It's swollen. It will be a while when I return to the city." Emily replies with a sigh.

"Well, your foot's not broken, and Pilot kept you company."

"Pilot is the one who got me help. She remembered the cabin when we walked past it and came here. If it weren't for Kate, I'd still be sitting on the forest floor." Emily beamed; the man turned his head to look at Kate, who had sat down on her chair, head lowered but in her peripheral vision, saw everything.

50

"Oh." Kate heard the disapproval in his voice, causing her to look up at him to see the man frown.

"Kate has been wonderful to me." Emily continues, not noticing her son's closed-off expression. "She walked me back to the house, bandaged my leg, and fed Pilot & me." Surprise crossed the man's face as he stared at Kate. "Did you do that for my mother?" Kate hesitated before nodding once. "Of course, she did!" Emily says. "What is this? Twenty questions? Are you ready to go, son? I know you work tonight, and I don't want to keep you waiting, Joel." Joel nodded, turning back to Kate, saying almost grudgingly. "Thank you." Kate nodded wordlessly. Joel helped lift his mother to a standing position and walked slowly as her mother limped forward. Kate carried Emily's right boot when they made it to the truck. Pilot leaped into the back seat while Joel seated his mother, clipping the seatbelt around her waist.

"It was so good to meet you, Kate." Emily beamed when her son took the boot and closed her door. Kate smiled sadly.

"You too, Ms. Emily." She says. "If you need any cleaning services, you have my card." Emily nodded as her son started the truck. Kate waved goodbye as they drove out of the woods. She saw Emily waving from the window before the car left toward town.

Kate lowered her hand and turned back to the cabin. There, she picked up her wares and started washing them. The silence of the room echoed loudly, deafening her ears. It had been so long since she had actual human contact. Kate's eyes began to blur, remembering the man's face when he recognized her.

She thought she would be used to this. But although no words were spoken, she felt the sting of rejection.

Loud and clear.

Chapter Seven

"'There was a ding, and Ruby winced. Emily and Joy gaped at the white fluffy cloud turn from a six to a seven…

"Well," Ruby says meekly. "Maybe a little."

Ding!

"Okay! A lot!...'"

Kate looked up from the paper with a frown.

"*Hmm.*" She tapped the pen beside her lips to think about what to put down. The sun basked down into her room, beckoning Kate to join her outside, but was too distracted where she sat on her desk, leaning back on her chair, her face pensive as she… Kate's face brightened!

Leaning forward, she put her pen to paper and started writing, smiling as the words in her head poured onto the page: Kate's story of a small town affected by a magical spell that caused their lies to be revealed in numbers getting bigger with each lie. The main character witness what is happening to her friends and neighbors. Kate beamed, seeing in her imagination that her character, Ruby, tried to grab the cloud atop her head in a fit of anger and desperation, laughing aloud when the character fell into the town's fountain. Kate felt free in her element, scribbling fantastic tales that allowed her to escape the world to one of magic; making the impossible. *Possible.*

Kate put down the pen with a contented sigh when she finished the middle chapter; picking up her work, she skimmed through the reading before laying it back down beside the empty bowl that once contained cereal. Picking up her phone, she saw the clock read 11:55 am.

She sighed. Raising her arms to stretch them, her stomach rumbling with newfound hunger. Kate rose from her chair, picking up her bowl to go outside to the kitchen, where she washed and placed the wares on the dish rack to dry before going to the fridge to find something to eat. Kate frowned when she peered into it, seeing a carafe of orange juice, butter, a carton of milk and half a loaf of bread.

"Hmm." She closed the door. There was nothing to eat. After many days of working on her job and writing projects, Kate didn't have time to go shopping. Of course, she ate to build her strength for herself and her child. The days were a blur, for maintaining her home seemed unimportant. Kate sighed as she placed a hand on her growing belly. She looked out the curtained window at the sun that streamed onto the wooden table.

"I guess I have to go shopping today." She muses. "That means going into town for…" she trailed off with a shudder. Kate was not looking forward to that. The townspeople still gossip about her and what happened in the inn. Now that she was four months into her pregnancy, Kate was not looking forward to another helping of sneers and mocking jabs.

Mrs. Roth made sure Kate was not welcome in town. No matter how short her visit was.

But it was either drive eight minutes or drive forty-five to the next town to shop in comfort. Kate checked her account on the phone, finding she had enough money before packing her bag pack with her wallet, cell phone, and keys. Kate put on her fleece poncho before stepping out into the cold air.

The supermarket wasn't crowded when Kate pushed her cart to the first aisle that greeted her. She inhaled, picking up the different scents the produce aisle offered. Pushing the cart, Kate stopped at a cart full of delicious apples, each with different colors, sizes, and tastes. She picked up a bright red apple examining for any imperfections before putting it down, eyeing the Granny Smith curiously.

There was a recipe for apple crisp in Emily's book. She thought. *I wonder if it was granny smith or...* she trailed off when she heard giggling. Kate lifted her head sharply; she looked around, seeing workers packing produce and two older women laughing amongst themselves.

Kate breathed. Picking up a produce bag and placed five Macintosh apples along with granny smith, cherries, fruit cups and plum tomatoes when the idea to make homemade tomato sauce came to her mind. She left the aisle satisfied before walking down the coffee and tea section, where she bought a container of loose tea leaves. Kate noticed block chocolate for sale and her mouth watered; leaning forward, she looked for the most affordable, finding one to her liking before putting it in her cart.

The shopping experience was pleasant for Kate. She always enjoyed coming here for the products and brands: Kate bought juice, soda pop, bottled water, flour, yeast, sugar and chocolate bars.

Kate felt she belonged once again as she observed the store patrons examining prices as they prepared for the holiday season. Pushing her cart, she walked; picking up what she touched. Kate was placing a gallon of milk when she heard laughter making her turn.

Two women stood by the meat aisle she stood in moments ago. They were giggling as they watched Kate, who gripped her cart tightly; before pushing it forward, she heard one say:

"Cinder-whora has come out of her shack." Kate stiffened. She forced herself to look away, but their whispered jeers continued as she picked up a package of

mozzarella and ricotta cheese before leaving the dairy section… feeling their mocking eyes stab her back.

Kate walked until she was sure they were gone. She stopped to look behind her and breathed in relief, only to take in a wonderful smell. Kate looked to her side and saw a large buffet stand lined with delicious hot food from: Korean chicken wings, fried shrimp, white and fried rice, fried chicken, mac & cheese, baby back ribs, and vegetables.

Kate picked up a container and started piling food into it. Her mouth watered as her belly gurgled with hunger. Kate was closing the second lid when she felt it… a sudden push within her stomach. Kate gasped quietly, looking down at her middle hidden by the poncho; wonder and awe course through her as she felt, for the first time.

Her baby kicking.

Unconsciously, she placed one hand on her middle while the other pushed the cart, making her way to the cash register. It was something she had never felt before, the first sign that life was growing within her. Warmth filled her chest, whilst she gently clasped her middle; a loving smile crossed Kate's lips.

Kate stood online, placing her spoils onto the conveyor belt and paid before packing her groceries into the cart and pushed it out of the store. Kate felt the cold sting of early winter on her cheeks, waking her from her trance. Opening the back of the van trunk, she packed her bags wordlessly; struggling with two or three, but the rest was light. Kate was placing the last of the groceries when she heard her name called, making her raise her head to see the tall, handsome face of Nolan Roth walking forward, pushing a cart full of paper bags. Her eyes widened when she saw the baby seat where his daughter, Esme, had her back facing Kate.

Nolan slowed the cart face full of surprise. He was in a foul mood when he left the house with Esme, as his wife and her rich friends prattled the latest rumors and gossip. His blood boiled when Camille spoke cruelly of Kate as she told the girls how she tried to pin her baby on Nolan. Reweaving the same tale, she said to her friends. Camille's side-eyed glance at Nolan was jeering as she told them that Kate was sleeping with another man before she met Nolan and walked out on her upon knowing she was pregnant.

"The home wrecker thought she could get away with it. She wasn't showing, so when she met Nolan, she used him, thinking she would get a free meal ticket and endless luxury." The girls snickered.

"What a tramp!" one says.

"Why do these poor girls always believe they can have any rich guy they see?" Camille shrugged as Nolan clutched Esme in his arms, face burning, while he sat on the armchair of the parlor.

"This is what I tell you, girls," Camille says wisely. "Give the rich gold, we turn it into more gold, give it to the poor, and they demand more handouts." The girls nodded in unison.

Nolan stepped out of the parlor, explaining that he needed something in the kitchen. He overheard his staff talking about going to the supermarket as he walked. Nolan immediately volunteered to get away from the house. He hadn't expected to see a familiar face amongst so many familiars.

A face he was glad to see.

"What are you doing here?" he asks. Kate stared at him before grabbing the cart and push it for the cart rack. "Kate! Wait!" he followed her, pushing his. Kate ignored him as her eyes stung, whether of tears or coldness she didn't know. All she knew… She had to leave!

"K-Kate!" Nolan tried to keep up as he saw her push the cart to the cart shed.

"*Leave me alone, Allen*!" Kate cries. Nolan froze, surprised that she said his first name.

"Wait!!" Nolan looked at her pleadingly. "I don't mean any harm. I just wanted—

"To what!?" Kate pushed the cart into the shed. She spun around, eyes blazing. "Why don't you leave me alone? I want nothing from you!" Nolan stopped aghast.

"I…" he started. "I wanted to apologize for how I acted at—

"I don't want to hear it! You've done nothing but bring me suffering! Just…" she stomped past him, fist clenched. She didn't want to talk to him, much less acknowledge his presence.

"Please, Kate!" Nolan pushed the cart forward and walked beside her. "I know you're angry with me! But give me a chance to make things right." They were by her van now, and Kate had stopped going into her bag to find her keys.

"Kate?"

"*WHAT*?" Nolan flinched, then glanced to see if anyone was watching. No one was.

"Kate I..." She watched as he sifted his words carefully before finally, he says. "How is the baby?" Kate froze. She didn't answer for several moments; instead, her gaze turned to his daughter, who watched her with wary boredom. She lifted her gaze back to Nolan.

"That is none of your business." She says. "What happens between my child and me is none of your concern!"

"I want to know if my baby is—

"*Your baby* is sitting freezing to death!" Nolan looked down and remembered Esme. He looked at Kate, pained, as she glowered at him with bloodshot eyes.

"So, don't bring yourself into matters that don't concern you!"

"Kate." Kate found her keys. Opening the door, she climbed in, starting the car. "Kate! Please don't go. I—" a loud screeched made Nolan pull the cart protecting his child. He saw Kate back out of the parking space before the large van pulled away for the road.

☙

Kate cried home, wiping her eyes every few minutes as she drove slowly on the road. By the time she made it back, her eyes were bloodshot and her nose stuffy. She parked her van, going to her trunk pulled out her groceries: starting with the light bags before taking the heavy ones. Kate grunted when she pulled a gallon of water and milk into the house with both hands; her legs trembled as she walked to the table after kicking the door closed. Kate laid her bag of milk and water on the floor before sitting down and burying her face in her hands. Her tears had long dried up, but her nerves were still uneasy. Everything was going so well. She believed she was making progress, starting to forget her woes despite her encounter with the women; everything was bright, but why did fate have to be so cruel?

Nolan. It had been months since she had seen him: months where she cried silent tears for the man who not only took her heart but broke it as well. She believed Nolan was like her. Kate thought she found her kindred spirit when they talked for weeks on end about literature, fantasy, hopes, and dreams. She had put trust in a man she thought she knew. She had poured her secrets into him that could now be a weapon because of his lies to her.

There was no point in fighting for her innocence. Kate could do now was move on. But there he was. Entering her life again, coming with a cart full of food as he pushed his cherished baby girl. The thought sent a pang through Kate. All those things she had wanted from him… gone! Unbeknownst to her, he had already claimed the traditional family unit. She could not be envious of Camille, but she was. Kate was jealous. It was a feeling she didn't like; it rankled, burned hot, and heavy. But it was there.

Nolan. His eyes were warm as he gazed at her; his smile was both shy and gentle. Kate remembered one evening as they sat in a park late at night on the swing, counting the stars, tracing them to form the constellations, laughing when Nolan couldn't trace the image of Orion's belt.

"You have an imagination." He griped. "Your brain runs on magic dust, not cogs that need to be oiled like me." Kate laughs.

"That's because you traded magic for logic." She teases as she swung. "You chose to live off cold, inanimate material, not dreams.

"Dreams." She continues. "Is what connects us to the other world. Without dreams or magic, we would never have stories." Nolan smiles with a chuckle.

"You're probably right."

"I am right!" Kate teases. Nolan laughed before he, too, pushed himself on the swing.

Kate smiled at the memory, lifting her head from her palms, tracing the fine lines with her eyes. Such a magical time: the summer of magic and dreams of… Nolan startled when he looked at Kate; not of fury or disgust like she expected from the others. No, Nolan looked almost… Kate shook her head.

"He was trying to get me in trouble." She tells herself. "If I had stayed, he would have called the police or worse. His wife would have seen us…" she shivered.

"No." she breathes. "I won't let that happen again. Nolan is not part of my life anymore." She nodded, rising from her chair. Kate started unpacking her bags.

I won't have any dealings with the Roth's. She thought resolutely. *They may run this town, but not me!*

Chapter Eight

Kate woke up to an overcast morning. She sleepily opened her eyes to the sound of chirping birds singing outside the cold pane glass. Kate saw them perched with quiet wonder at the different colored creatures as they pecked on the wooden stand going about their day. Her gaze moved from the window to her writing desk. She smiled sleepily, thinking of the second world she birthed in her mind. A young couple from different classes comes together, finding friendship in one another's company.

Kate snuggled against her pillow. Thinking how her main character walks down the beautiful city after living for years in the country. Her character, a woman, was window shopping before she bumped into her love interest. Kate couldn't help but smile; she knew these meetups were cliched, but it was a cliché she loved amongst all others.

She felt a push from within her. Kate looked down and smiled tenderly at her middle; she wore a simple white sleeping gown that hugged her body, keeping her warm. It was enough to show Kate's protruding belly, hard but smooth to the touch, especially as she held it, hugging it lovingly.

"Good morning." Kate's voice was a caress, afraid to break the peace between her and her growing treasure. Kate closed her eyes, breathing slowly, feeling her baby moving in her expanding womb.

BUZZ

Kate opened her eyes with a gasped at the familiar noise from her phone's alarm clock. Kate groaned; turning onto her right side, she lifted a hand to hit the button on the phone; she didn't have to look at the screen to know.

It was time for work.

Kate grabbed a breakfast bar, washing it with milk, when her phone buzzed, revealing an email from SQUEAKY CLEAN alerting her of an emergency meeting at the headquarters. Kate sighed.

"I hope no one's accused of stealing again." She murmurs, pocketing her phone. Kate grabbed her bag and headed out of the cabin.

Kate entered the cleaning office to find a group of familiar faces sitting down on one spot; a feeling of anxiety crept into her when they all turned to look at her, but to her relief, their faces weren't angry or disgusted.

"Kate," Ben says. "You're just in time. Have a seat." Kate obeyed, sitting down as her manager, Ben, talked. The meeting started with the announcement of their second annual Christmas party. *She didn't plan ongoing.* Being in crowds still made her nervous, and going out, dressed up, brought back fear of the townspeople who turned against her. Kate listened to the rest of the meeting half-heartedly until Ben brought up something new.

"I need twelve of my five-star cleaners today for a job with a large family house," Ben announced before calling names. Kate didn't pay attention; she was already thinking of the houses she had to do today.

"Kate!?" Kate started.

"Yes, Ben?"

"I need you to go with the girls to the large mansion," Ben replies. "I know you have to work with Mr. Victor. Millie will go in your place while you come with me and the rest to Mr. Roth." Kate froze.

"M-Mr. Roth." She stammers. Ben nodded. "Wh-where does he live?" she asks, hoping, no, praying it was not the same Roth. Ben said the town's name… a shiver ran down Kate's spine. She hoped this day would never come. As Ben went about the task, Kate felt pain in her stomach; it was not the baby but her mounting terror. Kate was to work for Nolan, sweeping and mopping his grand mansion.

"Kate?!" Kate woke at her name.

"Y-Yes?" she says.

"I need you to come with me and the others." He says. "I need to hand out business cards and new t-shirts to wear when you get to the house." He smiles. Kate nodded as she and her co-workers got up.

Kate lingered, her mind whirling with worry even as she put cleaning supplies in large blue buckets. Kate could not talk her way out of this. Her schedule had already switched. She couldn't fake illness or lie about a doctor's appointment, and Kate definitely couldn't tell her manager the truth. She feared for the safety of her child.

Although, the town believed she was pregnant with another man. Camille Roth knew she would use it to her advantage to play a harmful trick to have her ostracized even worse. Kate placed her hand gingerly atop her right cheekbone. Wincing, when she felt a pang under her half-swollen skin, seeing in her mind's eye the unruly woman from the bar. It was supposed to be a quick trip. Kate thought as she held a stack of Squeaky Clean promotional brochures.

Each store in town rejected her when she asked to leave a few in their shops; leaving Kate no choice to go into the local bar that late evening; after a ten-hour shift. Kate's back ached, her eyes heavy with exhaustion as her stomach growled for her and her unborn child.

She would be in and out. *To not call attention to herself.* Kate entered the bar hoping to speak to the owner but was met by Emily's son, who she whispered her request to leave the advertisement, explaining her jobs specials. Joel, Emily's son, nodded once after making her request, stating with a murmur:

"You can leave them on the table." Kate thanked him, asking if his mother was alright; noticing Joel eyes harden before grunting "she was doing better." Kate turned to leave when a cackle made her turn to see the woman; her drunken swagger marred as she staggered toward. Face contorted to an ugly jeer as she insulted Kate.

"He doesn't seem to be seduced so easily." She slurred in front of everyone. "Yet when I did it, he hated me and..." her lips quivered as her eyes grew shiny and red. Kate took her insult wordlessly before she turned to leave. A shriek made Kate turn only to feel pain burn her cheekbone; she staggered back. Her hand flew to her cheek where she was hit by the butt of the beer glass the woman held as she screamed.

"WHY DOESN'T HE LOOK AT ME LIKE THAT!!?" Too stunned to answer, Kate could only watch as patrons, including Joel, grabbed the woman, him ordering, "Janey! Stop it!"

Janey's shrieks echoed in Kate's ears before she fled, a hand atop her growing belly before the police could be called.

That was four days ago.

Kate wasn't ready to face the town again. She closed her eyes, mind full of questions about what the woman meant and her rising fear of being discovered, possibly fired, leaving Kate unemployed.

"Kate?!" Kate started. She turned around to see one of her co-workers call out to her. "You alright?" Kate nodded dumbly, trying to hide her fear with a smile.

"I'm fine," she spoke. "I just have my head in the clouds."

"Well, you better hurry. We're leaving to take the van to the house. Do you need a ride?" Kate shook her head: she knew where to find the home.

65

"You go ahead, Rachael," Kate says. "I'll meet you at the house. I brought my car with me, and I can't afford to pay the meter in the city." Rachel nodded before walking away. Kate took this moment to use the bathroom to change, switching her old shirt for a new one that fitted snugly on her growing belly, but she didn't mind.

Please don't let me see them. Kate thought. She took a breath to steady herself before opening the door to the restroom.

The house looks different. Kate could not help thinking as she drove up the front of the mansion, where the blue van stopped. Kate parked her car next to it and stepped out into the cold winter air. Carrying her supplies, she walked to her co-workers, who had gathered their cleaning tools and walked inside the sizeable brown door decorated with a large wreath. Kate entered the familiar foyer where her co-workers stood next to a woman who introduced herself as Mrs. Clover, Roth's head of household. She listened as the woman explained how the Roth's wanted their home cleaned and to be mindful of the family's belongings.

"As soon as you're done, the interior decorators will take over." Mrs. Clover explains. "We'll be handing you walkie-talkies to different teams, so buzz me, and I'll call the decorators." Everyone nodded.

"This mansion is big. So, we'll split up into teams of four." Ben nodded, calling his team; he split them into teams: Kate in the second group with two others. Once assigned, Mrs. Clover gave them the tour, directing them through the house. Kate marveled at the rich interior of the mansion, remembering her last visit.

Kate shuddered. Her hope was granted when she and her co-workers, Joe, and Alice, were led upstairs. There, Kate and her team were assigned to clean the spare bedroom. Kate felt her stomach twist with envy when she saw the nursery. Her pulse quickened as she admired the luxurious room full of expensive toys, a crib, and changing table. She decided to work here with her co-workers, taking in the abundance of the rich. If only for a moment.

"Hey!" says Ben. "Good luck, you three." Kate and her co-workers nodded. "When finished, look for me, okay?"

"Okay." Mrs. Clover nodded at them.

"Please be careful. These items are very breakable, especially the crystal chandelier."

"We'll get the ladder." Said Joe. "I'll clean the chandelier while you, Kate, work on putting the toys away." Kate nodded before proceeding to pick up more.

"Hey! Is Mr. and Mrs. Roth here?" Alice asks. Kate's back went rigid; she rose slowly, holding a few stuffed animals. Mrs. Clover shook her head; that simple gesture thrilled Kate as the woman replied.

"Mrs. Roth went shopping with her daughter, and Mr. Roth is at work. They won't be home until evening."

ᘓ

Kate worked with ease throughout the day. Her mind made brush strokes on the canvas, painting the world as outside she toiled away, cleaning within the sleeping beast. But the beast was fed, so the fear of being devoured was far from Kate's grasp. Kate scrubbed the dirt, dust, and grime of the posh rich. She couldn't help but smile at the irony as she helped her co-workers on each floor, doing what her body would allow her if it meant bending, stooping, and pushing. The hours went by uneventfully; she listened to her co-workers as they chattered about the house, giggling about celebrity gossip. Kate smirked, adding her two cents that made everyone laugh.

Kate looked up as Mrs. Clover announced the chef had prepared a lunch of rice pilaf, flank steak and roasted potatoes and asked if anyone would like some. Everyone agreed, and Mrs. Clover led them to the kitchen, where they served them. Kate ate hungrily; all that work had worked an appetite; the food was delicious, the meat well done, and the rice fluffy; she went for seconds. Kate felt safe. No one in the house recognized her, and she could truly enjoy the presence of people's company.

While everyone else worked downstairs, she smiled as she cleaned the last room of the day. Kate stood alone in the office room, wiping the oversized desk with cleaning spray: she had already dusted, swept, and wiped down the windows. Her hand fell lovingly up on her middle as she cleaned before finally pulling back with a sigh. She had done it. Kate turned from the desk, throwing her rag into her bucket; she pulled off her gloves and face mask, dumping them in the waste bin. She stretched, letting out a tired groan as she faced the window: the sky had turned dark despite the overcast day; she took out her phone unthinkingly to see the time seeing it say 4:47 p.m.; pocketing the phone, Kate watched the landscape of the upper floor with a gentle smile. *It was lovely.*

A click made her whirl around with surprise, quickly turning to fear.

ᘓ

 Nolan stood back against the door as he peered at Kate. He hadn't seen her in weeks. When Nolan cast her aside, choosing his reputation, rebuilding his family, letting his wife ruin her; while he turned a blind eye to her laments for help as her home and job were taken away, leaving her destitute, alone, save for...

His eyes widened. Nolan's feet involuntarily broke the space between him and Kate, who looked at him with wide, frightened eyes. She prayed not to encounter him: to know the man she once loved who destroyed her life. Who made her carry hurt to this day; Kate couldn't heal.

Kate was the first to react. Moving as fast as she could, she picked up her broom and went for the garbage pail to pick up the waste bin...

"Wait!" Kate paused, but it was to her detriment. Nolan stepped forward in fast strides; fear turned to terror. Kate let go of the broom; she backpedaled on the carpet until bumping against the curtains. She gasped as the second body radiated from his heat; despite the room's warmth, her hands flew to her stomach, bracing herself.

The months had not been kind to Kate. Her cheeks, once round, were sunken, leaving dark circles like splotches and bright eyes gone. Although fearful, he saw wariness in her brown irises.

She had seen many tears. Nolan thought as he lowered his gaze to her middle. Her sky-blue shirt with the logo "SQUEAKY CLEAN" in big, bold white lettering lifted slightly to reveal taut, round, brown skin.

Nolan gasped; stepping back, he looked at Kate, her face no longer fearful. It was closed, unreadable.

"Y-You." he breathes. Kate didn't answer, just lifted her hand and lowered her shirt, covering her pregnant belly from him and the world. Nolan saw that simple gesture. He stared at Kate, who looked away, not meeting his gaze. The act alone made his eyes shine as his face twisted in grief.

69

"Kate…" he breathes thickly. Nolan stepped forward. "Kate, I…" Kate looked at him distrustfully; seeing the grief on his face, she didn't respond. Instead, she started to bend.

"Kate!" Kate flinched back as he stepped forward.

"Stay away from me!" Nolan froze at the command in her words. He stopped.

"Kate," He breathes. "pl-please I… I didn't…" he faltered, looking at the woman he hurt. No amount of apologizing could take back the months of suffering.

"*I never meant for this to happen.*" He whispers. Kate looked at him; her face melted from fear to enraged.

"Never meant?" she echoed with all her strength. She pushed Nolan, causing him to let out an "Oof!"

"Never meant!" She screamed. "You lied to me! You tricked me into becoming your mistress! Y-you said you would be there for me! But you told your wife where I lived! You got me fired from my job, **you, your wife**—I never want to see you again!"

"Kate, please, don't be upset! Think of the baby!"

"You have no right to talk about my child!" she yells. Nolan stepped back, afraid.

"I know, I'm…" he paused. "Please, let's talk. I—"

"There is nothing to talk about," Kate says through clenched teeth. But Nolan stepped forward, blocking her.

"Kate… Please." Kate stepped back, closing her eyes, fist clenched. He stared at her, seeing her face.

"Who did this to you?" he spoke, seeing the dark bruise on her right cheek. She didn't answer. He eyed her carefully, taking in her changing body; her face tired, her cheeks, look sunken, concerning Nolan. Especially with her condition.

Nolan stepped forward, placing a hand beside her head to touch the cold glass. He looked down at her stomach, seeing her belly move up and down the roundness of her middle as he stared wonderingly at her expanding womb. He looked at Kate, seeing her cheeks red under her dark caramel skin. "How long?" he whispers. "How far along are you?" Kate didn't answer. "Please, Kate. That's all I want to know." Kate stared, seeing his pleading eyes to know the welfare of his... Kate looked away; her fist raised to her chest as she whispered in a low voice.

"Four months."

"Four months." Nolan echoed. He looked down at her belly. Warmth filled his chest as he stared at it, as a smile pulled at the corners of his mouth. "*Four months.*" He breathes, lifting a hand to touch… Kate knocked his hand before it felt her treasure. Nolan looked up, startled, as Kate glared at him. "You will not touch me again!" She spoke angrily.

"Ka—" Nolan started, but Kate was faster. She bent down and picked up her bag and cleaning supplies. Kate sidestepped and walked out of the room. Leaving Nolan alone in his clean office.

Chapter Nine

Night swept over the tiny town, ending the overcast day. Snow was expected to fall for the Christmas week, less than a week away. The Roth mansion was decorated in gorgeous splendor. The spirit of Christmas possessed the interior: warm and inviting, especially with the upcoming Christmas Eve celebration that was to take place in the house.

Camille had talked about the party preparations as soon as she entered the office. Nolan sat on his office chair, his ears deaf to his wife's prattling of the need for more workers to serve their wealthy guests.

"We need nine more staff to help with the cooking, serving, and a bartender. I…" Camille stopped, seeing his face half covered by his right hand. "Nolan? What's wrong?"

Nolan lifted dull gray eyes to stare at his wife, his mind on many questions, but one stood out the more: "Did you know Kate was working as a cleaning maid?" What he did say was…

"*Nothing.*" He suddenly felt ten pounds heavier. It didn't help that he was still wearing his suit. Nolan didn't change as he intended to. It was irrelevant when he saw her in his office.

Seeing her sweeping his polished floor, Kate didn't notice him, his face the picture of shock and wonder as he watched her. Why was she here? Did she know she would get in trouble because of… Nolan didn't know why he came into the room. He had a meeting in the morning. He was tired, but it was far from his mind as he entered the room and closed the door behind him.

Nolan's mocha skin prickled with heat where he sat in his office; hours after Camille left, stating he had a lot of work and would take dinner in his office. Camille nodded before leaving the room when he promised to talk about the event in bed. Nolan's thoughts were a jumble, repeating the scene, thinking from every angle; what he could have done better with Kate.

Dinner arrived by a maid on a large silver platter. Nolan pulled off his suit coat and tie when the dish was lifted, revealing a large steak with all the fixings by his chef. Nolan ate with slumped shoulders, despite the meal being delicious. Still, every time a piece of steak entered, his stomach felt like a boulder, heavy to digest. Dessert came after he ate his Panna Cotta in silence.

Now it was 9 p.m. Nolan stared blankly, his right face hidden under his fingers: his body heavy. Still, his mind was not at rest as he thought of Kate, seeing her again after so many months. Months where Nolan spent going on fancy trips with his family, rebuilding his marriage as he vacationed in ocean view villas, and eating expensive exotic delicacies. But behind his smiles and witty banter, Nolan knew Kate was still here. Kate, under the public shame of the town for her "attack" on Camille, while he discoursed business deals, Kate was living in a run-down cabin in the woods.

Gossip was the main currency in this town, and he got full of it when he returned after hearing nasty rumors about Kate and her child. Rumors spread like a plague infecting the once kind town-folk, leaving a diseased husk, the remains of what made him love this town.
Nolan blinked wearily, his eyes going dull, akin to black. He could not help remembering when Kate turned to look at him, her eyes filled with panic, once full of warmth as she gazed at Nolan. It was replaced with fear. He was not expecting to see her on his estate. With the restraining order still in

effect, this was the last place he expected to see Kate, much less work as a maid cleaning, dusting, mopping, and sweeping… For him.

Nolan's stomach twisted at the same time his heart gave a throb of pain, seeing for the first time Kate's belly. He groaned at the memory of seeing her stomach rounding with pregnancy. Nolan remembered the look of shock on Kate's face, discovering he was married: knowing she was pregnant with his child. All that Nolan told her… Was a lie.

Kate, belly taut and growing with his child, made Nolan feel warmth for the first time in months. Seeing Kate filled his chest with emotion, the girl he ruined, the woman he still cared for. Nolan closed his eyes, lowering his head.

I have to do something for her. Nolan thought. He pondered this, thinking of ways to help support Kate and his child. Nolan knew visiting her was out of the option: Camille always kept an eye on him.

He had difficulty trying to persuade Camille to let him pay for Kate's bail. How was he going to help her? He knew Kate wouldn't accept anything from him after her ruined reputation; she never took his money in the past, which made him admire her in the first place. Kate was honorable. She would take care of herself and her child. Alone. Nolan opened his eyes and looked down. It was then he noticed a blue card on the floor with the logo of Kate's shirt. Curious, Nolan picked up the card.

SQUEAKY CLEAN

"Make your home squeak as you enter."

He smirked at the motto. There wasn't much on the card, just its date of establishment, website and… his eyes grew bright as he stared at the location of the main headquarter: one of them situated downtown. A plan hatched in

74

Nolan's brain. He knew how he could help Kate and his child. Nolan entered the master bedroom to find Camille awake; he had set his plan in motion. He closed his eyes with peace of mind, knowing he could finally do right for the one he had wronged.

☙

Nolan woke up early to dress quietly while his wife was still asleep. He showered and dressed quickly, moving with precise movements, his body working mechanically as he put on his shirt, buttoning it.

"Nolan?" He was fixing his tie when he paused. His back stiffened.

"Yeah?" Nolan turned to see his wife sit up from their king-size bed, her blond hair array.

"Where are you going? It's—Camille glanced down at the clock—" 6:45 in the morning." Nolan smiled to hide his worry.

"I know." He says apologetically. "But I have a meeting this morning at the office. I want to get to the city early to beat traffic."

"Then get an Uber," Camille yawned. "That meeting isn't for five hours." Nolan came forward, picking up his suit jacket.

"There are some documents I left there. I want to go through them one last time." She didn't answer, just looked at him.

"Since when have you needed to do last-minute checking?" Camille asks. "You're the best in getting people on your side."

"I learned it from you." Nolan teases. Leaning down, Nolan kissed his wife on the cheek, where she had injured herself months before.

"I'll see you this evening." He purrs. Camille smiled seductively before kissing him on the mouth.

"I'll hold that to you," she says, pulling back from their kiss. Nolan smiled, but it didn't touch his eyes. Instead, he picked up his briefcase and left the master bedroom.

Nolan raced down the hallway and the stairs; someone called his name, making him scowl. He turned to glare before he stared, surprised to see the nanny carrying Esme in her arms.

"Oh, it's you, Chantel." He smiles at the matronly woman. "What are you doing up so early?"

"Esme just woke up, so I'm going to feed her." He nodded. "Are you alright? You look unease."

"I'm fine." He smiles as he went to kiss his daughter on the cheeks. "Good morning, princess." He cooed, "be good to Chantel." Esme cooed, and he couldn't help but smile.

"I have to go to a meeting this morning. So, I won't be back until this evening." He turned to leave.

"Wait? Did you eat?" But Nolan was walking for the door; he called over his shoulder.

"I'll grab something to eat in the city!"

CB

Nolan sat in a small white corridor. His stomach twisted with nerves of fear of being discovered; his face, especially of late, had been plastered all-over high-end magazines. Nolan was spotted by the receptionist when he entered the building and asked what floor was for the cleaning service. The female receptionist ogled after he thanked her before taking the elevator to the 9th floor. Nolan spoke to one worker, telling them he had a meeting with the owner. Now, Nolan sat impatiently in the uncomfortable seat briefcase on his lap; he lifted his right hand and looked down at his Rolex to see it was 8:35 a.m. Nolan heard a door open, and the manager said the owner was ready. He rose, thanking the man before walking into the small but colorful office of the owner of Squeaky Clean.

"Mr. Roth." Nolan smiles at the tall brunette, glancing to see the nameplate. "It's a pleasure to meet you, Ms. Lauran."

"Likewise. It's not every day we are graced by someone as successful as you." She gestured to him to have a seat, which he did. "Can I get you anything? Coffee? Tea? Hot chocolate?"

"No, thank you." she nodded before leaning on her chair.

"What is it I can do for you today?" Nolan hesitated.

"Well, I'm not sure where to start." He admitted sheepishly.

"Is there something wrong?"

"No, not at all. You see, that's why I am here… my wife had told me she needed your service at my home yesterday."

"Was there a problem?" Ms. Lauran asks, concern in her voice. "If there was any dissatisfaction that my workers had done, please let me—"

"No! No! That is not the problem. The people who worked at my home did a wonderful job!" Nolan spoke. He continued praising their professional manners and service.

"Well, we're happy to help you, Mr. Roth. It is quite an honor to know that you or to say your wife picked us, especially before your Christmas celebration." Nolan smiles. "Our service is always welcome, and our staff is always ready to help."

"Speaking of staff." Nolan seized this opportunity while he had it. "There is someone I like to discuss. One of your cleaning crew I met yesterday, Ms. Kate Alma." Mrs. Lauran's eyes widen.

"Oh, did something happen to Kate?!" she gasps.

"Oh no, on the contrary, she was excellent. Quite a hard worker."

"She is." Ms. Lauran sighs, leaning back in her chair. "Kate has only started working for us for a few months and already surpassed all expectations."

"Expectation?" Nolan inquired.

"Yes. At first, I was concerned when Ben told me about her. She is so young, and I feared for her safety with a baby on the way. She's a sweet girl, but you know how it is. We have to see everyone as a liability behind closed doors. We don't want anyone getting hurt and risk a lawsuit." Nolan nodded.

"But Kate, I never saw a woman work so hard in three months. She gets so many five ratings from people she worked with. She is attentive, giving us a good name for our company."

"That is good." Nolan listened with a surge of pride at Kate's accomplishments. "I am glad to know she is doing well. But as you said, she is with a child. Aren't you apprehensive that all this work could put her child in danger?"

"Ben voiced this to me as well." Ms. Lauran says. "The first two months, she worked seven days a week to clean five homes daily." Nolan froze as he sucked in an involuntary breath. "But since she started to show, Kate has changed her schedule to make herself more comfortable; she isn't working those hours anymore, but it still concerns me how much she still does." Nolan nodded, committing the new information for later use. "I'm sorry, I never asked; how do you know Kate?"

"Oh." Nolan felt nervous for the first time. "K-Kate is an acquaintance of mine."

"Really? She never told me that. Granted, I heard Kate doesn't converse with many people. She mostly keeps to herself. Only coming here to get supplies or if there's a meeting. But I'm getting off-topic; what is it you wish to know about Kate?" Nolan squared his shoulders.

"I am here because I wish to show my gratitude to Ms. Alma. To all your staff who worked at my house." He says. Nolan opened his briefcase. "I know it must be hard on a single mother. She has to work to care for herself and a newborn, so I want to reward her."

"That's very sweet of you, sir." Ms. Lauran beamed. "That would mean a lot to her and my staff."

"The thing is," Nolan looked sheepish. "I know Kate, and she doesn't enjoy being treated as if she is a charity case. If she found out I wanted to award her, she would not accept it. That is why I need your help."

"My help?" he nodded, smiling.

"I want to give Kate a gift from me without telling her. Make it look like she was given a prize or someone from her job wanted to reward her for her hard work."

"Ooh! Like a surprise!" Ms. Lauren squealed. Nolan nodded.

"Yes, that's what I meant. Let Kate believe it was a gift." Ms. Lauran thought for a moment.

"There is our annual Christmas party before the break," she says. "this is the year that we give out bonuses for the workers. I could give it to her."

"Yes! A bonus!" Nolan says.

79

"But she hasn't been working for me long," Ms. Lauren adds with a frown. "Only those who worked a year can get bonuses." Nolan's face began to fall. Was his plan starting too…?

"Unless I can give it to her in private. Tell her it was from a Secret Santa. That way, she wouldn't expect a thing." Nolan's face brightened.

"Yes," He agrees, "That would be perfect."

☙

Nolan entered his home that evening in high spirits. His day was perfect following his meeting with Ms. Lauren. His meeting with his rival company ended when they merged their thirty-million-dollar company with Nolan's. Now he had control over the tourism and hospitality sector. Although he was pleased, his mind focused more on the upcoming week: Christmas. Kate. Kate would not suffer during the holiday. Nolan made the final arrangements to ensure that she and his child would have a comfortable life. Nolan sat down in his office chair in his room with a smile; he closed his eyes.

"Kate." He breathes warmly. "I will right the wrong I've done to you." he heard noises coming from outside his door before opening it; he sensed his wife.

"Nolan?!" she says. He opened his eyes to look at Camille, his smile still on his lips.

"Camille." He spoke. Camille, believing the smile was meant for her, smiled seductively.

"You look cheerful." She says.

"Should I not be?" Nolan asks; Camille walked forward.

"Well, you did say you had a meeting today. By the looks of it, it was successful."

"It was." Nolan's lie was smooth as he grinned. "You're looking at the new co-founder of Nirvana tourism."

"I knew you would get it." She beamed. Nolan rose from his chair.

"Was there any doubt?" he walked to his wife and kissed her passionately.

"No, it's what I tell the girls," Camille says, pulling from their kiss. "You can talk out of a hostage situation as long as you come out. They can do what they want with the others." Nolan made a face.

"You didn't tell them that?" Camille smiles deviously.

"You have a way with words." She says silkily. "It's how you got this town to kowtow to you. You have them wrapped around your finger. It's what I told Kate." Nolan froze. He looked at his wife.

"You said that to her?" he asks. Camille smiled, nodding once. Nolan felt a throbbing pulse in his heart, but his smile was sweet as he said casually.

"I'm ready to eat."

Chapter Ten

The new year had finally come as the world turned on its axis, allowing the past to drift away for the future. January came with a blanket of white, fluffy snow that shrouded the sleepy town in a winter wonderland. Roofs were covered in glittering powder hiding the homes of the people who hunkered down, not ready to face the stress that snow came in its aftermath.

As the houses crowded under the blanket of white, one home sat alone amongst the tall pine trees that shook flurries down onto the earth. The red brick cabin stood out in the sea of snow. Its outward appearance was bright and merry. The dull brick of yesteryear was scrubbed away by nature's hand, making the once shabby cabin become a beacon to all who were lost; smoke wafted silently from the chimney, giving the cabin a homey look as snow blanketed the forest.

Kate took in the sharp, crisp air of peace and tranquility, feeling and listening to the sounds of nature amongst deafening snow. The woods were tranquil save for the falling snow that fell from the trees, the chirping of birds that sang in the background, its sweet trill echoing in the forest. She took in the beauty with reverence, the birth of beauty after a milliard of chaos. Kate woke up after a long, blustery night. Snow pelted her window where she lay in bed shivering, despite the heat of her electric heater; she listened as the wind knocked snow in heavy torrents. She had hoped that her roof could withstand the fury as she turned onto her back and stared at the black ceiling of her room where she lay.

When Kate opened her eyes, she was greeted by the view of white, no longer pounding and relentless. This snow was thick, soft, and billowy as if someone spilled sugar over the forest, she thought with a smile before turning around and walking out of the bedroom. She gazed at the scene with wonder; words of magic weaved in her mind of ice castles that only appeared in winter of heroes who stumbled upon this castle of ice to find secrets and treasure. Kate smiled at the word treasure just as a stirring in her stomach made her look at her fleece poncho at the visible mound that contoured her middle.

"It's beautiful out here." She whispers. Kate turned her gaze to a small picture she held in her left hand, a black-and-white image outlined by a figure who could not see but could hear the world through her mother. She leaned back in her seat, resting her back on the tree trunk. Lifting her hand, she peered at the ultrasound picture with loving tenderness, tracing the silhouette of her baby.

Kate, laying on the doctor's bed; watched the machine image seeing with brown eyes as a figure moved up and down: the wand the doctor held glided onto her smooth, taut, slimy belly, pointing to the image of hands, feet, stomach, spine and finally head. She stared, enchanted by the moving picture, her eyes stinging with unshed tears. Kate asked for a picture to take home, which the doctor readily granted before announcing that her child was healthy.

"You are doing well, Kate." The doctor spoke. "Just don't overexert yourself with your job."

"I won't," Kate answers, but she hardly paid attention as she stared at the hard copy of her treasure.

Kate hugged the picture to her breast, and wetness slid down her cold cheeks.

Our baby is healthy… Kate thought softly. *She's safe… Nolan.*

Twilight began to take root as the sun, once hidden by the remnants of clouded light, dispersed and began to set over the horizon line, bringing the end to a long, sleepy day on the lavish mansion in the woods. Nolan stared at the setting sun of winter; the orange glow cast its fiery blaze as it set forth to bring light to the other side of the world. He stood in his office under cover of darkness, peering out of the wide window, his face hidden, passive as his dark gray eyes, the color of midnight, gazed outward at his estate. Snow covered the front of his home, shrouding the driveway, trees, and fountain in white. The spray froze over, turning the bubbling streams of water into magnificent tendrils of clear ice crystal that pointed in different directions, making it resemble an elaborate outdoor chandelier.

It was a new world. Nolan couldn't help thinking. A world of quiet, of rest, despite the brutality of old men. Winter was natural. The best nature could offer. Free to all who took the time to appreciate her.

He smiled a tiny smile as he gazed past the trees, seeing the last sliver of the sun's appearance where he stood tall, proud, powerful... *Alone.* The word plunked like a stone in a well that whispered praises in its ripples. He didn't have to worry about human shortcomings and flaws: he was a man who could do no wrong. The man who smiled at interviews, broke dirt at new construction sites for a million-dollar hotel, donated to charities, and clinked glasses full of sparkling champagne.

 Continually wearing the same mask surrounded by the gold he created, the touch blinded everyone, making him glitter like the king he made them believe he was. Nolan's heart throbbed; it pulsed hot like stinging needles through his left chest. He let out a breath; leaning forward, his left hand touching cold glass while the right lifted upward to his heart. Nolan felt his body buried with heat; his lungs felt heavy as they burned, making breathing difficult. Nolan heaved, looking down at himself with worry.

"What's wrong with me?" he gasps. His chest squeezed, and his back went rigid. He took deep, fast breaths, listening to his breathing in the hot air that seemed to burn his throat. Nolan looked up five minutes later; his handsome face had a thin sheen of sweat, his breathing no longer heavy and hot as the pain in his chest began to subside. He looked at his hand on the glass, seeing the condensation around his hand; when he pulled his hand free, he saw his handprint on the glass.

Nolan lowered and peered at his palm, wet and cold but strangely soothing. He let his hand fall as he looked at his chest where he still grasped it, his fingers curled, gripping the fabric of his shirt; he was still staring at it when the door opened, and Camille entered. Lights flicked on, making Nolan blink at the sudden brightness.

"Nolan?" Nolan spun around to face his wife, who walked forward dressed in a rich outfit of gold sequins.

"Yes." He spoke. His voice came out rougher than he meant, and Camille stopped, eyeing his appearance.

"What are you doing in the dark?"

"I… nothing." He replies. "I was just watching the landscape." He nodded at the window.

"Oh." Camille crossed her arms, her face turned annoyed. "You mean the white out that graced our home."

"You sound bitter?" he says, lowering his hand from his chest that stung a little, but was manageable.

"We were supposed to be in the Mediterranean today. I was supposed to be soaking in a tub of rich herbs while sipping wine. Not being buried by disgusting snow." Nolan frowned inwardly, but his smile was in check when he spoke.

"I know." He walked forward. "I was looking forward to dining on some freshly caught oysters."

"Or fresh fruit. Now I'm stuck eating boring food." He raised an eyebrow.

"Boring? You mean our fantastic dinner of lobster, which I currently smell." Camille made a face.

"We need a new chef. Tony is too boring. I need variety."

"Tony is a good chef." Nolan defended. "He is using locally fresh ingredients."

"That's the problem. It's local." Camille replies as if local was a slug she stepped on. "I want to dine on what we can't get here. These townsfolk tastes are so mediocre." Nolan frowned, feeling ire at his wife's talk. Once upon a time, he would have gotten angry, ending with them fighting. Nolan looked away with a sigh.

"I'll have Tony ship ingredients from Europe." He conceded. "He can order wagyu, swordfish, whatever you want, once we return from vacation."

Camille beamed, nodding. Nolan stepped back, placing a hand on his left chest.

"Good. Maybe we can also get an Italian chef."

"I'm not firing, Tony," Nolan says.

"Why not?!"

"He knows how to cook for me." He says. "He's also a good man with a loving family."

"He can get another job," Camille says loftily. "He should be lucky you took him in and put—"

"I'm not in the mood to argue, Camille," Nolan says, voice hardening.

Camille stopped to get a good look at him.

"What's wrong?"

"It's nothing, just heartburn." He lied. Camille thought little of it; instead, she nodded.

"Go ask the maids if they have something. I'm sure they carry antacids or whatever the poor use." Nolan wanted to glare; instead, he nodded. He walked past Camille, who followed him, letting go of his chest.

Kate sat down with a contented sigh on the floor in front of the crackling fireplace, illuminating the living room where she sat on an oriental sitting pillow, the picture of ease as she braced her back on the heavy coffee table. The rest of her morning was spent in silent solitude. Although lonely, Kate reveled in the peace by keeping active: she cleaned and organized the baby's room, making sure nothing was a miss, taking in the new items she purchased.

Kate smiled as she touched the hard but sturdy wood of her brand-new old fashion rocking chair, her eyes softening at the thought of rocking her child to sleep when the nights were dreary. By midday, after a hearty lunch, she went to her room and researched on her laptop, listening to her radio about the winter storm. Kate scribbled down stories with ferocity, writing about the couple as they experienced a conflict in their relationship that would tear them apart. She cried quietly as she wrote, tears splashing on the pages as the love interest said goodbye to her before walking out on the main character.

Kate sniffed, feeling the main character's grief as she went along her day, always with a smile that hid her heartache. She stopped writing to catch her breath, feeling for the woman on paper; it didn't help that Kate felt her baby kick, which brought on more tears but this time of happiness.

Night had fallen on the cabin when she stepped out of her room, stomach rumbling with hunger. Craving cheese for dinner, she made grilled cheese, making different varieties, adding pepperoni slices, sliced apples, and ham with Swiss. All this she made, along with a cup of homemade cocoa. Kate munched on her sandwich, tasting the apples' cheesy goodness and sweetness. Classical music played on the radio, low and soothing, making her feel warm as she hummed to the tune.

This is so peaceful. She thought, listening as the logs popped into the hearth. Kate finished her dinner with relish before having a dessert of roasted marshmallows on the open fire; taking a sip of her hot cocoa, she tasted the rich flavor that flowed warmly down her throat.

Kate sighed contently, gazing at the fire as it danced; it seemed to respond to the music, seeing it twist and flow back and forth, giving heat. She stared at the flames, her brown eyes reflecting the orange glow that saw visions of the future past beyond the fire. Another body beside her, his arms wrapped around her petite frame, seeing his smile, his hair blowing in the central air, his gaze warm as he looked at her; dark gray eyes glowing in the firelight before he closed them, leaning forward toward…

She touched her lips, remembering the heat of his, hot, gentle. Kate huddled into herself, feeling warmth surge beside his flesh, yearning, warm against her. Kate wrapped her hands around her stomach, eyes half-closed as she leaned her head against her shoulder: a sleepy smile on her lips as she thought of what used to be, of fantasy, of dreams, of…

Kate fell asleep.

☙

Nolan woke with a gasp! Chest heaving as he breathed fast and heavy, sweat beaded down his brow as he sat up, feeling the hot room, the source coming from the massive lit mantle. Nolan turned his head to see his wife as she lay in bed, au natural, save for the blanket that covered her lower body as she lay on her stomach fast asleep. Spent. Nolan looked from his wife to stare at the mantle that burned the logs, its fiery flames making the room stifling as he kicked off the sheet and laid his feet on the carpet. Nolan panted. His chest burned with discomfort despite taking an antacid from his workers. His stomach roiled as his chest throbbed; not even a dessert of ice cream quenched his burning heart. He had some relief when he played with Esme; his just turned two-year-old: making her laugh as he showered her with love until Camille brought the nanny to take Esme so she, Camille, could be 'showered' by Nolan's love.

Nolan obeyed with a wry smile, but inside he was sick. After performing his husbandly duty, Camille went to sleep immediately as Nolan collapsed, losing consciousness to the world: seeking refuge in the realm of dreams. Nolan wiped his brow of sweat as his right arm wrapped around his middle, his lower half, semi-covered by the blanket; his bangs covered his eyes as he thought of his dream: a dream still so fresh in his mind. Not a dream. A memory. A moment with Kate. His chest throbbed as he lifted his head to peer at the curtained window revealing the pitch blackness of the night: seeing Kate as she walked down the hall, her eyes sparkled as she wore a strapless red dress. He stood tall in his suit, drinking in her beauty as people parted to stare at the beautiful woman who had eyes only for…

Nolan looked down at himself in the gloom. He couldn't see much, but he knew the silver band wrapped around his left ring finger. The band symbolized his bond: a bond he strove to rebuild by aching piece. Nolan felt a shudder run through him.

"*I'm doing the right thing.*" He spoke to the darkness. A sting hit his chest, but he ignored it as he turned and walked back to the bed; the blanket felt cool as he covered himself.

Nolan didn't go back to sleep.

Chapter Eleven

May crept upon the Forest-Bend with benevolent grandeur. After months of late snowflakes of march that melted into the form of April showers, spring drenched the earth, moistening the ground with its watery blessings, foretelling the promise of a cloudless sky and balmy days. Mother nature kept her promise as she walked the land; her flowing train dragged on the soil, leaving freshly grown flowers in her path as she walked, leaving her essence along cobblestone, and concrete, before coming to a stop on grass tall green spruces, a babbling brook and a small brick cabin.

Kate stood quietly within the small quarter of her bedroom, in front of a full-length closet mirror, where she watched the figure staring back at her: a stranger she had never realized was with her. The stranger stood on long legs, her toes perfectly pedicured, laid on smooth hardwood. The figure wore loose-fitted pants that complimented her body, hiding her swollen legs, knees, and thighs before stopping at a sphere where her belly used to be. The sphere was large, perfectly smooth, and taut over dark brown skin; one line streaked the middle of the sphere as if the globe was cut in half but was stitched up with dark thread. Hands smooth and slender held the globe. Its gentle touch made the sphere react; the stranger smiled, making her round face glow with full cheeks, soft red lips and brown eyes that sparkled in the light.

The image smiled at Kate as she mirrored her smile, shy at first but warm and sweet...

"Beautiful." Kate breathes; lifting a hand, she touched the cold glass coming in contact with the stranger, her doppelganger. Herself. Kate let go of the glass, turning her back on her reflection. Her long black hair swished slightly as she walked to her bed, where she left her maternity blouse; where Kate put it on, the light material slid smoothly before she sat down on the bed next to a pair of slip-on shoes putting on her socks. Kate slipped on the shoes before walking out of the room.

CB

The town was a buzz with excitement as Nolan walked the paved sidewalk; his feet clopped on designer sneakers as the townspeople whispered, gawked, and smiled at the newcomer. Him. Nolan felt eyes bore into him with his family, attempting not to call any attention to himself as he walked his wife to his left, as Nolan pushed the stroller containing his daughter. People watched Nolan through open shop doors and windows of the quaint old fashion stores. Nolan tried to take the popularity of all in stride, but his chest blazed; everywhere he looked, he was bombarded by grinning sycophants who thought he could do no wrong. Camille reveled in the attention, basking in the praises of the lower class who doted on her and her daughter.

"Nolan?" Nolan started before looking at his wife, watching him with a trained smile.

"Y-Yes." She frowned.

"I said I'm going shopping. Take Esme for me." Nolan blinked.

"Don't you want to spend time with her?" he asks, glancing down at his toddler, who slept in her stroller. "You haven't spent time with Esme in weeks."

"I'll spend time with her later," Camille says loftily. "There are a few things I want to see in town while we're here. I can get my nails done while you wait for me." Nolan shuddered.

"I'll go for a walk," he murmurs. "I need to go to the pharmacy." She nodded. "We can meet at the diner at 2:30 pm." Camille made a face before smoothing it out quickly as onlookers stopped a stare at the wealthy couple.

"Okay," Camille says too sweetly. She leaned forward and kissed Nolan to the townspeople's ooh's and awe's by their display of affection; but felt hollow as Nolan answered her kiss. Camille broke the kiss first; smiling coyly at him, despite her smile didn't touch her eyes before she turned and walked down the street.

The rest of Nolan's day was slow but comfortable as he breathed a sigh of relief. Nolan went to his favorite spots: first taking Esme to the bookstore, where he sat down in the children's section, reading to her before purchasing a few books to take home. Next, he went to the men's grooming store, where he was greeted warmly by the owner, whom Nolan talked adamantly about what was new in stock; Nolan ended up purchasing a shaving kit and shoe polish. Esme cried as Nolan stepped out of a watch store. Picking her up, Nolan glanced at his watch to see it read 2:01 pm.

Time to eat. He thought, feeling his stomach rumble as he smiled at his daughter, cooing.

"Are you hungry, my little Essie?" Esme looked at him, pouting. "Do you want food?" he nodded, making her nod. "Let's get lunch and wait for mommy, okay?" she nodded, making Nolan smile as he pushed the stroller. Nolan ate with relish, chomping down on a thick bacon cheeseburger and shoestring fries. The diner was crowded with patrons who sat in booths eating, drinking, and talking as waitresses waited and served in teal uniforms. Nolan listened to the people chatter about life and work while he ate, admiring the culinary creativity of the diner. He fed Esme chicken strips that Nolan had cut into bite-size pieces; Esme smiled at him as she chewed, and he grinned back, enjoying the sort of peace of the diner.

"Nolan!" Nolan looked up after taking a sip of coke to look at Camille, who was watching him angrily. Nolan's good mood suddenly sank.

"Camille?"

"Why didn't you answer me?!" she demands, side-stepping over a patron who passed by her.

"Y-You called?" It was then he saw the large number of bags that were held in both her hands.

"Oh, Camille, I'm... I didn't know." He says. Camille clenched her teeth as she said tightly.

"Maybe you were too busy stuffing your face with greasy food to pay attention to your wife's needs." Nolan opened his mouth to protest.

"Excuse me, ma'am." They both looked to see a waitress. "I'm sorry, but you are crowding the walkway. If you are not ordering anything, I will have to ask you to leave."

"Are you telling me what to do?" Camille's voice was low; before anyone could answer, she turned to the worker, eyes blazing.

"How dare you say that to me! I know people in high places who can't tear this pathetic hovel to the ground! You don't tell me what to do! Where is your manager?!" the waitress stepped back, stunned, afraid.

"Camille, stop!" Nolan rose and grasped her wrist. "This waitress has done nothing wrong." Nolan looked at the waitress apologetically. "That won't be

94

necessary getting your manager. She's, my wife." Camille glared as the waitress nodded. Nolan sat down in the booth, feeling eyes on him and his wife.

"Sit down, Camille." He spoke calmly.

"So, you're taking her side!?" she shrilled.

"I'm not taking sides. Just please sit down while the waitress gets you something to drink." The waitress nodded eagerly. Camille glared at the woman.

"I want a diet coke." She orders. The woman shrank back before nodding. Camille placed her bags on the chair before she slid into the booth, not concealing her disgust. The room seemed to let out a collective sigh as the patrons who watched the scene returned to their meals. Nolan sighed just as the waitress came back moments later with a tall glass of diet coke along with a menu.

"If you need anything, just let me know." Nolan could hear the waver in her voice. Nolan thanked the waitress, smiling apologetically as his wife stuck her straw, not even glancing at the waitress who walked away.

"*I can have her fired.*" Nolan swallowed at his wife's harsh whisper before looking away.

"I know." Nolan spoke; his stomach began to knot tightly. "she's only doing her job. She didn't mean any harm."

"She harmed me by being in my presence." Camille hisses. She looked at him with disgust on her face. Nolan couldn't help but notice the scar on her right cheekbone. "She's lucky this is as good as she can get. For everyone in *this* town." Nolan didn't answer. Instead, he turned his attention to the window, seeing the passersby as they went about their afternoon.

Nolan and his family left the diner after he paid, leaving a tip for the poor waitress who witnessed his wife's wrath. Carrying Camille's bags, the three of them headed back to their black Mercedes; Nolan was loading the trunk with the bags, feeling the afternoon heat on his back despite his white shirt. Camille hooked Esme to her car seat before shutting the door. Nolan was just closing the trunk after loading his spoils when a flash of white caught his eyes, making him pause to turn. His mouth went dry. Dark gray eyes grew wide as Nolan stared at the figure dressed in elegant clothes. A shiver ran down his spine.

"Nolan!?" Nolan looked at his wife. "What's wrong?"

"I…" Nolan turned his head and saw the figure was gone.

"I have to go!" he pressed the button the trunk began to close.

"Go? Go where?" Nolan looked at the street, scanning to find…

"Nolan!?" Camille yells. "What are you doing?" Nolan handed her the car keys and started to jog forward.

"I forgot something I wanted to buy." He called. "I have to get it."

"How are you going to get home?!" Camille cries, but he was already running down the street, calling over his shoulder, he says truthfully.

"I'll take an Uber!" Before turning a corner, running past people to find the figure in white. The woman he knew he saw just moments ago.

CB

Kate breathed. Taking in the sights and smell of the quaint town, admiring the new shops she hadn't stepped into after her self-exile. The town glowed with new life as she passed old fashion stores that sold toys, clothes, shoes, watches, baked goods, and candy. Kate entered the sweet shop with awe,

96

taking in the warm, inviting smell of hot chocolate that melted in a giant chocolate fountain, reminding Kate of the chocolate river in *'Charlie in the Chocolate Factory'*. She examined the large jars of sweets, picking out the best and her favorite with clear plastic tongs that she placed in a medium-size bucket.

She usually wouldn't purchase so many sweets, but today was a good day. Kate started her day in the supermarket, gathering groceries for the last time before her due date, purchasing fruit, meat, juice, milk, eggs, bread, sugar, flour, and pre-made foods. Kate was just driving into town about to go to the post office when she marveled at the beauty; seeing the smiling faces in the open shops; she was overcome by curiosity. So, driving her car to the town square, she took her first steps into the alien town that shunned her.

Kate placed the heavy tub on the register. The cashier's eyes were wide when she took in the amount; she smiled sheepishly before paying, thanking the man who didn't recognize her before leaving the store.

Kate walked in the afternoon sun, taking in the sun's warmth as she explored the streets window shopping and occasionally picking up a few trinkets to decorate her home.

I feel so free. Kate thought as she made her way down the street, pausing when she saw a group of women giggling. She lowered her head as she walked past them, breathing when she was a yard away from them. She may be free, but knew she was still not accepted. Kate looked up to see the town's clock post-reading 4:36 pm.

Time to go home. She thought, turning her head only to see an expansive window that displayed baby items such as clothes, shoes and rocking horses. Kate marveled at a white and yellow ball that stood high atop the display window. Unconsciously she touched the glass, her eyes riveted to the ball: her mind peering into the future, seeing herself rolling the ball on the ground with small hands. Kate entered the store, the door chiming for the bells that hung above her. She walked as if in a dream as she gazed at the baby store, the interior reminding her of a play-place for babies.

"Can I help you?" Kate started waking from her trance; she turned to see a young woman with red hair.

"Oh!" Kate apologizes. "I'm sorry, I got distracted."

"Is there anything I can help you with?" the woman smiles kindly.

"Yes, I wanted to purchase the white and yellow ball on the window." The saleswoman beamed.

"Of course, ma'am." She pointed to a basket in the back that contained multi-colored bouncing balls. Kate thanked the woman before going to the basket, examining each toy but not seeing the one that was on display that Kate asked about.

"Oh, let me check downstairs, ma'am." The clerk said. "I think we should have a new shipment of them." Kate smiles as the woman says she would return. Feel free to look around the store. Kate thanked the woman before looking around admiringly. She had already purchased enough clothes and disposable diapers but could not help eyeing the clothes and bibs with interest. She was passing by the birth cloths when she saw a table containing silver music boxes and chests.

"Oh!" Kate picked it up; lifting it, she peered at the bottom that held the turning knob. Kate turned it and listened to a beautiful tune played from the silver box; she looked at the price. "$115!" Kate stared at the music box, thinking of her account: she had enough to get her by until she could work again, but… although the box was cute, she had to focus on other finances. Kate sighed, placing the box back on the table as it trilled sweetly.

I've been so busy thinking about the baby's primary needs that I forgot to buy toys. Kate thought, placing a hand upon her swollen belly. She smiled just as footsteps came, making her turn to see the clerk.

"Here we are!" she says. Kate beamed as she walked forward.

"Thank you so much." Kate breathes; the woman handed her the ball; Kate tested its weight, even giving the ball a test bounce. "It's perfect." She adds, passing the ball to the saleswoman, who rang it up on the register.

"That will be $33.79."

"That much!?" she gasps. The woman nodded. "I didn't know it would be so expensive."

"Yes." The clerk replies. "It's made of a latex-free material; it hasn't been sprayed like most balls you would find in other toy stores because the smell could make the baby sick. And it's heat resistant and puncture-proof."

"Then it's worth the price." She noted with a weak smile.

"Oh indeed. These been selling like hot cakes." Kate nodded, then sighs.

"I'll take it." The woman smiled and nodded. Placing her candy bucket on the counter, Kate started to shrug off her backpack as the clerk pulled out a bag for the ball.

"What are you doing here?!" Kate looked up, startled; her right hand pulled halfway from her bag, that kept gripped her wallet. She looked to see a tall, curvy, mocha-skinned woman standing by the door.

"Ms. Jackson." The girl beamed. "How was lunch?" The woman ignored her as she glared, black eyes narrowed at Kate.

"Wh-what?!"

"Is something wrong, Ms. Jackson?"

"Yes, there is." Ms. Jackson says. "Why are you in my store?!"

"I... excuse me?" Kate says.

"You heard me! You got a lot of nerve coming here after all you've done!"

"Wh-What? Wh-who are you? I did nothing wrong. I just wanted—"

"What did she touch?" Ms. Jackson turned to the clerk.

"What?" says the clerk.

"What did she do? Did she touch anything valuable? Our expensive shipment?" Ms. Jackson demands.

"I don't know. I was in back I—"

"I did nothing wrong!" Kate cries.

"You sure as hell did! I know all about you, home-wrecker!" Kate felt as if she had been slapped in the face.

"What?"

"I know what you did to Camille and her husband." Kate was aghast; her wallet slipped from her fingers. "You trifling snake come to my store thinking you can do what you want, but not here. I know your ways." Kate pulled her hand from her bag.

"Please, Ms. Jackson, is it?" She spoke respectfully. "I don't mean any harm or disrespect. I didn't know this was your store. All I wanted was to purchase something; that's all I—"

"What did she buy, Jean?" Ms. Jackson spoke as if Kate hadn't answered.

"Uh... just a ball."

"Put it back. She will not have it."

"What?!" Kate felt warmth rising in her chest. "You can't do this!"

"It's my store. I can do what I want."

100

"I have money. I was going to pay—"

"With a card you and your boyfriend stole, no thanks." Kate opened her mouth to protest.

"What's going on here!?" The women turned to see Nolan, who stood tall as he entered the back door of the store. Ms. Jackson's face turned from disgust at Kate to a cheery smile as she said.

"Nolan, what a surprise to see you." The woman, Jean, stood to attention, gaping at the handsome man who walked forward. Kate shrank back, placing an arm around her stomach.

"What is going on?" Nolan spoke, stopping close, but not too close, to Kate.

"Nothing Nolan, just taking care of a little problem."

"And that problem is Nicole?"

"We have an attempted shoplifter." Kate raised her head in shock. She opened her mouth, but Nicole continued haughtily.

"This woman claimed to be paying for my merchandise with stolen money."

"That's not true!" Nolan looked at Kate, who cries out passionately. "I was to do no such thing." The woman sniffed disdainfully.

"I'm sure."

"Enough, Nicole," Nolan replies, he looked at the clerk. "What was she going to buy?" Kate looked at the woman pleadingly, but the woman lifted the ball. Nolan's eyes widened for a moment in surprise before he looked at Kate, who looked away as Nicole added.

"I don't want people like her ruining my store."

"Let her pay for it." He spoke. Kate looked at him with surprise. "If she has the money, she should pay."

"No!" Nicole glared at Kate. "I want you out of my store."

101

"Nicole!" Nolan protested.

"Get out, or I'm calling the cops." Kate shuddered before obeying with a nod; wordlessly, she picked up her bucket of candy, her eyes downcast as she side-stepped the two adults before walking out of the store with stinging eyes.

Nolan watched her leave to the jingle of the door closing behind her; he saw her walk down the street. Words were spoken, but they fell on deaf ears as he stared, head lowered, the familiar throb pulsing on the left side of his breast. Nicole beamed at him as if nothing had happened, tossing back her curly black hair as she said merrily.

"What can I do for you, Nolan?" Nolan raised his head to reveal stormy gray oculars. He pulled out his wallet. Opening it, Nolan pulled out a black rectangular object before slamming it on the counter.

"You can start by ringing up that ball." He replies solemnly.

∞

Kate walked, head lowered for her car, cheeks stained with tears as she clutched her stomach, protecting her child from the harsh words of the store owner. Her belly roiled as the baby felt every emotional upheaval Kate had injured. People passed by her, whispering as they recognized her; no one took pity on the single young mother; instead, they mocked her, whispering past gossip. It didn't stop the new flow of tears as Kate made it to her van, opening the trunk to put her candy bucket inside.

"Kate!" Kate looked at the voice to see Nolan running forward, holding a large blue and pink bag. Kate looked away and started to close her trunk.

"Wait!" Nolan stopped in front of her, gasping.

"K-Kate I…"

102

"Leave me alone, Allen." She spoke, her voice defeated. She wasn't in the mood to talk. Nolan stared, seeing the tear tracks on her cheeks. Instead of answering, he lifted the bag in front of her.

"Here." He says. Kate eyed the bag, seeing a hint of white and yellow.

"I don't want it." Nolan gaped at her.

"But why?" he spoke, surprised.

"It's not mine."

"But..." he stepped forward. "I bought it for you." Kate hugged her middle.

"I don't want your charity." Nolan stared at her in shock; he stared at the woman and how the sunset glow cascaded down her beautiful body. He looked away, seeing a small crowd begin to form.

"I know." He whispers. Kate didn't respond. "But I want you to have this. It's a gift. I want you to have it. I want your child to have this." He saw the crowd, but for the first time, he didn't care if they saw him with Kate. Kate lifted her head to watch him see the weariness on his handsome face. Kate nodded once. Nolan, seeing the nod, extended his right hand. Kate raised both hands and took the ribbon strap before pulling it away, barely touching his hand. Kate put the bag in the trunk before shutting the door.

"Thank you." Nolan nodded, watching her sadly. He wished he could say more but let Kate walk away slowly, her eyes downcast as she walked to the driver's seat; Nolan stepped back when he heard the engine's thrum watching as she backed the car before it turned and drove slowly down the street... His hand clasped on his chest.

☙

Nolan sat back in his office chair with an exhausted sigh. Night had fallen hours before. After Nolan saw Kate drive away, he turned back to the whispering murmurs seeing their confused but giddy faces as they spoke about the scene that played out most was the same unkind stories of Kate and her violent attack on Camille, but one stuck out the more:

He, Nolan Roth, had given Kate a gift.

Nolan passed through the crowd as their murmurings echoed painfully in his heart. Nolan drove home on Uber in silence, looking down at his palms and tracing the lines that etched his flesh. Once home, dinner was announced, and he sat down with his wife and child in the dining room; Nolan ate wordlessly throughout the meal. Although the meal was delicious, Nolan missed Tony's down-home cooking. As he ate, Camille was on the phone, pausing to take another bite of her meal, ignoring Esme, who squealed for her attention despite being fed by the nanny.

"What was so important that you had to buy?" Camille asks, making Nolan jump.

"What?" Nolan started at the question.

"You left me." Her eyes narrowed. "You left me to drive our stuff back home; Esme cried out for you throughout the ride home!"

"Oh," Nolan says. He had forgotten his ruse at the baby store after the incident. He looked down at the large slice of lasagna, his expression sober. "It's not important." He finally says. "They didn't have what I wanted."

Camille stared, face pensive, as Nolan ate.

"You mean to tell me you rushed out on your wife and child for a non-existent quest?" her eyes narrowed. Nolan lifted his glass of wine and drank.

"Yes," He answers, placing the cup down. "That's exactly what happened." Camille stared for a long time, her eyes narrowing. The nanny watched the scene with a curious gaze, pausing to feed Esme.

104

"What is so important that you would abandon your wife?"

"I didn't abandon you, Camille," Nolan spoke gravely, not looking at her.

"There was something I had to do, something important."

"More important than your wife, it seems," Camille spoke snidely. Nolan rose from his seat.

"I'll be in my office."

Nolan sat up abruptly, looking down at his desk and feeling the pain coursing through his being. Pulling out the secret compartment revealing a dissolvable antacid, ripped the sealed package. Fortunately, he had a bottle of sparkling water by his table. He broke the quarter-size chalk tablet into pieces before plopping it on the lip of the bottle. It fizzed to life but would take time to dissolve.

Nolan sat wearily, thinking about Kate seeing her again after so many months, seeing her standing in the store after following her. He didn't want to make himself known; he hung back after seeing her leave the candy store, watching as she wore a white lace poncho over a blouse, her face in the sunlight looking as beautiful as the day while she explored the town, she once said was a capsule to tradition and quaintness.

Nolan smiled as he saw her enter the baby store; not wanting to go inside, he saw the back-door entrance going around the back; he stopped near the door, seeing Kate pick up the music box. Watching her smile as she gazed at the trinket. Nolan's gaze traveled to her belly, seeing how much it had grown: the last time he saw it was a bump. Now, a giant sphere seemed to swallow Kate's petite frame. It amazed him; he wished he could touch it, feel the bond between his child, to feel the warmth of... he started when Kate gasped the price, seeing her crestfallen expression as she placed the trilling box back on the display table. Nolan pulled from the view to stare at the streets, his face pensive, an idea hatching in his...

"What are you doing here?!" Nolan started. He turned his head to glance at the new voice, only to jerk back when he saw Camille's friend, another lackey, to her gossip empire. Nolan listened as Nicole spoke harshly to Kate, seeing the woman's face full of disgust and ire at the quote-unquote mistress who tried to ruin his and his wife's reputation. Nolan didn't think, just reacted; he came forward, ignoring the pang in his heart when Kate shrank back from seeing the sadness, knowing that no one would help her for past deeds, the suffering he had put upon her. Nolan opened his eyes; he involuntarily closed to look at the green bottle. Sitting up, he took the bottle and drank the watered-down medicine, feeling the cold sensation go down his throat, wishing it could take the fire away forever instead of giving him momentary relief.

He felt hot. He wanted...

Kate sat in the living room by the light of the fire. Although the season was getting warmer, she could not help feeling comforted by the firelight that made her skin glow. After a big dinner, Kate washed the dishes before sitting on the sofa, weary by this afternoon's events. The tears that were shed dried up hours before leaving her tuckered out. She didn't want to remember that terrible incident at the store; instead, she focused on it after she left. Seeing Nolan.

Kate was shocked to see him as she packed to go home, seeing the man who wronged her and her child. He didn't look well. That was Kate's impression as she saw him after their last encounter. He looked thinner, his cheeks sunken, and his face, although handsome, looked ashen as if he was coming off a sickness. It seemed ironic to Kate, for the rich never got sick; they were another being higher than humans, at least that is what she believed; she had a firsthand account of their power, the malicious way they used to get what they wanted and have it successfully.

But seeing Nolan, seeing his eyes once mysterious and gentle, now dull as he gave her the bag, made Kate feel a pang of what she didn't know. Kate laid a hand on her middle. She looked at the blue and pink bag that sat on the coffee table. Kate lifted the bag in front of her and opened it. A small smile formed on her lips as she saw the yellow and white ball; lifting it from the backpack, she gazed at the round object, feeling the large smooth texture; Kate's smile widened before she placed the ball back in the bag when she heard a sudden trill.

Surprised, Kate opened the bag to see amongst the tissue paper a small object that too was wrapped in paper. Curious, Kate lifted the palm-size thing before unwrapping it. Kate's eyes widened, her breath caught in her throat as she gazed, eyes stinging at the silver music box: the very box she picked up. Questions pooled through her as she stared, examining the music box from all angles. She could not believe it, but there it was in her hand. Nolan had bought her the music box, the specific one held at the store. No one else was with her unless...

He saw her pick it up. Nolan had followed her. She, Kate, unbeknownst to her, had a pair of eyes watching; not with disgust or mocking but of... Kate turned the knob of the music box and listened to it play, placing it on the table. She entwined her fingers, eyes closed, her shoulders trembling as hot and wet tears slid down her cheek, not of sorrow or defeat but...

Gratefulness.

108

Chapter Twelve

Night drew its midnight curtain upon the town, closing the chapter that told a story of warmth and sunshine with the hint of humidity that spread over the small town with the promise that summer was on its way. Kate raised herself with an effort peering down at her middle, trying to see past her swollen belly to look at the black duffle bag containing the items she would need on her last trip to the hospital: the last time she, Kate, would be pregnant.

In a matter of days, she would give birth to a new life: a life she carried amongst ridicule for several months. Side eye glances, snide remarks, all the while Kate scrubbed floors, dusted rooms, cleaned houses and apartments until they sparkled. All this she did, trying to reconnect with her fellow humans, to find companionship in a town she still held dear to her. Kate turned from her baby bag with a sigh, her hands behind her back as she stood in the kitchen. Her back had been hurting her of late. Kate woke up to terrible cramps that spread from her lower back to her stomach.

The baby kicks were even stronger as she went about her day doing last-minute preparations for her home. Kate stepped out of the bathroom in her nightdress, clicking off the light as she walked in darkness, knowing her way to the bedroom by heart. Kate shut the door before she climbed into bed, covering the large down comforter atop her. Kate stared at the window, at the pitch blackness as an owl hooted outside her window as she snuggled close to her pillow.

I can't believe how time flies. She thought softly. It feels like only yesterday that I came to this town, hoping to start a new life after the hustle of New York.

Kate reminisced to her old life, going to school, playing outside with the neighborhood kids, having adventures in imaginary worlds where she was the hero and was tasked with saving everyone. Kate thought of her parents, her father especially thinking of the days she spent with him, whether at home or at his college job, where she watched him proudly teach bright-eyed students of history; telling them of man kinds past the good and the bad, how in the ashes life sprouted for the next generation to cultivate.

Kate could not help but smile. She was a daddy's girl that hadn't changed despite everything else. She had risen from the ashes of pain, betrayal, heartache, and rejection, but...

Have I cultivated enough for her? She thought as the thought hung in the air; moonlight entered the open window, casting its heavenly beam upon Kate, but she didn't notice it, for she was fast asleep.

☙

Kate awoke with a jolt! Her eyes opened to the sudden pan that rocked through her body. Kate gasped, her hand grasping at air as she sat up, breath hot and heavy as she blinked back the sweat that blurred her vision. It was hot, so boiling. Kate threw her legs over the bed and sat up more properly. As soon as she did, hot pain squeezed her chest and stomach.

Wh-what? Wiping the sweat from her eyes, she reached for her phone. Light blinded Kate momentarily, but it was enough to show her the screen reading: 1:12 am.

"O-oh!" she gasps, looking at the phone. She looked down, breaths coming out short and fast as realization hit her. Kate didn't think, just reacted.

110

Pushing herself off the bed, Kate staggered on trembling legs through the dark, still gripping her phone. She walked down the hall. Her keys were on the table along with her slip-on shoes that she felt with her feet, slipping them on. Kate's breaths were labored as she walked to the door, pausing just a moment to pick up the duffle bag that felt heavier as she shut the door and walked on shaky legs through the pitch night. She let out a scream as pain pulsated through her stomach. The night echoed with her cries. She felt the hot sticky night press down her body, but didn't care as she pressed the unlocked car key button, and its lights flicked on in the darkness.

Kate opened the door to the driver's seat, shoving her bag into the passenger; putting one leg, she hopped in before shutting the door. Kate fumbled with the keys in the dark, her mind telling her to turn on the light, but the pain…

"**Kiya**!" Kate screamed. She forced herself to concentrate, to let her hands stop shaking, breathing. She felt the key in the ignition before turning it, feeling the thrum of the engine roar to life. Kate put the car in reverse. Turning the steering wheel, she maneuvered the car expertly before driving out into the night.

Traffic was light on the highway, but Kate drove slowly, stopping on the side of the road every few minutes when her stomach cramped, causing her to scream with pain. The clock on the dashboard was no help, as her contractions grew worse with every pause. Sweat beaded down her face despite the A/C on full blast; her chest heaved as if her lungs could only hold ounces of air, but she drove, staring at the road with concentration, grateful that the highway wasn't heavy with traffic. She would take her time, just like the old fable.

She nearly cried out with joy when she saw the sign reading hospital. Kate sped up just a little so as not to call attention to the police; the thought made her shiver, not wanting another encounter with them. Although their intentions were noble, Kate was not ready, not…

Kate parked her car in the closest spot near the hospital, eyes stinging with tears of relief and pain. She gritted her teeth as she grabbed her bag, opened the door, and walked on trembling legs. Kate entered the general hospital, the large doors sliding back, letting cold air cascade through her. She looked with pain-filled eyes at the hustle and bustle of doctors and nurses walked back and forth in clean sterile scrubs. She stepped forward, passing the onlookers who saw faces unfamiliar, judging, as they took her in silently. Kate ignored it all as she stopped in front of the reception desk where a young woman sat.

"Hello, can I help you?" Kate's lips trembled. The words she wanted to speak could not pass her lips. The woman stared at her for a moment. "Is something wrong, ma'am?" she asks when she saw Kate's state. Kate nodded. "Are you in pain of any kind?" Her lips trembled as she nodded. "If you are injured, please go to the emergency room." The woman pointed down a long corridor.

"You can have a seat there until you're called by a nurse." Kate shook her head. The woman frowned. "Ma'am, if this isn't an actual emergency then please…" The woman's words fell on deaf ears as Kate turned her head to see two officers come into the hospital her eyes widen when she saw them walk right for…

Her water broke!

Kate's head pulsed, lightheaded, disconnected. An involuntary gasp escaped her lips as pain she couldn't describe stabbed her back. Someone gasped! She vaguely saw the police step back in alarm before looking down to see a puddle of wetness on her shoes. Arms gripped her as the world swayed forcibly. For a moment she saw nothing but blinding light before it came into focus, and she saw a man with sandy blond hair and wide eyes speaking to her frantically. Kate stared. She was on the floor; she wondered how she got there as people she didn't notice before, crowded around her.

"Ma'am! Ma'am?! What is your name?!" Kate started at the familiar question. Her throat felt tingly from disuse. "Ma'am! How many months are you?!" Kate blinked. The question struck a chord. Suddenly, everything came back into place. She was in the hospital. She was going into... Kate screamed!

ʒ

Kate gasped! Her chest heaving, trying to take sips of crisp sterile air. Her eyes stung as sweat and tears streaked her face while nurses crowded around Kate barking kind commands at the young mother who strained, panted, and pushed. Kate was carried into the maternity ward by the nurses and doctors who lifted her from the floor, her night dress drenched in fluid by the time a bed was brought to the main entrance.

Kate sobbed, frightened for the life inside her, fearing she had failed, that her child... Kate was carried away, her right arm connected to an I.V drip as she was led away.

"M-My b-bag?" she whimpered. A nurse by her side, smiled.

"It's right here, honey. Right on the bed." Kate nodded tearfully, grateful for the nurse's kindness. "Can you tell me your name?" Kate hiccupped and tells them. "That's a pretty name. Now Kate, can you tell me how you got here?"

"I-I drove."

"Alone?" Asked another nurse. Kate nodded.

"Kate, do you know when the contractions started?" Kate sniffed.

"No… all I know is I woke up at 1:12am to pain. My back and st-stomach were hurting so much."

"So, you drove alone?"

"Y-yes." Kate felt tears stream down her eyes. "I had no choice!"

"Why didn't you call 911?" asks the first nurse.

"I-I live in the woods." Kate gasps. "I-I didn't know this would happen. I was due in four days."

"What date?" Kate tells them. "Oh, honey, these things happen. You have nothing to be afraid of." Kate hiccupped. "Just hold on. We're going to take care of you, alright."

"Is your husband coming to the hospital?" Kate shivered, shaking her head as a new realization hit her. Nolan.

"No," she confessed weakly. "I'm alone." The nurses looked at her with sympathy.

Kate sat up on the bed, her brown eyes full of pain. Nurses stood on each side of her arm, supporting and soothing her as she screamed. Kate squeezed the nurse's hand in her right as she pushed, following the doctor's instructions through the turmoil. Her body felt severed in two, her ears ringing from her screams, her pleas…

"I can't do it!" she wailed.

"Yes, you can, Kate!" They say firmly. She shook her head. "You can do this! Don't be scared. We're right here for you! Do it for your child. They need you!" Kate stared tearfully; her eyes burned with sweat stuck to her forehead.

She felt so weak, frightened, alone… Kate thought back to the days she was with Nolan at the memories they spent in the summer of magic where she told him her dreams, her hopes to become a writer. Her quest to bring back fantasy to the hearts of those who forgot it.

She had forgotten about that world: the work she created to escape the harshness of reality to play in its realm, but not to forget that reality is needed, so they could grow and be independent. To leave a mark even as they danced in make-believe.

She wanted that. Kate was tired of being alone. She wanted to make fresh stories. New memories. The past was gone, but her present. *Her future…* was right here… Kate nodded. She turned her head, seeing past the window that showed dawn breaking in the east to look at herself at her swollen belly that housed her treasure: her pearl Not of price… but great love.

"The babies crowning!" the doctor announced. He looked up, beaming at Kate. "You're almost there, Kate! Just one more push." Kate nodded, then took in deep, gasping breaths before letting out a scream one last time.

A piercing wail echoed in the room. Kate looked down, her ringing ears reacting to the new sound.

"It's a girl." Kate blinked sweat from her eyes that grew with wonder as the doctor lifted the tiny figure, its body pink, its wails telling Kate to… Kate lifted her arms, her eyes glistening. She clutched the figure in her arms, supporting its rump and back as it cried. Involuntarily Kate let out soft shushing sounds at the infant with pink skin, tuffs of thick black hair and…

"Kate?" she looked up to see the nurses smiling down at her. "The baby." Kate nodded wordlessly. Carefully, reluctantly, she handed the baby to the nurse. She stared, mesmerized, as the nurse weighed the baby, handling her with care even as the baby cried once more, missing the warm body it had lived for so many months.

"6 lbs. 4 ounces." The nurses announced. Before taking the baby to another table, Kate was being taken care of, but her eyes were only on her child; vaguely aware of being told about the afterbirth when the baby, now wrapped in a neonate blanket, cap and diaper, was carried to Kate's awaiting arms.

Kate felt the stranger's weight under the crook of her arm, warm, still, yet so familiar: after months of feeling it twist, punch and kick, whether sleeping or waking, its tiny body left its impact, alerting Kate to a pang of hunger, sleep and attention, she was finally here. Kate stared at the tiny creature with silent awe, amazed that this came from her; she, who had no friend in the world whom her fellow man, betrayed, cast out, had done something like this. Kate didn't think she could perform blessings to make miracles become real instead of books, but she had done it. The proof was right there before her eyes, in her arms. Round brown eyes peered upward with blurry wonder.

"Hi." Kate breathes. The baby girl watched her silently as Kate smiled down, lovingly drinking in her treasure.

"Kate?" Kate looked up to see the nurse smiling at her.

"Yes?"

"We want to know if you have the strength to answer some questions." Kate nodded, answering all she could before the nurse came to the important question.

"What will you name your baby?" Kate looked down at her daughter, who slept peacefully. She caressed the side of her child's pink cheeks, reminding Kate of pink flowers that used to grow in her family garden.

"Rose," Kate says. "Her name is Rose."

"Will she have a middle name?" Kate nodded.

"Sophia Emily," Kate answers.

"That's a unique middle name." says the nurse as she jotted it down.

"Sophia was my mother's name." Kate looked down at her child. "And Emily is a friend I saved last year." The nurse smiled, nodding before leaving, promising to have a baby crib brought to her. Kate nodded, but her eyes were still on her baby.

"My little Rose," she whispers. "We're all we have now." Kate leaned forward and kissed her cheeks.

"*But we're going to make it.*" Kate breathes before she fell asleep.

Chapter Thirteen

Nolan felt sick. His chest throbbed, and his heart burned as his work and life, declined. The weeks into May took a turn for the worse as poor status for his company when the stock market took a downturn affecting him and his investors, who took a chance on his company. Nolan was doing damage control coming from meeting after meeting; answering, demanding his workers to make everything right to do what he said with assertiveness.

Nolan spoke through conference calls with people worldwide, trying with all his might not to lose their trust in him, making promises as he swallowed antacids, trying to soothe the fire in his throbbing chest. That was Nolan's routine for the past weeks. He had stayed in the city, signing papers by day and going to sleep in his private suite, collapsing on his king-size bed by night. Nolan entered his home in a daze after two exhausting weeks, greeted by his maids, who welcomed him happily, asking if he was hungry.

"Chef Luc just made a mushroom ravioli with soup."

"No, thank you, I… maybe later. Right now, I need to rest." The maids nodded.

"Oh, Ms. Camille, have guests this evening." Said another maid. "She and her girlfriends are in the parlor." Nolan grimaced as he walked up the stairs.

"Shall I tell Camille that you're home?"

"No," he says gravely, feeling the familiar throb of pain. "Leave her, I… I need to be alone. If she asks for me, tell her I'm in the office." The maids nodded and left, leaving Nolan to climb the staircase. He was near the top when a door opened, and the nanny entered the hall carrying Esme, who, upon seeing Nolan, burst into tears.

"Nolan!" she gasps. Nolan's head pain sharply upon the extra noise.

"What's wrong with her!?" he demands, too annoyed to be kind.

"I don't know. She was fine a second ago. Maybe you scared her."

"Scared her?" Esme hugged the nanny close.

"Are you alright, sir? We haven't seen you in weeks."

"I'm fine," He spoke gruffly. "Can you keep her quiet? I need some peace." The nanny nodded before walking away. Nolan lifted a hand to his chin, feeling the rough stubble of beard growing on his face. He didn't have to imagine how he looked: no wonder Esme was afraid of him. Nolan closed the door to his office, turning on the light. He walked to his seat, collapsing on it with a groan, his bangs tickled his eyelids that dropped as exhaustion overtook him and he fell...

"Nolan!" Nolan jolted awake, his eyes flying open as he gasps to see Camille who stood across the desk, her usual scowl of annoyance on her lovely face.

"Camille? Wh-what...?" he glanced down at his table where a small digital clock read 8:08pm. Surprised, he looked at his wife, heart hammering.

"What are you doing here?" he asks hoarsely.

"I came to see you." her tone was not warm. "I came to talk to my husband to demand answers to a few questions. I had to wait while I was with my friends." Nolan's hand landed on his left chest as he looked down wearily.

"I'm not in the mood tonight, Camille." He spoke gravely. "I've had a long two weeks, as I'm sure you of all people should know."

"Oh, I've noticed." Camille crossed her arms over her chest. "You and half of your millionaire friends have been all over the news." Nolan winced. "But that's your problem, not mine." He looked at her, dark eyes stormy.

"What do you want, Camille?" He spoke coldly. "If you've come to berate me for my shortcomings, you'll have to take a rain check."

"Don't you talk to me like that, Nolan!" she hisses. "It wouldn't take me two minutes to pack my luggage and take Esme with me to Europe." Nolan's spine when rigid, but his words were colder.

"Oh, so you finally acknowledge we have a daughter. And here I thought Esme was just your off again on-again accessories." They both glared at one another.

"Like your mistress." Camille spat. Nolan had enough. He rose abruptly to his feet, nearly knocking his chair to the floor.

"You leave her out of this!" he snaps.

"Oh, I would. But it seems you cannot."

"What are you talking about?"

"It seems you can't go anywhere without being trusted. It makes sense why you were so distant last week. You were still hung over your whore." Nolan felt as if he had been slapped in the face.

"Camille." He spoke voice low. "Do not say that in front of me. You will never speak about Kate in that manner." Camille lowered her arms; hands clenched tightly on her hips.

"I gave you a second chance. I let this marriage go on for us, for our daughter." She glared at him with icy green eyes. "I go to your mistress. I sabotage her life, so you are clean to the eyes of everyone in this stupid town. I made sure that baby isn't yours, that she is looked down on as nothing but a gold-digging gnat, and this is the thanks I get? You go behind my back and see the pregnant wench, making all I've done, what we've done for nothing!" Nolan stared at her with surprise.

120

"Y-you… you know." She glowers at him. "H-how?"

"Why don't you ask, Nicole?" she spits contemptuously. "Apparently, she witnessed you paying for a gift for that whore after she was caught stealing from her store and—

"That's enough!" Camille stopped at the roar that escaped Nolan's burning throat. "I told you not to call Kate that!"

"Oh, then how about a thief, because that's what—"

"Nicole is lying! Kate didn't steal from her. I saw she was going to—"

"Wait? How did you know that?" Nolan froze. "Were you following her?" Nolan flushed. He looked away. Camille stared with mocking laughter. "Oh, isn't that wonderful?" Her tone was mocking. "While I was waiting for my beloved husband, he was out in town, stalking his mistress. Playing all innocent when he wanted to see his used goods."

"I never said that Camille," Nolan spoke gravely. "I just… I just wanted to see how she was doing," he confessed.

"So, you buy her gifts? You just noticed she was short on cash, and you so gallantly offer to pay for. Because you're such a gentleman." Camille's tone was sardonic.

"She wasn't short on cash." He grumbled. "Kate was going to pay for her items before—"

"Before Nicole saved her store from a would-be thief. Good for her."

"So, what!?" Nolan lifted his head to glare at his wife. "So, I paid for Kate. I saw her being treated unfairly by your lackey for something I did. Not Kate, not my child!—they don't deserve—"

"Of course, they do!" Nolan was stunned. Camille looked at him coldly; her forehead wrinkled as her eyes narrowed.

121

"You don't understand, but I do. You don't seem to see into the future, but I can. What if the truth was found out that you fathered a child with your mistress? The tabloids would have a field day. People online would go back and forth about us, whether we should split up, and what of the mistress? She would be all over the news getting free publicity and riches as your company, **your** empire, crumbles. Esme will grow up knowing that her daddy couldn't keep it in his pants and why mommy hates daddy all because of her!" Camille sneers 'her,' with such revulsion it sent a shiver down Nolan's spine.

"I did what I had to do to maintain the perfect family everyone says we are," Camille spoke. "You chose to stay. I made sure your hands were clean of Kate and that baby. No one will ever know. We rule this town and the people. *Our hands are clean.*"

Nolan stared at his wife with newfound eyes. His mind raced on Camille's cruel, *truthful* words. A shuddering gasp escaped his lips as he looked down at his desk. His chin lifted involuntarily, making him look unwillingly at his wife, dark gray to her green. She leaned forward and kissed him; long, hot, *passionless*. Nolan took it all without complaint. Camille pulled away first with a smile.

"I love you." She breathes. Nolan didn't answer. Camille stepped back, letting go of him, turning elegantly.

"Oh, by the way. Kate had the baby." Nolan's eyes widen in alarm.

"What!?" she paused, turning to halfway to look at him with a nod.

"Susie saw her at the hospital two nights ago." Camille's smile was uncaring as she pushed back a lock of hair.

"Kate's water broke right in front of everyone in the hospital. Susie says she was screaming, refusing to answer questions until she was led away," She chuckles. "must have been ashamed to admit who the dead-beat father was." She smirked. Nolan didn't react to the insult. Kate had…

"She gave birth!? I-is it a boy or a girl?" Camille shrugged.

"She didn't stay for the delivery," She smirked. "just thought you should know. Like it matters. You do not need to worry about the likes of them." Nolan didn't respond, just stared. Camille left the room, closing the door behind her. He stared at the door, his gray eyes sunken, stinging…

∞

Kate looked up at the sudden knock coming outside her front door. she stared, startled, where she sat on the edge of her bed; wondering who could come to her at this time of night. She waited silently after the first knock, expecting it would go away; thinking it was a deer that occasionally came by her home.

 Another knock followed, loud but not demanding. She looked from her open door to peer down at the large white crib where her treasure lay. Kate spent the better part of her evening taking care of her child. After having a bowl of thick creamy lobster bisque for dinner, Kate started her new nightly ritual of caring for her baby: she washed Rose in a bucket careful of the umbilical stump, once dried, she put on a new diaper and gently slipped on a white onesie.

Rose cried. It was then Kate scooped her up tenderly in her arms, taking her to her bedroom, where she had moved the crib two days before. Kate soothed and caressed her child as she pulled back her nightgown and breastfed Rose before laying her on the crib, where Kate just sat watching her lovingly at the tiny creature.

She rose from bed, wincing as she took a step forward, placing a hand upon her swollen stomach that descended slowly, her body healing after giving birth. She was in her living room when she called out warily.

"Who is it?"

"It's Nolan!" Kate froze at mid-step just by the door, her eyes wide as a growing question, and fear, crept into her.

"Kate!?" she dare not move or speak. "Kate! Are you there?"

"Go away!" Kate was surprised by her raised voice.

"Kate, please let me in! It's me!"

"I know it's you!" she called out, glancing back quickly behind her before looking back. "what are you doing here!?"

"I…" there was a pause. Kate stood near the door, listening. "I heard about the baby." She froze. This time, she stepped back with fear.

"Please, Kate, open the door."

"Why should I trust you!" Kate was angry as the sting of tears threatens in her eyes. "Go away! Or I'm calling the police!"

"I promise, I'm not here to cause trouble," Nolan called. "Please, open the door." Kate hesitated, hearing the pleading in his voice. Kate looked down at herself in her light nightgown. Kate unbolted the lock before opening slightly, her eyes downcast, unable to meet her visitor.

Nolan stood outside her door dressed in a navy-blue business suit that, in the dim light, Kate could make out how rumpled it looked; her eyes traveled to his face that was half hidden in darkness: Kate stared at him somberly as he gazed at her with wide but tired eyes.

124

"What do you want, Allen?" Kate's voice was firm. Nolan blinked at her, forgetting he was in the dark, humid forest.

"May I come in?" Kate didn't respond right away. When she spoke, it was controlled.

"I think it's best that you didn't." Nolan stared. "You are not welcome here. I don't know how you found my home, but please leave."

"Kate, wait!" Nolan placed his hand on the door just as Kate closed it.

"Kate." He spoke calmly. "Look at me."

Kate didn't.

"I have no ties to you, Allen." Nolan looked down.

"I know, but Kate, you just had…" he stopped. Kate looked at him then, seeing him wince, his right hand on his left chest.

"I know you don't trust me." He continues. "Not after what… please, this child…" He looked at Kate. "I want to see the baby, just once." As he stared at her, Kate heard the pain in his voice, seeing his eyes. Kate hesitated…

Kate spun around at the cry coming from her room. Nolan looked up at the sound with surprise. Before he could react, Kate had let go of the door and left the room. Nolan hesitated for a moment before opening the door fully and entering the house.

Nolan closed the door. He looked curiously at the small living room; fire crackled quietly in the mantle, illuminating the room with a warmth Nolan had only felt when he was with Kate.

Subconsciously, he took off his suit jacket and placed it on the black leather sofa before walking peering forward at the house. Although small and empty save for furniture was clean; his footsteps were quiet as Nolan walked down the hall, passing the first two doors before… he stopped just a yard

125

from Kate's room. Nolan stared at the young mother, who stood cradling something white in her arms; he heard soft hushing as she rocked the small creature, who cried softly as Kate cooed gently.

Nolan stared, his chest warmed as his heart throbbed and released it was a pain different from the others; his mind didn't tell him to reach for an antacid. He didn't feel stressed. Today's stress felt distant. All that was left was this pain, this warmth.

He welcomed it.

Kate turned her head to see Nolan standing by her door, his expression full of awe as his eyes met hers. Pleading. Kate met his gaze with wariness but understood what he wanted. Kate gestured with a nod at her bed. Nolan stepped forward into her room. He took in the room's interior before he sat down on the bed. Kate watched him before slowly she stepped forward as Nolan involuntarily lifted his arms as she leaned forward. The baby let out a small cry as Kate gently passed her child into Nolan's warm arms.

Nolan peered down at the baby, spellbound, in his enormous arms. She was so light as if he was holding a loaf of bread. Nolan shifted his arm, and the baby settled into his body, bright brown eyes peered blearily into glistening gray eyes as he memorized every feature from her browning skin, her silky black hair to her tiny nose, her small mouth, before looking down, counting ten little fingers. He counted twice. Nolan raised his head to see Kate, her head turning to the closet, but it was enough to show moisture had formed in her left eye.

"Is it a boy or a girl?" he breathes a pang of guilt him for not knowing.

"A girl." Nolan nodded.

"She's beautiful," He whispers. Kate nodded wordlessly. "What is her name?" Kate looked at him, then lifting a hand to her chest.

"Rose." She spoke gently.

"Rose." He whispers. Nolan looked down at the child. "Hello Rose, it's nice to meet you, I'm…" he stopped, voice tightening. Kate watched him, seeing his mouth half open, sunken cheeks growing red before he closed his lips. He swallowed hard.

"How did you get to the hospital?" he asks after a long silence. Kate's eyes stung painfully. She looked away.

"I drove."

"Alone?" she nodded. "Were you due on time?"

"No," Kate spoke. "I was due yesterday." Nolan's eyes widen as he did the math in his head.

"How did you know I gave birth?" it was Nolan's turn to look away.

"Camille." He confessed. "One of her friends saw when you entered the hospital." Kate nodded slowly.

"When did you come home?"

"Two days ago," Kate answers. Nolan noticed her middle was still swollen after pregnancy.

"They said your water broke in front of doctors and nurses." Kate flushed with embarrassment. "Did you go into labor there?"

"No." Kate looked at him. "It was here in this bed." Nolan froze. Kate told her harrowing tale of that night.

"You went through this by yourself?" his voice was full of awe. Kate nodded once before stepping forward, picking up her daughter in her arms.

"I had to do what was right for my daughter." She spoke firmly. Nolan nodded, then sighed.

"When Esme was born, I was at my wit's end." He says. "Esme was induced, but when she was born, her heart dropped and…" he trailed off, shuddering at the memory.

"Camille was three days past her due date, but the doctor had told her that the baby would take her time, but Camille couldn't wait… she wanted her body back." He adds bitterly. Kate had placed Rose into her crib before she turned to at him, face unreadable.

"It's getting late." Kate says. Nolan looked at her, surprised. "You need to go home, Allen." Nolan grimaced.

"You need not call me that." Kate saw him lower his head, face grave.

"Call you what?"

"Allen." He spoke. "I never enjoy being called by my first name." Kate looked away.

"It's what your wife told me."

"That doesn't mean I like it. Nolan is fine." Kate looked at him.

"It's time for you to go." Nolan looked at her sadly.

"Can I see her again?" He asks, getting to his feet. Kate looked at him sadly. She shook her head.

"But why?!" Nolan gasps. He looked at her, stunned. Kate wrapped an arm around herself, eyes downcast.

"If the town sees you with me, it will call attention to Rose. I won't let my daughter suffer for my past."

"B-But." Nolan was still thunderstruck by Kate's words. "She's, my child! I have the right to—

"No," Kate interrupts face firm. "You relinquished your right to Father Rose when you and your wife ruined my life. My daughter won't grow up being mocked because of the damage by you." Nolan heard Kate's words with horror.

"Y-You can't… Kate, I, she's mine…" Nolan protested weakly.

"No, she's not. The whole town believes you're not the father. I wish to keep it that way for her sake… and mine."

"Your own!" Nolan echoed. He felt his temper rise. "How can you deny my right to be a father to her!? She's I… I don't care what the town says, they can mock me all they want. I don't care what—

"But I do!" Kate cries. Nolan froze, seeing the look of anger on her face.

"You don't know what it's like!" Kate spoke. "what it's like to be alone. To be cast out by society, to be the center of malicious gossip. Humiliated every day by people I once called friends; to be attacked..." She swallowed, her throat tightening as her eyes burned. "To be afraid of the ones who sworn to protect you for fear of getting arrested for a crime you didn't commit." Tears spilled hot and wet down her cheek.

"To work for ungrateful people cleaning their homes just to put food on the table as you build a home from nothing. I had to do this. All while carrying a child to term." Nolan stared silently.

"You don't understand, but I do." Kate continues. "Do you know what the town or the world found out you had a child with me? The media—" she shuddered— "they would find me and my daughter and put us on every tabloid magazine about Nolan Roth's mistress and love child. They would never leave us alone. For each waking moment, they would take photos of us while strangers jeer about the *worthless whore* who got into bed with a married

129

man and got pregnant on purpose to get your money. Rose would grow up in the spotlight of malicious people, by kids her age, she would be shunned, just as I was!" Nolan listened to Kate's tearful lament, his face twisting with pain. Kate looked away.

"I can take the town and their ways. I can endure them, but I won't succumb my daughter to it. They believe she's another man's child. I can accept that. All I want is to live in peace." Kate wiped her eyes at the silence that followed. Nolan's eyes glazed over. He opened his mouth to speak. But no words came.

"I'll show you out." She whispers, not meeting his gaze. She turned for the door.

"Wait!" she stopped to see him look at her. "Le-let me…" His throat worked. "*Let me say goodbye to her.*" Kate hesitated for four heartbeats before nodding once. Nolan walked to the crib and peered down at his daughter, who slumbered silently. He leaned over the crib and kissed her cheek.

"Goodbye Rose." He whispers thickly. He pulled back and turned, following Kate out of the room.

Nolan picked up his suit jacket, putting it on silently. Kate walked to the door, and opened it, letting the warm night in. Nolan looked at the room one last time before walking toward the door.

"I'm sorry." He whispers, looking down at her somberly. "For everything, for what I, what Camille…" he trailed off.

"*Goodnight, Mr. Roth.*" Nolan looked at her sadly before walking out into the clear night. Kate watched him go silently, only closing the door when she saw his car turn slowly for Forest-Bend.

Chapter Fourteen

September finally arrived, putting an end to the three-month heat. The humidity lowered, making everyone take in a collective sigh when the first northerly breeze, cool, comforting, came down upon the city. Nolan stood as passersby's, the size of ants, walk by his tower. Not knowing they were being watched by a man who, for the past months, struggled to keep his business afloat as his empire began to fray at the seams.

Nolan's dull gray eyes rose from the ground below him to the skyscrapers; seeing glass reflect the sun that displayed high over the buildings. He heard the door to his office open; his secretary announcing he had a phone call from one of his business partners.

"Tell them, I'm busy." Nolan's voice was gruff from disuse. The secretary obeyed before shutting the door, leaving Nolan to continue staring; listening to the silence as his heart twinged with pain. A pain to this day never left.

Nolan drove all night. Passing shadowy fields of corn, his mind replaying what he tried to deny. Camille's actions to have the perfect family: to destroy another life just so he was left untarnished, great, proud, *untouchable*. Nolan tried to deny it. To want what was his... Kate's anguished voice sent a shiver through him: hearing everything his wife said thrown right back; not with bitterness, but through a year of exile, rejection, and cruelty; while all the while he knew... *and did nothing about it.*

Nolan closed his eyes at the memory as he rest his head on his steering wheel. How could she be so cruel!? How could Kate think of what the town thought of her? To deny his child, it was...He would tell her she was wrong. What she was doing was selfish to his daughter, to *him*... Pain, sharp and hot flared his left chest! Nolan gasped aloud, only to groan, clasping his chest.

That was four months ago.

Nolan looked up from the floor of his office to stare out the window, his expression somber.

"Mr. Roth?" Nolan didn't turn around to look at his secretary.

"Yes?"

"Your wife's on the line. She wants to talk to you." Nolan sighs. He turned around.

"Thank you." he says.

Nolan sat in his limo an hour later, staring out at the city through tinted windows. His driver drove aimlessly per Nolan's order, allowing time to pass until it got late, and he would drive home in his car. His stomach twisted. Although, he had Esme, Nolan was not looking forward to being in the same room, much less *presence* of his wife. Nolan sighed as the limo turned and he saw the city cathedral. He watched admiringly at the exterior; noticing people walking, including a woman dressed in white.

"**Carl**!?" he pressed a button and the front window of the limo opened. "Go back around the church!"

"No problem, Mr. Roth!" Nolan felt the car thrum under him as the car turned, but then stopped at a stoplight just in front of the church. Nolan cursed but stared out the window seat, gazing with wide eyes at the young woman who reappeared again; carrying a small infant in her arms as she climbed the red-carpeted staircase. The limo drove.

⊱

Kate walked into the enormous cathedral with awe and trepidation. The height of the curved arches and buttresses made her tiny as she walked the long red carpet, her flats barely made a sound as she passed the seats, all empty, save for one where a middle-aged nun sat toward the end of the seat where the podium stood mighty along with its gleaming pulpit, red chairs, and large golden cross stood in the middle.

"Excuse me?" Kate's voice was a whisper, not wanting to break the peace of the sacred place. The nun turned her head and smiled.

"Greetings, child." She spoke. "How may I help you?" Kate felt a shift, making her look down at her child, who was watching the church with clear brown eyes.

"I'm here for the christening with Minister Winston," Kate replies.

"Oh, you must be, Kate." Kate nodded. "It's nice to meet you." The woman stood up and step out of the seated bench. "I'm Florence." She shook Kate's hand.

"Nice to meet you, ma'am."

"And this is your daughter." Kate smiles, looking down at her daughter, who wore an all-white christening dress with a matching bonnet.

"Yes, this is Rose." Kate spoke gently. The nun smiled.

"I will tell minister Winston, you're here. Please, have a seat." Kate nodded and obeyed. Florence stepped forward and bowed to the cross before walking away to a brown door where she entered. Kate sat on the pew watching the interior of the church, her brown eyes bright with wonder, but timid. This was a big day for her and her daughter. Kate looked down and smiled.

"Are you ready, Rosy?" she cooed. The baby looked at her quietly, her brown hands closed into fists as she stared. Kate's eyes pricked as her breath hitched. She thought about her decision she made two months prior where she laid silent in her bed within the cover of night while Rose slumbered. Kate knew the choice would not be easy; after falling rock bottom. She worried for Rose's future: a future that seemed so predictable in its despair. She didn't want her child to live a life of solitude. She wanted to see her grow in joy by people who loved her for her, not for what she represented.

Kate clutched the back of Rose's head, supporting her back. She closed her eyes, praying quietly she only hoped to be the best person, the best mother she could be.

"Kate?" Kate started at the voice. She opened her eyes to see a man dressed in professional priest attire.

"Minister Winston." Kate smiles. He smiled down at her as the nun stepped forward.

"Are you ready, child?" she asks. Kate felt her chest tingle with numbness, but she nodded, rising from the bench. Minister Winston walked forward to the center of the church where a stone object that resembled a birdbath. Pure, clear water reflected the bright halo of white light as Kate listened to the minister, who explained what he was going to do, liberating Kate's fear, but not her worry.

"Do you have a witness?" The minister asked kindly. Kate clutched her child protectively before she shook her head. "All right, let us be—"

The door to the church opened.

The three adults looked up as an unknown figure stepped into the large room. Kate's eyes widen when she saw the familiar stranger out of breath, his hair tousled as if blown by a sudden gust of wind. Nolan.

"Excuse me, young man." Minister Winston looked just as surprise at the well-dressed stranger. "But this is a private event. The church visiting hours are not until tomorrow."

"I-I'm sorry." Nolan spoke as he walked. His eyes were only on Kate. "I didn't know this was a private event, I—"

"What are you doing here?" Kate breathes. She didn't move from her spot, afraid. "How did you—?"

"I saw you." Nolan stopped half a yard. "I saw you in my car, I…" he stared at her gently. "*I had to see you.*" he breathes. Kate's eyes widen.

"Son?" says Minister Winston. "I have to ask you to leave." Nolan finally looked at him.

"What is this event?"

"This is a private christening." Nolan let out a surprise breath. He looked at Kate, seeing her dress. Her long hair hung in waves past her shoulders. In her arms was Rose, who turned her head, watching, her tiny fist in her mouth.

"Y-You're having the christening?" he breathes. Kate nodded wordlessly just as the nun stepped forward.

"Son, you need to leave." Flo spoke, Nolan took a step back.

"*Kate.*" He whispers his eyes glassy, pleading, what his mouth could not. Kate stared before turning to face the minister.

"Minister Winston, he's with me." She spoke.

"He is?" he asks, surprised.

"Yes."

"Who is he to you? If he is causing you any harm, I can call the police." Kate winced at 'police.'

"That would not be necessary, sir. Nolan, he's—"

"*I'm her friend.*" Nolan spoke. Kate looked at him with surprise as he stared at the priest, boldly.

"I've known Kate for a long time. She and her daughter are very dear to me." He spoke firmly. "I'm sorry to interrupt your service, but I wish to be for the christening of Rose."

"It's a double christening, son." says the minister. Nolan blinked, surprised he stared at Kate, who looked away. Nolan watched her for a long time before looking back at the priest, face somber.

"I understand." Kate looked at him as he adds. "I want to be a part of this for both of them." The pastor nodded as the nun stepped back turning to her.

"Are you sure, Kate?" she asks. Kate nodded.

"It's alright, Ms. Florence. *He can stay.*"

"Would the father be joining us?" asks the minister. Kate didn't answer.

"No." Nolan replies sadly. The pastor nodded.

"Let us begin."

The ceremony was a quiet, joyful affair. The minister spoke in a deep, resonating voice about the blessing he was to bestow. Nolan listened as the minister spoke of guarding oneself against temptation and sin. Nolan stared at Kate, seeing her face and head held high, cheeks red with emotion as her brown eyes sparked the way he remembered her when they were together.

Kate's slender fingers entwined with his, speaking about their future, her dreams of having a family after being alone for so long. Nolan's eyes stung. Kate had been alone as the town scorned, mocked, and jeered her; all the while trying to build a home after leaving hers. To sustain a loving environment for her daughter. Her only companion was to grow, heal, and love.

And he was going to take her child away.

Nolan's stomach punched from within. The moment hit him hard as he realized his selfishness. This wasn't about Rose. Kate was right… Nolan didn't deserve, didn't *earn* his right to call himself father to his daughter.

"Son? Are you alright?" Minister Winston looked at him, as did Kate and the nun witnessing, as Nolan raised his head, revealing tears that slid down his cheeks. He nodded once. "Alright. Now, we shall proceed with the christening, Kate?" Kate nodded before proceeding on taking off the baby bonnet.

"Can…" Nolan's voice was thick. "Can I hold her as the pastor pours water on her?" Kate looked at him with surprise as the nun says.

"It is up to the mother to decide." Kate looked at Nolan before she smiles softly.

"*We can do it together.*" She replies softly. Nolan answered her smile with his own. Together, the adults grasped Rose, lowering her head over the large dish. Nolan entwined his fingers into Kate's, supporting their daughter's head. Rose cried as the pastor spoke the sacred words pouring water atop her head. Rose wiggled and wailed, but Nolan and Kate gently shushed her together until she calmed; watching her parents quietly.

They lifted Rose at the same time, Nolan letting Rose go first. Kate pushed back the tears as she clasped Rose to her chest, shushing her when she let out a small keen. Nolan watched her silently, his heart filling with warmth. "Kate." says the pastor. "It's your turn." Kate nodded before looking at Nolan.

"Can you hold her for me?" she asks. Nolan hesitated, surprised by her request. His cheeks tingled as his tears dried in the cool church. He stretched out his arms.

Nolan watched with quiet with pride as the pastor spoke with the same pomp, giving his blessing to Kate. Nolan held Rose, who watched him with wide curious eyes. He smiled down at her and she lifted a hand to his chin, feeling his warmth on her soft, warm, caramel skin.

She is so much like Kate. He thought softly. No one would know she was Nolan's. A flash of sadness coursed through him, but it faded quickly, replaced with resignation. It was for the best for his daughter. She would grow up free, not under the microscope of public scrutiny. Nolan watched Kate lower her head, and the pastor lifted a cup full of water to Kate's forehead, seeing tears stream down her cheek.

It was a new beginning, not just for Rose, but for Kate as well. She was purging her past crime as the town saw her: never knowing he was the real criminal of them all. Kate would always be an outsider, but he knew who she was, had always be... Kate lifted her head from the baptism alter; her chest heaved a sigh of relief. Her gaze landed on her child who turned her head, hand in her mouth before landing on Nolan who smiled at her tenderly.

"That's it." Said Winston with a smile. Kate as Nolan got to his feet. Kate thanked him and Florence, asking if she could take pictures with the pastor holding the baby. The first five minutes were a joyful one as photos were taken. The pastor and nun beamed as Nolan took pictures of Kate with them, as well as the baby.

"Let me take a photo of you two." Said Florence. Nolan hesitated before nodding while Kate, though reluctant, complied. Together they stood Kate holding Rose while Nolan laid a hand on the mother's shoulder. The camera flashed.

☙

Kate and Nolan stepped out of the church. The setting sun hidden behind a building. Kate held Rose, seeing a long black limo that was parked on the curbside. Nolan stared as he stopped beside her.

"So," He whispers. "This is it." Kate nodded, not looking at him. Nolan sensed the wall she built, closing him once more. She was alone.

"Is that your car?" she nodded at the limo.

"Yes." He spoke. "Do you need a lift home? I have plenty of room I—"

"I brought my van," Kate murmured. Nolan nodded; looking back to his limo, seeing his driver step out of the driver's side.

"*Thank you*." He started; raising his head to face her. "*For being here for her.*" He looked lovingly at Rose, who watched him. She yawned.

"You're welcome. I'm glad I was on the road when I saw…" he trailed off.

"Aren't you supposed to be at work?" Kate's tone was slightly reproachful. Nolan sighed.

"I needed a break." He says gloomily. "Besides, my company hasn't been doing so great. It's nice to have something good happen for me today." Kate didn't reply. "Kate?" She looked at him, face wary. Nolan sifted his words carefully before saying.

"You know what's best for, Rose. I won't interfere in your choice to keep her safe and living a happy life… you are all she has, I won't…" he trailed off, voice tightening as he spoke.

"Just let her know she is loved. That her daddy…" he swallowed. "Her daddy cares about her." He closed his eyes as pain throbbed in his chest.

"Of course, I will." Nolan opened his eyes to see Kate's sad smile on her beautiful face. He nodded.

"*And you*." he spoke. Nolan lifted a hand before placing it on her shoulder. Kate stared at him, eyes shining she bobbed her head. Nolan felt his eyes sting with tears; lowering his head, he kissed Rose on her plump cheeks before Kate walked down the stairs.

"*Goodbye, Kate*." He says. Kate turned her head, meeting his gaze.

"Goodbye, *Nolan*."

Nolan's chest lifted, his breath hitched as he watched Kate look away and walked carrying her child. Nolan walked on stiff legs to his limo, where his driver opened the door. He watched her walked the sidewalk before turning a corner and was gone. Nolan entered the limo wordlessly, before closing his eyes as the thrum of the engine started under him.

Chapter Fifteen

Spring had finally arrived in the small town, bringing the kiss of warmth after so much cold. The earth warmed, waking the slumbering forest with life as green leaves, colorful flowers and chirping birds that sang merrily to the morning rays that rose, casting its light on all who took the time to notice its rays.

Kate laid asleep as the sun's rays entered her room through the window. Her breaths were slow and deep as she slept peacefully, unaware that the morning had begun. Something bounced beside her; shaking her bed along with Kate. Laughter, sweet and excited, echoed in the room and in her ears.

"Mommy!!" Kate didn't respond, but she was smiling as she turned to her side facing the window as the figure bounced, calling out to Kate to… "Wake up! Wake up!" Kate opened one eye and smiles at the two-year-old toddler who bounced on her bed, her tiny hands closed into tight fists as she jumped on her legs, calling out to Kate.

She didn't think, just reacted. Opening the other eye, Kate turned, sat up, and scooped up the child in her arms, tickling the girl child on her stomach. The child's laughter grew to hysterical giggles as her mother blew raspberries on her stomach; her legs kicking as Kate showered her daughter with kisses.

"Good morning, Rosy!" Kate cooed. The child beamed.

"G'mornin, mommy!" She chirped.

"Did you sleep well?" Kate asks Rosy, Rose, nodded happily. "Would you like breakfast now?" Rose nodded, bouncing up and down on Kate's thighs.

"Breakfy! Breakfy!" Rose crowed. Kate laughed.

"Okay, mommy will make breakfast. What about some yummy chocolate chip waffles?" Kate smiles, thinking of the waffle batter she made the previous night. Rose clapped her hands as Kate scooped her up in her arms and out of bed.

Three years had passed for the young mother as the world changed; with each turn on its axis, so had Kate, growing from every experience that she learned and thrived not just for herself but for her daughter. Her Rose.

Kate smiled as she poured batter into the prepared waffle iron, hearing the sizzle when it came in contact with the black ridges before she closed the lid, allowing it to cook. Kate stepped to the side where on the stove a pan of sausages browned on one side. She turned them with her fork as music, sweet and whimsical, played in the background on her radio.

"Waffy! Waffy!" Kate turned and grinned at her child, who chanted happily in her chair. Had it really been three years that Kate brought her treasure into her home? It felt like only yesterday that Kate was holding up her arms as her baby girl took her first shaky but purposeful steps on barefoot to Kates; her tears of joy of her daughters' accomplishments: from her first tooth, her first words, to every first she could count and record.

Kate placed a plate of waffles covered in syrup, sausages, and scrambled eggs she cut into bite-size pieces. Rose squealed before thanking her mother and took a bite. Kate beamed as she sat down in her own seat and dug into her plate of waffles, eggs, and sausage with relish.

"Mommy!? What we goin' do to'dy!?" Rose asks. Kate smiled happily, especially since today was her day off.

"Well, today mommy has to do some errands," Kate answers. "Mommy has to go to the supermarket for your special birthday cake." Rose eyes widen.

"Can I have it now?"

"No, honey." Kate replies. "You have to wait until your birthday."

"When is my birthday, mommy?" Kate laughs after sipping her juice.

"Soon honey. You will have cake and ice cream." Rose's eyes widen at that, making her laugh.

"I want cake and ice cream now!" Kate shook her head.

"Not yet, Rosy. But until then we have errands to run, okay." Rose nodded. "Now eat your breakfast, sweetie, so we can go."

03

Nolan Roth stared at the road with silent drudgery, driving mutely to the small town that had changed; growing in quaintness, joy, and pride, not just for the town but for the man, the family, who put their town on the map for tourism. Nolan turned on the winding road; gray eyes focus as his mind tried to block out the silence coming from his luxury van. Nolan's chest throbbed as he felt the familiar pain on his left breast, he ignored it as he lifted a hand to the rearview mirror, adjusting it to peer at his five-year-old, with her mother's eyes, staring down at the tablet that chimed quietly each time she touched it with a small finger. He glanced at his wife, who was staring down at her phone shopping online, her head resting on her fist. Nolan sighed, then reached to turn on the radio.

"What are you doing?" Nolan didn't glance at his wife, who was eyeing him with annoyance.

"I'm turning on the radio."

"I can see that. My question is why?"

"I just want some background noise."

"Well, don't," Camille spoke. "We don't need noise about nothing." Nolan stopped the car at a stoplight. Turning to his wife, he got a proper look at her from professional tan skin and long blond hair.

"Fine." Nolan pulled from the radio. He turned his attention to Esme. "How was school, Esme?" Esme didn't respond. "Esme?" Esme looked up at her father, who smiles at her, though the rear window.

She shrugged.

"Come on, Essie." Nolan encourages as he drove. "What did you do in school?! I'm sure it must have been exciting." The child hesitated, thoughtful.

"Umm…Mrs. Tolins taught us about plants," Esme spoke.

"Plants? Wow," Nolan spoke. "What about plants?" He saw her face grow excited.

"We learned how plants grow and how they make photos to eat?" Nolan chuckles, ignoring his wife's dismissive noise as he tells Esme the correct term.

"Monday, we're going to bring home our bean plants." Nolan nodded.

"Are you excited about summer vacation?"

"Yes, daddy. Can Cherry, Flora, and Julie come to the summer party?"

"Of cours—"

"No!" Camille snaps. Esme shrank back at her mother's command.

"Why mommy?" she asks. "They're my friends."

"Yes." Said Nolan, surprised by Camille's outburst. "We have plenty of—"

"Because their parents aren't like us." Said Camille, dropping her voice.

"So, that shouldn't mean they can't co—"

"We have plenty of people already coming. We don't need their company. It's bad enough Esme has to play with the scholarship kids." Nolan didn't respond, but his eyes widen at the insult. Esme lowered her head and returned to her game as Nolan saw from the mirror her sad face. His chest squeezed.

The day went on like any other day. Nolan shopped alone whilst Camille and Esme got manicures. Nolan felt the eyes of all who knew him. Some smiled and talked to him, but the conversations were all the same. The town had changed over the years with the addition of new stores, modern with old fashion sensibility; stores ranging from cafes that made as well as sold expensive coffee, an ice cream bakery that sold baked goods along with homemade ice cream, an antique store, and an exotic, specialty market. The once small town that thrived was now a hotspot for newcomers who wished to explore or build a home in the old town. All thanks to him.

After his past investors bailed on him, his company had taken a turn. Although still rich, Nolan saw firsthand how the economy hit his beloved town; so, going to the mayor, he invested his money in tourism once more to make his town on the map. Nolan sighed as he walked the paved streets. The town was forever grateful to him and his wife. Nolan took the praise all in stride, but inside… He was hollow. Alone. Nolan sat down on a stone bench beside the town's fountain (built by Camille). Head lowered, he stared at his lap. The familiar throb in his chest pulsed as he exhaled hot CO_2, wishing he had some water to take his antacid he had bought more at the local pharmacy. People walked past him, going their merry way to their jobs or spending time with their families. He looked at them enviously; seeing their smiles, hearing the laughter of children as they splashed one another with water. He frowned inwardly thinking of the past years: the fall of his company, that regained momentum after so much loss, the coldness of his wife who took joy in being cruel to others who were not in the circle of sheep she called "friends". Nolan stared wordlessly at the town folk. He had everything, but yet…

"Daddy!" Nolan started, turning his head he saw Esme running wearing a purple fairy tulle skirt and holding a wand. Nolan smiled as she ran with Camille behind her.

"Hi pumpkin!" he croons. Esme stopped.

"Look what mommy got me!" she pointed to her skirt at the same time brandishing her wand in his face. Nolan smiled just as his wife came forward, holding large multicolored bags in both her hands. He raised an eyebrow.

"Had fun shopping?" he spoke casually as Camille stopped beside him.

"Daddy! Look at my wand!" Esme chirped. Nolan looked at her as he held her wand, examining it.

"It's lovely, Essie." He spoke.

"I'm going to show it to my friends at the party." He handed it back to her as the kids at the fountain splashed cheerfully. Nolan stared at Camille.

"You look like you bought half the stores." He spoke.

"Half these stores have nothing special," Camille replies. "I'd be glad when I get to 5th avenue, at least I know half the items I purchase are worth more than what the town folk put in their products." Nolan frowned as she put the bags on the bench.

"Are you ready to go?" before he opened his mouth, Esme says.

"Mommy, can I play in the fountain?" Camille and Nolan looked at the fountain, where the children splashed their hands and feet. Camille grimaced.

"Absolutely not!" she snaps. Esme pouted.

"But I want to play with the kids in the water!"

"That water is dirty, Esme! You're not getting sick because of those urchins."

"Camille!" Nolan gasps. "They're only kids!"

"Yes. Children covered in germs. I'm not trying to get sick because of them."
Nolan nostrils flared.

"Yes, of course." His tone was sardonic. "For a moment I actually thought
you were concern for your daughter's welfare. I should have known your
main concern was about yourself." She glared at him as Nolan rose to his feet
and started picking up her bags.

"*Let's go, Esme.*" He spoke voice low.

"But I want to play in the fountain!" she whines.

"You heard what your mother said. We're going home." Esme broke into
tears, all the kids stared at her, pausing in their play to see the mother take
Esme's arm and pull; the child hitting her with small fists.

Nolan felt a headache throb in his temple when he made it to his car.
He and Camille had argued back for the whilst Esme kicked and screamed,
causing everyone to stare and whisper. Nolan wanted to curse them for their
gossipy ways, wanting to get home as soon as possible as he shoved the bags
into the trunk.

"Don't shove my bags like that!" Camille screeched. Nolan glared at her.
They were alone in the parking space. His temper rose as his heart burned.

"They're inanimate objects! I'm not hurting them!" he snaps.

"Don't you dare snap at me!" she screeched.

"So, what!? You do it all the time! How is this any different?" He adds
bitterly.

"You are doing it in front of our child, is what's different."

"Oh, so you want to give me grief when Esme is not with us." They both glower as Esme sniffled quietly. The wand she held moments before laid broken in her fit of temper.

"You bring your own problems to yourself. I'm not the one with a failing company that you have to kowtow to these simple folks just to make yourself look righteous."

"If you hate my stance on how I do things, then don't stay!" Nolan yells. "I'm tired of you complaining about my failings!"

"Then I'll take Esme with me! If you're so tired of me and my ramblings." Camille hisses, glaring. Nolan froze, staring at his wife with shock. Before he could respond, he saw Camille turn her head. Nolan watched as her face turn redder with anger as her eyes narrowed. He turned his head and paled.

Kate stepped out into the parking lot where she had parked her car. In her hands, she held a long light pink fabric which she wrapped behind her. Nolan, Camille, and Esme watched as she, Kate, wrapped it around her back, where two little arms clung to her neck. They watched as she tied the fabric before fixing her back, which was followed by a childish giggle and face that came with the laugh. Kate walked to the trunk of her car and opened it to her back and the child's, who was wrapped in the cloth like a carry-on backpack. The family watched as Kate pulled out a gray package before stepping back to close the van door.

"Mommy, what's that?" the girl child asks. Nolan started at the voice. It struck a chord, twisting his insides.

"It's something important for mommy's job," Kate spoke. "I have to go to the post office to have it mailed." Kate turned to her side as she says this, not noticing the family watching her. The child nodded.

148

"Ready to go, sweetie? We still have to get decorations for your birthday."

The child sang "Birthday! Birthday!" As Kate walked forward. Nolan stared, his dark gray eyes full of tenderness as he saw the young mother and toddler. His hand clasped his left chest.

"*Must be nice*." Nolan started at his wife's voice. He looked at her, her face was a scowl.

"What?" her scout turn to a cruel, but knowing smile.

"Knowing you don't have to worry about carrying a child, that's not yours." Her smile grew snide. Nolan didn't answer, just looked at her.

"Who is she?" Esme asks. Camille smiled down at her child.

"*No one important, my darling,*"

Chapter Sixteen

Nolan woke up to a bright Friday morning as he opened his eyes to the ceiling fan that turned on medium speed, bringing air to his already cool room. There was a shift, and he saw an arm wrap atop his stomach. Nolan didn't have to guess as lips brushed his left cheek, he laid still; seeing her smile in his mind's eye; perfect; fit enough for the front page of Vogue magazine.

"Good morning." She purrs. Nolan looked at her, but his voice was emotionless as he answered.

"Good morning." Camille, unaware of his tone, beamed. As always, her smile didn't touch her eyes.

"How did you sleep?" she asks. Nolan shrugged on the bed; his head rested on the pillow.

"Fine." She frowned.

"Aren't you going to ask if I slept well?"

"I don't have to ask because I know your bedtime routine." He smirked.

"You are more well rested than anyone else."

"You know me well."

More than I like too. He thought but didn't say it aloud, instead he said gravely.

"I got to go to work." He sat up, but Camille lay a hand on his bare chest.

"Stay," she purrs. "You can afford to be a little late."

"No, I can't." Nolan spoke, his mind flashed of his new financial intake after the sudden decline of the Stock Market.

"I have a meeting at ten." Continued Nolan. "Besides, I promised Esme I would take her to school." Camille frowned at the meeting, but her face was nonchalant when she spoke loftily.

"Esme can be driven by the nanny; you can miss one day."

"I already missed three weeks of not spending time with Esme because of my job."

"She'll understand. Besides, you can make it up to her." Camille says with a shrug.

"A promise is a promise." Nolan pulled himself, letting Camille's hand fall from his chest. "I won't miss out on spending time with her." He got up from bed. He heard Camille grumble but ignored it as he stared at the open window.

"Why do you suddenly care about Esme's wants?" Camille grumbled. "She's only five. She won't remember this promise. It's the same as all the others you made." Nolan felt heat climb up his chest.

"*I've always cared.*" He turned to face his wife. "I don't like breaking my promises to my daughter." Camille didn't answer as she sat up from the bed, her long hair slid off her shoulder.

"Yes." Her tone was snide. "I thought you almost forgot we have one, especially since you've been closed off to her after deciding to stay to work on our marriage."

"Don't start this, Camille." He spoke, voice grave. "I'm in no mood to argue."

"Whose arguing? I'm stating a fact." Nolan's chest burned.

"Then maybe you should look in the mirror." He says. "You're no different from I am. At least with me, I don't pawn my child off to the nanny after

151

showing her off to your rich friends." Camille glowers. Nolan took a moment's satisfaction before walking to the bathroom to change.

Breakfast was tense as Nolan ate a slice of quiche with blueberry lemon scones. Esme talked excitedly as he and Camille ate; both adults not looking at one another until Nolan rose from his empty plate.

"Come on, Essie!" he says, Esme beamed, nodding. "Can you get her bag for me, Chantel?" The nanny nodded and walked out of the room.

Esme lifted her arms.

"Pick me up, daddy!" Nolan smiles. He was just bending when Camille said. "Aren't you going to give me a hug?" Esme looked up at her mother just as the nanny came with her bag pack.

"No!" Esme says.

"Essie!" Nolan gasps. "That's not nice, go give mommy a hug." As he said this, the nanny helped put on her backpack. The child shook her head.

"Essie." Said Chantel. "You must hug your mama."

"I don't want to." Nolan tried to coax his daughter, but to no avail.

"Will you hug me?" asks the nanny. Esme beamed and obeyed, hugging her. Camille glared at the nanny before Nolan scooped Esme up in his arms.

"Time to go, princess." He says. Esme clung to his neck and waved goodbye to the nanny and maids.

Except Camille.

C3

Nolan drove to work after driving Esme to school, giving her a stern talking about not hugging her mother. Esme's words still haunted Nolan as he drove to work, knowing that his own five-year-old understood what was happening around than most children.

152

"*All mommy does is use her phone than play with me. She's not nice!!*" Nolan shuddered even as he tried to defend Camille, but he knew his actions were halfhearted.

The meeting with his business partners went well enough as they discussed stats and the still stagnant market where people still put their hope and trust on mountainous lines. Nolan sat in his office room listening as more bad news seem to spew from the advisors' mouths; telling him how business won't be returning to normal for another two years. His acquaintances spoke amongst themselves once the meeting was over. Nolan couldn't help a twinge of ire as his friends complained about selling their boats or not being able to vacation in private resorts; he hadn't realized how noxious they were until now. Nolan rose to his feet.

✂

It was just after 1 pm when Nolan drove out of the city; to where he didn't know. It was too soon to drive back to the house. Although no one would be home, it still filled Nolan with dread. He drove quietly as the radio played in the background. Nolan's stomach growled, but he had no appetite: it had decreased considerably. He who ate ravenously at any meal ate half-heartedly. He missed the meals prepared by his old chef. To this day, Nolan still regretted ever firing Tony, not just for Tony, but for many other things as well.

Nolan parked his car in his VIP spot in the small town. His eyes were duller than ever as he stared dejectedly out the window. Why had he come here? Nolan's stomach rumbled under his suit, reminding him he hadn't eaten in hours. He didn't even have a cup of water.

Nolan let out a breath as he reached for his glove compartment and pulled out a hanger, allowing him to park here. Second, to the mayor, Nolan and his family were the most powerful residents in town. Nolan grunted as he opened the car door and left. He walked the not-so-busy street with an air of disinterest. The town was as beautiful as always, but with tourist season a month away, the town and its people felt empty, preferring the days when it was busy, when he could see his town bursting with life. He sighed as he walked the paved street, eyeing now and again the windows of each store stopping in front of a sneakers store taking in the new brands with semi-curiosity. His hand lifted to his chest.

Something knocked against Nolan's left ankle.

He looked down, surprised to see a yellow ball stop at his shoe. Curious, he bent down to pick it up. Slapping feet on the pavement made him look up to see a child wearing a navy romper and clear jelly sandals. Her brown skin glowed in the sunlight.

Nolan's eyes widen as he stared at Rose stopped two feet from him standing by a pole watching him with quiet brown eyes that glowed in the sun's light. Nolan's voice got stuck in his throat for the name he wanted to say as he stared at the baby girl.

"Rosy!" Rose turned her head as a tall elderly woman with silver hair came forward. Rose ran to her an grasp the woman's right leg.

"Rosy can't run away like that." she chides gently. "You can't leave, Emily, okay." Rose nodded, then lifted a finger, pointing at Nolan, who still held the ball.

"It's not her fault!" Nolan spoke involuntarily at the same time he took a step forward. "Sh-her ball rolled away and came to me. I…" he trailed off. Emily's eyes had widened as she stared at him.

"I'm sorry. Please don't be mad at her. Her ball rolled to me. I'm Nolan Roth." Nolan lifted a hand. Emily, who had recovered from her shock, eyed him, face pinched.

"Oh, everyone knows who you are, Mr. Roth." Nolan was surprised to hear the reproach in her voice. She didn't take his hand as she added. "You are very famous here." He stared at her.

"Y-Yes." He mumbles. Nolan lowered his hand, seeing her brow furrow.

"Emmi, ball!" Rose spoke, pointing at her toy. Nolan saw Emily's face soften as she looked down at her.

"H-Here." Nolan extended his arm as Emily picked up the child.

"Take the ball, honey." Emily says, but her face was not kind as she looked at Nolan. "Take the ball from the nice man so we can go to the park, okay." Rose nodded but didn't move. Nolan tried to smile.

"Here you go, honey." The child looked at him for the briefest of moments before taking her ball wordlessly.

"What do we say, Rose?" Emily spoke. The child looked at him.

"Thank you." She says in a small voice. Nolan smiled tenderly at the child, his gray eyes brightening at the simple display of gratitude.

"You're very welcome, sweetie." Rose was put down and Emily took her hand with a nod at Nolan before starting to walk…

"Wait!" Nolan turned to look at the woman and child, hands on his chest as he stared with pain.

"I-Is she doing alright?" Emily's eyes widen for an instant before they narrowed.

"I am not enclosed to discuss that with a stranger." Nolan felt as if he was stabbed in the chest. Emily turned away and the two people crossed the street, with Nolan watching.

☙

Nolan sat in his office chair with a silent sigh, burying his face in his hands as he breathed in and out. His body felt heavy, especially after having an enormous dinner; the day's excursion had made Nolan devour his meal with vigor. But despite feeling full, Nolan felt the wall of forgetfulness he built crumble. Today's problems and worry came crawling back tenfold. Nolan let out a shuddering breath as he looked up just as the door to the office opened and Camille stepped into the room, her usual look of fury directed toward him.

"What do you want, Camille?" his voice, even to him, sounded annoyed.

"**I want her fired**!" she yells.

"Who?" Nolan's eyes drooped, ready to hear another tirade.

"The nanny." Nolan, expecting the maid, looked up with surprise.

"What?! B-But why?" Camille scowled.

"Like you don't know." She says. "You saw how she acted. How Esme treated her, she is putting my child against me! Esme was rude to me this morning, and that nanny is to blame."

"You're overreacting, Camille."

"Overreacting!!" she screamed.

156

"Shh!" Nolan shushed her. "Yes, you're overreacting about nothing. Esme loves you, she's—" Camille sniffed. "Look, I spoke to Esme today telling her what she did was wrong!"

"Yes. Because she clearly listens to you, the nanny and the maids who work for us. Not her mother, who went through fifteen hours of labor." Nolan scowled.

"So, this is jealousy. You get slighted by the child you ignore unless it's an event or party and suddenly you blame the hired help for doing their job." Camille glared.

"Chantel has tried to take over this house for far too long." She hisses. "I'm taking back what's mine. Esme is mine, this house is mine, you're mine."

Nolan had enough.

"Why do you even care!?" he yells. "Since when has this become you!?"

"You have no right to speak to me that way!" She cries.

"**What is wrong with you**!?" Nolan demands.

"**I'm pregnant**!"

Nolan froze, his anger that exploded imploded in his face. He stared at his wife, stunned.

"Y-You're what?" she looked at him as she gestured to herself.

"*Surprise.*" She says. Nolan, who had risen to his feet during their fight, stood stunned. His wife was…

"When?" she smiles, but it didn't touch her eyes.

"Today." She says. Camille stepped forward and took Nolan's hand before placing it on her flat stomach. Nolan let out a gasp. "You're going to be a daddy again. Baby number two." Nolan froze, his eyes wide at her statement.

Nolan pulled his hand from hers, still shell-shocked. Camille stepped back, turning her back on him.

"Chantel will be fired as soon as school is over." She says before walking out of the room.

Nolan didn't respond. Camille, she was… Nolan collapsed back on his chair unable to speak, sweat beaded down his brow as if he ran a marathon.

Baby…

She wanted control. She ran this town with a silk glove hand but let her worshipers slid between the cracks, laughing as their screams of reverence echoed in the black. But she still wanted more.

Number…

She destroyed the lives of countless people who were a slight out of place in her perfect world. Taking what was hers, but could not stand when others tried to take what she own, what she ignored because it would ruin her reputation and now…

Two!

Nolan felt his heart race, his hand clasped his chest, his pupils dilated as realization cascaded down over him.

He was to be a father again to Camille. The mother to his child was to bear another: a son or a daughter. A child that would be trapped with her damaged lifestyle… and let her. To save his marriage, his reputation his… Rose looked at him with quiet shyness, her brown eyes so much like her mother. A mother with a gentle strength, her vast knowledge, her love of the unknown and the fantastical. A mother who had been outcast by sneering whispers and sideway glances.

Nolan's throat tightened; his brain was on fire! He had no one to talk to. He was alone with the burning brand on his chest.

"*Kate.*"

∽

Kate looked up to see darkness from her curtain window.

"Kate?" Kate turned her head to Emily, holding a white piping bag with the decorator's tip. Pink frosting peeked out from the light squeeze of the old woman's hand.

"Oh! Sorry, Emily." Kate smiles turning her gaze away from the window at the warm May night where she and Emily stood in Kate's small kitchen where for the past hour and a half, Kate learned to make shells, ruffles, fleur-de-lis, and rosettes following Emily's piping pattern and frosting directions. Kate watched and followed piping each careful design with pink buttercream acting as paint while her clear piping bag was her paintbrush as she squeezed, lifted, swished, swirled, and pulled to see her handiwork come to life. It was so much different with her pen on clean paper but yet ended the same. Art was born by her hand.

"See! You're a natural!?" Emily beamed.

"Thanks to you." Kate smiles as she pulled back from her line of rosettes. She just made each line in one chain, reminding Kate of a necklace.

"I wouldn't know what to do without your help." Continued Kate. Emily waved it away.

"Think nothing of it. I just can't wait to see Rosy's face tomorrow."

"Me too."

"You're going to have to hide the cake with a towel or foil, so she doesn't peep at her birthday cake." Kate nodded.

159

"Now, shall we get started on the big roses?" Kate laughs, nodding, eyes sparkling.

"Yes." She spoke. "I am."

Chapter Seventeen

Nolan opened his dull gray eyes to reveal a bleak, overcast morning. Rain pelted quietly on large clear glass forming water droplets that stained the window, obstructing Nolan's view of the grand skyscrapers of the city. Nolan gazed at a weary quietude. A flash of lightning streaked the high, gray, clouds followed by the rumble of thunder. He looked at the large white blanket that covered his torso and legs; a blanket familiar but not his own. Nolan sighed.

He had finally gotten some sleep.

Time hadn't been kind to Nolan as he sat in his hotel suite alone save the company of drizzling rain and a growling stomach. After finding out about Camille's pregnancy, his mind was a whirl of frazzled nerves, his body was on fire. He felt sick. Nolan left his office. It wasn't around midnight when he entered his bedroom; discovering that his wife was asleep, he went to his closet, packed his clothes into a duffle bag, along with toiletries, before leaving the room. All was quiet when he entered his car and drove out of his estate, to where he didn't know, just anywhere!

Nolan paced in his suite at the bomb, Camille dropped on him. He who had negotiated business plans, he who had broken soil for construction sites, he who sailed on yachts, dining on high-class delicacies: the most powerful man in the world… Nolan felt pain grip his chest. Collapsing to his knees, he realized with horror that he was having a panic attack. Alone, frightened, with none of his staff, his family: knowing he was suffering through this. Nolan heaved, taking hot shaky breaths despite the cool temperature he felt hot. Nolan was burning, yet… he preferred this than being with his wife.

His wife!

161

Nolan spasmed. His hands clenched the downy fabric of the blanket as he thought of the years he had injured by his vindictive wife: she ruined other lives using her glamor, her power to destroy. Allowing her to do this witnessing as well as adding to the destruction. He had ruined lives.

Nolan had smiled as his competitors crumbled to dust; his hands on the chess piece as he called 'check mate' to the hundreds of people he ruined. People tried to get in his favor to gain an advantage, but it was all in vain: those who tried were punished by him or his wife just like Janey and… Nolan convulsed. His hand clasped his mouth as he thought of Kate. A promising mistress of the written word, now... Her reputation tarnished; her daughter's future stained because of her. Of him.

Nolan let out a broken sob, sweat and tears streamed down his cheeks. "*K-Kate.*" He rasped. As he climbed into bed, his body weakened after his shakes and spasms subsided from the panic attack.

Despair overwhelmed him. Despite getting good news, he just wished it didn't have to be from Camille. A child. A new baby was to come into his life again. It was too early to know if he was to have another daughter or a son; it didn't matter to Nolan as long as they were born healthy, not how Esme was in her first minutes of life. His child would receive nothing but the best care, he or she would have the best clothes, the best shoes, nothing but the best. Never having to lift a finger as staff fed, changed, and played. All the while he worked. Missing out on the early years as he had for poor neglected Esme, his treasure, his joy, just like… Nolan's breath hitched. He dared not think her name.

Now it was morning. Nolan's mind no longer felt crushed by desperation could think of the name of his child. She looked so small and delicate. Her eyes were clear, bright just as he remembered her during her christening. Nolan smiled as he remembered his Rose as she smiled whilst her mother carried her on her back, seeing joy in them both, that life moved on without him and he was...

"I have to do something for her." He spoke to the emptiness. Nolan tried to think about what he could do for a daughter he hardly knew. Nolan realized with a pang; that he didn't even know his own child's birthday. Rose, from the way he saw her, looked maybe two or going to be two?

"Argh!" Nolan lifted his hands to his head. "What do I do?" he had to do something, something good in the tempest he created.

A gift. He thought. He will get Rose a gift. He remembered hearing Kate say something about a birthday. Could it be for her or her child? It didn't matter. Nolan raised his head, a plan hatching as a smile crossed his features.

"*I know what I have to do.*"

☙

Evening came gray, wet, and soggy in the forest above and below. The last of the May showers left its remnants on the earth so in days to come, blossoms of vibrant colors would cover the brown soil. Pink and white balloons danced within the confines of the brick cabin. Kate smiled warmly as the sound of giggles echoed around the small house.

"Mommy!" Kate turned her head as a bright face girl dressed in a simple old red fashion dress entered the room. Kate marveled just as Emily walked forward into the living room.

"Oh, Emily!" Kate breathes. "It's beautiful." Emily beamed as Kate touched the fabric of the dress, seeing the red and gold embroidery on the middle of Rose's dress. Rose laughs as Kate asks to "Spin around so mommy can look

163

at you." Rose obeyed in the light of the small fireplace. It seemed to make the dress flow like sails on a boat.

"It's lovely," Kate spoke.

"And best of all, it's very versatile," Emily says. "Rose can wear this every day she can play and get dirty and won't have to worry about it getting worn out." Kate nodded.

"I wouldn't mind a dress like this myself." She says. "For home use, that is."

Emily chuckles. "You said you got this made at the antique store?"

"Yes. You have to go there, Kate. You'll love it. I know how much you like old-time antiques."

"Someday," Kate mumbles. "Thank you so much for the dress."

"You're welcome, dearie."

Honk! Honk!

Both women looked up at the sound. Emily checked her watch.

"Oh, how time flies." Kate rose from the sofa as she sat.

"Let me cut you a piece a of cake for the way home."

"All right." There was a knock as Kate went to the kitchen whilst Emily went for the door. Pilot was lying near Rose barked when the door was open and a tall handsome man came into the room, kissing his mother before saying.

"Is the party over?" Kate smiles as she sliced a piece of pink rose swirl cake, revealing a delicious white chocolate cake that had hints of pink marble swirl in the three-layer cake.

"Hi, Joel!" Kate spoke as he closed the door.

"Hey, Kate! How are things?" She nodded.

"Good. How was work?" Joel shrugged.

"Work is work." He eyed hungrily at the table and saw it was full of pizza slices, chicken wings, and lasagna.

"Help yourself, Joel," Kate says. "I'm just wrapping a few slices of cake for you to take home." Joel nodded gratefully before going to the table and taking some pizza.

"You girls' had fun?" he asks over a mouthful. Kate nodded as she wrapped the cakes in thin foil. Footsteps made Kate look to see Rose in her red dress.

"Hi Mr. Joel." Rose chirped. Joel swallowed and beamed.

"Who is this!?" he says, feigning surprise. "Is this a real live princess, I see?" Rose giggled.

"It's me!" Joel kneeled in front of her.

"Wow!"

"All that's missing is her crown," Emily laughs, stepping into the room after using the bathroom.

"Or wings." Joel chuckles. "Did you have a wonderful birthday, hon?" Rose nodded.

"Mommy got me a tent!" Rose says.

"Wow! That's awesome." Rose took Joel's hand and pulled.

"Come see tent!"

"Oh no, Rosy." Emily says. "Joel is tired."

"I don't mind, mom," Joel says, getting to his feet. He let Rose guide him to her room. Emily and Kate chuckled as she finished wrapping the cakes and food.

"Thank you for coming, Emily," Kate says earnestly.

"Oh, dearie any time. I love coming to your birthday dinners." Kate smiles. Laughter made the two of them look to see Joel carrying Rose with Pilot walking beside him.

"That tent is awesome!" he says. "Who put on the lights?"

"I did." Said Kate.

"I need this for me and Ivy when I go camping." He says with a laugh.

"Thanks for the cake." He adds as he and Emily headed for the door.

"I put some food for you and Ivy, too." Kate says, as she and Rose waved goodbye to her guest. Emily and Joel waved back as Pilot barked before driving away. Kate closed the door, locking it behind her. Rose rubbed her eyes as the sandman spell took effect on her treasure; glancing at her kitchen clock seeing read 7:56 pm. Kate got to work.

First, changing Rose from her dress, replacing it with her nightgown. There, she read a story to Rose, who listened with sleepy interest before going to sleep; the mother kissing her goodnight before shutting the door. With a sigh, she headed for her room, where she removed her clothes, grabbed her towel, Kate headed for the bathroom to shower.

Twenty minutes later, Kate, dressed in her light nightgown, was quietly packing the food to save for another day. She glanced at her countertop where her cake sat half-finished; a feeling of pride surged for her handiwork, remembering Rose's face when she saw her mother's masterpiece: her eyes lit up as she clapped whilst she and Emily sang Happy Birthday as Kate took photos of every moment.

I must get them printed so they can go into the photo album. Kate thought.

Quiet rapping from the door made Kate pause, putting the lasagna away. She was so busy she didn't bother to check outside the window, curious; she walked to the window and peeped out, but all she could see was the silhouette of a car. What brand? She didn't know. She walked to the door. "Who is it?" Kate called. Her voice was full of authority despite her pulse raced.

"*It's Nolan.*"

She froze eyes wide as she heard the voice, but it didn't sound right, it scunded... Kate unlocked the door and cracked it open just enough to see the face that went with the voice of a man who stood tall, but there was a disheveled look to his appearance. Gray eyes looked into her stunning brown eyes that were glazed with despair; even as he held a large box in both hands. "N-Nolan?" Kate breathes. Nolan smiled, but it was weak.

‍ ‍

Nolan took in the warm air of the night. Darkness surrounded him save for bright white flood lamps that cast their beacon where he sat on the curved bench. He stared at the open window that viewed the kitchen; watching her move; appearing and disappearing behind the curtains that showed her silhouette. He closed his eyes, remembering how Kate saw him, her eyes wide as she looked at him when she opened the door; Nolan stepped inside, holding a large gift. His gray eyes swept the home he hadn't entered in over two years. Banners hung on the walls as balloons hovered in different directions, their silent appearance telling him that there was a grand celebration.

For a celebration he was late.

Nolan groaned, burying his face in his hands.

"Nolan?" He started, opening his eyes. Lifting his head from his hands to look up to see Kate standing quietly.

"Y-Yes?" He breathes, he could not help staring at her eyes wide as she stood tall, dressed in a lovely nightgown holding, to his surprise, a cake. "Here," she says as she pushed the plate forward. There was a slight clink of the fork that scraped the plate's surface. "I thought you'd like some cake." Nolan stared at it, surprised. Not just for the cake, although it was beautiful and cut thick, but was surprised because she was serving him. Again.

Nolan was faint with hunger when he placed the boxes on the floor. Kate watched as he slowly rose to his full height, only to tip over to the side of her table. Kate caught him with a cry before sitting Nolan on her sofa. Nolan's eyes were half closed when he felt something cold touch his cracked lips. He tested the liquid, tasting something sweet before he drank readily. Nolan was almost himself when Kate came in with a large slice of lasagna that he ate hungrily, feeling the pangs of hunger leave him. Now he stared at the cake in his hands, gazing at the three layers that contained pink frosting that held it together.

"Nolan?" Nolan started looking at Kate, who had been watching him silently sitting on a black swing.

"Aren't you going to eat?" she asks.

"Oh!" Nolan looked at the cake. "Y-Yes I-I was just…" he trailed off.

"What?"

"Nothing." Nolan picked up the fork. Cutting a piece from the cake, he lifted it to his mouth, chewed, then swallowed. His eyes lit up. Looking back at the cake, he ate another piece.

"This is good." He spoke. Kate looked away, hiding a small smile.

"Thank you." Nolan took another bite, eagerly.

"Who made this?" he asks over a mouthful, then froze, realizing he was being rude.

"I did."

"You did?" Kate lifted her shoulders to her ears.

"I had help." She says modestly. "Emily showed me how to make the cake as well as decorate." Nolan, speechless, nodded.

"It's delicious." Kate nodded quietly, not meeting his gaze. Nolan ate quietly, unable to bring up more to say. He took a large bite of the dessert, thinking how this was his first birthday cake from his second born and it was made by the woman he… Nolan looked down. Melancholy returned, making him chew with less vim. Kate stared at Nolan, noticing his hollow cheeks, telling Kate how much weight he lost in the three years she had seen him. She looked away.

"Thank you." Kate turned her head.

"For what?" Nolan didn't look at her as he placed the empty plate on the side of the bench by his thigh.

"For doing what you did for me." He spoke. "No one would help, much less feed someone like me." Nolan looked down when he says, "Me."

"Anyone would do the same." She murmurs, looking away. Kate pushed herself on the swing gently.

"Not for me," Nolan's voice was grave. "Not after what I've done." Kate didn't answer for several seconds. When she spoke, it was stating a fact.

"You're the richest man in the country." She replies. "Anyone would do the same for someone like you." Silence. Nolan turned his head to look at Kate. Her nightdress billowed lightly as she swung on silently; he could not help

169

noticing how lovely Kate's face was as her hair flowed in the slight breeze as her hands gripped the metal chain handles. Nolan's cheeks warmed. Looking away from his ogling, he asked.

"How was the party?"

"Good," she spoke. "We kept things quiet, just the four of us."

"Four?" he looked at her.

"Me, Rose, Emily, and Pilot girl."

"Pilot?… girl?" Nolan looked confused.

"Pilot is Emily's dog." Kate stopped, then realized her error. "Oh, you don't know her."

"I do." Kate blinked, surprised, as Nolan looked down.

"The woman, Emily… I saw her yesterday with Rose." Nolan spoke. "I take it she watches her while you're at work?"

"Oh," Kate spoke after a moment's pause. "She does. She's Rose's babysitter." Nolan nodded, storing this information.

"She seems, um… cold." Kate blinked slowly.

"Cold how?"

"It's probably nothing. I mean, she doesn't know me, and she had every right to not tell me about… Rose." he trailed off.

"Did you ask about her?" Nolan opened his mouth, then closed it. He looked down.

"It wasn't my right to ask." He finally spoke voice sad. "I have no claim on your child. Emily was right to refuse my question."

"She does," Kate replies. Her voice was unreadable as she gaze at Nolan, who was looking at the palm of his hands.

"Does she know?" Nolan whispers after a long silence. Kate looked down at her lap.

"Yes." Kate breathes. Nolan nodded wordlessly.

"How much does she know?"

"*She knows everything.*" A slight breeze caused her nightgown to blow. "Emily knows you're the father, as well as her son."

"When did you…" he swallowed, before continuing. "Tell her?"

"Before Rose was born." Kate closed her eyes. "She heard about the rumors. How I harmed cam…" she stopped. Nolan winced. "She wanted to know my story. To know why her son told her to keep away from me." Nolan looked at her, eyes shining. His skin prickled with needles that stabbed his back as his chest clenched.

"Emily listened to me." Kate breathes; she raised her head with a gentle smile on her lips. "She believed me. She was the one who volunteered to take care of Rose when I returned to work. Until I left Squeaky Clean.

"**What**!?" Nolan gasps; she nodded. "When!? Wh-Why!"

"I found a better job in the city," Kate explains, she shrugged. "I'm a published author."

"You…" he breathes stunned by her announcement his chest squeezed but not what he was used to "*You did it.*" he whispers.

Kate looked at him eyes widening slightly at his words. A tiny wistful smile lifted the corners of her red lips. She nodded once.

"Wow." He spoke. "C-congratulations." She thank him quietly, even as a new revelation came to his startled mind. "But then…" he paused before saying in a trance. "That's why the money was given back…"

"What money?" Nolan froze.

"I…" Nolan started, his cheeks burned. "I wanted to help you. It was before Christmas after I—this was before Rose was born!" he adds hastily when Kate stared at him distrustfully.

"We're you having me followed?"

"N-No! I-I swear! I-Kate—it wasn't like that—I had found your business card in my office, and I didn't want your boss to tell you I gave you…" Kate blinked, seeing Nolan babble.

"*You were my secret Santa,*" She breathes. "all those years ago, even after Christmas when I…" she trailed off. Nolan groaned.

"I knew you wanted nothing from me." He says, "I know you work hard but I couldn't—then I saw you in my office and your condition—I wanted to do something!" he looked down pushing back his hair.

"I'm sorry. I didn't want you to think I was treating you like a charity case. I…"

"Thank you." Nolan raised his head, taking in Kate's warm eyes, as she looked at him gently.

"I would have given more as Rose got older, but when you left Squeaky Clean I—" Kate shook her head.

"What you've done was enough. I just didn't know it was…" Kate smiles softly. "thank you," she breathes, "for helping her." Nolan's chest squeezed but it was a pain he didn't want to lose as he stared at her.

"You're welcome," Nolan whispered. Kate nodded before looking into the dark trees. An owl hooted in the distance as crickets chirped in the grass.

"How old is Rose?" Kate looked at him. Nolan faced Kate with sad, pained eyes.

"*She's three.*" She whispers.

"Three." Nolan stared at the house; his heart squeezed. "*Three.*" He whispers.

"It's amazing how time flies." Kate followed his gaze, a small smile on her lips.

"Yes," she agrees. "It does." Nolan turned his head to look at her. He smiled weakly.

"I like the swing." He noted. "Did you build it?"

"No. I had it installed. I can't climb that high." Kate pointed up to where the chain hung on a thick branch in the darkness. Nolan looked before nodding at her.

"It's quiet here." He spoke. Kate nodded, letting herself swing. "You forget you live in a town full of smiling faces and lending hands."

"It's like that for you," Kate replies, her face turned somber. "But behind the smiling faces, there are whispered secrets." Nolan looked at her.

"That would be preferable to their false smiles. At least I know who they are. Instead of trying to pretend to like me." He mumbles.

"What are you doing here?" Kate asks. Nolan started.

"You didn't just come here to give Rose a gift." She spoke calmly. "You could have just given it and left. You wouldn't stay this long without a reason." Nolan stared at her eyes, black, despite the flood lamps. He sensed the shift. All pleasantries were gone from Kate as she looked at him firmly. Nolan couldn't stall any longer.

He looked away.

"*Camille and I had a fight.*" Nolan's voice was low, tired, even to him: he didn't know why he says this in front of Kate, but he had no one else to talk to. No one who understood, who knew he was... "We had a fight." He repeated. Kate stared at him before looking down.

173

"Married couples fight all the time." She whispers. "It's normal."

"Not ours," Nolan spoke gravely, as he entwined his fingers and rested his chin on it. "Our relationship was never built on love and happiness. Only conformity." He adds bitterly.

"Did she say that to you?" Kate looked away when she asks this.

"No." He replies, his voice even more tired, regretting the words. "I did." Silence. Nolan looked at her face sadly; it didn't help when he saw Kate's frown, her left hand on her lap clenched into a fist.

"It is something I'm not proud of." He spoke, looking at her pleading. "Looking back, I see I wanted to hurt her. To feel something other than contempt." Kate's expression didn't change.

"But you're still together," Kate spoke. "You're working things out. You're sorry about the past and you, your wife, and your daughter are better now."

"That's what it was at first." he sighs. "To you and everyone else. To everyone, we're the perfect family who had survived a storm stronger than ever before." He looked at her anxiously, but Kate merely nodded. "But our boat was sinking from the start. All we can do was put a bandage on the cracks."

"Why are you telling me this, Nolan?" Kate asks. "This is something that should be discussed with your wife or a counselor, not your mistress." Nolan flinched at the title. He looked at her, pain and regret on his face. "You still didn't answer my question of why you are here?" Nolan opened his mouth but hesitated to speak.

"Did Camille tell you it was Rose's birthday?" her tone was low, accusatory.

"No, I…" Nolan started, then stopped shifting his thoughts, debating on truth or lie:

He went with the truth.

"*I wanted to see you.*" Kate's eyes widen, she stared at Nolan, who looked at her sadly. "I wanted to see you and Rose. I… I didn't know when her birthday was. I wanted to do something. Something good after so much bad, go somewhere that someone knows the truth about what I am." Kate, who had stared after his confession in shock, grew grave.

"I don't know you, Nolan," Kate spoke quietly, glancing away. "You lied to me."

"I didn't lie!" Nolan looked at her, shocked.

"You hid you were married." She looked at him firmly. Nolan stared, unable to come up with a rebuttal. Instead, he looked down. "Everything you've done and told me was a lie. One minute you're sweeping me off my feet, the next you get a restraining order for a crime I never committed."

"I know the truth!" Nolan looked at her, eyes wide. "I know what Camille done."

"But it doesn't change the fact that it happened. That *you* let it happen." Kate spoke solemnly. Nolan looked away; his throat worked. Kate stared at him grimly for several moments. Before he looked away, she let out a breath.

"I'm not mad at you, Nolan." She murmurs. "I've come to terms with it. You have every right to not trust me. If I was in your shoes, I would have done the same, but it doesn't change anything."

"You don't trust me." Nolan whispered. It wasn't a question. He closed his eyes, his chest squeezing with pain that he had grown accustom too.

"I want to know who this person really is." Kate spoke. "That the man I had fallen in love with three years ago was real, not a fake." Nolan was silent. The pain grew stronger. Kate stared at him for a long time before letting out a sigh. Looking down, she pushed herself on the swing once more.

"He wasn't lying," Nolan spoke. He opened his eyes and watched her, hand on his left chest. "That man you met three years ago was not playing games. He was not trying to hurt you, that man he… he still exists." Kate didn't answer. She felt a twinge in her chest even as she changed the subject.

"If you wanted to be there for Rose, you could have called me." She spoke, not meeting his gaze. "My number is still the same. I would not have prevented you from seeing her."

"I didn't know if you changed your number," Nolan mumbles. He let out a breath, shoulders slumped. "Besides, she wouldn't want to see me. Rose doesn't know who I am. She would fear me."

"How do you know that?"

"I saw how she saw me yesterday. She didn't want to come near me."

"That's because I taught her not to talk to strangers," Kate spoke. "She did the right thing. But that's because she saw you as a stranger. If I had been there, I would have told her you were a friend of mine." Nolan frowned. "Rose is not at that age to ask about her father. She's too busy being happy to think about such topics." Nolan nodded slowly, leaning his head back against the tree trunk, his eyes half closed.

"*I ran away from home.*" He confessed.

"Wh-what!?" Kate looked at him wide-eyed with surprise. "B-but why?!" Nolan looked down at his open palms, seeing the lines etched in his hands. "*Camille's pregnant.*"

Silence.

Nolan's eyes dulled as he confessed to the woman he hurt. He risked a glance at Kate, surprised by her calm expression.

"*Congratulations*," Kate spoke. Her voice was devoid of any emotion, only resignation. Nolan didn't answer; just watched as Kate swung quietly.

"Thank you," he mumbles wearily.

"When did you find out?" Kate asks after another silence.

"Last night," Nolan spoke, "It was a shock. One minute we're fighting about firing Esme's nanny, the next…" he trailed off.

"Is that the night you ran away?"

"Yes." Kate looked down.

"I take it you are not happy about the news." Nolan looked at her, startled.

"What!?" She didn't look at him. "Ka- I…" he paused. "I am happy, I just…" Kate bobbed her head. "Kate? Please look at me." Nolan breathes. Kate lifted her head, and he saw her face was distant.

"How long is she?" Kate asks.

"I…" Nolan hesitated before he whispers truthfully. "She found out yesterday. I didn't, then Camille said everything was hers and I… I had to escape."

"So, your first thought was to come to your mistress." Nolan winced.

"Please don't call yourself that."

"But it's what I am."

"It doesn't apply to you," Nolan says. "You didn't, I was—"

"But you did." Kate's voice was accusatory. "You knew, and you lied. You hurt your wife and child for a naïve fling!"

"You're not a fling, Kate," Nolan spoke firmly. "You were never that to me. I care about you and still do."

177

"Cared enough that you and your wife plotted against me!"

"It wasn't like that!" he was on his feet.

"Then what was it!?" Kate sprang from the swing, eyes stinging, but her voice didn't waver with her anger. "You tell your powerful wife that you slept with a poor, gullible girl and get her pregnant; only to be ashamed of your affair, and love child getting out and ruining your reputation. So, your wife bribes me to abort so that *you* can continue living in perfect bliss. Erasing the momentary blot on your flawless record!" Nolan stared at Kate with shock. "Wh-what?" he gasps. "H-how? Who? Who told you this?" Kate looked away; hands clenched.

"It doesn't matter." Nolan's face burned with anger now as he step forward. "It does to me, Kate! How could you assume I would do this to you? That I would kill my child for my reputation."

"Why don't you ask Camille?" Kate retorts. "She's the one who calls the shots in this town."

"Did Camille tell you this? Did she…" he stopped remembering the night he went to see Camille in the hospital: believing everything she tells him, what Kate did… Kate stood glaring.

"She made you think I didn't want the baby." Nolan breathes, stunned.

"Not just her." She glared at him. "*You* made it pretty clear that you wanted nothing to do with my child." Tears pooled down her cheeks. "But it doesn't matter. Not anymore. Camille got what she wanted. No one knows, will never know the truth." Nolan stared thunderstruck at her. Dark gray irises stared at the lonely woman; his heart hammered, making his pulse beat under dark skin that grew cold hearing his wife's plan, to his own… his eyes stung as he stared at the weeping mother.

"Kate," Nolan whispered. He lifted a hand to touch her shoulder, but she flinched back. "I'm sorry I… I didn't know I…" Heat flashed within him. "If I had known, I would have stopped this, I…" he trailed off, thinking of his promise; all the steps to keep his family unit. Kate sniffed.

"It's time you left." She spoke thickly. Nolan opened his mouth to protest when a cry made the adults look up at the house.

"Rose." Kate gasps. Before Nolan could react, Kate was running for the house. Nolan hesitated for half a second before he followed behind her. Kate opened the door with such force it rattled the walls, her eyes fearful as she cried out.

"Rosy!" Rose sat on the floor between the living room and the kitchen, her bright eyes wet with tears as she looked up, arms raised as she cries.

"Mommy!" Kate ran and scooped her up in her arms, shushing her child, crooning.

"Mommies here sweetie! Shh! Mommies here."

"You ran away!"

"No, mommy didn't run away. Mommy was outside. Mommy is so sorry for leaving you alone." Kate felt wetness pooled down her cheeks. "Mommy won't leave you again, I promise." Rose sniffed, clinging to her mother's neck. Kate placed her lips against Rose's cheeks, kissing the tears away.

"Mommy!" Kate looked to see Rose looking at Nolan, who stood face flushed after hearing Rose scream. Kate stared as Rose watched quietly clinging to her mother.

"It's alright, sweetie." Kate breathes. Nolan watched quietly, seeing Kate relax but still hold her daughter protectively.

"Mommy who's that?" Rose spoke loud enough for Nolan could hear. Kate looked at him before saying.

"He's a friend of mine, Rosy." Rose looked at him, face scrunched in thought.

"He gave me my ball," Rose spoke, remembering.

"He did?" Kate asks, looking at him. Rose nodded. "That was very nice of him to do that." She adds. Rose nodded.

"Where did you go, mommy?"

"I was outside, honey, talking to Mr. Nolan," Kate answers. She said this as she walked to the black sofa and sat down with Rose.

"Him?" Rose asks, pointing. Kate nodded.

"Hi Rosy," Nolan spoke, tongue dry. Sweat formed on his forehead. Rose started, then hid her face in her mother's chest. Kate let out a tired laugh.

"Don't be shy, honey." She breathes. "Say hi." Rose shook her head.

"Don't you want to see what present Mr. Nolan got for your birthday?"

"Presents?" Kate nodded. Rose looked at Mr. Nolan curiously.

"Yes. Mr. Nolan got a big present for you." She nodded at Nolan. "He wants you to see it." Nolan, surprised, nodded, closing the door behind him. He stepped forward before lifting a large, red-wrapped gift. He took pleasure in seeing Rose's eyes light up with wonder.

"Would you like to open your birthday gift?" Kate asks. Rose nodded, then crawled off her mother's arms. She walked forward as Nolan kneeled on the floor, smiling with nervous excitement as his child walked to the box, her brown eyes showing uncertainty as she stared at him.

"Happy birthday, Rosy," Nolan whispers softly. Rose started at her name. She turned her head to Kate, who had gotten up from the sofa and was

180

standing behind her. Kate nodded. Rose looked back at the man before lifting her hands to the box, attempting to open it.

"Mommy, the wrappy won't come off," Rose says.

"L-Let me help you." Nolan volunteered, lifting his own hand as he ripped a side of the box. The long rip made Rose start. Expecting a present, she helped Nolan tear the paper; both adults saw as Rose's face lit up with wonder as the last paper was torn off, revealing a large box containing a toy kitchen. Rose squealed.

"Mommy! Mommy! Look!" Kate smiles.

"Wow!" Kate says. "It's so pretty." Rose nodded, beaming at Nolan.

"What do we say, Rose?"

"Thank you." Nolan smiles.

"You're welcome, honey." He breathes, before picking up a short package in different wrapping paper.

"This is for you." he breathes. Kate's eyes widen even as she started to decline the gift.

"No." he spoke gently. He placed it in her hand. "I want you to have this." He smiles at her, taking Kate back when they spent together, walking in the park, as he listened to her speak, seeing the warmth in his gray eyes.

"Opee! Mommy! Opee!" Rose chirped. Kate hesitated for a moment before lifting a hand to the top of the seam and tore off the paper. Nolan watched with bated breaths, a sad but hopeful smile on his face. Kate gasped! Nolan and Rose stared as Kate peered down, eyes shining with unshed tears at the scarlet leather-bound notebook. Nolan had searched all over town for a gift that would be perfect. He knew jewels and dresses didn't appeal to Kate and he almost gave until he stopped at a store that sold books, pens and…

Nolan's smile grew, his chest squeezed not of pain but of joy as he saw Kate look up at him and breathed with reverence.

"Thank you."

Chapter Eighteen

The next two months were long in the small town. The lazy days of summer had finally arrived with sweltering heat, trips to summer side beaches, and tourists who came far and near to the quaint town that reveled in the summer of celebrations and fun. August came with a high commemoration for Forest-Bend annual fair. People chatted excitedly about the event commemorating the last week before school began and the vacation ended. Much to every child's dismay.

Water splashed down Nolan's face, wet and refreshing, waking him from his sleepy haze as morning rays glided from the window. Nolan raised his head to stare at his reflection. His face no longer looked gaunt, instead of sunken cheeks: his cheekbones were fuller the way he remembered after regaining his appetite back and gaining muscle from his previous weak body. Dark gray eyes peered back at Nolan, calm but bright as he stared at himself, a half-smile on his face.

A grunt made Nolan turn to see a groggy, flushed face from Camille, who grimaced as she entered the white bathroom supporting herself on the sink. Blurry green eyes looked up to see Nolan, who looked away, but his eyes watched her through the mirror as she staggered.

"You look cheerful." Nolan didn't look at her but says coolly.

"Should I not be?" he saw as his wife walked past him to the other side of the sink where she sat on a plush stool. Camille's sallow cheek had a tinge of green as she laid a right hand on a ball-size bump that stuck out between her hips. Camille grimaced, lifting her left hand to her face.

"What's wrong?" Nolan asks, but he knew the answer. Camille didn't do well during pregnancy. After three months, Camille still looked sickly. Rashes and acne covered her face and body, and lack of appetite made her moodier due to bouts of violent vomiting that concerned Nolan.

"You know what's wrong." Her tone was biting. She didn't look at him. "Did you put on cologne? Because it's making me sick."

"I didn't put on anything," Nolan replies. "I just woke up."

"Well, something smells." She grimaced. "And it's making my stomach hurt."

"How's the baby?" He asks quietly. Camille grimaced as she leaned back against the wall.

"Ruining my body." Nolan's lip twitched, but his voice was kind of attempting to extend the olive branch.

"I know this isn't easy, for you. Especially, when you carried Esme I…" Nolan trailed off, sighed. "I will do what I can to make *you* both comfortable." As he said this, Nolan kneeled in front of Camille, placing a hand on her knee. Camille didn't answer, just stared. Both adults watched one another: green to dark gray. But there was no warmth: no joy, only a mutual truce that stemmed after three months of silent seething, passive-aggressive comments, and lust.

The only bright spot was *Esme* and their *son.*

☙

Kate hummed quietly as she opened the brown shiny box containing her mail. The small door swung open, revealing a large stack of white envelopes containing letters from unknown companies and businesses. She picked up the letters and placed them in her purse before closing the lid, locking it with a key that she too placed in her bag. A shift on her back made

Kate turn her head and smile lovingly at her daughter, who watched her quietly with wide, curious eyes as she hung on her mother's back.

"Ready to go, Rosy?" she cooed. Rose nodded. Kate turned away from the P. O Box to walk outside to the bright August afternoon.

Kate marveled at the town's fair. In all the years she had lived here, she never attended the festival. It only began three years ago when Rose was still a baby and still feeling the sting of being an outcast; she avoided any events and functions for her own peace of mind.

But today would be different. *Kate wouldn't be alone.*

"Kate!?" Kate turned and smiles at the familiar faces of Emily, her son, his girlfriend Ivy, and Pilot. Emily stepped forward and hugged her.

"You made it!" she says.

"Yes." Kate smiles.

"Pilli!" Rose cries, bouncing on Kate's back. Pilot barked and stepped forward but was held by her leash.

"I'm so glad you came. Did you just get here?" asks Emily.

"Just a few minutes ago," Kate admitted. "I was taking in the sights." Kate untied Rose from her back and placed her down. Pilot went to the child and licked her face. Rose giggled.

"Well, let's get going," Joel says. "Mom, me and Ivy are heading to meet Tony and James."

"Alright," Emily says.

"We can meet at the food stands at 2 pm."

"We'll save you a seat." Said Joel, smiling. Kate and Emily nodded, and the young couple left hand in hand.

"What do you want to do first?" Emily asks. Kate hesitated a moment before saying softly.

"There's a bounce castle I want to take Rose." Emily nodded, smiling.

"Okay, let's go there." Kate smiles weakly before picking up Rose. The two women walked.

Unknown to them that someone was spying on Kate.

The rest of the fair was an exciting experience for Kate and Rose. For Rose, everything was new and vibrant; the small town she had seen as quiet but also full of mean faces was now smiling and bright. The people and places she walked with her mommy, Emmi and Pilli, look to Rose like a magic book: full of rainbows, laughing children and yummy smells.

Kate felt she belonged. The years of banishment that marked her seemed to dissipate, replacing exile with hope for the kind mother. She saw her child bounce happily with children her age in the inflatable castle. Rose waved merrily at her mother, calling out to "***Look what I can do***!" Kate found herself enthralled by the activities as she walked the streets where vendors sold ice cream, kettle corn, and funnel cake. To the local shops that sold their wares on discount for the tourist who came for the festivities and take back home as souvenirs.

"Mommy!" Kate felt Rose tug her leg. She leaned down to see Rose holding a package of strawberry seeds.

"What's this?"

"It's seeds, honey,"

"What are seeds?" Kate tells her. "Baby plants grow in the paper?" Kate chuckles.

"The seeds are inside the paper. You have to pour the seeds in the ground."
Rose's eyes widen, making Kate laugh. "Would you like to grow
strawberries?" Rose nodded eagerly, making Kate smile. Kate bought the
seeds along with a small pot containing mint. She and Rose left the store in
the august sun, where Emily and Ivy looked up from their ogling.

"Joel just called," Emily says. "He's waiting for us at the food benches."

"Good. I'm starving." Ivy said. Emily giggled as the girls walked. They found
Joel, who saved them a seat. He had already had a plate full of fair food when
he saw them telling the girls that the line wasn't very crowded.

"Why didn't you get me something?" Ivy griped. Joel smiled apologetically.

"It's all right, Ivy." Said Emily, placing her bags beside Kate who kept them
under the table. "What are you two getting?" Emily asks Kate and Ivy.

"That fried chicken Joel's eating looks good," Ivy says, eyeing Joel's plate.
Kate nodded in agreement before she and Ivy walked to the vendors before
splitting up to go on two different lines. Kate's mouth watered as she saw the
vender selling funnel cake on the menu: it had been so long since she had the
fried treat dusted in powdered sugar.

"Kate!" Kate turned her head and was surprised to see Tony, the chef and
Joel's friend, standing online across from her, grinning. Kate beamed.

"Hi Tony!" she says. "How are you?"

☙

Sweat beaded down Nolan's front brow as the August heat beat down his
dark skin. Nolan bore the torment of the summer heat but the wrath of his
wife and daughter was a whole other story.

"*I want ice cream!*" Nolan looked down at the pouting face of Esme, her
cheeks shiny with sweat but also with a sunscreen that protected her skin

187

from harmful rays. Nolan heard a grunt and turned to see Camille standing, one hand on her middle as she wore a designer dress with matching summer hat, which to Nolan seemed too elaborate and big to wear to a town fair. Camille walked forward as people parted, some watching the couple, but most were watching Camille's dress.

"Daddy!" Esme cries. Nolan felt his arm tug at her hands.

"You didn't have to come." He spoke, his tone was calm, his face unreadable as he stared at Camille. She glared at him.

"And let you run around while your pregnant wife is home alone." She hisses low enough for him to hear. Her stomach twisted queasily, and she hunched in on herself.

"Camille?" Nolan stepped forward, but she raised herself once more. He could see her cheeks were flushed. "Maybe you should sit down," Nolan adds. Camille didn't answer. "Why don't you both find a shady seat and I'll get us something to eat."

"I'm not eating fair food." She says with disgust.

"**Daddy! I want ice cream!**" Esme yells.

"I'm coming, Esme," Nolan says patiently. To Camille, he asked. "What do you want?"

"Water and…" Camille took in the smell of fair food. Her stomach twisted, but she pushed back her. Nolan, noticing her gaze, said with a knowing smile. "I'll bring us some ice cream." Camille nodded. Nolan told Esme to go with her mother and find a seat, while he walked to the shady trees where ice cream and food truck vendors sold food. Nolan got on-line with a grateful sigh; glad to get a break from his wife who grew worse with each passing

188

second, her… *And Esme*. Nolan remembered her displeasure when he told her she was going to be a big sister throwing tantrums in front of the maids. Nolan had to buy her gifts to pacify her, now she had no nanny to step in. Nolan sighed as he held two large waffle cones on an ice cream holder that supported a plate of funnel cake and a bottle of water in hand. Nolan walked in search of his family when he heard a giggle that made him turn his head. Nolan stared wide-eyed to see her face flushed, her eyes dancing as she stood talking merrily to his old chef. Nolan's mouth went dry seeing his two acquaintances, one he fired unfairly for his wife's whim and…

Kate's smile was bright as she spoke. Nolan noticed in her hands she held two slices of pizza, and funnel cake, along with two bottles. Nolan could not help smiling gently at her involuntarily. His footsteps carried him forward stopping when he saw a woman stopped next to Kate, grinning, holding her own plate. Nolan stopped watching as the woman spoke to Kate; seeing Kate nod before they both walked away. Nolan's heart sank. He turned and walked away, face pinched.

"Daddy!" Nolan looked up to see Esme sitting across from Camille on a small rectangular bench. He walked with little enthusiasm to them, passing a table before handing Esme a cone, who took it without a thank you.

"Took you long enough." Grouched Camille. Nolan didn't answer, instead handing her the cone. Before sitting beside Camille, entwining his fingers on his propped elbows. Camille watched him, seeing his grim expression as she licked her ice cream, which to her surprise was delicious.

"What happened now?"

"I don't want to talk about it," Nolan spoke in a monotone. Esme licked her ice cream. Nolan untwined his fingers to pick up a napkin. "Esme, you're making a mess of your clothes. Clean your shirt."

"No!" Nolan frowned.

"You heard what I said, Esme. Don't argue with me."

"No!"

"Listen to your father!" Camille orders.

"No!" Camille eyed Nolan's face saying: 'she's your problem.' Before lifting her cellphone. Nolan sighed, then looked away from his daughter. Esme frowned when she saw her father's defeated expression, her ice cream dripping all over her top. She looked down. Nolan looked across him and was surprised to see the woman, Emily, sitting across a tall handsome man, but that was not what made his eyes widen: it was the small child that sat cradled in the old woman's lap.

Rose sat comfortably, watching quietly the world around her with bright brown eyes. Her hair was different. Nolan couldn't help noticing the clips and bubbles that held her shiny black hair. Nolan watched the adults wordlessly, his eyes softening when he saw Kate and the woman, he saw earlier come forward holding plates of food: seeing Kate sit next to Emily. Gazing as Kate took Rose from Emily and sat her down beside her with a slice of pizza that Kate cut into bite-size pieces.

Nolan smiled tenderly.

"What are you smiling at?" Nolan started before he could protest 'nothing.' Camille craned her neck and saw them. Nolan saw her face flicker from shock before turning to a scowl her green eyes harden as she glared at the mother. Esme turned her head to see the family, her face pinched as she

190

looked at Kate and the child. Nolan saw as his daughter gazed at them, her green eyes narrowed like her mother's.

"Why is *she* here?" Camille's voice was full of derision.

"To enjoy the fair." He stated quietly. Nolan glanced at Camille whose lips curled, making her look unattractive.

"Who are they?" asks Esme, turning back to her parents. No one answered. Nolan felt his chest squeeze before looking up to see Rose feed herself, smiling up at Kate who beamed. She raised her head... and her eyes met his. Nolan saw her eyes widen as her face, turned to surprise. Her gaze roamed to his daughter and wife, before landing back on Nolan. Nolan felt a hot hand turn his chin, making him look at his wife, who had a smile on her face before she brought her lips to his in a kiss. Nolan started! *He hadn't been kissed by Camille in months.* He felt her tongue enter his mouth; involuntarily his tongue touched hers, but as he started to close his eyes, it was over... Camille pulled away abruptly and craned her head, a wicked sneer on her lovely face.

 Nolan glanced quickly to see Kate's face flicker from surprise to pain. It was then Nolan realized it was a ploy: Camille had used him. Her face said it all. *"You may have slept with him. But I still have him."*

Nolan felt the taste of his wife turn bitter. He looked at Kate, eyes wide, pleading, but Kate's expression was no longer shocked, only resigned. She looked away, and he saw her face soften as she looked at her daughter.

"Who is that mommy?" Esme asks. Camille looked at her daughter, her face softening in the rare moments when she was in the company of her friends.

"Someone who isn't like us." Camille spoke.

"What do you mean?"

191

"She's poor, Essie." Nolan opened his mouth as she adds. "You are never to go near them, understand."

"Are they bad?"

"No." Camille's smile was cruel. "She's worse: *a naïve fling.*"

"Camille, *stop*," Nolan warned in a low voice. Camille glanced at him as she licked her cone silkily.

"I'm just protecting my child from people who try to take what's not theirs." Esme nodded as if that was the most important wisdom on earth. She looked at the mother and child with a frown. Nolan was too stunned to react. He was going to have to talk with Esme alone or… Camille entwined her hands in his and squeezed hard. Her face showed she read his mind and would not let that happen.

A chill ran down his spine despite the heat.

෬

The rest of the fair was enjoyable for the adults, toddlers, and German shepherds, partaking in the festivities as the town prepared for the grand finale. Kate tried to enjoy the festival, but her mind went back to Camille Roth's face: it had been years since she saw the woman. When last she saw Camille, she was being carted to the ambulance on a stretcher from Kate's '*attack*'. Now seeing her with her sneering grin as she took no, claimed Nolan, sealing their love with a kiss.

Kate didn't feel the pang of jealousy. If anything, she felt humble: who was she to judge? Nolan: in his confession to her about his marriage, that behind their smiles was a tempest of loathing, seething respect… and misery. *Kate knew all.* But it still hurt seeing the couple and child sit as the perfect family. She walked to where Emily, Ivy and Joel stood, where a crowd was slowly

192

growing across from Joel. She saw a bright red convertible with a man inside who looked to be trying to start the vehicle.

"What's happening?" Kate asks.

"They're trying to fix the Convertible for the parade." Said Joel, gesturing with a nod. "Ben, Luke, and Paul are trying to see what's wrong." Kate nodded, wrinkling her nose as the potent smell of smoke mixed with odorless carbon monoxide emanate from the car. Emily glanced at her watch.

"The parade starts in twenty minutes." She says, looking up. "We should find a spot to sit down and see the show." She nodded in agreement. A gaggle of giggles made Kate turn her head to see a group of women huddled together, pointing; it didn't take her long to know it was Camille's brood of spoiled housewives. The woman looked up, meeting Kate's eyes before nudging her companion, whispering something that made her friend look at Kate.

The woman smirked, then called on her other friends, who saw and started pointing and laughing. Kate's eyes burned but she looked away, turning her attention back on the parade preparation: but she still felt their eyes.

"U-uhm, I'm going to find a restroom," Kate says, voice thick. Emily and Ivy nodded as Joel stared, transfixed, at the float. "I'll meet you at the parade— save us a seat." Kate left her bags with Ivy before turning, eyes stinging, head lowered, when she heard someone whisper by her side.

"*Cinder-whora.*"

Kate couldn't breathe. She clasped her daughter tightly, ignoring the ache in her shoulders. Her vision blurred as her eyes stung even worse. Kate walked quickly eyes down as she dodged the faces of the people whether of the town or tourists, she didn't know, all she knew was they were set of eyes in the crowd that knew the stigma she carried: The Scarlet Letter that marked her with…

Kate came to a complete stop. Lifting her head, she saw she was standing by the town hall. People congregated, some sitting on the stone steps while others sat on portable chairs. Kate watched glassy eyed as the onlookers walked the streets laughing while children played on the sidewalk. She let out a breath before walking steadily to the town steps. There she sat with an exhausted sigh. She felt a shift, making her gaze at Rose; relieved the child was fast asleep; smiling gently she shifted Rose, cradling her head in her arm; watching her child sleep, unaware of the cruelness that she endured, not witnessing the fear and anxiety she faced daily.

Kate rested her head atop her child's head, curtaining their face. Kate closed her eyes.

"Mommy." Kate opened her eyes and smiles.

"Hi Rosy," She cooed. "had a nice nap?" Rose nodded, looking around.

"Where's Pilli?" Kate looked up. She had completely forgotten about the others in her haste.

"I'm not sure, sweetie," She admitted. "But we'll find them." Rose nodded, then yawned. Kate rose to her feet.

"Come on, honey, let's find the others and see the parade." Rose smiled, taking her mother's hand. Kate guided her down the staircase and turned… Kate froze, her body hot with the summer heat turned icy cold. Her mind went blank as she stared at…

ᴄ౩

Someone screamed!!

Nolan turned around with shock as an ear-splitting scream echoed through the town. Camille and Esme turned as Nolan saw people scrambling, clutching their children as husbands ran, protecting their families.

"Nolan! What was that?!" Camille gasps. Nolan didn't answer. At that moment, a bang made him turn to see the red car hiccup to life. People stepped back at the same time listening to the screams as visitors ran!

"Let's go!" Nolan commands. Taking his wife and daughter who protested, pulling them, where he didn't care. He had to save…

"What's going on!?" Nolan turned his head, feeling Camille turn her head to see her friend Susie's eyes, tear-stained, clutched Camille almost collapsing on her. Camille pulled from Nolan's grip.

"Camille!" he cries. She ignored him.

"What is it, Susie?"

"She's insane!"

"What?"

"Daddy!" Esme wailed. Nolan picked her up as Susie rambled brokenly.

"Susie, what's wrong?!"

"She has a gun!" she gasps. "She shot Tina!"

"Who did!?" Nolan demands. Just then Joel, Ivy, Emily, and Pilot came by with no sign of…

"Joel!" he called. Joel turned his head, surprised.

"Mr. Roth?"

"What's going on!?"

"We don't know!"

"Son?!" Emily cries. "We have to leave!"

"I'm sorry I-I have to get my family to safety!"

"But do you know—?"

"I don't—"

"She's gone crazy!" Susie says. They all looked at her as she added. "she didn't want to be reasoned. She just started shooting!"

"Who did!?" Ivy cries.

"Janey!" Susie confessed. She looked at Camille. "she's after us! She wants revenge on you!" you have to run Camille!" Camille froze, fear for the first time passed her face as Nolan stared at her stunned.

"Where's Kate!?" Ivy spoke. Nolan turned to look at her.

"Are you sure?" Camille squeaked.

"I don't know." Emily looked at her worriedly. "she went to the bathroom and took Rose and left her bags with—" more screams Nolan put Esme down but held her hand.

"We can't stay here." He spoke. Everyone started running; following the crowd who ran, trying to get away from the pandemonium. Sheriffs ran in the other direction when they heard bullets echo in the air, making everyone duck and cover. Nolan saw Joel and Emily, seeing the old woman struggling to keep up, only to trip and fall with a cry.

"Mom!" Joel cries. He ran back to help her. Nolan didn't think, just reacted: he went to Joel who swung his mother's left arm over his shoulder and Nolan, swung her right over his. Together they carried her as Esme and Camille ran.

"Come on!" Nolan cries as the sound of sirens came from the distance, getting louder with each passing second until everyone stepped under a cover of trees where the ambulance was waiting. Nolan helped Joel get his mother to the truck, telling them she was injured.

"Th-thank you!" Joel breathes. Nolan nodded as Ivy came running, hugging Joel. Nolan stepped back, knowing they were being taken care of. He walked to Camille and Esme where they sat on a bench. Esme was sobbing when she saw Nolan. Nolan breathed heavily as he stared at her.

"Are you alright?" he asks. Before anyone could respond, someone ran forward saying: "she's got a hostage!"

"What's happening?" Camille demands, Esme sobs, Nolan went to her, and she embraced him.

"I don't know." He spoke. Susie, Nikki, her husband, and the other housewives came forward demanding what happened, doting over Camille.

"Are you alright?" asks Nikki's husband to Nolan, who nodded.

"Do you know what happened? Susie says she shot Tina."

"What?!"

"It's true." Said Susie. "I saw her. She just came out of nowhere and pulled out a gun and…" she trailed off, sobbing. Nolan shuddered.

"I heard Janey has a hostage?"

"Yes." Someone came forward and says this, adding. "Janey has a mother and child hostage!"

"Why would she do this!?" says a woman. Ivy came forward, face pale. Nolan walked over to her after giving Esme to Camille.

"Is Joel's mother alright?" he asks. She nodded. Nolan could not help noticing she was still holding a large quantity of bags.

"Are you alright?" she opened her mouth to speak then closed it, nodding when Joel came forward trembling. Ivy turned to him.

"Joel?" he looked at her with pain. "I-Is mom—"

"No, it's… I know who is held, hostage." Everyone looked at him, surprised.

197

"Who Joel?" Joel gulped, his face ashen.

"It's Kate."

Nolan felt the ground under him vanish, the air he breathes cut short as his heart stopped, and his mind went numb.

Ivy screamed.

℘

Kate wanted to scream, but her throat was too dry. Even if she could, she didn't want to break the unearthly ringing that rang in her ears despite all around her, noises, strong and commanding reverberating through her body. Kate felt warmth course through her, bringing back circulation to her fingers; her eyes that were focused on the metal barrel of the pistol had blurred, changing as she raised her head and saw the face that came with the deadly instrument.

Janey stood in dirt-covered jeans and a bloodied top. Kate could not help staring at the crazed woman once as beautiful as the best as she stood beside Camille; only to cast her out for what reason. Kate didn't know. Kate felt a spasm on her left leg, making her glance down to see Rose, her eyes wide as she clung to her for dear life.

Kate woke at that. Her eyes, her senses came flooding back as she remembered all, even as Janey hissed obscenities at the police who tried to get the upper hand to free not just her but…

"*L-let my daughter go.*" Janey turned her beady, wild eyes on Kate, who held her hands up conciliatorily. Janey's smile was cruel as she took a step forward.

"**Stop right there**!" someone shouted. Janey turned her hand and shot at the sheriffs, who ducked for cover. Rose screamed. Kate started to bend when Janey screeched.

"Don't you move!" Kate froze.

"Mommy!" Rose wailed.

"It's okay, baby." Kate was shocked to hear the panic in her voice as the gun was pointed back at her.

"Make a move, and the brat gets it!" Kate didn't move.

"Pl-please," Kate whispered. She moved slightly, trying to shield her child with her body. "T-take me, let my child go. She's innocent." Janey hisses.

"Kate!!" Kate heard the familiar voice but didn't turn.

"Well, look who it is!" Janey's smile turned mocking. "Mr. '*I'm too good for you*!!'" Nolan, who appeared breathless was immediately held back by the sheriffs.

"Let me go!" he roars. Kate turned her head for a second before looking back at the woman, staring at Nolan with venom.

"Let them go, Janey!" he yells.

"Sir, get back!" Nolan looked at them pleadingly. Kate took Janey's distraction to put Rose behind her as Janey sneered. Blood pulsing in her ears; Kate felt dazed, but she had to protect her only love.

"Why did you come here!?"

"They did nothing!" Nolan cries.

"Why didn't you choose me!?" she screamed. Janey's face melted from a sneer to agonized. "why do you side with the likes of her!?" she pointed her gun at Kate. Nolan froze.

"What?" he choked. The sheriff let him go, and he stood tall, his face full of shock.

"Your marriage was on the rocks!" Janey screamed. "I knew you didn't want Camille, but you stayed! You could have had me, but no…" she turned her baleful glare at Kate. "You chose to be with some stranger, some girl!"

"Janey, please, stop this." He spoke. Nolan heard the sheriff whisper close to him, "*Let her keep talking.*" He took a step forward.

"Don't hurt them." Nolan continues. "You need help—let them go. Leave Kate and the child out of this!"

"This whore has done nothing but hurt us!" she shrieked.

"There is no us!"

"It could have been!" Janey screamed. "Why did you choose her—I knew you far better than everyone else?"

"Janey, this isn't the time for—"

"It's all Camille's fault! You did this to me—She did this to me!" Nolan froze.

"What?" Kate saw from the corner of her eye something red. She took a step back.

"You ruined my life! Camille turned me into this!" Janey pointed to herself. "I was once like you! I was powerful, but you and Camille blacklist me!"

"What?!" Nolan looked at the woman with horror.

"You could have been happy if you just had me, not your witch of a wife!" she hisses. "You could have had me, but she ruined it!" she glared at Kate, who froze.

"What did you do to get him to choose you?!" Janey demands. "what do you have that I don't!" Kate remained silent.

She heard the rev of an engine.

"Janey!" Nolan lifted his hands in surrender. "I had no idea this happened to you! What cam—what we did. I didn't know. I'm sorry you had to go through this, but this isn't the way." He took a step forward. "Holding Kate responsible for my actions won't make me love you." Janey's face crumpled. "You don't love me?" Nolan hesitated before shaking his head.

"I can't love a person who would harm my family." He spoke. "But killing a family isn't the way to get what you want," Nolan took in a breath. "please let them go. Let Kate and my *daughter* go free."

Silence.

Janey's eyes widened as she stared at Nolan. Sheriffs looked at one another. Kate froze.

"The rumors weren't true!?" Janey gasps.

"Yes." Nolan looked at Kate as he says this. Janey's face darkened with rage. She swung the gun from Kate and pointed it at…

"*You son of a bi*—!!" that was all she got out when the sound of a car vroomed fast! Officers jumped out of the way just as Kate scooped Rose, as Nolan ran for…

BANG!!

Kate landed on something soft. Something or someone wrapped themselves in a cocoon, protecting her and Rose as they on concrete. Kate heard a grunt, and a wail followed by screams, men barking orders to **"She's pinned!"**

"Get her out! Help the others!"

"Kate!" Nolan cries. Kate looked at him, dark gray eyes wide with panic as he held her and Rose.

Kate passed out.

"Mommy!" Rose's screams echoed as the shouting may lie. Nolan felt fear as he stared at Kate's prone body, her eyes closed as her head laid on Nolan's chest. Fear overtook him as he saw her.

"Kate!" Nolan sat up as Rose cries for her mother. Sheriffs came forward as Nolan held her, getting to his feet that shook. A female sheriff picked up Rose. The child thrashed wildly, her eyes still on…

"**Mommy**!!"

Nolan's heart squeezed as he heard the piercing screams of his child. Esme had tantrums. She would scream, and today was no exception. He had comforted her with toys and treats, but with Rose. Her screams of terror will forever haunt him… He placed Kate on a stretcher where EMS came and saw him carrying her; they barked questions at him, but he couldn't respond. He turned his head to the sheriff, who was still holding Rose.

"*Let me have her*," Nolan replies softly, lifting his arms. The woman hesitated before handing Rose to Nolan. He lifted a hand to her head, unable to look at Kate. Not like this.

He could not lose her. Everything happened so fast. Did the bullet… If he lost her, how would he live with himself knowing his child was an orphan.

All because of him!

Nolan embraced his daughter tightly, feeling her racing heartbeat, knowing her pulse didn't recognize him as his daughter and son would.

Oh, Kate. Nolan thought, his eyes began to burn as moisture start to brim—

"Rosy!!"

"Mommy!!" Nolan turned his head, he saw in astonishment; Kate sitting upright the EMT trying to order her to lay back down but he knew she was not listening as she stared at Nolan, no… Her Rose.

"Mommy!!" Kate raise her arms instinctively, her eyes glassy with tears as she cries.

"Rosy!" Rose thrashed harder, kicking Nolan.

"R-Rosy W-wait!" he started.

"Put me down! Put me down!" Rose screeched. Nolan struggled for a moment as she kicked his stomach before putting her down. Rose ran; an EMT lifted her and into Kate's awaiting arms. Kate embraced her daughter, smothering her treasure with kisses and tears; mother and child cried together as Nolan watched the tiny family as sheriffs and EMS workers bustled about, but Nolan didn't notice as he stared.

Kate raised her head. Tear tracks lined her beautiful face. She smiles tearfully at him and mouth "*Thank you.*"

Nolan smiles sadly, as he mouthed, "*You're welcome.*" Kate nodded. Someone called her name, making Nolan turn and see Joel and Ivy run forward toward the truck.

Chapter Nineteen

Nightfall had passed over the lonely brick cabin. The wind blew rustling the forest trees, sending cool air of early September turning the august heat into chilly relief. Kate, in the fireplace's light, gazed quietly at the blazing fire that fed off the fat logs; releasing heat into the living room. She looked down at her coffee table that held her cellphone and a portable writing desk that contained paper of her written work, a long envelope stamp and pen. Kate smiled wistfully, listening through the silence to hear her daughter as she slept safe and sound from the fear of the past few weeks. She closed her eyes.

Life had returned to normal for the small town after Janey's rampage. The first few days, people far and wide saw the spectacle of the madwoman and her revenge. After being checked out, Kate found out she was one of the lucky ones to survive the mad woman's wrath; she had found out that Janey had shot Tina, Joanne and many other women who were part of Camille Roth's circle of friends and a few tourists who were injured during the stampede as everyone ran for their lives.

Kate's relief was profound when she was reunited with Emily, Joel, Ivy, and Pilot, her adoptive family, safe from the ordeal. There were no deaths. Only the shooter. News broke out days later of the fate of the once proud Janey who met her end by the collision of the out-of-control car. Janey's reign of terror was over, but her words of denial and betrayal still hung in the air.

Camille… *Nolan.*

Nolan came to her cabin three nights later, asking how she and Rose were doing after the attack. Kate received a few cuts, but Rose…

"She's afraid to go into town," Kate whispered. Her eyes downcast seeing her Rose sobbed when Kate had to go into town: She couldn't forget her daughter's terrified expression when she saw sheriffs walking by the closed town hall. Kate soothed and comforted Rose, but her own fears were still fresh, causing nightmares that woke her up each night.

Nolan's face full of grief and pain as she retold their harrowing tale of fear and recovery; he took Kate in his arms whispering, "I'm sorry," to "It's over now." Kate sniffed, feeling his warmth, forgetting where she was. All that existed was her, and Nolan… just like it used to be before… Nolan looked at her, his eyes tender, loving… lowered his head…

Kate pulled back!

"Kate—?" Nolan started. Kate's eyes shining with tears, his scent and warmth still on her body as she said firmly…

"You have to leave."

"Wh-what?" Kate brush the tears from her eyes, but they still fell.

"You can't be here." She spoke. "I… you… this is wrong." Nolan stared.

"What's wrong?"

"You!" Kate spoke. "You and Camille had done this to Janey."

"Kate." Nolan took a step forward. Kate stepped back.

"Why did you blacklist her?!"

"Kate I—?"

"Is this what you do to people?" Kate demands. "Ruin their lives when they out use your usefulness? Pretend to be kind until they slip up, then their damage goods!!?" She screamed. Nolan stepped back; pain crossed his face.

"Kate please." He spoke. "I know you're upset. I know how scared you were for what Janey did, but please, you must know I had no part in this. The blacklisting, it was all Camille I would…" he stopped.

"But it had something to do with you!" Kate's eyes narrowed. "Janey must have done something that would make Camille retaliate. Why she would ruin her life as she ruined mine!" She clenched her hands into fists.

"You've done nothing but bring suffering to people, you, your wife." Kate shook her head. "I fell for your lies when all along you have done this to others, hurting them as you did me, using me as a fling."

"That's not true!" Nolan cries. "K-Kate pl-please don't… I-I care about you. I never felt so safe with anyone than when I'm with you." She saw Nolan's eyes shine as he clutched his left chest. "I don't want to lose you again. To see Rose, to wonder if she would live without you. You're the one who made me feel happy, who made me feel normal. Who treated me with kindness. Who never saw me as a rich person I… I should have never hidden my marriage from you. Camille." He grimaced. "I have paid for hurting my wife, but you…" he stepped forward. "Rose… I care about both of you." Kate's eyes widened as he gasps his chest heave fast as he stared at her.

Her eyes narrowed.

"What about your daughter?" Nolan froze. "What about your unborn child?"

"I…" Kate clutched her chest.

"How can you say you care about me and Rose when you have a family to care for?" she spoke in a low voice. "How can you say I make you safe and happy when your true happiness is waiting for you at home!?" She glared at him. Nolan stepped back seeing her face darken, her eyes cold.

"It's evident you have no loyalty." Kate reproached. "It only shows me you're selfish. **A coward**. To choose whatever is convenient when you won't take accountability

206

for your actions… But I won't have that. I won't be your second home for you to run. I won't let Rose and I be your play family that you can put away when you get tired."

"Kate." He breathes thickly. "Kate, please, I…" Nolan's voice broke, his throat tightened as he watched her, pleadingly. She stared at him for a long time. She stepped forward, walking past Nolan…

She opened the front door.

"Goodbye, Mr. Roth."

She opened her eyes slowly to look at the fire that blurred hot tears slid down her cheeks.

RING! RING!

Kate started at her phone, which broke the silence. Kate looked down at the screen, seeing the name of her agent on her caller ID.

"Hello." She spoke thickly.

"Kate!? Oh my gosh, is it really you?"

"Yes." Kate cleared her throat.

"Oh, my gosh! I'm so sorry I'm so late! I saw what happened on the news…" She babbles about the events that Kate experienced when her agent asked; pouring apologies for not coming to town and asking if Kate needed anything.

"No really, I'm fine Alex," Kate says. "Just a little shaken."

"I don't blame you, hon." She smiles as she spoke with Alexa, talking about her book.

"I'm sure you got a hefty check this week." Kate half smirked, remembering when she saw how much in royalties she received; she had never seen so many zeros before.

"I couldn't have done it without you," Kate replies.

"Oh, pish posh! I knew your story would make it big." Kate, and her agent laughs. "speaking of big, I have news." She sang.

"What is it?" Kate asks, curious.

"How do you feel about an author interview?" Kate froze.

"M-me?"

"Yes. Writer's Digest has selected you for a one-on-one meet up in New York City. They want to meet the woman who made the NY Times bestsellers list." Kate was on her feet.

"M-me!" she gasps. "Th-they want to interview me?"

"Sure do." Said Alexa. "So, what do you say?" She turned her head to the hallway where Rose slept peacefully in her room. She turned her head to the fireplace that popped before finally opening the door where she exited into a town that could never accept, much less believe, in her innocence. She will forever be looked down as... *A fling.*

Kate smiled.

"*Yes. I'll do it.*"

❀

Water sloshed and burbled in the deep white shell shape sink of Nolan's bathroom. Nolan stared as water slid down his face after splashing the element upon the heat that burned his body.

The weeks that passed were grueling for Nolan. After leaving Kate's home, Nolan drove all night through the dark road, his eyes burning, his vision blurring every few minutes, causing Nolan to stop his car on the side of the road.

Kate.

Nolan groaned as he rest his head in his hands, shuddering as he remembered Kate's words as she looked at him with revulsion at the man, she truly saw him as. The man who burned bridges with a smile as he turned a blind eye to his wife, who buried the enemies who entered their perfect circle.

Nolan grimaced. No, there was no perfect circle, no perfect smiles, perfect family. He had said so himself years before and now he was paying the price for his words. He was not whom he made Kate believe. Through the smiles, the gentle caresses, their talk of dreams. It was a ploy caused by him. He had done this many times, bringing people in with his award-winning smile before bringing the hatchet to their unsuspecting heads.

She was right. He thought.

Nolan felt the familiar wetness as a new flood of tears pooled down his cheeks to his chin. His breath hitched.

"Kate... Rose..." he turned from the sink.

"*I'm sorry.*"

Chapter Twenty

Nolan felt the weight of years in two long months. Outside, leaves had turned from evergreen to golden crackling orange; the once oppressive heat of summer was long gone as the north brought down a cascade of cool breezy wind that rustled trees bringing crisp air to all who breathed in.

But inside his mansion, everything remained the same. Nolan sat in his office alone, in the dark, save for a small lamp that glowed brightly on his desk. Except for him. With dull gray eyes, he stared into the distance; sadness, replacing the spark of his former confidence, showed in his dejected gaze across his room: all-powerful, trapped, alone.

The months had not been kind to him. His face, although handsome, looked gaunt. Aged. His stride once confidant was now slow as if he had to get up and walk from point A to point B. Nolan missed work. Ignoring urgent calls of the meetings he missed; the once prominent investors begging him to save his company, but he didn't care as he sat in his chair, the memory of the last two months still on his mind.

Kate hated him.

In the years of watching her from a distance, her eyes, once gentle, had turned hard. She had cast him out when she realized he was a terrible person. Nolan was a coward. He had messed up everything ever since his affair to his wife, but instead of owning up to it. To apologize for hurting Kate. He had let his wife take her wrath on her; breaking down a foundation that was still growing; only to destroy it with her and the help of the others: the small town he adored was tainted by him and Camille. Despite the years, no one had forgotten Kate's crime and after Janey's revenge on Camille, everything Kate had worked hard to rebuild was crumbling at the seams.

He never forgot Janey's face when she spoke of her love for him. How her life turned for the worst when Camille had her blacklisted making her turn to the bottle and a life of crime: she was gone now, but Nolan could not help feeling responsible. He wasn't there when Camille ruined her life; but he might as well have, despite disgusted at her advances; wanting to fix what he deemed fixable for the sake of his child. Even if it meant closing himself off to others except for Kate: the one woman who made him happy, who brought him back when he lost everything except his empire. Janey must have seen this. She knew Kate had broken through him, a side to him that was weak in others like... Camille. Nolan twitched, his open palm curled into a fist.

He and Camille were a scourge. Camille, with her ironic smiles, her nose held high, took glee in the suffering of others. She had used the town as her pawns to take down a signatory person who had done no harm except love him. And he, he had taken advantage of the girl when he felt the first taste of freedom from the witch; he was now ashamed to call his wife.

Nolan raised his head, his gray eyes narrowed, burning with a new emotion other than despair. The door opened, and the lights flicked on when Camille walked into the room with an aura of pride despite her appearance as she stood tall in high heels, her belly hidden in her designer maternity blouse. Camille opened her mouth to speak.

"*Why did you blacklist Janey?*" Camille looked at him, mouth agape.

"Wh-what?!" Nolan's eyes darken despite the bright light.

211

"You knew all this time and never told me." He rose from his chair, his body trembling with weakness and anger.

"Told you what?" Camille spoke. Nolan growled, making her pause at mid-step. "what's wrong with you?!"

"Me!" Nolan yells. His body and chest burned, but he didn't care in two strides. He was in front of Camille, who stepped back, apprehension on her face.

"Nolan?!"

"Why did you do this to her?!"

"To whom?!" Nolan lifted a hand, and she flinched.

"To Janey!" he bellows. "why did you ruin her life?!"

"J-Janey." Camille took a moment before saying. "I've done noth—"

"Liar!" Nolan stepped forward.

"You're not making any sense I didn't—"

"If that's true, why did she try to come after you and your friends?" Nolan's cheeks flushed red as his eyes flashed. "Why, when she had a gun pointed at my head, did she say you blacklisted her!" Camille stared at him, stunned.

"I—"

"Was that what you meant when you said that she will live to regret trying to seduce me at the party?" he demands. "You made sure she becomes destitute living on the streets, drinking, causing havoc with others."

"H-How did you—?"

"THE TOWN" Camille stepped back. "The town and your gossipy lackeys told me what you've done to her, what we've done!"

"We?" Camille spoke. She had recuperated, finally understanding Nolan's ranting.

212

"Don't tell me you actually feel sorry for that worthless wh—"

"Stop!" Nolan snaps. "Just stop, Camille! You have no right, no precedence to talk about her after all you've done!"

"All I've done!" Camille scowled. "Is save you from that backstabbing slut from ruining this family."

"So, you blacklist her!"

"I did what I had to do to teach her a lesson," Camille tossed back her hair. "and it worked. Janey never came near you after the town rejected her."

"So, you would let her harm others to protect yourself?" Nolan demands. She glared at him.

"What happened at the fair was completely unexpected," she says. "what she did to Tina and Joanne was terrible, but they lived. We've covered their hospital expenses and donated to the town. And after what you did for that old woman. Everyone sees you as a hero."

"But at what price!?" Nolan shouts.

"The price is you getting more allies on your side. The people love you, and that will bring more wealthy investors and friends." She smiles. "As far as this town knows, we can do no wrong."

"But you have!" he cries passionately. "Janey went insane! She wanted to kill you!"

"*Janey* is **dead**!" Camille hisses through clenched teeth. "Whatever lies she was going to or had told the town, no one believed her."

"Are you hearing yourself right now!" Nolan says. "Do you realize all this could have been prevented, that Emily, Tina, and Joanne would have been safe if it wasn't for us! This would never have happened if you just left things alone."

"You mean let her sleep with you?" she says cruelly.

"I would never sleep with her. I swore to make this marriage work."

"But yet women can't seem to get enough of you." Camille mocked snidely.

"Those women you think I'm attracted to don't hold a candle to how I feel about—" Nolan stopped, stunned at what he had said. He looked away.

"*Kate*." Camille finished with a sneer. "That naïve gold-digger who taught you about hopes and dreams, about make-believe and fairy-dust," she laughs mockingly. "The woman who carried your bastard to live in the woods."

Nolan looked at her, eyes blazing.

"Rose is not a bastard!!" Nolan growls, spacing each word. "You will never call my child that to my face."

"Oh, so her name is Rose, then my apologies. I'll make sure the girls know when they come over."

"You will not hurt Rose as you did to Kate!"

"Who said I'm hurting? I'm just warning my friends to keep their children away from—"

"ENOUGH!" Camille stepped back, her hand falling to her stomach. Nolan glared down at her with venom, his gray eyes storming as he looked at his wife with hate.

"Listen Camille. I had enough of your vindictiveness, taking your wrath on me fine. It was well deserved, but you've gone too far." He spoke angrily.

"You can ruin my life for my past transgression, but you will never—" Nolan stepped forward as she stepped back.

"EVER! Harm Kate and Rose!"

Silence.

Nolan took grim satisfaction in Camille's frightened expression as he walked past her.

"Then I'll tell everyone!" he spun around. Camille stood glaring at him with malicious triumph. "The girls, the town, the media! They'll all know about the affair." Nolan didn't respond. For several seconds, he didn't speak. He turned for the door...

"*Goodnight.*"

☙

Nolan felt free for the first time in weeks as he drove down the empty road later that night. His mind felt clear, his hands steady on the wheel as he passed the slumbering town. It was just after 8 p.m. as he drove, feeling giddy as he resolved himself to see the woman he loved. He made his decision. The next several days were full of tension as he, Nolan, waited on bated breaths for the town's reaction to the truth: that he fathered a child outside his marriage. Camille had invited her friends that evening after dinner, which was tense and uncomfortable. Nolan had wanted to spend time with Esme, but Camille snatched her away to be with her friends.

"*She deserves to be with her mother to teach her how to be a true woman,*" Camille replies. Nolan didn't respond, just left the room before hopping into his car. Nolan made a turn onto the side road that led to a dark forest; a smile formed on his lips as he pulled in front of the familiar brick cabin in the woods. Nolan stopped the car.

Kate. He thought, looking at the familiar window and door, thinking how he would right the wrong by first apologizing to Kate and Rose before taking them both in his arms, promising them his heart and love. Nolan opened the

215

door and walked out into the November chill; he was surprised that the curtains were drawn closed, and the lights were not on.

Maybe they turned in early. He mused before raising a fist. He knocked on the door.

No response.

Nolan stared at the door, straining his hearing, wondering why Kate didn't open. He glanced down at his watch and saw it read: 8:45pm. Looking up at the door that was illuminated by his car knocked again.

"Kate!?" he called. "K-Kate, it's me!" No answer. Nolan stepped back, puzzled, concern on his face. Kate wasn't the type to leave abruptly. He remembered her telling him she had no other family, but now... had Kate moved?

Nolan stepped back... Was Kate and Rose?... Nolan turned his back on the door and walked to the window and tried to peer inside, but the curtains made looking inside difficult. Nolan stepped from the window to the side it was there he saw. Kate's van was gone. Nolan stepped back, his head going lightheaded as he backed away from Kate's home.

Kate... Rose... he thought, panicked. What happened to them? Hundreds of terrible scenarios ran through Nolan's thoughts, causing his chest to thrum with pain.

Were they evicted? Nolan thought, afraid. Was Kate not able to pay the rent that she and Rose are living in a... New thoughts came to mind, making him shudder.

Did Camille tell her friends? Making them go to town to tell the real estate seller to buy back the house. Camille would be more determined to make Kate suffer after their fight. Anger burned in his eyes as he whirled around and ran

216

for his van. His phone rang in his car; seeing it was Nicole, Nolan punched the green button.

"What is it, Nicole?" he spoke tightly, no pleasantries in his voice.

"N-Nolan, oh thank goodness!" Nicole's voice was breathy. "You have to come home now!"

"I'm on my way now." He says but was surprised to hear the fear in her voice. "What is it? What's going on? Is it, Ess—?"

"Camille! It's Camille she's—" at that moment, a scream echoed in the phone line, making Nolan jump.

"Nicole!?" he cries.

"Something's wrong with the baby." Ice water pooled down Nolan's spine. His child, his son…

"Nolan!!" he heard Camille scream. Nolan drove faster, heart in his throat as Nicole screeched.

"Call 911!!"

೮

Nolan rode in the back of the ambulance truck fifteen minutes later. Words were barked as the EMS asked questions that Nolan could not answer, not just because he was scared, but he didn't know his wife's conditions. Time seemed to have slowed down when Nolan entered his home, calling out to Camille! Susie and Nora came into the foyer with tears in their frightened eyes as they took him to, their upstairs parlor. It was there Nolan found Camille laying down on a large chaise gasping heavily. Her eyes were wide when she looked at Nolan, who kneeled down beside her, fear in his eyes, taking her hand in his cold ones.

"What's wrong with her!?" he exclaims. The girls mumbled out shaky explanations as Nicole told him she had called the ambulance before he got here. Nolan's heart raced with panic for his unborn child. It was too early for Camille to give birth. Something had to be wrong, his child…

"Where's Esme!?" he looked from his wife to the others. Nora pointed and turned his head to see Esme huddled in a small corner, staring at him with wide, frightened eyes.

"Essie…" he breathes. He rose. Camille cried out, making everyone jump. Nolan turned back to Camille, soothing her as best he could, but his attempts were feeble.

"Daddy?" Nolan turned his head to see Esme close beside him, her cheeks red as she stared at him tearfully.

"E-Esme." Just before he could speak, sirens echoed outside the window.

"They're here!" Nicole cries.

Nolan sat staring at his wife as she took in air, her eyes closed. He held the pale icy hand, trying to warm it, but Nolan felt it would never be warm again.

Please let my child live. He thought pleadingly. His mind drifted to his Esme frightened face as she saw the EMS put Camille on the stretcher. Nolan lifted her in his arms, seeing her cheeks red with tears; his daughter didn't deserve this, she was too innocent to pay witness to such adult tragedies. Feeling her heartbeat fast beside his chest was a testament. Esme called to her father, waking him up from his trance.

"Y-yes Esme?"

"What's wrong with mommy?"

"Mommy is not feeling well," Nolan tells her the half-truth. *"She and the baby are sick."* Esme, whose face curl with discontent at the word 'baby', looked at him with wide eyes. *"The baby is sick?"*

"Yes." She looked at her mother as she was pulled on the stretcher that Nolan followed before looking at her father.

"Why is it sick?"

"I don't know." Nolan's eyes stung; his throat ached as he continued thickly.

"I don't want him to be sick." Esme looked at him before saying quietly, tears running down her eyes.

"I don't want him to be sick, too."

∞

Nolan buried his face in his hands as he sat in the hospital. Doctors had rushed to aid Camille, who had woken up only to scream at the pain before being led away from surgery. Nolan sat for hours praying that his wife and child would make it, especially his child: who was innocent in all this would be born to a good safe life. Without love from his mother, for Nolan knew once his son was born, he would get full custody of his son and daughter. Camille would fight, but he knew her love was for herself and what her influence could do for her.

He knew what she had done to Esme before she got sick and that alone told him he would make Camille pay just as she made Kate pay for falling in love with him.

"CODE BLUE-NEONATE!"

Nolan looked up, startled at the double doors that blared the alarm. Doctors and nurses came bustling dressed in surgical gowns from within the room Camille was in. Nolan rose to his feet.

219

"Doctor! Wh-what's happening!" the doctor looked at him just as the nurses came with an incubator. "Doctor!?" Nolan stepped forward as Camille screamed before nurses cried.

"His heart rate is dropping!" Nolan froze. He took a step forward. The first doctor bard his way.

"Please, sir, you have to wai—"

"My child!" Nolan howled. "What is wrong with my son!" he tried to push past them, but the doctor shut the door, leaving Nolan alone. He paced, waiting to hear the screams stop from his wife and hear the cries of his child. Nolan's mind drifted to his second born, who he barely knew but wanted to know, who vanished with her mother to parts unknown without his knowledge because to claim his child would be the end of her and Kate's reputation.

Nolan thought of Kate as he paced, seeing her smile as she wrapped her arms around him after a tough day of work and he would forget his… the door opened, making Nolan stop to look at the doctor, who walked wearily out.

"Doctor?!" the doctor looked at Nolan, his face professional, but… something was wrong. "D-Doc…" Nolan breathes. The doctor removed his surgical cap.

"Mr. Roth." He spoke calmly. Nolan's eyes stung.

"Is it Camille?" He spoke weakly. The doctor blinked.

"No! No! Camille's alive." Nolan breathes a sigh as the doctor explains she was stressed but was now in stable condition.

"They're taking care of her as we speak." Nolan nodded again, but he smiles, asking the most important question.

"What about the baby? What about my son?" the doctor's face grew grave as he looked away from the door. Nolan stared at him with surprise; shouldn't this be the part where the doctor would smile and say his child was alive and healthy… the doctor looked at him, his face firm, sadness was in his brown eyes.

Nolan froze.

"*No…*" he whispers.

"I'm sorry, son." Nolan felt his world crumble, his body ripped in half. He was still standing but his mind had drifted; his ears rang. He was not in the hospital. He was alone. Trapped. Powerless.

Nolan didn't realize he sat down. It wasn't until his eyes were glassy with salt water as the doctor spoke, but Nolan couldn't hear the doctor who patted his shoulder and walked away. He didn't watch him go. Instead, he saw with blurry eyes his open palms, the deep lines that traced his center hands. Water spilled onto it… Nolan's eyes glazed, the dark gray irises clouded, becoming stormy. His heart gave a throb, but he didn't feel it as his body went completely numb.

He did not resurface.

C3

Kate opened the door to her cabin at 1 a.m. Flicking on the lights, she carried Rose who slept peacefully, oblivious as her mother laid her on her bed; warm and safe in her pajamas that Kate put on before they drove from the last rest-stop into Connecticut. Kate smiled as she pulled in her suitcases, the spoils that she brought from the Big Apple.

She sat on her bed with a contented sigh. Tired, but her ecstatic mind couldn't rest. It was what she needed. Her smile grew as she thought of Rose, seeing her treasure eyes grow wide as she took in the bright, tall skyscrapers, and beaches of the Empire state with awe after her interview with the famous magazine; promoting her newest novel that would entice new, eager, readers, and future book-babies in the work that would allow her to dip her toe into different stories.

Kate lay on her back with a sleepy smile as she kicked off her shoes; listening to the quietness of her home.

It's good to be back. She thought.

Chapter Twenty-one

Three years later.

Time passed with every ticking of the universal clock, like a pulsing wound measuring the passage as the earth spun on its forever rotation: changing seasons, nature, people, and town. Nolan stared at the thriving city below, watching the world move on without him, whether they knew of his existence. Dull gray eyes peered as cars drove, appearing to Nolan like toys as people walked higgity piggity in an ant swarm.

"Nolan?" Nolan closed his eyes, but his voice was thick when he says.

"Yes." A pause soon followed before there was a shifting of paper and the click coming from a ball-point pen.

"How are you doing today?" Nolan took in a deep breath before letting it out slow.

"Fine." Another pause. Nolan waited three heartbeats before he added. "I am doing fine." A shift followed by a beat; he didn't have to turn to know that pen was scribbling on paper. It had been two years and that sound always filled him with dread.

This was his life now.

The years that past had come and gone like a hurricane; destroying a town, leaving an aftermath of destruction that to this day was still trying to pick up the pieces. The first year was hell. After the death and funeral of his baby boy, Nolan had fallen into a depression; the first weeks comprised him staying alone in bed in his guest room drinking or eating, his body growing

223

weaker where he laid. Silent tears, streaming down his eyes as he mourned. He rarely talked to anyone, preferring solitude than people's company. No matter how it was affecting his staff who quit, leaving his home in disarray, his wife who left to do whatever she wanted, or his daughter who he pushed away; not wanting to taint his child with his stigma. Nolan laid his head on the cool glass pane. His bangs tickled his nose, but he ignored it when his name was called.

"I'm listening doctor." He spoke. The doctor looked at him with calm beady eyes as Nolan turned. He saw her dressed in a black suit, her legs crossed, writing pad and pen on her lap.

"I was saying you look better than how you looked last time we met." She says. Nolan tried to smile, but his lips barely twitched.

"Thank you." he spoke, she nodded smiling at tiny smile before she was serious.

"How are you holding up?" Nolan shrugged as he walked to the large sitting chair and sat down. "Have there been any changes at home or at work?"

"Work is work." Nolan replies quietly.

"What about home? How is Camille doing?" Nolan grimaced.

"Still drinking and shopping her way until the money stops or until she passes out." The doctor nodded before scribbling on her notepad.

"So, she's started drinking?"

"Correction, she's never stopped." Nolan replies.

"So, she's been drinking more since your son's death." Nolan shuddered before looking down. He nodded. "Have you started—"

"No. I swore to never do that, not while Esme…" he trailed off.

"This is the first I've heard you say your daughter's name." Guilt made Nolan cringe back in his chair.

"That's because I'm trying to save her. Trying to protect her."

"From whom?"

Nolan looked down.

"*From myself.*" A beat followed by more scribbling.

"Why do you believe that?" the doctor spoke calmly. Nolan raised his head to see the psychiatrist lean forward in her chair.

He didn't reply; thinking of Esme, the daughter who he neglected letting the maids take care of her, watching as she transformed from a spoil child of five into a subdued girl of eight years old.

He thought of Esme cries after her brother was laid to rest. Esme had came into the room where he and Camille sat not looking at one another when she came in and wanted Nolan to play with her. Nolan, still stricken with grief ignored her before she came to her mother who snaps at her to 'be quiet!' Esme had cried then but Nolan, who would defend her, had no strength instead, left the room, shutting the door behind him.

He voiced this to the doctor, who wrote it down on her pad, listening with professional interest. Nolan still could not believe he was here talking to a shrink but after his company had fallen on hard times; he was not at the right state to control his company, so his friends suggested he see a professional so he could work out his problems and fix his business. It took Nolan half a year to open up; confessing to all he had been through, all his secrets, except one, and that Nolan knew he could not, would not expose to his doctor. The one secret that would end the lives of the people he harmed more than his wife and daughter.

Nolan left the doctor's lavish office feeling ten pounds heavier with slump shoulders as he drove home, his body tense as his stomach roiled with hunger as he prepared for the on-slot that awaited him. Nolan watched the city streets turned to farmland as he left downtown behind him; he had a lot of work to do and the unfriendly distraction from his already miserable home made his chest throb with the familiar agony.

He sighed heavily as he turned into the car and drove silently. He tried to focus on other matters, but nothing came. Everything was the same, same road, same town, same everything. He was just driving when he saw the familiar mailbox that stood out in a wooded patch he knew if he made a left, would take him down a slope that stopped at a familiar red brick house. Nolan's pulse stuttered when he drove, his hand twitched at the wheel, wanting his hand to push the car blinker, directing it to go left to see the small home and its inhabitants, he…

He…

Nolan drove past the mailbox and down the road, seeing the hint of the small town come into view from a distance. His eyes and chest stung.

"Good evening Mr. Roth." Nolan entered the foyer to find his new maid holding a basket of clothes.

"How was your day?" Nolan nodded.

"What's for dinner?" he asks, stepping forward.

"I believe chef Lehman is cooking lobster." Nolan nodded.

"Where's Camille?" Nolan asks, stiffening, for he knew the answer. He saw the maid frown before saying begrudgingly.

"Upstairs in the parlor."

"Is she awake?"

"She's asleep last time we checked." Nolan sighs, then nodded.

"I'm going to see her. Where is Esme?" he asks as he walked upstairs.

"In her room." He winced before nodding as he made his way to the parlor.

Nolan cracked open the door to the parlor, peering inside to find boxes opened and scattered about the bright, cold room. He stepped inside wrinkling his brow as he saw the mess from packaged paper to… Nolan felt something hard under his foot he looked down and saw to his dismay a dark blue bottle of wine, empty: there were a lot of bottles scattered amongst the room ranging from different sizes and colors each of whom was empty. Nolan turned his attention to the person who he wanted to see, the woman who lay passed out on the long chaise, her blond hair half covered her face; beside her was a wine glass containing a pink liquid.

Nolan stared down at Camille, gray eyes unreadable as he saw his selfish wife; the wife he could not escape after the death of his son. Camille during the first week was unresponsive; she refused to talk and only stare at nothing: her friends had tried to comfort her, but instead of lavishing them with the attention she pushed them away, choosing the finest bottles of wine to drown in forgetfulness. As the years went by, Camille became unstable, firing anyone who tried to defend themselves when she went on a drunken tirade, making working for her unbearable. Luc left, cursing her and the family in a fit of rage after Camille insulted him.

Nolan felt as if his late chef placed a curse on them as he stared at his drunken wife, who stirred before opening blurry green eyes. Nolan and Camille stared down at one another, not speaking, but there was a shift; the air became thick with animosity and… a noise made them both look up at the same time. Turning his head, Nolan looked to see his eight-year-old standing by the door watching them with somber, green eyes, a book tucked under her arm.

"*Esme.*" Nolan's voice croaked at her name; Camille didn't speak, only watched her with an unreadable expression. Esme watched them first, her father, then mother before watching them together. Parent and child stared at each other for what felt like an eternity before Esme turned her head and walked away. Nolan felt his chest squeeze, seeing his daughter's dejected coldness toward him. Out of everyone, Esme took the brunt of his and Camille's abuse. Not of words or with fists, but by neglect and abandonment.

Camille lifted her glass and drank from the contents with an air of lethargy. Nolan watched her. Despite she went to the best doctors, she still was a shell of her former self: her normal vain, cruel, vindictive self. Nolan shuddered.

He didn't know which he preferred.

"What?" Nolan looked at Camille, who spoke, glaring at him with blurry bloodshot eyes.

"*Nothing.*" He spoke, voice grave. He looked away toward the door where Esme stood before getting up and walking out of the room.

Chapter Twenty-two

Nolan reclined in his office chair one afternoon with a sigh. His face was half covered by his right hand. The sound of silence vibrated in his ears as Esme sat reading her head lowered closed off to the world.

He had woken up in his usual guest bedroom. There he got dressed for work. As he was walking the hallway, he passed Esme's room making him check on her as he did every night to ensure if she was all right. But today he decided to visit her only to find her wide-awake reading.

He, surprised, walked inside causing Esme to look up, startled by his presence.

A frown creased Nolan's face as he looked at his daughter. A muffled bang and a shriek made them both start! Nolan saw Esme shrink back on her bed; it was then he realized Esme would be alone with her mother all day; had been with her all year through her drunken rants.

He couldn't bear to leave Esme alone with her.

"Get dressed, Esme." He spoke voice rougher than he meant to. Esme stared at him warily but obeyed, closing her book before she got out of bed.

The day slipped silently, on Esme's part, making Nolan uncomfortable with his own child. He hadn't spoken to her in months, maybe years, after he closed himself like a hermit, wallowing in grief. It seemed like he had just emerged from a deep sleep, yet he didn't feel refreshed. Nolan thought at his company, communicating with investors; It hurt Nolan to see his child like this; Esme closed herself off to Nolan: The one person who defended, no protected her from Camille.

He frowned at that as he looked at Esme, who read, her long hair hung down her face, curtaining herself from the world.

"Esme?" He spoke, voice thick. She didn't respond, making him call again to see him with quiet green eyes. "What are you reading Essie?" Esme blinked once before looking back down at her book. A fresh twinge struck Nolan before he stood and went to her. She avoided seeing him as he knelt beside her.

"Esme?" Esme tried not to look at him. Nolan could see that, his throat ached. "are you mad at me?" Esme looked at him for a moment before looking away.

She didn't answer.

"Did daddy do something wrong?"

Silence.

"Why don't you talk to me?" Silence. Stinging eyes accompanied a burning sensation in Nolan's chest.

"Can you talk to me?" he asks.

Esme didn't answer or look at him.

Nolan looked at her lap, that held the book. Gingerly, he took the book and closed it, just putting his finger on the page she was reading.

"The Adventures of Rose Garden." He read aloud.

"*It's Guard-den.*" Nolan started at her quiet voice.

"Guard-den?" she nodded, looking at him for the first time. "Oh." He spoke. When observing the manga cover, he noticed an illustration of a girl dressed in pink. Nolan flipped through the pages of the chapter book with pictures of the same girl with caramel brown skin.

"She's pretty." He noted. To his surprise, he saw Esme nod, her cheeks growing pink with excitement.

"She's a girl that turns into a magical princess who fights monsters to protect the kingdom," Esme spoke. "She's not a real princess, she's a poor girl who lives in the woods with her mommy."

"Oh." He got the gist of it. Nolan found himself enthralled by his daughter, as she explained the main character and her heroic adventure.

"Are there more stories from this book?" he asks, looking to the back to find that this was the first of three series. "Where did you get this from, Essie?"

"Ms. Lehman, let me borrow it." She replies.

"The chef?" Esme nodded.

"She said her daughter finished reading it and said I could borrow it, but I have to give it back." Nolan nodded with a frown as he flipped through the pages before closing the book.

"Have you finished the book?"

Esme nodded. Nolan looked at the front cover again and came across the author's name: Victoria Starfield. A plan hatched, making Nolan smile weakly, but genuinely.

"You should have your own copy, Esme." he spoke. She looked at him, puzzled. "Why don't we go to Barnes & Noble to get this." He pointed. "And the rest of the series." He rose to his feet.

"Can we?!" Nolan nodded, his chest thumping, extending a hand as he spoke.

"*Let's go.*"

Despite the heat, the afternoon was pleasant; Nolan's time with his daughter eclipsed it. *He missed his Esme.* He'd been too busy with meetings and doctor appointments. Her smile, laughter, and stories about new toys made him feel old. *She made him recover better than any doctor's-prescribed medicine.* She helped him forget the troubles of the previous months. It was just him and his daughter.

Nolan and Esme came back to the mansion late that evening, laughing together as they carried their spoils into the glittering foyer. Nolan was light, his gray eyes bright from his adventure, even when Camille staggered into the foyer with a look of annoyance, didn't daunt him.

"What's all this noise?!" she demands. Esme was the first to break the happy bubble. Her lips curled downward as she looked away. Nolan, still smiling, said.

"Nothing." Camille's eyes narrowed, her hand atop her head.

"Well, keep it down!" she snaps. "What are you cheerful about?" Camille asks, looking from Esme to Nolan.

"Nothing. We just spent all day in the city, that's all. Right Essie." Esme didn't answer, only nodded. Camille blinked.

"She was with you the whole day?"

"Yes, is that a problem?" Nolan saw her expression; Esme's absence was unknown. Camille's eyes narrowed.

"Why didn't you tell me she was gone!"

"She's my daughter Camille! I can take her wherever I want!"

"Not without me knowing. She's my child too!" Heat rose in Nolan's cheeks.

"I took her out with me to work, then we went out and came back. *Safely*! You make it sound like I kidnapped my daughter!"

"***How do I know that wasn't your intention***!!" she hisses. Nolan stepped back, stunned. He stared at Camille for a long time before looking down at Esme, who stood, face closed as she stared down the marble floor.

"Esme, go take your bags upstairs to your room," Nolan says. Esme obeyed; Nolan looked back at his wife with quiet fury.

"Listen here, Camille." He spoke in a low voice. "I don't know whom you think I am but get one thing straight. You will not accuse me of taking my child for malicious intentions."

"Oh. So, you what? Decide to take *my* daughter out for fun? That's a first and for what?" Nolan clenched his hands on the bag straps.

"I took her out to get away from you!" he barks. Camille looked as if he slapped her. Before Nolan could react, she let out a wail, bursting into tears and ran away. Nolan stood stock still before letting out a sigh. He walked upstairs to his room with his wife's sobs echoing in his ears.

Chapter Twenty-three

"Nolan, how was your week?"

Nolan looked up from where he sat with a smile, as he looked at his doctor. The past few weeks had been pleasant, even with the lingering tension. Nolan felt a sense of relief he hadn't felt in months.

"Good." He answers. The doctor nodded, pen and legal pad in hand.

"You look different from the last time we met."

She smiled and asked, "How so?"

"You, haven't stared aimlessly out the window." She says. "You look better. Casual and well rested. I would see you in your suit and tie."

"I took a few days off." He replies. The doctor nodded, making a note of it on her pad.

"That's good." She says. "The last time you told me about your company not doing so well that things have not worked out for the better. That is why you spent your hours working." Nolan looked down.

"That was part of it." He spoke. "I was working to fix things, but when my company got better, I didn't want to stop working. It was distraction from… *you know*." He mumbles.

"I know." Looking up, he saw the doctor's smile.

"It was nice to meet your daughter." She says, changing the subject. Nolan, grateful for the change, smiled. "She is a lovely girl."

"Thank you." Nolan replies. "She is."

"Is she part of your recent change?"

"Yes." He spoke. "Esme has been a great joy to me. She is the best medicine I can prescribe." He chuckles, making the doctor smile. "We have a big weekend ahead of us."

"What plans?" Nolan tells her. "Well, I know you deserve this after so much hurt." Nolan nodded, then sighs. "I won't keep you and your daughter waiting. When are you free to come again?"

୦ଽ

Nolan left with Esme in toe saying goodbye to the doctor. As father and daughter, Nolan and Esme visited the museum, played in the city park, and enjoyed a horse ride across the city. Nolan and Esme entered the hotel suite late that evening. After having dinner at a restaurant, Nolan tucked Esme to bed after reading a chapter of the adventures of Rose Garden. Esme was near sleep when Nolan got up from her bed.

"Daddy?" he looked down at her.

"Yes, Essie?" Esme's eyes were half closed.

"Are we still going to the bookstore?"

"Yes, honey." Nolan whispered.

"Will we see Victoria Starfield?"

"Yes."

"Will she sign my book?" he leaned down and kissed her forehead.

"I promise you will." Esme nodded, then closed her eyes. Nolan sighed, exiting, then closing the door. Nolan walked to his bedroom suite. He went to bed after undressing.

"***Wake up daddy! Wake up!***' Nolan woke up to bouncing, he opened his eyes to see Esme grinning down at him. Nolan sat up, his smile genuine when Esme crowed.

"Today we go to the bookstore!" Nolan laughs, glancing at the time he saw it read 7:45 a.m. chuckling he said.

"Victoria Starfield isn't going anywhere, Essie. We still have time." Esme nodded. "until then, why don't we have breakfast."

"Okay!" Nolan smiles as Esme jumped off the bed.

"What do you want for breakfast?"

"Pancakes!" Nolan smiles as he got up from bed and reached for the phone to call for room service.

The whole Saturday went by in a blur as Nolan spent time with Esme doing whatever activities were within the indoor pool and watched movies in their suite; Nolan let Esme get her nails while he got a massage, before relaxing in the tearoom with a cup of tea and English shortbread cookies. Before Nolan knew it, it was six o'clock and he and Esme got ready, leaving the suite hand in hand, Esme laughing as they headed out into the city.

A crowd of children, ranging from Esme's age and older, and their excitedly talking parents crowded the bookstore when they entered. Nolan to felt giddy who Ms. Victoria was.

She must be huge if adults are this excited. He thought. Although he enjoyed reading the adventures of the magical girl, he couldn't help but wonder about what made her so popular.

Nolan passed a group of what looked like teenagers dressed in pink holding mini parasols that resembled the character's wand.

"Daddy!?" Nolan looked down at Esme, who was pointing to a large poster board with the picture of the newest book in the series.

"Can we get it, daddy, please?" Nolan smiles.

"Of course, honey."

"**Attention everyone**!" came a female voice. Everyone quieted to hear the announcer. "**Those who are here for the book signing for Ms. Starfield, please make your way upstairs to the preteen section of the store. Once you buy her book, you are free to go upstairs, and have it signed!**"

Nolan smirked as everyone, including the teens, hurried upstairs.

"Let's get the book, Essie," Nolan spoke. Esme beamed and nodded.

Nolan's feet ached as he stood in line forty-five minutes later. Fatigue took hold of him as he stood with Esme, along with many adults and children, each of whom held a new copy of the latest book.

"Daddy?" he looked down at Esme, who looked at him. "Why is the line taking so long?"

"Because everyone wants to meet Ms. Starfield." He replies. "We have to be patient so we can get to see her." Esme nodded and sighs. Nolan could feel her inpatients and he empathized with her wanting to go back to the hotel: his feet ached from standing and he wished he could use his status to get him online faster. Nolan sighed just as up ahead he heard laughter, followed by a group of people leaving ahead of him: he was ten people away from meeting the mysterious author. Craning his neck, he saw a flash of white when a child blocked his view before letting out a squeal in the front row.

Nolan looked at her daughter and smiled at her. Esme smiled back, clutching her book, showing the cover of Princess Rose Garden flying on her parasol holding a black treasure chest.

"Next!" Nolan started, realizing it was his turn. Taking Esme's hand, the two stepped forward to see a woman standing in a casual suit beside her sat the author, who wore a white lace blouse holding an old fashion feather pen in her right hand.

237

Dark gray eyes widened with shock as he stared at the author of his daughter's favorite book. Eyes glowed with joy meeting her next patron grew wide as her smile froze on her face. Nolan stared thunderstruck as the woman looked at him with large brown eyes that glittered in the light. Esme stepped forward, a nervous smile on her childish face as she placed her book on the table, broke the spell. The woman blinked. All traces of shock gone, replaced with a kind smile that turned their attention on the little girl who watched her with awe.

"*Hello*." She spoke. Nolan stared at her, unable to speak.

"Hi," Esme says her voice didn't break as she looked at her idol. Victoria Starfield pulled Esme's book forward.

"How are you doing this evening?"

"Good ma'am and you?" Nolan blinked, surprised by Esme's manners. He looked at the woman, who smiled.

"I'm doing well. That's very nice of you to ask." Esme blushed before nodding, thanking her.

"Now who am I making this out too?" Victoria opened the book to the front of the page that was blank. Esme considered her father, uncertain.

"T-To Esme!" Nolan's words came out as a gasp, as if forcing the words was difficult. "I-It's for my daughter." The woman looked at him. Nolan felt those eyes bore into him, making him want to fall apart or cry. She looked at the child, smiling.

"Esme." She says. "That's a pretty name."

"Thank you." Esme spoke, cheeks flushing pink. Victoria picked up her pen and wrote in the book.

"How old are you, miss Esme?" she asks.

"I'm eight." Victoria nodded, eyes going wide.

"Wow. You're a big girl. How do you like my stories?" Esme beamed, awed that she called her miss the way adults were called.

"It's awesome!" Victoria smiles. "My daddy's been reading it to me every night."

"Oh!" Victoria looked at Nolan, who froze. "That's very sweet of him." She replies. "You have a wonderful daddy." She nodded.

"He's the best daddy in the world!"

"I'm sure he is." Despite Victoria's calm tone, Nolan felt a sharp pang of anguish. She looked back at Esme.

"Well, here you are." She closed the book and handed it to her. Esme took the book as Victoria added. "I hope you enjoy and thank you for coming to see me."

"You're welcome and thank you." Nolan nodded, placing a hand on her shoulder he says.

"Come on, Esme."

"Esme?!" Nolan froze. He looked down to see Esme turn to the author, who held out a bookmark with a pink tassel.

"This is for you." Esme's eyes widen as she reached out to it.

"Thank you." Esme smiles. Victoria nodded and with one last look at Nolan, she looked away, her smile appearing as she looked at her fans.

ℭ𝔰

Nolan drove back to the hotel in silence as his daughter squealed about meeting her idol and getting a free bookmark. Esme could not wait to read the book as she chatted, not noticing her father's somber expression. After a late dinner, Nolan put Esme to bed when she started to fall asleep on her dessert. Nolan collapsed in his bed, shivering as he covered himself with the cool sheets as his mind drifted to the author…

Kate.

Kate had changed in the past years. She no longer looked like the shy person he had seen seven years ago. Her cheeks looked fuller instead of gaunt, her eyes were glittering with confidence instead of anger as she banished him from not just her home but from her life. Forever.

It's been three years. Nolan thought. *Three long agonizing years where I've been in the darkness of grief, pain, and loss. I never knew, I always thought…* he trailed off, his chest squeezed with guilt. Kate had evolved over time, achieving something remarkable that she often talked about. She left, life continued. Nolan's eyes stung. He could not bear to think of his baby boy, pale and still as he cradled him in his arms. Nolan's eyes drifted to the open window, where he could see the city building across the street.

She remembered Esme. He thought softly. Kate treated her with kindness and respect, even though I ruined her life with my lies and cowardice. She still treated her kind and me… her face appeared in his mind's eye. It was not cruel, nor was it friendly; it was professional, calm, so different from how she used to look at him. Nolan closed his eyes as his heart throbbed, his mind still on meeting his daughter's favorite author, thinking about what he could have done better, wishing he could turn back time as a new question filled his mind just before he fell asleep. He had seen Kate, but where was…

Rose.

Chapter Twenty-four

The evening event had finally come to a tiring but enriching close for Victoria Starfield. Night had come cool and inviting, putting an end to the hot summer months of June, July, and August, to the mellow crispness of September. Victoria stared out the window of the bookstore to see the dark glittering city that illuminated hundreds of thousands of mini lights that guided the late visitors to whatever destination they so choose.

It had been a wonderful evening full of awe-inspiring faces as they took in their idol. Victoria sighed. She still could not get over that she was now revered: to everyone who saw her face they would think she was a great lady, a queen among queens, but to her she was still the hardworking writer who earned a living by cleaning homes for the rich and comfortable while bringing food on the table and keeping a roof over her and her treasures head. To her, she was still Kate. Shy, hardworking Kate who made a home from nothing with her quiet patients, gentle strength and an endless supply of imagination and ink.

Kate smiled as she looked at her reflection through the dark glass. Seeing the lace white poncho she wore, she still could not believe it was her: with her manicured nails her long hair quaffed and shining to her glowing face Kate was still in awe at her transformation to her alter ego; NY Times Best-Selling children author Victoria Starfield. It was uncanny seeing herself as such a person, but her agent insisted, she looked the part.

"You need to look like a star in human form!" she says. Kate sighed.

"Kate?" Kate turned to see her agent Alexa standing behind her holding to large Barnes & Noble bags.

"You've finished." Kate says, smiling.

"Sure did. You're ready to go? I'm sure you're tired after all that signing." Kate saw her grimace, but she smiles. "bet you're glad this was the last stop on tour huh?" they were walking now, and the store clerks says goodbye to Kate who waved.

"It's a little bittersweet." She admitted with a sigh. "It was so nice to meet all those smiling little faces, but I'm eager to see my own little face back home." Alexa nodded.

"Me too. But you earned this, Kate."

"I still can't believe I've been touring for two months."

"Pfft! This is nothing. Just wait until your international tour." Kate shuddered as they stepped into the elevator.

"I'm not ready for that, Alex." she says. "I don't think I can bear leaving Rose while I'm across the sea. I can't take that."

"Then bring her with you. Rose would love to see England and France."

"Not yet. She's still so young." They were on the first floor now when Alexa yawned.

"Tired?"

"I'm ready to sleep for five days." Alexa says. Kate smiled, feeling the weariness of the day take hold of her. "How do you like your suite?"

"It feels fit for a goddess, not a mortal like me." Kate admitted. Alexa laughed. "I still don't know how you got us a suite at the Ritz Carlton." Alexa tapped her nose, winking.

"I'll never tell." Both women giggled before entering a city taxi and drove away.

C3

Kate laid her head on her pillow under the cover of darkness. Alone, save company, was the light of the crescent moon. Kate stared out the open window with a full stomach, heavy eyelids but a heavier heart; she was glad she had the suite to herself for she could not answer Alexa why her eyes stung before tears flowed hot and wet down her soft cheeks.

Kate thought her secret was safe.

After years of living under a pen name she thought, no, hoped that people from her past would not know that it was her and would use their newfound knowledge to take advantage, making Kate feel like the timid creature who was mocked and jeered all those years ago instead of... Kate closed her eyes. She didn't expect to see him.

After three long years as her writing career grew to a nighttime project to a full-time job, Kate thought she had no dealings with the town and its inhabitants. But there he was in all his glory. He had come into her life and was not alone. Nolan still looked underweight, his hair looked longer, glossy, under the fluorescent light and his eyes... dark gray irises that sparked with excitement become extinguished as she saw him and... his daughter. Kate hadn't seen the child since she was an infant when Nolan begged to talk to her in the parking lot while she struggled not to fall to pieces for the man who hurt her so terribly.

Kate hugged her middle as she saw Nolan in her mind. She was grateful that the child didn't recognize her. Esme was too young to know the truth. All she knew was she met her idol and was given a gift. Kate opened her eyes to see darkness; wishing to be home with her daughter whose gentle touch and words of joy, helped Kate forget her troubles.

Soon. She thought, closing her eyes once more. Kate didn't want to think about her past; only *now*. Nolan was not part of her life. She was free from the stigma that he and his family brought and still encircled the townfolk's. *Kate was safe.*

The next day was Sunday. The morning was sunny and bright, but rain was promised to make landfall on the heads of mortals. Kate packed quietly of her clothes and gifts to take back home when her agent knocked on the door telling her she was heading down for breakfast. Kate called, saying she would join her in a few minutes before calling Emily and asked how Rose was doing, to which Emily said cheerfully.

"Wonderful!" Kate smiles as she heard Rose's voice and spoke to her daughter, feeling last night's melancholy melt away.

"We have a surprise for you, mommy!" Rose says happily. Kate laughed.

"So does mommy." She says.

"What?"

"I can't tell you, Rosy, or it wouldn't be a surprise." Rose groaned. Kate spoke to Rose and Emily before hanging up. Kate left the room and took the elevator down to the restaurant that was dressed in fancy fall colors for Halloween was right around the corner. Alexa waved to Kate, and she came forward and sat down on the side corner of the table.

"Did you order already?" Kate asks. Alexa nodded as a waiter came with a menu and a coffee press. He poured hot coffee into the women's cup.

"I'll be back to take your order, ma'am." Kate thanked him, and the man left. Breakfast was a fine affair. Kate was served French toast with eggs benedict. She and Alexa talked merrily, complimenting the chef before leaving the restaurant, with Kate tipping the waiter generously. Kate pulled her suitcase to the main desk to checkout, handing them the hotel keycard, waiting for the front concierge.

"Ms. Starfield!!" Kate turned and froze as she saw the familiar face of Esme Roth running, her hair bouncing as she ran.

"Esme!" Kate paled when she saw Nolan, who skittered to a stop when he saw her. Esme ignored him as she beamed up at Kate.

"Hi Ms. Starfield!" Kate started staring at the child. "Do you remember me?!" Esme asks her face started to fall after she didn't respond. Kate's smile was genuine as she leaned forward.

"Of course, I do." She says kindly. "You're Esme, correct." Esme nodded, beaming. "How are you doing, sweetie?"

"I'm good, thank you, and you?" Kate glanced up to see Nolan's face turn to stone, but his eyes were wide as she stared at her.

"I'm doing well." She says. "I didn't expect to see you again. Are you enjoying the book?" Esme's face turned sheepish.

"I didn't get to read it yet. I was so sleepy when daddy took me home. Did you know my daddy lives here too? He has his own special room."

"I didn't know that." Kate admitted. Nolan cleared his throat, making her and Esme look at him.

"Come on, Esme." He spoke calmly. "Let's leave k—Ms. Starfield alone. She has important things to do." Kate caught the slip of his words. She smiled down at the child.

"It was nice to see you again, Esme." Kate says earnestly.

"Where are you going, Ms. Starfield?" before Nolan could speak, Kate says.

"To my home." Esme's eyes widen.

"You have a house!?"

"Esme!" Nolan cries. Kate stood up straight with a light laugh.

"Yes. That's where my daughter is." She saw Nolan start at daughter.

"Wow." Esme spoke. "I didn't know you had a daughter."

"I do." Kate took her receipt and thanked the clerk before looking at Esme.

"She's six years old." Esme nodded. As Nolan's face went blank with shock.

"What's her name?" Kate smiles at her.

"Rose."

"Just like princess Rose Garden." Kate grinned.

"The very same."

"Wow." Esme breathes. Kate smiled before lifting a hand to shake Esme's.

"It was very nice talking to you again," Kate replies gently. "I can't wait to tell my daughter about you." Esme looked down. "Oh! Don't cry, dear." Esme nodded but gripped the front of her skirt, as her wet cheeks turned red. Nolan stepped forward and placed a hand on her daughter's shoulders. "Come on, Essie." He whispers. Esme looked at Kate, who waved before picking up the handle of her rolling suitcase and walked away.

⋈

Nolan watched her go chest aching. He lifted a hand to it as his throat tightened watching the woman enter the taxi before it carried her away. Esme cried quietly, making him look down at her. His chest burned as he stared pityingly at his daughter, who would never see her idol again… just as he could never be with Kate.

Chapter Twenty-five

Monday came stormy and bleak over Forest-Bend. The smell of rain was heavy as clouds turned to stormy gray. Nolan drove silently, watching the cityscape as he drove from his doctor's appointment to go home after a long day of work: the meetings felt longer and more tedious as ever as he sat with different members from his board. Nolan listened to all that needed to be said and done, but his mind was on other things that prevented him from concentrating. Not even his trip to the doctor helped as he sat on the large chair talking about his weekend with Esme.

Nolan's stomach squirmed as he drove out of the city, wishing he could talk to someone about this, whatever this was. Kate. The name sent a thrill of pain and pleasure about seeing her again in the main lobby. Seeing her dressed in a simple blouse with jeans, her hair glossy and long as he saw her the other night. He saw in his mind's eye as Esme ran, letting go of his hand to see Kate at the front desk. Surprise overcame him when he was face to face with his daughters' biggest fan: watching as Kate spoke kindly to his daughter who spoke about his private suite. She was still kind to Esme. Everyone was, but he knew it was his status.

No one dared to be cruel because they feared him.

Kate didn't acknowledge him; only spoke to her. Nolan interjecting when Esme's questions got too personal. But it didn't stop Kate from answering her question: she was so patient, so gentle…

"*My daughter.*" Nolan's hand convulsed on the wheel as he heard Kate say the words that still cut him deeply.

"*She's six years old.*"

Nolan's stomach clenched, making him drive slowly. Thankfully, he was in the countryside when cows pastured, and corn grew.

Rose.

Still, after all these years, he wondered if his child still feared the town. Nolan's chest still stuttered when he remembered Kate standing stock still as the once proud elite took her wrath on the woman, she believed took his heart. Not his wife, but… Nolan shuddered.

Now as he drove, Nolan could not help think of his second daughter, remembering when he held her: it differed from the times he held Esme. A small part of him believed Rose was not getting the adequate needs for a growing child, but as he stood holding her while Kate laid unconscious, he felt her body light but strong, her bones fragile but had good dexterity, especially after feeling her kicks and screams.

Kate was raising her, keeping her in shape and safe from people who could do Rose harm, people like… Nolan's chest pulsed painfully. He gasped, clutching his chest just as he pulled into his mansion; fortunate no one could see him undergo his distress. His eyes stung as he laid his head on the steering wheel.

"You've caused nothing but suffering to me!" Nolan shuddered as Kate's words came back to him in a wave; seeing her angry tears as she told she would not be his play family he could run to… she won't expose her daughter to a monster like him!

Nolan gasped again, feeling his heart race, his breathing going shallow. He was having a panic attack. Nolan opened the door to his car, clutching his chest as he staggered to the house and entered. No one greeted him and he was grateful, he could not explain to the maids what was wrong and Esme…

he had closed himself off once again and now she was alone while he was left to brood in silence for the crimes that he done, but someone else was paying the price for… Nolan collapsed on the parlor as he heaved trying to take in air; he was alone again, trapped in the endless circle where he was revered by all but hated by the two women; who he tore her bleeding heart, leaving a hole where was once meant for him.

He closed his eyes.

CRASH!!

Nolan stirred as the sound of rumbling reverberated through his body, waking him up from a fitful sleep. Thunder shook the room as he opened his eyes blinking tiredly as he sat up from the sofa, feeling stiff for sleeping in an uncomfortable position. Nolan rubbed the back of his neck, massaging it as the sound of rain pelted the window. He sighed as he let go of his neck to pick up his phone as it buzzed.

"**Tornado warning across the tri-state area, effective now until…**"
Nolan clicked off the phone. His head ached, making him bury his face in his hands, feeling the day's stress and despair on his back like a heavy blanket. Screams made Nolan stiffen as he heard the familiar voice of Camille. He didn't want to be disturbed, but he knew he had to face her in order to get upstairs to change and have dinner.

A new sound made Nolan look up, turning his head for the door. He heard the childlike voice of his daughter, her own voice loud, angry… Nolan got up and walked out the room.

Nolan walked quietly as the sound of shrieks accompanied by angry shouts echoed in the room. Nolan heard the voices of Camille and Esme as their

249

voices grew louder. He heard Camille commanding Esme to do as she say but to Nolan's surprise, Esme shrieked. "NO!!"

"I am your mother!" Nolan stopped just enough to see Camille get in her face, her eyes wild. But Esme stood her ground as she shouted.

"You're the worst mom ever! I hate you!" Nolan saw Camille stepped back as if she was struck. She lifted a hand.

"No! Don't!" Nolan lunged. He caught Camille's hand, catching her by surprise. Esme stepped back, afraid and relieved. Nolan gripped Camille's wrist firmly.

"What is going on here!?" he demands. Camille hissed as Esme glared.

"Why don't you ask Esme!" Camille replies harshly. Nolan looked at Esme.

"Esme!?" Esme didn't look at him. It was then she saw she was clutching her book in front of her like a shield.

"What happened?" Nolan asks calmly. Esme didn't respond. Camille broke free from his grip and said.

"She was talking back to me! Her own mother!"

"What?! E-Esme is this true?" Esme looked up.

"She was being mean to Ms. Lehman!" Esme cries. "She was yelling at her just because I was eating dinner with her in the kitchen." Nolan looked at her surprised.

"You don't eat in there! You're not poor!" Camille shrilled.

"I eat there all the time!"

"Since when!?"

"Forever!!"

"You don't eat with the hired help!" Camille snaps.

"Why!"

"Because they're not us! She's the cook, not your friend."

"She is my friend!" Camille snorted a laugh.

"Why should you hang out with working-class people?! They're not like us. You should play with kids in your status!"

"I don't want to play with them!" Camille lifted a hand to her temple.

"Talk to your daughter, Nolan! I don't have time for this." She says. Esme let out a sound of disgust.

"You never have time for me!" Camille glared. "All you do is drink and yell at people!"

"Enough Esme!" Nolan intervened. Esme glared, cheeks red. Nolan stepped forward. "I know you're upset, but disrespecting your mother is wrong! If she says—"

"I didn't do anything wrong!!" Esme screamed. Nolan's eyes widen as she pointed at Camille.

"She did! I was defending chef Lehman, so she won't be fired by mommy like everyone else!" Nolan was stunned.

"She is not your mother!" Camille snarls.

"She's a better mommy than you! All you do is yell at people and ignore me! And at least Ms. Lehman is nice to me!"

"She's paid to be nice to you!"

"Camille, stop it!" Nolan exclaims, his head pounding.

"They work for us because they're poor and can't have what we have, so they have to be nice, otherwise they would be on the streets!"

"You're lying!" Esme cries. Camille's smile was cruel.

"I can tell the chef to stop talking to you or she's fired, just like the nanny!" Esme froze as did Nolan. "Would you like that, that she's—"

"Camille! Enough! You will not threaten the cook to—"

"I hate you!" Esme screamed tears burst from her eyes.

"Essie!" but it was too late. Esme dropped her book to the floor and ran for the staircase, yelling.

"*I hate you, daddy*!" Nolan's heart broke as he saw her ran upstairs and to her room, where she shut the door with a crash. Camille cackled.

"She's your daughter!" Nolan turned to glare, making her step back. But instead of yelling, Nolan turned his back and walked out of the foyer.

☙

Nolan didn't sleep all night. He tossed and turned on his guest bed as the evening events played in his mind, seeing his wife's disregard for human decency, to his daughter's look of anger as she said those three words. Nolan's chest, crushed by the weight of his daughter who witnessed the hand of life's cruelty; having to undergo the on-slot of her mother's temper tantrums, to his aloofness. Believing keeping her safe was to close himself because of the terrible things he had done to those who were close to him. He knew what he had been doing to Esme was wrong. He was no perfect father, but he tried to be the best he could be after Camille took her away when she was a baby; Nolan now, as he thought back to it, could not believe how terrible he was to let Camille take his daughter away: she was not fit for motherhood as he was not empathic. The words he said years before about conformity bit him hard. He was not a good father. He brought his daughter toys and the finest clothes but he himself never raised her it was always the nanny and now the cook who looked after Esme who gave her time in their own busy lifestyle taking care of a man who neglected his own flesh and blood. Nolan's chest squeezed as the truth hit him hard.

I'm... he thought before a shudder rocked through him. He curled in on himself as he closed his eyes, but it didn't stop the tears from flowing from his lids.

The sky was gray as black storm clouds envelop the town, fat with the promise of rain, thunder, and lightning. Nolan awoke groggily to the sound of rain hitting the glass. His eyes were dull, his head ached despite his deep slumber. Slowly, he sat up from bed before resting his face in his hands. A scream echoed, making him stiffen, thinking it was Camille. He was in no mood to argue. Footsteps came fast, followed by frantic knocking from his door.

"Mr. Nolan! Mr. Nolan!" surprise took him. It wasn't Camille but... he got up from bed and opened the door, revealing one of his maids who looked at him frantically.

"What is it, Joyce?" the maid looked at him with a frightened expression. "It's Esme!" she cries. "**Sh-she's gone!**"

Nolan froze. His dull eyes grew wide as his body went cold. The maid went on, but it fell on deaf ears as Nolan stepped out of the guest room and ran not to get Camille or call the police but for Esme's room.

Nolan stopped when he saw the maids standing outside his daughter's room, some whispering, others crying; they parted for Nolan when they saw him allowing him to enter to find the room in shambles: closet wide open were clothes laid toppled to the floor, toys laid scattered in all parts of the room and the bed... Nolan stepped toward the canopy seeing the bed laid messy, the occupant... gone.

"No," Nolan whispered. Footsteps entered, and he saw Camille holding a bottle, her eyes bloodshot as she stared at the room, demanding what happened. No one spoke. Nolan turned his gaze to the door where another face, the cook, entered. The cook glanced disdainfully at Camille before going to Nolan, who stood stock still as he stared at the plump black woman.

"Mrs. Lehman." He breathes.

"Mr. Roth," she breathes. "she's not here!" Nolan felt the ground under him crumble, the world that was once visibly blurred. Suddenly, he was too scared to move from fear that his entire existence would dissipate. Camille screamed she dropped to her knees, but no one helped the woman, all eyes were on Nolan looking at him for council.

Nolan listened as his cook and maids spoke to him about how they looked everywhere for Esme, adding that the girls saw her bike was missing. "She must have ridden it this morning before Leah came to wake her." Mrs. Lehman cries. Nolan nodded, but his mind was not there. He had to wake up. This was just a dream! But why couldn't he wake…

"Nolan!" Nolan started at his name. He looked to see Camille staring at him with tear-stained cheeks. Nolan's eyes burned, but he ignored it, blinking back the wetness that threatened to spill.

There will be time to cry later.

"Call the police." He orders. Mrs. Lehman nodded as he turned to the maids. "All of you keep looking for Esme." The ladies nodded and left the room except for two that Nolan ordered to comfort Camille, which they obeyed, although reluctantly. Nolan walked stiffly. His body moved, but his mind felt severed from the rest of him. This was all his…

"Nolan!" Nolan stopped just by the door to turn to look at Camille, who was now sitting between the two maids. "where could she go!?" she cries. Nolan stared at her, seeing the woman as if for the first time her disheveled hair, her splotchy cheeks, her teary eyes that were wild. It had been so long since he had seen her cry.

"I don't know." He finally spoke. He didn't say, but he thought it with solemnly.

But I will find her and keep her away from you!

Camille looked at him as if she had read his thoughts. She wrapped her arm around her waist and sobbed.

Chapter Twenty-six

Black clouds covered the once blue sky in a blanket over the small town. Wind whooshed through the trees, shaking its branches violently as rain pelted the earth with fat but fierce drops of rain. All was still on the town, for no person dared to venture through the tempest for the fear of being blown away by the howling, merciless wind. No one except one. Esme rode fast on her bike. Rain pelted her yellow raincoat as she made her trip through the small town; she was surprised to find the once happy town that smiled at her be turned into a sad, gloomy empty place. Wood boards covered the store's windows as she rode through the town square, finding to her alarm that the fountain was not running. Esme peered down at the basin of the pool, seeing her distorted reflection by the howling gale. She looked up only to feel water pelt her face with icy needles that turned her cheeks pink with cold.

Esme shielded her face as she looked up at the swirling black and gray clouds; she was all alone her only company was her bike and her bag pack that contained her few belongings that she packed when she came to the idea of running away from home to go into town and visit the sweet shop or ice cream parlor but seeing both stores were closed because of the storm she had nowhere to go.

Home was definitely out of the question. She didn't want to face her uncaring mother to her father... Esme's eyes stung. She swiped her arm across her eyes as she hopped on her bike and rode away. It was hard for the wind kept pushing her back, making Esme pedal against the storm as the wind howled in her ears.

Esme rode through the town looking for anyone to help her. She remembered Leah, the maid, telling her if there was any danger to go to the police; but Esme had never seen a police station. She was never pointed to it by her, nanny, much less her father.

Esme felt tears roll down her cold cheeks as she thought of her daddy with angry tears of betrayal and heartache. Her daddy, who had been so good to her after so many years of being so distant, had closed himself to her again. He who took her to meet her favorite storyteller had ignored her, acting as if she didn't exist had listened to her mother more than she, who had yelled and screamed after she lost her baby brother had yelled and screamed again at her favorite person after her nanny said goodbye to her. Esme cried as she rode down a long span of road keeping to the sides so that cars would pass by. Water splashed her from top to bottom. Despite the rain boots and coat, Esme shivered. The storm raged on, growing stronger as she pedaled her way up an incline. Gritting her chattering teeth; she rode up the hill despite the wind that pushed her back and forth as branches fell nearly hitting her.

Esme screamed when a bolt of lightning streaked the sky before it was followed by a huge kaboom! Of thunder. Esme fell off her bike and cried out just as loose branches fell atop her.

"**Daddy!**" she screamed. But her voice was lost by the sound of wind and thunder. "Daddy!" Esme looked up and saw something up ahead. Going on her hands and knees she crawled carefully from under the branches; it was just in time, for at that moment she heard an earsplitting crunch. Turning her head, she saw a large tree tip forward ripping the earth up as it did to collapse atop her bike. Esme cried seeing how close she was to being crushed by the tree; shivering with cold, Esme stumbled on wobbly legs up the rest of the hill to find a mailbox standing tall.

Despite the storm, she turned her head and saw a declining slope that was covered in mud, water, and leaves. She was so tired. With all the strength she could muster, Esme walked down the decline. She had made it four steps when she slipped on the wet mud. There she tumbled, sliding the rest of the way down. Esme whimpered as she sat up a saw a house of red brick, but her eyes widen when she saw a signatory swing that swung back and forth in the wind.

଼

Kate hummed quietly as she stirred a pan of chopped browning sausages, bringing warmth that filled the kitchen for the evening meal. The house was quiet, Rose was napping on the sofa leaving Kate to work quietly on the menu of pizza and apple crisps: Kate had made the dough ahead of time allowing her to grate the cheese, warm up the tomato sauce she made the other night before finally cooking the sweet Italian sausages, sampling a bite to test for doneness.

Now. She thought, turning off the stove. Kate lifted the pan and scraped them onto a paper towel plate so the towels could drain off the fat and oil. All that's left is to work on the crumble for the apple crisps and cut & peel the apples. She smiled to herself as she placed the hot pan in the sink; running water inside it, she heard a yawn, followed by footsteps. turning Kate smiled warmly at her daughter, who walked into the kitchen.

"Hi Rosy!" she cooed. Rose walked to her mother and hugged her; Kate lifted her up. "Had a nice sleep?" Rose nodded, her eyes blurry still with sleep. She yawned.

"Whatcha doing, mommy?" she asks.

"I'm cooking the sausages." Kate replies.

"Are we still having pizza?"

"Yep." Rose's eyes brightened. "Until then, I have to work on the apples for the crisp." Rose nodded as Kate sat her down on the chair.

"Can I help?"

"Sure honey. You can help peel the apples with me."

Rose nodded, before looking out the window.

"It's raining outside."

"Yes, we're in the middle of a bad storm." Rose nodded. Kate took this time to get the apples from the fridge before putting them in a bowl. She was just washing them when Rose asked.

"Mommy, can I play on the swing?"

"No Rosy, it's too wet and dangerous to go outside."

"What's dangerous?"

"It means it's not safe to play."

"But that girl is outside on the swing." Kate, who had put the bowl on the table, looked at Rose with surprise.

"What girl?" Rose pointed outside. Kate followed and looked out the window to see a young girl sitting lonely on the swing. Kate's eyes widen as Rose asked.

"Who is she, mommy?" Kate stared for three heartbeats before she turned and ran for the door; slipping on garden boots, she orders Rose to "Stay here." Before opening the door, umbrella in hand.

Kate stepped out into the gale, her footsteps squished in the wet mud as she walked carefully through the yard. The wind had lessened somewhat, but she could still feel the icy chill as it stung her hands; but it didn't matter to Kate as she stared at the child, who was watching her with sad eyes.

Esme watched her quietly where she sat, her coat matted in mud: the child's hair was wet, too tired to cover her head with the hood. Kate stared at her with quiet concern, wondering how this child; the child of her former lover, made it to her home.

"*Esme.*" She breathes.

Esme started before looking down. It was then Kate saw she was missing a shoe. Pity overwhelmed Kate as she stepped forward, shielding the rain from Esme. She leaned down to her eye level.

"Esme?" Kate spoke. Esme looked at her as tears slid down her eyes. Kate lifted a hand. "Come Esme, let me help you." Esme looked at her for a long time before taking her cold hand. She placed it in Kate's warm ones. Kate watch wordlessly as the child leaped off the swing before walking shakily on her legs. Kate winced, realizing the child was wearing one boot. Before she could, react, Rose poked her head from the open door.

"Mommy!" she cries. Rose saw Esme and her eyes went wide.

"Go inside honey!" Kate tells Rose. Rose obeyed, allowing her and Esme to enter. Esme took in the house's sight with wide eyes. She had never been to a stranger's house before, not like this in its... Kate closed the door, startling Esme. She looked up to see Kate lock the door, placing the open umbrella on the floor under the window.

"Mommy?!" Kate turned to see Esme and Rose. Rose was on the sofa watching Esme fearfully but curiously whilst Esme watched her with wonder. Kate hid a smile before taking Esme's hand.

"Come sit down, Esme." Kate says. She guided Esme to the kitchen there she sat her down on the chair. Esme was still watching the house with keen interest. It wasn't until Kate called her name for the third time did, she wake up.

"Are you alright?" Kate asks. Esme stared it was then she had realized who she was in the presence of...

"Victoria Starfield!" She gasps. Kate smiled weakly but nodded once.

"Are you okay, Esme?" Esme looked down at her wet coat and missing boot.

"How did you get here? Can you tell me?" she looked at Kate, who kneeled before her.

"I rode my bike." She spoke.

"In this storm!?" Kate asks. Esme nodded.

"What happened to your bike?"

"I-It got crushed." Kate's eyes widen.

"Are you hurt?!" Kate gasps. Instinctively, she lifted a hand to her arm, patting Esme.

"I don't know," Esme's voice sounded glum. "One of the tree branches fell on me."

"Oh, dear!" Kate gasps. Esme stared, feeling the warmth of the room and Kate's touch. "I'm so glad you're alright and not hurt." Esme's eyes half closed. She was so tired. Seeing this Kate spoke gently.

"Let me take off your coat and get you cleaned up okay, sweetie." Esme nodded.

"Mommy?" Esme looked at Rose, who was standing behind a corner.

"Mommy, who's that?"

261

Esme stared at Kate, who was watching her daughter lovingly. Kate pulled off Esme's wet coat as she rose to her feet.

"This is a special friend of mine." She says kindly, making Esme's eyes widen. "Rose, come say hi to Esme." Rose stepped forward, looking down at her feet, she says shyly.

"Hi." Esme blinked, remembering her manners, she says.

"H-Hi."

છ

Nolan sat huddled within himself. Minutes, felt like hours as the clock ticked mercilessly on the large grandfather clock within the parlor. Hours felt like days as he sat, his mind unable to rest as it whirled repeated the same questions with no answer. Answers, he so desperately wanted to know.

Where was Esme?

Nolan sat as sheriffs talked, asking him and Camille questions as offices searched his house for the millionaires' daughter. Nolan answered the questions as best he could, but his mind felt weak from the emotional strain at the thought of his beloved daughter all alone during a storm that threatened the small town.

"And you say she was gone this morning?" asks the female officer.

"Yes." says the maid, relaying what Nolan and Camille already knew. Nolan felt sick to his stomach. It didn't help that he had not eaten since yesterday; now his stomach churned with pain and fear as he thought of Esme. He didn't care about his company or his connections; the only thing that mattered was...

"Mr. Roth!?" Nolan started at his name. He looked up with bloodshot eyes at the officer, who spoke. "Can you tell me?" She says. "Has your daughter ever tried to run away before?" Nolan stared as the question struck a chord.

"Of course, she wouldn't!" Everyone, including Nolan, turned to see Camille glaring at the officer. She sat on the other side of the chair where Nolan sat, glowering.

"So, you're saying she never ran away before?"

"Why would she do that!? Where could she go?! She's seven!"

"*Eight*," Nolan spoke. Everyone looked at him, including Camille.

"What?" It was Nolan's turned to glare.

"Our daughter is eight years old, Camille." He spoke his voice hard. "If you had been paying any attention other than your tablet, you would have known that. Instead of spreading your drunken malice through this house, you would have *noticed* **that your daughter is missing**!" he bellows. Camille shrank back.

"Mr. Roth?" The sheriff spoke, breaking the tense silence. "Do you know why you daughter ran away?" Nolan looked at the officer.

"*Camille and Esme had a fight.*" He answers.

"About what?" Nolan tells them, leaving nothing out. His heart ached when he told the officers that Esme said she hated him.

"So that's what caused her to run away?" Nolan buried his face in his hands. He nodded once.

"Do you know of her favorite places she likes to go to?" asks the female sheriff. "Friends?" Nolan raised his head slowly; revealing, pained, dark gray eyes.

"I don't know any of her favorite places."

263

"Does she have—"

"No," Nolan spoke. His voice was a growl as he turned his glare to Camille. "She's *not* friends with any of the kids in this town."

"You must find her!" Camille cries.

"We'll do our best, ma'am," says the officer. "But with this storm, most of the landlines are down. It's not safe out there for a child. She could be crushed by a fallen tree or…" he trailed off. Nolan shuddered.

"We'll try to search for her tomorrow, but until then, I'm sure she is hiding someplace safe." Nolan nodded, but he didn't feel comforted. He watched as the officers left the room, escorted by the maids, leaving him alone with Camille. Nolan rose to his feet.

"Where are you going!?" Nolan didn't turn around as he says through clenched teeth.

"To find Esme." Camille stared at his back with surprise.

"In this storm, you heard what the police said."

"What other choice do I have, Camille." He whirled around, eyes blazing. "I have to do something! I can't just sit here knowing that my daughter is out there in a middle of a super-storm!"

He glared at her.

"At least I'm taking action." He murmurs. Camille rose to her feet.

"Your action is to go out in the wet and get killed!" she demands. "How does that help us?"

"Us!" Nolan shouts. In three long strides, he was in Camille's face. "For the last three years, you've ignored your daughter as you wallowed in your pity party!" He towered over her as gray eyes blazed with fury. "While I seek help; you missed every *appointment*, drank *every* bottle of alcohol, including the

264

cooking wine, and fired every hired help that stood their ground against you!" Camille stepped back, alarm and fear on her face.

"As far as I know." He spoke low. "There was no us! At least I'm trying to be proactive instead of inactive. At least I'm trying to get penance for the wrongs I've done than pretend to care to look good for the police!"

Silence.

"You don't think I care?" Camille breathes in shock.

"I know it." He snarls. Camille raised her head, and her eyes were full of tears.

"I didn't know this would happen," She breathes. "It was supposed to be my night but… It happened so suddenly one-minute Esme and I was fighting the next… *I felt wetness between my legs*." Nolan stared at her, his eyes wide as he stepped back in shock.

"That night." Camille clasped her hands in front of her.

"*It was as if it knew*," She murmurs. " Knew that I was a terrible mother, knew Esme didn't want to be a big sister; knew that it would be hated… it didn't want to live inside me. Because it wasn't loved." Nolan's eyes stung as he heard Camille's painful confession. She looked at him, green eyes dull.

"He had your eyes. He was so small but… *he had your eyes*." Nolan's chest pulsed, as his eyes blurred.

He turned his back on her.

"*I'm going to find, Esme*." His voice was thick as he spoke. Camille raised a hand, but Nolan walked for the door. He stopped turning slightly to look at his tearful wife before walking out the room.

Chapter Twenty-seven

Kate hung up her cell phone with a sigh as she stood in her bedroom. Night covered the forest where branches toppled from the howling tempest that laid waste upon the wet earth. Kate saw the result of the storm with worried eyes, concerned that one of the shaking trees outside her window would collapse upon her humble cabin. She was thankful that it didn't happen, but only time will tell. When the pounding rain had ceased to a sober drizzle, the wind had finally died down, easing Kate's fear, although she kept a brave face for her daughter and… their guest.

Kate looked down at her hand, thinking of the child who crept silently into her life once again. The child with long blond hair and wide curious green eyes took in every bit of Kate's home. Kate couldn't help comparing her to a young bird that just opened its eyes, seeing the world for the first time eager to explore every nook and cranny.

Once Kate removed Esme's wet coat and socks, she took Esme to the bathroom; there Kate brought out a clean towel that she wrapped around Esme, who shivered. Rose watched Esme as Kate went to her room shutting the door quietly after telling Esme she would find her something to wear. Once in her room, Kate called 911 but to her alarm, the lines were busy with so many emergencies happening during the storm, who knew when help will arrive or if they considered this as a big emergency that Kate had brought in the child of wealthy parents: *who destroyed her reputation.*

"Mommy!?" Kate looked at the door.

"I'm coming, Rosy!" she called.

That was several hours ago. Now, with night blanketing the cabin Kate could finally think through the situation. Esme Roth. Esme didn't complain when Kate took care of her. Esme washed in the tub while Kate sat on the toilet seat, making sure she was safe, a fluffy robe in hand that she gave to the child once she was clean. Kate had put the child's clothes to wash in the laundry room; Esme watched her do this with awe as Rose stared her curiously. Kate next gave Esme her old shirts to wear since Rose's clothes were too small. Esme thanked Kate as she stared starry-eyed at her favorite author.

Once the child was clean, Kate led Esme to the living room where she sat her down and ask the child why she ran away. Esme looked down sheepishly, unable to look at Kate. It took some prodding before Esme confessed the truth. Kate's eyes widen at the child's tale, but she hid the shock as she listened to Esme.

"I'm so glad you're all right, Esme," Kate spoke when Esme fell silent.

"Are you going to call my daddy?" she asks sadly. She looked at Kate and Rose who sat on her mother's lap. Kate hesitated.

"Do you know your daddy's number?"

"No." Kate sighs.

"I can't reach your daddy without his number. Your parents must be worried sick about you." Esme didn't respond. "But until this storm ends, you'll have to stay home here."

"You mean you're not going to make me leave?" Esme looked at Kate, eyes wide. Kate shook her head with a small smile.

"You can stay until the storm passes. Tonight, I'll call the police and let them know you are here with me, okay." Esme nodded.

267

"Until then, you can stay for dinner." Just as she said this, Esme's stomach growled audibly.

"Mommy I'm hungry." Rose whined. Kate smiled at Rose.

"Okay, hone," Kate says. She looked at Esme, asking with a kind smile. "How do you feel about making pizza?"

⚬

Kate opened the door to her small hallway; it was a quarter past eight when she peeked to see Rose fast asleep on her bed. She smiled lovingly before closing the door softly. Kate walked down the short hallway to the living room where she found Esme laying on the leather sofa covered in a large downy white comforter. Kate sat up on a makeshift bed with pillows and sheets to make the child stay more comfortable. Esme sat up when she saw Kate, who smiled.

"Are you alright, Esme?" she asks. Esme nodded.

"Were you able to reach the police?"

"No." she saw Esme let out a breath. It was relieved; Kate noticed even as she continued. "But with the storm, it's hard to reach them,"

"Oh." Esme paused. "Ms. Starfield... do I have to go home?" Kate was surprised by the question.

"Why? Don't you miss home?" Kate asks. She tried to sound chipper as she sat beside her. "I'm sure the maids and chefs are worried sick about you." Esme nodded sadly.

"And your parents, I know they must miss you terribly."

"Not my mommy," Esme spoke glumly. Kate winced inwardly.

"I'm sure she does and your daddy." Esme didn't reply, her eyes downcast.

268

"My mommy isn't nice to me." Esme finally spoke. "She does nothing but be angry and drink yucky juice."

"Yucky juice?" Kate spoke. Esme told her. Kate shuddered. Esme looked at Kate sadly. "mommy does nothing with me, and daddy doesn't play with me since my baby brother died." Kate watched as tears flowed down the child's cheek.

"Oh, Esme." Kate breathes.

"Can I stay here with you and Rosy?" Kate sighs sadly.

"I'm afraid not, honey." Kate breathes. "If you stayed, your family would miss you terribly." Esme sniffed. "I know it seems bad right now, but I know your daddy is anxious about you. He loves you very much."

"But won't he be mad at me?"

"I think he'll just be glad to know that you're all right and not hurt by the storm." Esme nodded, then yawned. "time for bed, Esme." Esme nodded. Kate tucked in the child, placing a kiss on her forehead.

"Goodnight Esme."

"Goodnight, Ms. Starfield," Esme says before falling asleep. Kate walked back to her room, closing the door behind her. Kate lay in bed five minutes later in her nightgown. Looking at the darkroom, silence filled the space, reverberating in her ears. She sighed, turning on her side. Nolan's face appeared in her mind, seeing his tall stature, his sad gray eyes.

Nolan. She thought before closing her eyes.

ᘒ

Nolan lay in the pitch blackness, alone in the dead silence of his mansion. The maids had turned in early that evening after Nolan came home after dusk. He had no appetite as he walked the cavernous halls, dazed, cold, and exhausted. He didn't find his daughter. The very walls seemed too big to Nolan as he walked aimlessly from room to room thinking of the past, his memories somber as his mind's eye relived every moment of his daughter; thinking of all the laughs he shared, the gifts he bought, the smiles he gave to his child before he closed himself off as he grieved for what could have been as opposed to what was.

This is all my fault. Nolan thought sadly as he lay on his right side, his eyes staring listlessly at the closed curtains that hid the night. He thought back to the years after his son's passing, remembering as he saw Esme cry, as she saw her brother be buried; seeing her green eyes cloud over, her cheeks flushed crimson as she begged to have her baby brother.

Nolan was too grief-stricken to react all he could do was stare at the tiny coffin being lowered into the earth. For several weeks Nolan didn't speak, he could not eat or sleep. Everything reminded him of how he had lost. He could not comfort his child or his wife, who sobbed for days, only to lash out at everyone who came close to her.

Including Esme.

Instead of being there to protect her, Nolan pushed her away. A part of him felt anger for his wife and child, who both didn't want the baby, but he, too, felt part of the blame. He had run away when Camille made the announcement, ran like a coward after years of loathing, fighting and **conformity**.

Nolan shuddered, cursing the day he ever said that word, wishing he could take back everything he said when he was consumed by pride and power. He would take everything back, but he knew he couldn't. It was in the past and his present… *his present…* Nolan's eyes watered. He closed his eyes, but the wetness came hot and salty upon his left cheek.

"*Esme.*" He whimpered.

Nolan let himself cry after holding it in for so long. The tears pooled down his sunken cheeks as he cried soundlessly. The sudden sound of the door opening made Nolan start up from bed to see the figure of his wife. Camille who stood in the main entrance where light shone in the background. Nolan stared at her, his face hard as she stared at him with bloodshot eyes. She had been crying but his eyes didn't soften as he stared at his wife.

"What do you want, Camille?" he spoke. Camille didn't answer, just looked at him pleadingly. "if you've come to fight or blame me don't—I know it's my fault!" he meant to growl the last part, but it came out thick. Camille opened her mouth, but nothing came out. Nolan took his time to lie back on his bed. He heard the door close, swallowing him in darkness. Nolan closed his eyes and tried to go to sleep when he felt an arm wrap around his waist. Nolan opened his eyes with surprise. He turned his head but could not see the face in the darkness. All he heard was her shaky gasps as she spasmed beside his back. Nolan listened wordlessly as more tears fell from his eyes. He laid his head back on the pillow, closing them as he heard Camille sniff. Nolan took her hand in his. She grasped it silently. No words were spoken but their silent language spoke loud in the darkness.

They fell asleep.

ᘓ

Nolan awoke groggily to the brightness as he opened his eyes. He saw rays of gliding light peeking from closed curtains. Nolan looked down and saw a white hand wrapped around his waist. Everything came flooding back as he stared at the arm that went with the body. He saw that body as he sat up from bed. Nolan felt stiff but well-rested as he peered down at Camille. He stared at her, her cheeks pink with sleep, her right fist pressed close to her mouth as her hair half covered her face.

She looks so… he thought, trailing off, unable to find the right word. Camille stirred before opening her eyes that looked up into his dark gray irises. They stared at one another for a long time; neither of them spoke.

A hard knock came on the door. Both adults looked up. Nolan sighed as he kicked off the sheets and walked on the cold floor to the door. Opening it, he saw it was chef Lehman gasping.

"Ms. Lehman!" he says voice hoarse but full of surprise.

"I'm sorry to wake you so early, Mr. Roth, but…" she stopped craning her neck to see Camille, who sat up and was rubbing her eyes with a yawn.

"Mrs. Lehman?" Nolan spoke. She looked at him.

"I'm sorry, sir, but we just got news this morning from the sheriffs. They said the storm has passed, and it's clear enough to go outside." Nolan's face, which was still tired, looked sad.

"Oh." He spoke. He heard Camille suck in her teeth and grumble something under her breath. "Thank you, Mrs. Lehman I—"

"That's not all." The chef was smiling at Nolan.

"They have a lead!" she says.

> *"They found Esme!"*

272

Chapter Twenty-eight

The first rays of dawn broke through the gray clouds, bringing light and truth to the small town as it erased the storm, but revealing the aftermath it laid waste. Kate hummed tunelessly as she whisked eggs in a large bowl. The house was silent as she made breakfast for herself, Rose, and Esme. Kate smiled gently as she thought of them remembering how she found the children: Rose, her body curled like a kitten as she laid in bed, oblivious to the world as she slept beside her new friend who hugged her close; her cheeks pink with heavy sleep.

Kate stirred the eggs in the frying pan, watching the eggs cook becoming an orange liquid into a light yellow solid that she scrambled with a spatula. A beep made Kate turn to the large waffle iron, indicating that the chocolate chip waffles she had prepared were ready.

"Mommy." Kate turned her head to see Rose standing behind her. Her right hand rubbed her eyes sleepily while her left held a pale warm hand. Kate smiled.

"Good morning, Rosy." Kate says, turning her head as she looked at her guest. "Good morning, Esme."

"Good morning." Rose said just at the same time Esme said. "Good morning, Ms. Starfield."

"Ready for breakfast?" Kate asks, going to the waffle iron lifting the lid, revealing four large golden-brown rectangles. Esme's eyes widen as Rose let go of her hand and walked to her seat and sat down eagerly.

"Waffles! Waffles!" Rose sang. Kate laughed as she placed the hot waffles on a plate where two other stacks sat. Kate turned off the stove where her eggs and sausage she cooked in separate pans before walking to the table.

"Did you have a good sleep?" she asks Rose, kissing her forehead.

"Yes, mommy." Rose smiles. Kate smiled as she pulled back a chair across from Rose.

"Sit here, Esme. Did you have a good sleep?" Esme nodded, walking over to Kate where she sat down.

"Yes, ma'am." Esme says. Kate nodded.

"Mommy, Esme slept in my room!" Rose beamed. Kate smiled and nodded as she plated the breakfast.

"I saw." Kate says. Esme blushed.

"Esme told me stories!"

"She did?" Kate looked at Esme as she placed a plate full of waffles, eggs, and sausages. Esme ducked her head. "That was very sweet of Esme to do that." Esme looked at Kate, who nodded approvingly.

"Rosy woke me up and asked if I could sleep with her," Esme admitted. "She said the storm was too scary." Kate nodded as she served Rose, pouring maple syrup on her and Esme waffles.

"Thank you, Esme." Kate says gratefully. Esme nodded sheepishly. "Well, eat up, you two." The girls nodded before digging into their waffles.

Kate poured the girl's juice before she too sat down and ate her meal. The room was filled with giggles and chatter as the two little girls talked happily. Rose asked many questions about the places Esme had been to. Kate saw her daughter's eyes grow wide with wonder; and Kate could not help getting enthralled by Esme's young life.

"You have lived an exciting life." Kate says to her. Esme squirmed. But her cheeks turned pink at the praise.

"My daddy and mommy took me." Kate nodded, although her stomach clenched when she says her parents.

"Is your mommy and daddy nice?" Rose asks.

"Rosy!" Kate gasps. "You're not supposed to ask that." She looked at Esme, who looked down.

"My daddy used to be nice." She says. "And my mommy is not nice at all."

"But all mommies are nice." Rose says innocently.

"Not mine." Kate looked down, knowing from experience how not nice Mrs. Roth could be. Rose thought about it.

"My mommy is nice." She says confidently. "She is nice to everybody." Kate smiles at that; Esme nodded.

"Your mommy is the best." She agrees. "I wish she was my mommy." She looked at Kate with wistful eyes.

"No! She's, *my* mommy!" Rose pouted. She got up from her seat and ran to Kate who chuckled.

"Honey." Kate says, picking her up. "mommy isn't going anywhere. I have plenty love to share." Rose shook her head, burying her face in her chest.

"I'm sorry, Esme." Kate says apologetically. "Rose is too young to understand." Esme nodded but her face was sad. Rose popped her head out and said.

"Mommy, can me and Esme play outside?" Kate glanced out the window.

"We'll see." She says, Rose whined. "Go finish your breakfast, Rosy." Rose obeyed, climbing off Kate. Esme continued her meal silently as Kate continued hers. The thrum of an engine made Kate look up again to see a car pulling up into the driveway.

That's strange. She thought rising from her chair just as she heard sirens blazing.

☙

Nolan sat in the backseat of the large SUV. His hands clenched on his lap. Outside he was composed, but inside he was giddy with nerves as he was driven down the winding road, to be reunited with his beloved daughter. Nolan could not rush fast enough when he heard the news that Esme was found; his eyes burned with unshed tears as he hurried to dress, not bothering to shower as the three simple words repeated in his head. Sheriffs came to the house after announcing to Nolan that they got a lead in the whereabouts of Esme. His eyes widen when the officers brought forth a destroyed pink bike from the trunk. Camille screamed, seeing the crushed bike as Nolan stared horrified at mother nature's wrath. Matters grew worse when one sheriff pulled out a yellow rain boot.

"This was found just outside town." Said a male officer. "She's close by."

"How do you know that?" Camille who hugged the boot to her chest looked at the officer with teary eyes. The officer smiled.

"We got a phone call last night. During the storm, all power was out, including land lines, but this person left a message telling us she had found a missing girl of eight and had her with her in her home."

"Did…?" this was Nolan whose throat tightened. "Did they…"

"Was it a threat!?" Camille demands, saying what he could not. "Did they want money!?" the officer shook his head.

276

"The caller didn't threaten your daughter. All they did was leave an address."

"Do you know who?" Nolan asks.

"I'm sorry, Mr. Roth. We can't disclose that."

"Why?!" Camille asks, her green eyes blazing. "How do you know that he or she is keeping Esme safe?! What if they have her tied up or worse!" Nolan shuddered.

"Come with us, Mr. and Mrs. Roth." Said a female sheriff. "we are now on our way to the address. If they have Esme held in danger, we will be ready." Nolan and Camille nodded before they entered the jeep. Nolan gripped his fist tighter as they drove.

Please be alright, Esme. He thought.

"Nolan?" Nolan turned to see Camille watching him her eyes glassy, red-rimmed. Nolan stared at her for a long moment in silence as the car drove under them.

"We're here." Both adults looked up at the same time. The officer turned on the siren, their own faces going grave. Nolan stared at the road, surprised at how far Esme had ridden her bike.

"Where?" he started. Just then, the car turned right and drove down a small decline. Nolan's eyes widen.

"Where are we!?" demands Camille. "Whose house is that?" Nolan stared at the familiar red brick house that came into view of the police cruiser's front window.

"No." he breathes. The cruiser came to a complete halt.

"Stay here." Ordered the officer. Nolan turned his head to see other cruisers stop and sheriffs come out, gun in hand.

N-no! he thought.

277

"**This is the Forest-Bend police**!" A booming voice echoed, making Nolan jump. He looked at the officer, who was now talking into a speaker. "**We are not here to harm you!**" He continues. "**We are merely looking for Esme Roth. If you have her, she is not to be afraid. Her parents are right here with us, and she has nothing to be afraid of!**"

Nolan stared back at the front window; his eyes wide, fearful not just of her child but… "**we ask you to come to the front door with your hands in the air!**"

"No!" Nolan gasps. Camille looked at him, surprised.

"Nolan?" But he ignored her. The officers who drove came out of the car. The couple watched as the door to the house open slowly before a face appeared, beautiful, frightened. Nolan froze. Camille stared.

"Is that…" she narrowed her eyes to get a good look at the woman who had her hands held high, her face unmistakable. Camille's eyes widen. The officers stepped forward shouting orders to "**Don't move!**" Nolan watched them go to her, seeing them finger their guns. Nolan opened the door to the cruiser.

"Nolan!" Camille cries, but he didn't listen. Nolan stepped out into the sunny morning. Debris from the storm laid all over the forest floor, but Nolan didn't notice as he stare wide eyed at the woman who looked at him with fearful doe-like eyes.

"Sir!?" says the officer as the female officer lifted a hand to push him back. "Please wait in the car." Nolan ignored him as he stared at her.

"Kate." He breathes. Kate watched him silently, her hands still in the air.

"Sir? Do you know her?" Nolan nodded.

"She's…" the slamming of the door made everyone look up to see Camille come forth, her face purple with rage.

"**You**!" she spit. Kate cringed, seeing Camille's fury. Nolan grabbed Camille's shoulder and pulled her back.

"Camille don't!" he started.

"You kidnapped my daughter!" she shrilled. Kate started, stunned.

"Put your hands up!" cried an officer. Kate obeyed.

"Stand down!" called the officer, who stood near Kate. The officers obeyed.

"Ma'am," he spoke to Kate. "did you call the police about the missing girl?" Kate nodded wordlessly. "Is she inside?" she nodded, not breathing.

"You can lower your hand, ma'am." Kate obeyed.

"Where is she!?" cries Camille. Nolan held her in case she tried to attack Kate, who let out a breath before breathing.

"She's in the living room." She turned and pushed the door fully to reveal Esme sitting on the large leather sofa, her hand covered with the blanket she slept with as she stared at the adults with wide eyes.

"*Esme*!" Nolan breathes. Camille dashed past Nolan and the others to enter the house. Kate stared at the other adults with wary eyes. She didn't react when Nolan entered her home. All she could do was stare at the officers.

A cry made Kate turn to see Esme, her eyes wet with tears as her father and mother wrapped their arms around her. Kate couldn't help smiling gently; the officers spoke into their microphones, but she didn't listen. All that mattered was this. Nolan and Camille asked for Esme's well-being, patting her making sure she was alright.

"We're so glad you're all right!" Camille sobs. Esme stared before looking at her father, who asked.

"How did you get here?" Esme tells them.

"Ms. Starfield found me and took me to her house." Nolan looked at Kate with wide eyes.

"Who?"

"Are you hurt?" Nolan asks quickly. Esme shook her head. Camille peppered her with questions until Nolan stopped her saying. "Essie has been through enough, Camille. She can tell us later." Camille nodded, before looking down at her child's eyes wet with tears.

"We're so glad you're safe!" she blubbered. Esme hugged her. Nolan sniffed before turning his gaze to Kate.

"*Thank you.*" He breathes with gratitude. Camille followed his gaze. Her eyes narrowed as her lips pursed. Kate nodded.

"Come on, Essie," Camille spoke. "Let's get you out of these clothes and go home." Esme looked at her mother, stunned.

"But I didn't finish my breakfast."

"You'll eat when you get home!" Camille's tone was sharp, making Esme shrink as her mother let go of her. "where are her clothes!?" she demands glaring at Kate. Kate opened her mouth to speak when Rose entered the room.

"Mommy?" Kate looked at her, not just her, but Camille, Esme, Nolan, and the officers looked at the child.

"Rosy!" Kate walked past the Roth's going to her. "I thought I told you to stay in your room." Rose stared at the strangers before shrinking back clutching her mother's leg. Kate sighed, then with a sad smile, she said.

280

"Rosy. Esme has to go home now." Rose looked at her with surprise. "Why mommy?!"

"Because her mommy and daddy miss her." Rose looked at Esme, who watched her sadly.

"Can she stay with us?" Kate shook her head. "Can I come with her too?" she asks.

Kate shook her head sadly. Rose's eyes went glassy as she opened her mouth. **"I want to go with Esme!"** she sobs. Nolan and Camille watched Rose with shocked eyes. Kate picked up her child, before looking at Camille.

"I have her clothes." She says calmly. "*I'll go get them.*"

☙

Rose cried as Esme was dressed and carried away by the hand by her father. Nolan held Esme's bag pack that contained her books. Nolan's heart broke when he heard Rose's wails as she cried not for Esme to go. Camille was already inside the sheriff's car when Nolan stepped out into the sun clutching Esme's hand; the officers rolled out of the forest leaving the S.U. V that waited for Nolan. He turned to Kate.

"Thank you again for everything," Nolan spoke quietly. Kate nodded once but didn't look at him. Rose cried harder, making Nolan look down at the child, wanting to comfort her, but didn't want to expose his secret. Esme let go of his hand and hugged the child. The sheriffs says "Aww!" in the background.

"I'll come back," Esme spoke kindly. She looked at her father. "Can I, daddy?" Nolan hesitated.

"Of course, you can!" Kate spoke she kneeled and smiles. "It was nice having you, Esme. Please visit me again with your mommy and daddy." She adds.

Esme pulled from Rose and hugged Kate.

"Thank you," Esme spoke thickly.

And they left.

Chapter Twenty-nine

Nolan closed the door quietly to Esme's room with a sigh. Night had come once again upon the small town, putting a close to a long but relieving day full of happy screams, joyful tears, and hugs. Nolan smiled to himself at the thought of the grand entrance his daughter received by the staff who stood waiting patiently when he called them, alerting them of Esme's safe return. Nolan was touched by the reception when he got out of the police cruiser carrying Esme the way he used to when she was young. Esme beamed when she saw the maids and chefs crowd around her, their eyes wet with tears as they patted Esme's hair and cheeks. Esme was pampered for the rest of the day, spending time with her father and staff whom she considered her friends. Nolan smiled sadly.

I must have Esme have children her age. He thought wistfully. Nolan entered his office, only to freeze when he saw he was not alone. Camille sat on the large office chair behind the grand mahogany desk. Nolan's eyes narrowed as a frown pulled at the corners of his lips.

"Esme's asleep." He spoke. His voice was not kind as he closed the door behind him. Camille nodded, looking at him with an expression he never seen on his wife's face. He stepped forward.

"That's… good." She spoke, she squirmed on the chair. Nolan walked forward.

"What do you want, Camille?"

"I…" she trailed off.

"If you come to argue about dumping the wine in the sink, I don't care what you have to say." His voice was cold as he stopped at the other side of the desk. Camille grimaced.

"I'm not here to talk about that." she spoke. Nolan's eyes narrowed.

"Then what do you want?" A pause. They stared at one another, cold gray to her nervous green.

"Esme..." his eyes narrowed.

"What about her?" Camille bit her bottom lip before saying quietly, her eyes downcast.

"Esme does not like me." Nolan's eyes widen at that before they narrowed once more.

"Oh! You've noticed." He says dryly. Another pause. Camille gave him a pained look, her lip jutted. Nolan stared at her for a long moment before he sighed. Turning his back on her, he braced against his desk, arms crossed.

"I think it's safe to say she doesn't like any of us." Nolan murmured. Another pause.

Nolan finally looked at her to find Camille slump back in the large office chair.

"She didn't want to come near me." She whispers. "All she wanted was to be with the maids."

"If you're planning on getting rid of the staff, I won't let you!" she looked at him aghast.

"I wasn't planning to." He looked at Camille distrustfully. She looked away sadly. "I didn't realize how much I missed." Nolan stared at her, but inwardly he was surprised. He looked away.

"*I know.*" He whispers. "It wasn't... easy not hearing, not knowing where she was."

"Not just that." he looked at her. "I hadn't realized how much I've missed these past three..." she trailed off.

"*Years.*" Nolan finished. He saw her wince.

"I want to do something for her." Camille looked at him, eyes glassy. He looked down.

"You can't turn back time." He spoke. She nodded wordlessly. "If they could, I would buy the machine in an instant." He saw Camille half smile.

"You were a better parent to her." Nolan shook his head.

"I'd like to believe that, but I know I wasn't. I missed half her babyhood and now this..." he trailed off. "She still wants nothing to do with me." He remembered how Esme clung to the maids and chefs as if she was afraid of him.

"What can we do?" Camille asks. Nolan looked at her.

"She needs kids her age." He spoke. "People who would look out for her besides the maids, in case this happens again."

"You mean allies?" Nolan grimaced.

"I mean friends. Girls and boys, her age so that she has someone to go to instead of being alone." Camille nodded.

"I'll call the girls," Camille says. "We can have a play date and—"

"I'm not talking about your girlfriends." Nolan interrupts. "I mean people of the town, those friends. Our neighbors." Camille stared at him; he could see her frown.

"Those..." Nolan glared at her. She huffed. "Fine." Nolan nodded.

"Good. I won't separate Esme from what she needs. Not again." Nolan says firmly.

"But how are you going to get Esme to play with those urch—children?" She adds quickly. Nolan felt his chest burn, but he sighed.

"I don't know how." He admitted. "I'll make a few calls. Maybe we can have a party." Camille nodded eagerly. "But with this storm, it would take weeks until everything is cleaned up."

"Well, there is my way." Nolan looked at her.

"What's that?" he stared, seeing the glint in Camille's eyes, her old knowing smile returning.

"There's always Christmas."

Chapter Thirty

Millions of silver droplets of light enveloped the dark night that blanketed the small town as winter had finally come in the form of frosty air and warm sweaters. Laughter echoed through the town as people walked, chatted, and sang merrily of old songs that invited people to join in the peace and good will to all men.

Kate stood outside town hall, staring warily at the open door decorated in green and red as the sound of bells and children laughing echoed within the grand hall. Kate gripped the silver clasp that held her cloak; warding off the cold and nip of jack frost as she stared with apprehension at the wide door that lead to reproachful eyes and vile snickers. Why had she come?

She was fine. She had everything ready for the holiday. Kate had no intention of going out. But fate had other plans as an invitation. Inviting children of all ages to celebrate at town hall where songs will be sung, food to eat and the promise of Father Christmas to arrive with presents to all good little boys and girls. All Kate had to do was RSVP and join in on the festivities, but all that changed when she saw who was hosting the party.

Why had she said yes? Kate questioned this for weeks on end as she worked on her novel, cooked, cleaned, and took care of her…

Warmth gently squeezed Kate's cold hand. Kate looked down and saw her treasure dressed in a long red cloak, her eyes wide with wonder as she listened to the sound of carols singing within the large building, her face eager to join in the fun. Rose looked up at Kate, her brown eyes bright with curiosity and excitement.

That's what made her come. To see that little face beam with joy, to have a childhood not marked with the stain of the past. Kate smiled lovingly at her child. She gently squeezed the small hand in hers.

"Ready to have fun Rosy?" Kate asks. Rose nodded, grinning. Kate grinned before looking back at the open door. Taking a deep breath, she walked up the stairs to go inside.

℞

Bright lights, laughter and smiles swirled around Nolan as he was bombarded by grins, handshakes, and joy by the grateful people of the small town. For hours Nolan was confronted by people who praised him and his wife for all the good they had done for this year Christmas party: Nolan had took full control of the festivities, to celebrate not just the holiday but to allow this chance for Esme to know the community. Children came to Esme wanting to play with her, allowing Nolan to shake hands with his fellow town's folk while Camille chatted happily with the mayor's wife and Camille's rich girlfriends.

We really do run this town. Nolan thought his perfect smile was plastered for all to see as children laughed and played excitedly waiting for old Saint Nick to arrive.

"Nolan?!" a boisterous voice called making him turn to see his friends who he invited to the party. Nolan was soon swept up in deep conversation with peers as they talked about the party. He drank eggnog glancing from time to time at his wife and daughter, who played with the town's children.

This is better than expected. He thought, glancing at new and old faces, including… Nolan froze. Dark gray eyes widen as he saw Kate dressed in red; standing beside her was Rose, who looked excitedly but shyly at the crowd.

"Daddy! Daddy!?" Nolan started before looking down at Esme.

"Y-Yes honey." He says shakily.

"Ms. Starfield is here, and she brought Rose." says she. "Can I ask Rose to play with us?" Nolan didn't respond for two heartbeats before he nodded. "As long as it's alright with her mother." Esme nodded, and he ran her green dress swishing. Nolan was distracted for the next half hour. His eyes roamed as they looked for Kate; his heart thrummed at the thought of seeing her again after three long months as the town rebuild itself after the storm.

"Looking for me." An arm hooked under his, making Nolan look down at his wife, who was grinning her award-winning smile. Nolan mirrored her smile, but his mind was still on Kate as he and Camille spoke to the mayor and his friends.

"This is the finest Christmas party we had in years." Said the mayor. He looked at Nolan, grinning. "If you ever think about running for office, you have my support." He winked. Nolan smiled.

"Oh, no." Nolan says. "I have enough on my plate. I don't want to deal with politics." Everyone laughed except Camille.

"You'll make a great politician, Nolan." says his friend.

"Yes," Said Camille, giving Nolan a look. "Why don't you?!" Nolan could hear the accusation in her voice, though it was cool. "You have allies who would support you." Nolan opened his mouth to speak when he saw Kate heading to the food table. Nolan chuckled as he surreptitiously pulled from his wife.

"If I ran for mayor, then I'll end up with grays all over my head." Everyone laughed, including the mayor. "Now if you'll excuse me, I'm going to get more eggnog." With a smile, he walked forward, ignoring the invisible daggers on his back that came from his wife.

Kate held her empty cup as she stood on the long, massive table that held food and drinks; her eyes landed on the large punch bowl that contained rich creamy eggnog. Kate reached for the silver handle and lifted a ladleful of the drink before pouring it into her cup.

"*It's good.*" Kate paused to bring the cup to her lips as she heard the familiar voice. Slowly, she turned to face the person who came with the voice. Nolan stood half a foot behind her, his eyes wide, as if stunned he spoke aloud. In his right hand held an empty cup with the frothy remnants of the eggnog still inside. She turned her gaze back to Nolan before looking down.

"So, I heard." She spoke. Nolan started at her voice. His heart gave a pang but not of pain as he stared at the woman, her long hair wavy as it fell down her back; her face, smooth, shining, not frightened or even gaunt like the last time he remembered her; right here at the very steps of town hall, she looked… *Beautiful.*

Kate walked away.

"Wait!" Kate stopped before looking at him, face wary when he adds. "Please, don't leave on my account." Kate didn't respond for several seconds making Nolan pulse quicken with nerves. He racked his brain to find something to say. Kate took this moment to look at the crowd of running children and chatting adults.

"Your hosting this party." She spoke, her voice neutral. It wasn't a question. Nolan nodded.

"Yes." Kate nodded before lifting the cup to her lips and sipped. Her eyes lit up as she tasted the sweet eggnog, thick and frothy on top with a pinch of cinnamon that floated on white foam.

"Y-You like it?" Nolan, who had watched her every movement, asked. Kate pulled the cup from her lips, looking down at the lip where red lipstick was shown on the cup. Not looking at Nolan, she replied.

"Yes. It's delicious," She paused. *"Thank you."* Nolan nodded. He too took a ladleful of the nog into his empty cup, before taking a sip. The two adults watched as the people interacted.

"How is Esme?" Kate asks quietly. Nolan looked at her, startled.

"Great!" he spluttered. "E-Essie is doing great better than great she's…" he trailed off. Kate nodded.

"That's good." Kate murmured. "I was worried about her, especially after…" she stopped. Nolan lowered his cup, looking down wistfully.

"We're all trying to move past this." He whispers. Kate nodded again.

"She was afraid you would be angry at her." Nolan sighs.

"I figured as much." He let out a breath. "It wasn't easy when she was gone, not knowing, expecting the worse."

"I understand." Nolan looked to see Kate watching him, a faint smile on her lips. Nolan smiled weakly.

"This party's for her." He admitted. "I want Esme to feel safe. To have the town look out for her." Kate nodded before looking away.

"She needs interaction."

"She does. She needs to be with children her age to have fun. To get dirty once in a while." Nolan spoke. Kate didn't respond but nodded once. The two looked to where the children played, watching as Esme was playing ring around the rosy with Rose and the other children.

"*She's beautiful.*" Nolan whispered. Kate looked at him, puzzled.

"Who is?" Nolan looked down sadly, fist to his chest.

"*Rose.*" Kate looked at him with surprise before she looked down, a tender smile on her lips.

"She is." Kate whispered. A pause.

"How is she?" Nolan looked at Kate with pain in his eyes.

"She's good." Kate replies. Nolan nodded once.

"I'm glad after seeing her cry…" he trailed off eyes stinging.

"*I know.*" Kate breathes. "Rosy cried herself to sleep after Esme left. She had grown attached to her." Nolan nodded. "I'm sorry." He started.

"Sorry!? F-For what?" Kate gripped her dress.

"*I'm sorry about… your son.*" Nolan stared at her with surprise. Watching the woman, he gravely wronged apologize to him. His eyes turned glassy as his chest burned.

"*Thank you.*" he spoke thickly. Kate nodded. "It hasn't been easy these past three…" Kate nodded again.

"Esme told me a lot of things during her stay." It was Nolan's turn to nod, his eyes downcast.

"She has been alone for too long." Nolan breathes. "I want to change that for her sake." Kate nodded quietly.

"She needs you," Kate spoke matter of fact. "You and Camille." Nolan grimaced.

"Mommy!" The two looked up to see Rose and Esme run forward, hand in hand.

"Daddy! Guess what!?" Esme chirped.

"What is it, Essie?" he asks with a smile as Rose went to her mother, who picked her up.

"Mommy Santa's coming!" Rose squealed. Kate beamed.

"Really?!" she says.

"Uh huh," says Esme, "mommy said he's coming with gifts."

"That's great!" says Nolan.

"Mommy said you'll be handing out the gifts." Nolan was surprised by this, but his smile was in check, as he says.

"I'll be glad to help Santa." Esme nodded.

"C'mon Rosy, let's go play in the bouncy castle."

"Okay." Kate put her down.

"Have fun, you two!" she says. The two girls nodded, waving.

"Okay mommy! Bye Esme daddy." Rose called before running away.
Nolan froze.

Time seemed to slow as he stared at the two little girls. His chest gave a sharp pang, making him involuntarily clutch it as he watched them go. Kate didn't notice Nolan's sudden distress. Instead, she walked away, leaving a pained Nolan, alone, as he watched his two girls play.

⑃

The rest of the party was a merry affair. People ate, chatted, laughed as children played tag and hide and go seek.

Kate and Nolan watched all this in a different point of view: Nolan being in the center of it all, while Kate hung in the distance, watching alone as the town's folk smile cheerily amongst each other. Kate closed her eyes.

"Kate?" Kate opened her eyes to see a woman.

"M-Mrs. Paige!" Kate spoke. The old innkeeper of the bed & breakfast smiled down at Kate warmly: her hair had turned silver and she looked grayer in the face, but her blue eyes were clear and kind as she gazed at Kate.

"May I sit down?" she asks. Kate was stunned for a few seconds before she said hastily.

"Yes, of course!" The old matron sat down. It was then Kate noticed she was holding a cane.

"How are you, my dear?" Mrs. Paige asks. Kate turned her attention back to her.

"I'm fine ma'am and you?"

"Not at the very best, but well enough, and you? I haven't spoken to you in so long. It's been what? Four years?"

"Actually," Kate corrected. "It's been six."

"Oh, my! How time flies! I see you every time you come to town with your daughter."

"I see you too sometimes at the supermarket," Kate says with a nod. Mrs. Paige nodded, smiling.

Nolan observed the festivities with vague interest as he watched Kate talking to the old owner of the bed & breakfast. He smiled tenderly seeing the matron pat Kate's shoulder before looking away, only to jump when he saw Camille watching him with narrowed eyes.

"What are you staring at?" she demands. Nolan opened his mouth to speak when a chorus of screams made them turn to see a tall, heavy-set man dressed in red and white.

"Santa!" all the children screamed, looking up from their play. Nolan smiled, grateful for the distraction.

"That's my cue." He says cheerfully. Nolan kissed Camille on the cheek before loping forward to the crowd, that surrounded Santa Claus. Camille watched him go with suspicion. She turned her gaze to where Nolan once stood before they narrowed to slits.

The celebration went off without a hitch. Children, young and old, came and sat with the hallmark of Christmas cheer. Santa clause smiled fatherly as children asked for gifts before being photographed by a professional photographer. Nolan smiled as he handed gifts wrapped in holiday paper, listening to the children ask for toys, video games, and electronics.

Christmas is sure not the same as it was in my time. Nolan thought as he handed a gift to a boy of seven years old, waving goodbye. He and Santa smiled.

"Next!" someone called. Nolan looked at the next child and froze when he saw Rose. Nolan stared spellbound as the child walked to Santa, who picked her up.

"*Ho! Ho! Ho!*" says Santa. Rose beamed at the man; her brown eyes sparkled with awe. Nolan broke from the spell and tried to smile as Santa asked her name and age. Nolan turned his back, going to the gifts.

"So, Rose, what would you like for Christmas?" Nolan waited to expect to hear her say toys.

"I want a daddy for Christmas." Nolan turned slowly from picking up a silver gift to stare wide eyed at the child. Santa clause who paused, surprised by the request let out a kind, "Ho! Ho! Ho!"

"Now that is a request I never heard before." He says. "Why do you want a daddy for Christmas?" Nolan saw Rose look up to stare at him before looking back at Santa.

"Because my friends have daddies." She replies.

"Ah." Said Santa. nodding. "Do you know your daddy?"

"No," Rose replies. "I ask my mommy can I have a daddy, but then she gets sad. I think my mommy doesn't know how to get one. I want a daddy to play with me and take me to the park." Nolan listened as the child went on hearing her wants, not just for herself, but for her mother, who always looked 'sad' when she sees other daddies. Nolan's eyes stung as he watched Santa talk patiently with his child: his words were kind, but underneath the words, could not make Rose's wish come true.

Nolan stepped forward with a big box.

"You have a Merry Christmas, Rose." Said Santa. Rose nodded, smiling as she took the box from Nolan.

"*Thank you.*" She says. Nolan smiled sadly at the child as she was given her picture before hopping off Santa and going to her mother, who waited to the side where other parents stood.

Chapter Thirty-one

The metropolis of downtown was vibrant and bright, illuminating the darkness. Nolan sat in the meeting room of his office, listening as his workers and clientele spoke over the past months; business charts were shown on PowerPoint presentations of the budget graphs as pie charts showed the slow increase of Nolan's company after years of stress after the collapse of the economy. Nolan listened, but his mind was on other things that didn't involve the future of his company.

"Mr. Roth?!" Nolan started.

"Yes?" he spoke.

"We wanted to get your take on these files." Nolan's meeting went on with him reading files, signing documents, and shaking hands. Nolan watched the party of businessmen file out, talking amongst themselves.

"Did you hear?" Someone says. "There's going to be a big snowstorm tonight."

Nolan rose to his feet, picking up his briefcase as he did; saying goodnight to his comrades, he left. The sky was gray when Nolan entered the parking lot alone, his stomach twisted, his head ached after being in so many meetings. For a moment, Nolan wondered if he was coming down with something as he entered his car and drove out of the lot.

Nolan drove through downtown. The nightlife of the cityscape hurt his eyes, making him yearn for the dark quietness of Forest-Bend. His mind felt cloudy as he turned, making his way out of the city and onto the highway. His stomach grumbled at meals missed: he had no appetite with the day's stressful meetings and the past weeks into the new year. He hadn't taken any time for himself.

"Guess it's time for a vacation." He muses aloud. But the thought didn't send a thrill of pleasure like it used to. Mainly because he had to plan his trip with… Nolan's hand gripped the steering wheel hard. No, he could not bear that. Nolan forced himself to relax as he drove out of the highway to the countryside; in fifteen minutes, he would be greeted by his maids, sitting down to a large, expensive gourmet meal whereas Camille prattled with her girlfriends who happily had forgiven her after her three-year absence. Nolan sighed, only to notice a change on the edges of his vision becoming blurry as his stomach that gurgled with hunger now twisted with nausea.

I'm getting sick! He thought, horrified. Nolan stopped the car on the side of the road. Thankfully, it was late at night, so no cars honked or curse him.

Nolan parked the car and groaned, resting his head on the wheel. He panted, his vision blurred in and out as a sweat slicked his forehead. Nolan's heart stuttered as he took in air, trying frantically to gain control. He closed his eyes, listening to the still night of January. Snow was coming soon to the small town; in a matter of hours, the town would be buried in white, and he would be trapped in his car sick or…

Nolan raised his head from the wheel, his eyes focused just enough for him to see the familiar road. He was too far from town and in his condition. Nolan turned his head and saw a mailbox in the darkness. Breathing shallowly, he made out a decline that led to… Nolan started the car.

⟆

Kate sat quietly in the living room as the fire crackled in the small fireplace. Heat filled the small space, making it cozy for the young author as she scribbled quietly on her latest project. Kate had spent the evening quietly after tucking Rose into bed after a dinner of Chinese food. Stomach full, Kate snuggled on her sofa with her lap desk and started writing her latest book baby. Kate was so deeply immersed in her work she almost didn't hear the quiet knock on her door. Kate looked up with a start. Glancing quickly at her wall clock to see saw it was after eleven.

Who could be here this night? She thought in wonder. The knock came again. Kate turned her head for the hallway, making sure that Rose didn't stir before getting up. Placing her lap desk on the coffee table, Kate got up and walked warily to the door. Flicking on the outdoor flood light she peered through her new keyhole. Her eyes widen, just as a voice said:

"*Kate?*" Kate stepped back. She hesitated for half a second before lunging at the door.

Nolan heard the clicks as the door unlocked. He waited patiently in the darkness, shivering in the cold night. The door opened, and he saw her, Kate, dressed in her flowing nightgown. She stood in the light; her face was full of surprise.

"Nolan?" she gasps. Nolan tried to smile, but it came out as a pained grimace.

"Kate." He whispers.

"What are you doing here?" she gasps. Nolan closed his eyes.

"*I need your help.*" He spoke weakly.

☙

The soft peel of a whistle pierced the silent kitchen where Kate stood by the stove, turning it off as quickly as possible so as not to wake her daughter. Kate lifted the whistling kettle before walking to the counter where a small teapot sat open revealing a mesh tea strainer that contained dried mint leaves.

Kate poured hot water into the small teapot, filling it all the way before placing the silent kettle back on the stove. Closing the teapot with the lid, she allowed the leaves to steep.

She was about to get some honey when a beep made her turn to her table. Nolan huddled in on himself. A warm blanket covered him, keeping him warm. He had watched Kate silently despite his blurry vision with quiet wonder when he jumped at the beeping sound that came from him. He looked down to see a white digital thermometer in his mouth. Kate stepped forward, face calm despite the gloom of the dark kitchen. Without a word, Nolan opened his mouth allowing Kate to take out and read the thermometer.

"102.4 degrees." She announced. Nolan nodded, then sighed. Kate looked at him as she turned off the device.

He looks so small. She thought. A gentle smile pulled at the corners of her mouth when she heard another beeping; this time coming from her microwave. Kate walked to the microwave and opened it, pulling out a steaming bowl of wonton soup. She placed a spoon in front of Nolan, who, after a moment's hesitation, picked up the spoon and began to eat. Kate turned, going back to the fridge. Nolan sipped his soup, feeling the warm broth fill his empty stomach. He felt his body relax as he lifted another spoonful into his mouth.

"Nolan?" he looked up to see Kate holding a plate full of food. "Is this too much?" he squinted at the plate seeing fried rice, chicken, and spareribs. His mouth watered.

"*No*," he spoke hoarsely, "*it's enough*." Kate nodded before placing it in the microwave to heat. While he ate, Kate lifted the teapot and mug and brought it to the table; pouring him a cup of warm mint tea, Kate watched Nolan as he ate; seeing him eat a wonton was heartening to her as she lifted a hand to his forehead. Nolan jumped, looking at her with surprise.

"Do you still have a headache?" she asks. Nolan, shocked by Kate's touch, nodded. "How about your eyes?"

"It's… it's still fuzzy." Kate nodded.

"I'll get you a cool compress." Without a word, she picked up the thermometer and left the room. Nolan looked down at his soup wearily, lifting a spoon he picked up a wonton and place it in his mouth; chewing mechanically, he closed his eyes.

He was so tired.

Something cold made him open his eyes. He jerked up with a gasp to look at Kate, who placed a cool gel patch on his forehead.

"Sorry," Kate spoke. Nolan shivered at the cold compress but nodded.

"It's… it's all right." He spoke. Kate pulled away. "It's so… cold." Kate smiles faintly.

"That's how it's supposed to be." Nolan lifted a hand to his head feeling a soft gel-like patch, that seemed to dull the fever; he lowered his hand as Kate walked to the microwave, he lifted the bowl to his lips and drank the rest of the broth. Nolan was just reaching for his mug of tea when Kate placed the food in front of him.

"Thank you," he spoke. Kate nodded before sitting down. Nolan could not help noticing she sat far across from him. He frowned inwardly before eating his meal.

The room was silent as the two adults sat. Nolan ate readily, feeling his appetite return, filling his stomach with warmth. He drank the tea that was sweetened with honey; by the time he placed the cup down, he had finished his meal.

"Thank you." Nolan spoke gratefully, looking at Kate with gratitude. Kate nodded.

"You're welcome." Kate whispered. She didn't look at him. Nolan looked down as he wrapped an arm around his waist. "How are you feeling?"

"Tired." His eyes half closed. Kate looked at him then.

"You're welcome to stay here for the night." She spoke. Nolan looked at her then.

"You've already done enough for me, Kate." He says. "I won't intrude on your hospitality any further."

"You're not intruding." She spoke slowly.

"I came to your house, uninvited. You've given me so much for someone who doesn't deserve it."

Silence. Kate looked at him sadly. Nolan rose to his feet. He would have walked out if he hadn't staggered. Kate caught him before he fell. Without a word, she guided him to the living room. There she sat Nolan down on the sofa. Nolan groaned.

"What's wrong with me?" he moans. Kate helped lay him down on the sofa, pulling off his shoes.

"Sleep Nolan." She whispers; she placed the red blanket on him.

"I'm sorry," Nolan spoke groggily. "I don't…" he trailed off, eyes half closed. Kate looked at him gently. She placed a hand on his forehead. "Sleep." She whispers. Nolan watched her weakly before closing his eyes…

He fell asleep.

Chapter Thirty-two

Nolan woke up to the smell of bacon. He stirred slowly on his bed, thinking that the maids had carried up his breakfast and left on a tray by his bedside. Nolan started awake when he heard a loud beeping sound. He bolted up, his eyes popping open as he looked up to see a red blanket that covered his feet. Surprised and confusion overtook him. Where was he? Nolan blinked the sleepiness away as he lifted a hand to his forehead to feel something soft and... he pulled it off his head; looking down, he saw it was a blue gel patch.

Wh-What? He thought.

The sound of sizzling made him turn his head to see a small fireplace, unlit, the logs blackened by... comprehension flooded through Nolan as last night came back: work, business meetings, driving home, the storm, his sickness... Kate. Nolan looked down at himself. He was half covered in the red blanket that had slipped off showing his undershirt. Nolan stared as he remembered Kate, seeing her as she took him in, giving him food and shelter as she nursed his fever.

Nolan lifted the back of his hand to his forehead again. It was still warm, but not as hot as he remembered. He lowered his hand and stared across at him, surprise and relieved that he could see again. Nolan smiled to himself.

BEEP! BEEP!

Nolan turned his head, hearing the sound that woke him as well as the strong smell of... his stomach rumbled under his shirt. Nolan looked down to check his smartwatch but was surprised to not see it on his wrist. Worry crept into Nolan when he looked down on the coffee table to find not only his smartwatch but his phone and wallet; beside them was a portable writing desk and a copy of a novel. Curious, Nolan kicked his feet from off the chair and picked it up.

"'*A Lonely Love*.'" He read quietly. He looked down at the author's name. Nolan's eyes widen as he saw Kate's name on print. He stared at the cover to see a woman dressed in white, her back turned to the world as she stood in a forest. Nolan stared at the cover with wonder. He opened the book.

CLANG!

Nolan looked up with a start, worried for Kate. Putting the book down, he got to his feet and walked for the kitchen. Nolan stood by the wall, he stopped at mid-step to see Kate making breakfast: a large frying pan, that had caused the noise was in the sink. Kate's back was turned to him as she worked quietly, taking out waffles from out the waffle iron before placing them on a plate that had a couple already stacked. Nolan watched her quietly, a gentle smile on his face.

"Mommy!" Nolan started. He turned his head to see Rose enter the other side of the kitchen. Kate looked down at her and smiled.

"Good morning, Rosy!" she cooed. Rose says, "Good morning," before looking at Nolan.

"Hi Esme's daddy!" Kate started. She whirled around to see Nolan who looked with surprise at Rose before looking at her face growing red under his skin. *Chagrined*.

"H-Hi." He breathes. Kate stared at him for a few seconds before she whispered.

"Hi." Nolan didn't know what else to say. Kate smiled kindly.

"Why don't you sit down, Rosy." Kate says. "And I'll bring breakfast for you and Mr. Roth." Rose nodded and walked forward. Nolan didn't move, unsure how to proceed.

"You can sit here." Kate gestured with a nod to a chair across from Rose. "O-Okay." He breathes. He walked forward, legs suddenly stiff, as if he didn't know how to use them. Nolan sat down as Kate carried a plate of bacon, eggs, and waffles. Nolan watched as Kate served the food, first serving Rose, then him, before finally herself. Nolan looked down.

"Nolan?" he looked up surprised. Kate was watching him with concern.

"Are you alright?" Rose watched him as she ate her eggs.

"Mommy? Why is Esme's daddy at our house?" she asks. Nolan started. Kate looked at her child.

"Because Esme's daddy wasn't feeling well last night." Kate explains. Nolan's eyes widen.

"He was sick?"

"Yes." Rose looked at Nolan.

"Is he going to be better?" Nolan was surprised to hear the sad tone in the child's voice. Kate looked at Nolan.

"I… I am better." Nolan spoke he tried to smile. "I'm not sick anymore, Rose. Your mother took very good care of me." He looked at Kate as he says this.

"Eat your breakfast, Rosy." Kate breathes; she cleared her throat quietly.

"Okay!" Rose chirped.

Nolan looked at the child with a tender smile. He looked back at Kate, who ate silently. Nolan lifted his fork and started to eat.

℘

Outside the window, snow pelted on cold glass. Old man winter made his presence known upon the forest as mother nature slept. But opposite the cold glass was warmth. Protective and inviting. Nolan watched with quiet awe at the small world he was transported to. Seeing Kate and Rose as they lived was an experience he had wondered about and dreamed during his lonely moments. Never in his life had he thought he would experience it. After breakfast, to which Nolan enjoyed; Kate let Rose play on her tablet while she cleared the dishes. Leaving Nolan alone with Kate.

"How are you feeling?" Nolan started. Kate's back was turned to him as she placed the dishes in the sink.

"Good," He hesitated. "Actually, I feel great." Kate turned to face him.

"No headache or blurry vision?" Nolan shook his head. Kate walked forward and placed a hand on his head. He gasped quietly, surprised again that she was willingly touching him.

"You don't feel as hot as before." She noted. Kate eyed him. "I'll check your temperature just in case, but you look better than you did last night." Nolan looked at her before looking down.

"Well enough to go home?" His voice sounded glum, even to him. Kate pulled her hand from his forehead, surprised.

"In this storm!" Nolan looked at her. "Nolan, you can't go out there! Not with this blizzard!" Nolan stared before turning his head to the window. Sure enough, snow fell in waves outside the glass pane. He shuddered. Kate took that as assent. She nodded.

"You can stay here with us until the storm passes." She replies resolutely. Nolan nodded, surprised by her tone of command. Kate walked to the sink and started washing.

307

The rest of the day was uneventful, but Nolan was awed by everything, as he spent it with Kate and Rose. Rose was shy at first coming to him, being used to her mother, Emily, and her family. Nolan noticed this, so wanting to break the distance between her, he showed her his smartwatch, to which Rose slowly warmed to him by asking questions. Nolan was awed by her inquisitive nature. The child was very smart for her age: she could tell stories from books she read so perfectly and draw pictures of whatever she saw with such authenticity that he wondered if she had lessons.

"No," Kate says with a smile. "Rose is just naturally talented." Nolan, enthralled by his daughter's accomplishments peppered Rose with questions, that she answers with a bright smile; it was then Kate revealed her daughter attended a special school for gifted children.

"She can read at a fifth-grade level," Kate explains. Nolan's eyes bugged wide when he heard that, making Rose laugh as Kate rose to her feet.

"Who's ready to make cookies?!" she says.

"Me! Me!" Rose squealed. Kate smiled, adding she had to set up the kitchen to make the cookies. She left the living room, leaving Rose and Nolan, who watched the child with a soft smile.

"What cookies are you making, Rosy?" he asks. Rose opened her mouth, then hesitated.

"Um, I don't know." She admitted. "But my mommy makes the best."

"I never had your mommies' cookies before." Her eyes widen.

"Wow!" she breathes. "I thought everybody in the world had them." Nolan chuckles just as Kate called Rose, saying, "she's ready." Nolan got to his feet.

"I want to see how your mommy makes them." Rose beamed and nodded. Involuntarily, Nolan lifted his hands to Rose and picked her up. Rose squealed with joy, saying: "You're strong!" Nolan smiles his chest puffed with pride as he walked to the kitchen.

Nolan sat and watched Kate and Rose with a gentle smile. It was a dream he didn't want to wake up from as he observed mother and child cream butter with sugar, beat in eggs, flavorings, flour, and baking levelers for the different cookie doughs.

"What's this?" Nolan asks when Kate placed a box full of different varieties of chocolate chips. He lifted a bag and read the label. "Toffee bits." Kate measured the chocolate chips before pouring them into the dough.

"I forgot I had those." She says, stirring the dough.

"I never saw them before or this—" he lifted another bag—"Cinnamon chips. Where did you get them?"

"I bought them in New York two months ago," Nolan nodded. "would you like cinnamon chips in the cookies?" he hesitated.

"Umm… I-I never had it before."

"Mommy?" Rose asks. "Can Esme's daddy help too?" Nolan blinked. Kate smiled.

"Sure. He can put the cinnamon chips and toffee pieces in the oatmeal cookies." Kate says. Nolan did his best with the cookies, stirring the chips and toffee pieces carefully; his hands felt awkward not use to mixing, scooping, and shaping the dough as he placed them on cookie sheets lined with parchment paper. Kate smiled at his awkwardness as Rose talked merrily. Kate placed the first two batches of cookies in the oven before cleaning up the dirty dishes.

"Where's Esme?" Rose asks Nolan. Nolan smiled.

"She's spending the night at a friend's house." He says.

"Oh! Like a sleepover!?" Nolan nodded.

"She won't be home until tomorrow."

"Can she come here and play with me?" Nolan hesitated. Kate, who heard everything, turned and spoke up.

"I don't think she can. Not in this storm."

"Aww!" Rose looked down, crestfallen. Nolan's heart gave a twinge seeing Rose sad. Nolan lifted a hand and placed it atop her head.

"Why don't you come to Esme's birthday party." Kate stopped washing to look at him wide eyed, but his eyes were on Rose, who looked at him with surprise.

"Birthday party?" he nodded.

"Esme is turning nine and I know she would be glad to see you, Rosy." He looked at Kate. "If that's alright with your mother." He adds kindly. "I would be honored if you and Rose came." Rose's eyes were wide with wonder. She looked at her mother as Kate looked at Nolan.

"Can we mommy?" Rose asked. Kate hesitated. She looked from her daughter to Nolan and back; her pulse raced, but her voice was quiet as she said.

"We'll see."

☙

Night had finally arrived in the woods, putting an end to the day blizzard that swept across the forest. Nolan leaned back on the sofa with half-closed eyes; a loving smile on his lips as he patted the back of his little girl, who stared sleepily at the roaring fire. Kate sat on a plump toile chair scribbling quietly on her lap desk. She looked up quietly to see the two people on her sofa. Warmth filled her chest as she closed her journal

310

revealing a leather cover. She smiled sadly, tracing the pads of her fingers on the etched design of the scarlet book. Kate turned her head to the large wall clock that read eight o'clock. Lifting a compartment of the lap desk she placed her journal and pen inside before closing it softly. Nolan opened his eyes, turning to see Kate stretched and groaned quietly before getting up.

"Time for bed, Rosy." Kate whispered. Rose didn't respond. Nolan looked down, surprised to see Rose fallen asleep on his lap.

"*I-I can put her to bed.*" He whispers softly. Kate shook her head before lifting her up with ease.

"I have to change her into her nightgown." She replies. She hesitated before adding. "I won't be long." Nolan nodded before looking back at the fireplace, feeling the warmth as the longs crackled and popped.

"Nolan?" Nolan turned his head to see Kate.

"Yes?"

"Would you like some hot chocolate?" Nolan hesitated, surprised, before nodding. Kate nodded and left the room. Nolan returned his gaze back to the fire before he closed his eyes.

03

The smell of chocolate filled the room. Quiet sipping and munching of cookies were the silent conversation between Kate and Nolan who sat on the sofa, apart from one another. Kate's foot was tucked in under her blanket as she gazed at the crackling fire. Nolan sat listening to the pleasant silence; his body felt warm as he listened to the fire, his hand held his cup of delicious homemade hot chocolate with cinnamon marshmallows.

Nolan stared at the flames, but it was a distraction as he glanced on and off at Kate; seeing her eat a cookie, sipping her drink. Nolan found himself captivated by her.

"Yes?" Nolan started. Kate turned her head to look at him calmly. "Is there something you need?" Nolan shook his head. "Is something wrong with the hot chocolate?"

"N-No," he says as he looked down at his steaming mug. "I-It's delicious," He took a sip, tasting the sweet yet spicy kick in the back of his throat as it went down. "The cinnamon's strong." He adds. "It's *spicy*." Kate blinked, then comprehension came to her.

"That's because I added a pinch of cayenne pepper." Nolan gaped at her. "Y-You did! But why?!" Kate half smiles.

"When I was experimenting on making hot chocolate. I decided to try something different. So, I added cayenne along with nutmeg and cinnamon." She shrugged. "I like how it tasted, but I never give it to Rose. She has her own hot chocolate mix." Nolan nodded, looking at his cup.

"It's unique." He replies. He took another drink before licking his lips. "I like it." Kate nodded before looking away back at the fireplace.

Nolan stared at her silently, seeing how the firelight glowed on her brown skin. Nolan saw as her eye's half closed; her body leaned on the arm of the chair: she was so close but yet so far away. Goodbye were the days when they talked on a night like this before. It was all… Nolan's chest gave a throb.

"Kate?" he whispers. Kate turned her head once more. Nolan had hunched in his shoulders, his hand on the mug's handle tightened.

312

"Nolan?" Kate spoke with concern. "are you alright?" Nolan shook his head. "is it your head? Are you—"

"No!" Nolan looked at her, his eyes glassy as he stared at the woman he hurt so terribly. "Kate, are you at peace?" Kate stared. "Are you happy? After all I've done? Are you at peace?" Kate stared, her eyes wide at the question, seeing Nolan's pained face as he stared at her with agonized eyes. Kate placed her mug on the table. The distraction allowed her to look away. Nolan's heart gave a painful squeeze.

"How?!" she looked at him, "how can you do this?! How can you sit here and be this way? After all I've done! After all I put you through. How can you still be so kind to me?" Kate looked at him for a long time, so long that Nolan wondered if she even heard him.

"I don't know." She breathes. Nolan didn't answer, just stared.

"How did you do it?" Nolan finally asked. "How did you make it? Your reputation was ruined. You had no friends to turn to. The town despised you! You were an outcast, all for nothing!" Nolan watched her with pain and grief. "How can you sit here knowing the truth about what I am, and still have the compassion to treat me like an equal?" Kate had looked away as he spoke his lament, *his…* "how can you live with your head held high for a crime you didn't commit?" Kate grimaced.

"*I don't know.*" Nolan placed his cup down and buried his face in his hands. Kate watched him silently before looking away.

"*You are not happy,*" Kate whispered. It wasn't a question. Nolan lifted his head.

"How can I be happy?" he spoke in a low voice. "How can I be happy with a town that smiles at me every day? To be greeted with warm handshakes, pats

313

on the back and inviting grins, knowing that my smiles are fake, my hands are numb, and my back is heavy with the weight of a seven-year crime. Not to my wife, *but to you.* How can I wake up each day knowing you have to suffer; that my own child had to suffer for the wrong I have done, as my wife dangles the key, preventing you from being set free from her malice?" Kate winced looking down, placing a hand on her chest.

"*I didn't suffer much,*" Kate whispered.

"But you still suffered." He shot to his feet. "I've known. For six long years, I've known what Camille's done," Kate didn't answer "you went through hell and all I did was let it happen. I believed everything she told me and I... **I let it happen**!!" Nolan nearly shouted.

"*Shh*!" she hisses. "You'll wake Rosy!" Nolan, who had opened his mouth, gasping, closed it. Looking with alarm, he turned to the hallway. Kate followed his gaze before sighing. She pushed back her hair.

"Yes," Kate admitted. "all this you've done and more. I have suffered, greatly so... Because of you and your wife." Nolan looked at her wordlessly. Kate didn't look at him. Instead, she picked up her book and started flipping through the pages idly.

"Why?" she looked at him. Nolan's face was ashen, his gray eyes somber. "Why did you let me stay? You could have cast me out last night. Let karma take its course as it did to me for years. You knew I had a home, but I came here. Twice. After you told me to never come back... *Why did you*?" Kate stared at him for a long time before she looked away.

"I don't know," she breathes. "I just, you seemed so..."

"What?" she didn't answer for a moment.

"Tired." Kate finally spoke. "Since I've known you, you were always well off. You were healthy, but now… after the incident." She winced. "You feel that the entire world is crushing you down and you're barely able to hold it up, much less yourself… I guess I wanted to give you a sanctuary from all this; that for one night you can feel normal instead of what you pretend to be." Kate looked at him. Nolan stared at her sadly, his shoulders that were tensed went lax. Nolan opened his mouth to speak… something wet slid down his cheek.

"How did you get past this?" he whispers. "All those people, Camille's friends…" Kate closed her eyes.

"I didn't," She whispers, "every day I still carry the burden. I am still labeled as a home-wrecker, a 'Cinderwhora.'" Nolan shuddered. "But I've made friends as the years' past. Friends who have become family to me and Rose." She whispers. People have forgotten about my faults, my naïve fling," She half smiles, "some have apologized for their actions toward me." Nolan looked down. "But it doesn't change the fact I'm still not welcome. I am still an outcast." Nolan raised his head, eyes wet with tears.

"I'm truly sorry for what I've done to you." he breathes. Kate looked at him with a sad but genuine smile. Kate patted the sofa.

"It's getting late." She spoke, rising to her feet. Nolan nodded. Kate picked up the plates and empty cups as Nolan sat on the sofa.

"Did you mean it?" Nolan started looking at her. "Is Rose invited to Esme's party?"

"Yes." Nolan breathes. Kate nodded.

>*"Then she'll be there."*

Chapter Thirty-three

Pink and white balloons fluttered merrily to the ground around Nolan's feet. He smiled, staring at the large, decorated party room. Crystal stones dangled above the ceiling, creating facets of light dance; making the room glow as they swung lightly in the breeze. The clicking of hard heels on marble came behind Nolan, who didn't turn but sensed his wife before warm hands entwined into his own.

"You're easy to sneak up on." She purrs hot in his ear. Nolan didn't respond. Instead, he slowly turned his head to face his wife, dressed in fine attire for her guests.

"Is everything ready?" he asks.

"Ready as it'll ever be." Camille shrugged. "Nikki and Joyce just arrived, and Esme is playing with Max and Fae." Nolan nodded.

"Good. I want everything to be perfect for Esme." He says. Camille opened her mouth when the door opened, and Esme came running into the hall.

"Mommy! Daddy!" Esme cries. Nolan smiled.

"What is it, Essie?" He asks.

"Everyone's here!" she squealed. Nolan grinned.

"Oh!" squealed Camille. "I'll go see if the other girls came." She started walking when Esme says:

"Ms. Starfield and Rosy are here too."

Kate stood in the grand foyer, looking with great awe at the main house. Rose stood watching the children as they ran around whilst the parents, mostly mothers, chatted merrily in large groups.

Everything was just as she remembered. The large brown door to the grand staircase that led to rooms of state and comfort. Had it been seven years that Kate stepped foot here? Seven years when she was inexperienced. Working a job, she loved by day to her career she adored by night: back when her life wasn't full of secrets; when truth was whispered by the man who held her hand, promising a new world. Kate closed her eyes.

"Ms. Starfield!" Kate opened her eyes. Rose, who was holding her hand, let go to run and hug Esme, who had arrived. Kate hesitated when she saw Camille and Nolan walk forward. She hung back as Rose and Esme hugged, jumping up and down, giggling.

"You made it." Nolan spoke, his smile warm. Kate nodded. She smiled weakly.

"Yes." Camille spoke voice low. Kate looked at her calmly, her pulse quicken but her words were polite.

"Thank you for inviting me and Rose." She smiles down at the two girls.

"Rose was so excited to come to the party." Rose pulled away from Esme to point to her mother.

"See! We got you a birthday present." She chirped. Kate smiles kindly to Esme, she stepped forward Camille stepped back with a frightened expression, but Kate merely bent down holding a large silver box, this she handed to Esme with a "Happy Birthday!" Esme took the box with a "Thank you." before beaming at her father, who smiles down at Kate.

"Why don't you put your gifts with the other presents, Essie," Nolan suggests. "You, Rose, and the other children can play while the grownups talk."

317

"Okay, daddy." She says. "C'mon Rosy." Rose nodded before running with Esme.

"Be good Rosy!" Kate called.

"Okay, mommy!" called Rose. Kate watched her daughter go with quiet worry seeing her as children laughed and waved at Esme while Rose was encircled by them. She looked down.

"She'll be fine." Kate looked to see Nolan and Camille watching her. Nolan, who had spoken, added. "The maids will look after them." Kate nodded but was not reassured. Camille, looking bored, said.

"I'm going to see how the food is coming along." Nolan nodded, but his eyes were still on Kate. Camille frowned before she walked away.

The rest of the party went off without a hitch. Children ran laughing as they played different birthday games. Kate sat in the party hall admiring the décor as she drank punch that was served by the waiters.

"Kate!" Kate turned and smiles when she saw Tony, the chef.

"Hi Tony." She rose and hugged the burly man.

"Long time no see." He says with a grin. Kate motioned him to sit down, and he did.

"How are things with your family?" Kate asks.

"Good, and you?" Kate nodded. "How's Joel? I haven't seen him in a while."

"I visited Emily just yesterday." Kate replies. "She's been so busy with the baby, Joel and Ivy haven't come out because they want to stay with their son." Kate beamed as Tony nodded, smiling knowingly.

Nolan watched the two adults in the distance, seeing his former chef talking to Kate. It was strange seeing them both laughing as they talked. A giggle made him turn his head to see a group of women from the town point and whisper. He followed their gaze and saw they were laughing at Kate. Anger flashed through him. He excused himself from the group he stood listening closely.

"Can't believe he's talking to her." He heard them say. "He should know better."

"His wife isn't looking to happy." Nolan followed their gazes to see Tony's wife standing with Camille and her friends glaring at Tony.

"Someone's in trouble tonight." The women giggled. Nolan heard enough. He walked forward to go to Kate's seat when Mrs. Lehman called, announcing lunch. All the kids crowed with delight before running to their seats, making Nolan turn back, shoulders slumped. He didn't care that Camille was watching him distrustfully before she turned her gaze to Kate.

Lunch was served in all its grandeur. Waiters and waitresses held and placed fancy meals on fine China plates while beverages were poured in crystal goblets. Kate could not help marvel at the extravagance, but a part of her felt that the party was too frivolous for a little girl. Rose ate with her mother, looking at the kids she made friends with; on and off she would wave to them, and they would wave back. Kate could not help but smile at her.

She's such a friendly child. Kate thought she looked up a saw one parent look at Kate, her face contorted with disgust before she looked away. Kate felt the sting before she looked down at her plate.

"Alright everybody!" Camille called after lunch was over. "It's time to say happy birthday to the birthday girl!" Everyone crowed and clapped, getting up from their seat. Kate hung back even as Rose got up and ran. Kate started to walk forward when she heard a giggle. She turned her head and saw two women watching her with a sneer.

"*Cinderwhora has come out of her shack.*" Kate hesitated, unable to move. Rose ran forward and grasped her hand.

"Mommy!" Kate woke at that. Looking down at her daughter, she smiled, before turning her gaze back to the women. Kate squared her shoulders and looked defiantly at them. The women gazed at her, blinking, before walking away.

☙

Nolan sang along with the chorus of voices to 'Happy Birthday.' Parents and children huddled around the massive three tier cake as Esme sat in the middle smiling as everyone sang to her: rich and poor, young and old. Nolan felt Camille's arm around his waist as she sang off key. Her grip was tight as if planting him, so he didn't escape. He had no plans on doing that, he would keep up appearance for his daughter. His smile was genuine as he sang, but his mind, like his heart, was still on Kate.

"Blow out the candles!" the kids squealed.

"Make your wish first!" the parents laughs Esme giggles before looking up at somewhere in the distance. She smiled, then blew out the candles. Everyone clapped merrily.

"Cake! Cake! Cake!" the children crowed.

"Alright everyone!" Camille called. "Please have a seat while the cake is cut and served." The kids hurried back to their seats, making the parents laugh.

Cake was served to every child and adult. Everyone groaned at the moist chocolate cake with pink frosting covered in a layer of pink fondant.

The room was silent except for the clinking of forks and the happy chewing from the children.

Emily would love this cake. Kate thought. She looked and saw Rose, her lips and cheeks covered in pink icing. Kate could not help but smile as she lifted a napkin and started wiping her daughter's mouth. Nolan watched the small family with a gentle smile. Esme ate her cake quietly as she sat with her parents, who sat on either side of her. Nolan smiled at her, and she grinned as Camille scrolled on her phone. Nolan frowned. Glaring at Camille for so long that Camille looked up to see his expression.

"What?" she demands. He smiled tightly.

"Must you be on the phone all day?" He says through clenched teeth. "we have company. You need not be on that phone." She glared at him.

"What I do with myself is my business." She says through clenched teeth. Nolan glanced at her phone before he snatched it from the table. "Hey!" He ignored her, getting up to his feet. He announced it was time to open gifts.

The next half hour of kids ooh'd and aah'd as they looked at Esme's gifts. The children marveled as Esme's eyes sparkled with awe as she ripped wrapping and tissue paper to see the wonderful presents; she received: from stuffed animals to princess accessories, clothes and…

"Wow! A candy machine!" every child gasped with wonder as Esme ripped the paper to reveal a red candy dispenser.

"Wow!" every child looked at the box enviously. Esme looked at Kate, who was holding Rose, who beamed.

"Thank you!" Kate nodded as Rose chirped.

"You're welcome."

"Who wants ice-cream!" Camille called.

321

"ME! ME!" everyone cried. Camille announced that ice cream will be served along with party bags. Kate sighed, ready to go home. It had been an eventful day. She was ready to return to her quiet cabin in the forest. Rose gorged herself on soft serve ice cream, covered in rainbow sprinkles. Kate smiled as she ate hers, making sure that Rose didn't get a brain freeze. Esme came forward and sat beside Rose, who beamed.

"Are you having fun, Esme?" Kate asks motherly.

"Yes, Ms. Starfield." She says. Kate nodded. "I like my candy machine."

"I helped pick it!" Rose chirped.

"You did?" Rose nodded before going into detail about what she did.

"Where are your parents, Esme?" Kate asks.

"Mommy and daddy went to the parlor." Kate was surprised to hear the sad tone in the child's voice. "I think they're fighting." Kate shuddered; she hid her worry with a smile.

"What did you wish for?" she asks, changing the subject. Esme smiled.

"Daddy says I can't tell, or it won't come true." Kate chuckles.

"You're right."

"Oh! Ms. Starfield, when will the next Rose Garden book come out?" Kate opened her mouth to speak...

    BOOM

Everyone turned toward the noise. The hall door was open for everyone to see Nolan step back as Camille step forward, her face twisted with fury!

"**You bastard**!!" Camille's voice echoed in the now silent hall. Rose whimpered as Esme cringed. Before anyone could step forward or react, Camille slapped Nolan across the face! Everyone gasped. Nolan staggered before catching himself, glaring at her.

"What's going on!?" everyone looked to see Tony step forward toward the couple; a few parents stood up and walked forward. Kate saw it was mostly Camille's girlfriends who tried to calm her down whilst a few children started to cry, including Rose and Esme.

"Let's go Rose." Kate whispered. Rose nodded. Kate looked at Esme and patted her cheek, wiping the tears.

"Happy birthday, Esme. Be good, alright." Esme nodded and sniffed. Kate picked up Rose and walked. Camille was carried back into the parlor when Kate stepped out into the hall; shielding her daughter's face from the open sliding doors that Kate had entered so many years before. Nolan watched her go, feeling the sting of his wife's blow.

"Kate?" Kate stopped to look at him for a moment before she turned away.

"Stop!" Kate froze when she heard Camille's voice. She turned her head to see the woman, her green eyes full of rage behind her, were her girlfriends, who stared as Camille shrilled.

"This is all your fault!" Kate didn't move, just watched the powerful woman as she… "You had to ruin everything!" Kate didn't answer. She felt Rose tremble and cry. Kate turned her head from Camille and walked away.

"Don't you turn your back on me!" Camille lunged.

"No!" Kate turned just in time to see Nolan come between her. He grabbed Camille's raised wrist. She screamed as her friends jumped forward in her defense.

"Stop it, Camille!" Nolan roars. He pushed her back hard. "Your fight is with me, not her!" Camille was caught by her friends, who stood her up.

"She's the reason this happened." She hisses. "she and her home wrecking ways. She's a leech, a whore!"

323

"Don't call her that!" he yells. "Kate is not a home-wrecker. She's innocent!" Rose cries, along with the other children at the party. "Camille, you need to stop! You're scaring the—"

"Daddy!" Esme came forward, her eyes wet with tears.

"Esme, go to your room!" Nolan orders.

"But why!?"

"**Go to your room**!" Camille snaps. Esme cried and ran past Kate, who had put Rose down and was using her body to protect her child.

"Camille, calm down!" Nolan continues. "You're scaring the children!"

"I don't care about those bratty street urchins!" everyone gasped. "She!" Camille glared at Kate. "she has no right to be in my house after all she's done!"

"This isn't Kate's—!"

"Why do you take her side!" she stepped forward. Nolan stepped back to protect Kate and Rose.

"Why do you side with this woman who tried to destroy our marriage!" Nolan stared, stunned. "Why must you affiliate yourself with her poor kind? She's done nothing but ruin everything!"

"Camille." Camille lunged and shoved him hard enough that he was pushed to the side.

"I've tolerated your presence in my house for too long! You and your brat!" She glared at Rose, who shrank back. "You think with you all dressed up like us, you can be accepted? That the town will welcome you back!?"

Kate didn't speak. Her throat tightened as her eyes glazed with unshed tears. Camille's face turned smug, cruel.

"No matter how well you become or how well you try to look, you'll still be a naive fling." Camille sneers. Kate froze. She looked at the people, the men and women, who mirrored their own disgust on their faces. Kate's eyes stung.

"Now get out!"

Kate didn't move for several seconds before she nodded shakily. Bending down, she picked up her sobbing daughter. Nolan watched in slow motion as Kate turned her back on Camille and walked…

"No!" Everyone looked at Nolan with surprise.

"Nolan?" Tony says. Nolan ignored him as, in two strides, he passed Camille, his left hand clenched as his right hand reached for Kate's arm. Kate turned her head in surprise, enough to see Nolan, tears streaming down her cheeks. Nolan took her arm and pulled her and Rose to face the crowd.

"This ends now!" he spoke firmly.

"Wh-what! What are you doing!?" Camille shrieked. Nolan let go of Kate and stepped forward, protecting her once more as he faced his guests: from his elite friends to the residents of Forest-Bend.

"Kate is not the reason for my marriage falling apart." He spoke.

"Nolan!" Camille screamed.

"What you believe about Kate, is wrong! Kate is completely innocent of the crimes you think she did." Nolan's heart thudded in his chest as he confessed. "**Kate never attacked Camille!**"

Everyone gasped.

"H-He's lying!" Camille shrilled. "Kate did sh-she attacked me! She's—"

"**ENOUGH**" Camille froze. Nolan glared at her for the first time with hate. "You have no right to say that about Kate! She's done nothing to deserve this or my child!" Everyone gasps. They all turned their gaze to, Kate, who looked at Nolan with shock.

"Nolan." Tony breathes. Nolan looked down. His chest squeezed with agony, ready to burst from his chest but he didn't back down.

No more lies. He thought. Nolan faced the crowd.

"*I slept with Kate!*" He confessed. "*Rose, is my daughter!*"

Chapter Thirty-four

The Roth mansion was cold and gloomy despite the brightly lit room that could be seen in darkness. Maids and staff cleaned quietly of the aftermath of the party. All was silent as they cleared dishes, packed glasses and polished silver, but all ears were strained as they listened to the confrontation coming from upstairs. Time had come to an agonizing crawl in the Roth mansion. Minutes felt like hours to Nolan as he watched the guest leave in droves after confessing his affair with Kate, telling the world or in this case half the town that he was the father to Rose leaving nothing out as he rectified the rumors clearing Kate's name of any wrongdoing that he and his wife had caused.

Kate left the house first, after Nolan ordered her. Eyes streaming with tears of joy or humiliation, Nolan was not sure. He added to the crowd apologizing for his actions before he walked out of the hall and into his office. He would have stayed there for the rest of his life, but Camille had barged in screaming at the top of her lungs off blaming him for ruining… "My reputation!" she shrieked. Nolan stepped back hours later, breathing hard as he stared at his wife, who stood, fist clenched, her face purple with anger.

"How could you do this to us!?" she screamed. "After all, I've done for you, our daughter!" she shoved him hard. "Why did you betray me!" "Betray!?" Nolan counters. "You call living under a lie a betrayal." He glared at her. "You call watching another human being suffer, love!? No Camille, I won't be that man anymore. I let my daughters suffer for my actions. I let Esme grow up with a father but never being her daddy. I let Rose." He winced. "Grow up believing she can't have a daddy because Kate had to punish for the actions we've done. I can't call myself a man when I have hidden like a coward. I can't call myself a father when I have to deny one child and reject another."

"So, this is what you'll do!? You will defy your wife, for your mistress!" Nolan stared at Camille for a long time. Seeing her red face; green eyes, and scar he believed Kate inflicted, resulting in her being the center of malicious gossip by day; only to weep lonely, silent tears at night.

To everyone, she was Camille Roth, fabulous, high-end. Beautiful. *But not to Nolan*. The pain that he carried for seven long years broke. His heartbeat was fast not with guilt or shame as he stared at her. Camille may be beautiful, but to Nolan…

She was ugly.

Nolan's chest rose as he squared his shoulders towering over his wife. "She's not my mistress, Camille." He spoke firmly. "She's her own woman. *A woman I love*." Camille looked at him, stunned. She slapped him. Nolan stepped back, hands on his face.

"I want a divorce!" Nolan looked at her before he smiles. Nolan put his hand down and stepped forward. He passed Camille and headed for the door. "Don't you walk away from me!" she shrilled.

Camille ran.

ങ

Kate laid in the light of a single lamp. The day events prevented her from falling into a peaceful sleep. Rain fell upon the trees, wet, and icy by the time she entered her house, shivering with cold, her eyes tear stained as she carried a sobbing Rose. Once inside, Kate soothed and comforted her daughter with motherly coos until Rose fell asleep.

Kate entered her room, shutting the door behind her. Numb with cold, she mechanically removed her dress and crept into bed and just stared at the sheeting rain outside her window. She closed her eyes. Night had fallen outside when Kate raised her head from the pillow. Her head felt heavy as she blinked, slowly listening to the rain that fell hard outside her window.

What am I to do? Kate thought sadly. This isn't what she expected. She thought she would go home free to her cabin, her life safe after being in the belly of the beast. She had tried to be brave for her daughter, tried to keep a brave face as she was laughed at and ridiculed by Camille's friends. Kate had accepted this even as Camille brought back the words that tore her apart. She bore it all for herself and her daughter. Never in all her years after the incident, she would be defended, by all people from the man she loved. Breaking the seven-year curse that followed Kate to the ends of the forest. Kate closed her eyes.

"Mommy?"

Kate opened her eyes to see Rose standing by the door, watching her with sleepy eyes. Kate felt her chest ache to see her daughter again. Kate lifted her arms instinctively. Rose climbed into her arms; Kate felt an agony of emotions flood away as she held her daughter.

"Mommy?" Rose spoke. Kate looked down at her.

"Yes, honey?"

"Why was Esme's mommy so mean?" Kate felt tears roll down her eyes as she hugged her child.

"Because mommy did something bad."

"Like what, mommy?" Kate sniffed. "Did you take her toys?"

"No."

"Then what? Why was Esme's daddy trying to save you like a superhero?" Kate had to smile at that.

"Because he was trying to protect us."

"From Esme's mommy?" Kate nodded. "Why?" Kate shuddered, but she gazed at her daughter with tenderness.

"Because he cares about you, Rosy?"

"Cares?" Rose echoed. "But isn't he Esme's daddy?"

"Yes. But he cares about you very much."

"But why?" Kate swallowed. She had feared this day. She was so scared of what Rose might think of her; she was at that age to ask about her father, but Kate was so afraid. She looked at her daughter before she took in a deep breath.

"Because Esme's daddy is your daddy too." Rose looked at her, puzzled. "Esme daddy is my daddy?" Kate nodded. "but how mommy?" Kate smiles at her before she took in another breath and tells her daughter everything: how Kate was all alone working on her stories until she met Nolan; how they had spent a lot of time together until she found out that Nolan was married and Kate thought she was alone once again, and heartbroken. Until Rose came and she wasn't lonely anymore.

"So, Esme's mommy put you in jail because she hit herself?" Rose asks.

"Yes. Mommy was sent to jail for a crime she didn't do. All the while I was carrying you in my belly." She poked Rose's tummy, making her giggle.

"That's not nice."

"It wasn't." Kate agrees.

330

"Then how did you get out?"

"Your daddy helped me." Rose nodded.

"But mommy, if Esme's daddy helped you, why didn't he tell Esme's mommy to not be mean to you." Kate sighs.

"I don't know."

"How come he never stayed with you? You're nice."

"He is married Rosy. What I did was wrong."

"But you said you didn't know that."

"I didn't. But when I did, I felt horrible." Rose stared at her quietly.

"But you're sorry for what you did."

"I am." Kate says. "But it's more complicated than that. Something that only grown-ups have to solve." Rose nodded, frowning at 'grown-ups.'

"Was Esme's daddy mean too?" Kate hesitated, thinking back to those years.

"No. He was still nice." Kate finally admitted.

"Did he see me when I was a baby?"

"Yes, he did. He saw you when you were three days old."

"Did he lift me up?" Kate nodded.

"He gave you a toy kitchen when you were three years old."

"Wow." Rose gasps softly. Kate chuckled.

"I have a picture of your daddy holding you."

"Really!" Kate nodded. She leaned to the right where her nightstand was. Rose watched quietly as Kate open a draw and pulled out a flat red box that she opened silently, revealing several photographs. Placing Rose beside her on the bed, she showed her the picture: showing the photo of Nolan holding Rose at her christening.

331

"*Wow.*" Rose gasps. Kate could not help but smile as Rose took the photo into her small hands, seeing the man she never knew. Kate placed another photo, this time with Nolan, Rose, and Kate.

"So, what do you think of your daddy Rosy?" Kate asks gently. Rose looked at her.

"He looks sad." She says. "Why does he look sad, mommy?"

"He was sad because he was happy." Kate explains. "He was happy to see you again and happy to be part of your christening."

"What's that?" Kate tells her until Rose let out a yawn.

"Time to go back to bed, Rosy."

"Can I sleep with you?" Kate hesitated for a moment. It had been a long day and right now she didn't want to be alone without her daughter.

"Alright." Kate says. Rose crawled under the covers as Kate put the photos away in the box before putting it in the drawer. Kate turned off the light and snuggled close to her child, who hugged her.

"Mommy loves you, Rosy." Kate whispered.

"I love you too, mommy." Rose says.

The small family fell asleep as rain pitter pattered on the window. Kate was vaguely aware of the sound of sirens before she fell under the sleepy spell.

Chapter Thirty-five

Kate gasped, feeling the tight, but warm embrace! She staggered back, her eyes wide, not of fear but with surprise. She heard Rose let out a giggle of joy.

"I-Ivy!" Kate gasps. Ivy held Kate, her body trembling with emotion.

"Oh, Kate!" she sobs. Ivy pulled back just enough for Kate to see her eyes shining with… "I'm so happy to see you!"

"I-Ivy." Kate breathes. "Wh-What?" Ivy hugged her again.

"You don't know how much I missed human interaction!" Ivy cries. Kate stood, confused and worried about the young woman. She wrapped her arms around Ivy's back just as footsteps came forward and Emily appeared. Seeing Ivy, she tutted.

"Ivy dear." Ivy stiffened but didn't move from Kate. Emily sighed, then smiled at her guest.

"Hello Kate." She says. Kate smiled nervously.

"Hi Emmi!" Rose chirped, running to her as she hugged her thigh. Emily beamed down at the child.

"Hello Rosy." She cooed, hugging Rose.

"How are you?" Kate asks.

"We're…" Emily saw Kate was still trapped by Ivy. "Ivy, let Kate go, you're scaring the child." Rose giggled as Ivy pulled away from Kate reluctantly, her face chagrined.

"S-sorry." She says meekly.

"That's alright." Kate smiles. She looked at Ivy. "what happened? Is there something wrong?" Ivy sagged, but Emily laughed.

333

"No, dear, everything's fine." She says. Rose walked to her mother as Emily added. "Ivy just been a little clingy these past few weeks. She and Joel haven't gone out since the baby." At the word baby Ivy started, she turned her head toward the hall.

"Baby!" she started. "Is he okay!? Is Jack hungry or wet!? Does…"

"Shh." Emily placed a hand on her daughter-in-law's arm. "He's fine dearie." As she said this, she guided Ivy down the hallway. Kate and Rose followed, walking the familiar hall of the house until they reached the living room where Pilot laid on the soft rug. Rose immediately went to Pilot as Emily sat Ivy, before sitting down herself; motioning to Kate to have a seat.

"I'm sorry," Ivy says, looking at Kate. Kate shook her head.

"It's fine, Ivy."

"No one can blame you." says Emily kindly. She smiled knowingly. "I was the same way when Joel was born." Ivy looked at her wildly.

"You were?" she asks. Emily nodded, as well as Kate.

"You're not alone in this." Emily soothes. Ivy sagged back in the chair.

"How did you take this?" she groaned. "I can't even use the bathroom without thinking if Jack needs to be fed or changed." Kate and Emily chuckles lightly.

"It will pass." Kate assured her. "When Rose was born, I couldn't leave the house for three weeks. Thankfully, I had enough food in the house."

"Lucky you." Ivy grumbled. "At least you were prepared." Emily tittered.

"Now dear," she replies. "I did say I will watch Jacky while you and Joel—"

"No! I can't leave him! He's so *tiny* and so **cute**!" Ivy looked at them tearfully.

"*I can't leave my baby*!" Emily smiles knowingly before patting Ivy's shoulder.

"How has your week been, Kate?" she asks. Kate sighed.

"Alright so far." She admitted.

"I'm so glad you came to visit us." Ivy nodded eagerly at Kate.

"It feels like forever since I've talked to another human."

"Why, you talk to me." Emily replies.

"Yes, but I don't know what's been happening in town."

"Nothing exciting I bet." Emily says. "The world hasn't changed that much while you and Joel were here." Kate swallowed, but her smile was in place as she admitted.

"I haven't been in town for a few days, so I'm in the dark too." Ivy groaned. Just at that moment, Joel entered the room, his hair in disarray, his eyes baggy, but his smile was genuine when he saw Kate as he held his son. Kate got up and hugged him, careful of the baby.

"How are you doing, Joel?" Kate asks, looking at him with sympathy. He looked so tired.

"Alright." He replies. Ivy had taken the baby in his arms and was holding her son with motherly tenderness.

"How is the world out there?" he asks. Kate smiled as he sat down.

"Still turning." Kate replies. Joel nodded, then sagged back in his armchair.

"When was the last time you two slept?" Kate asks. Ivy and Joel groaned.

"I don't know." They say in unison. Both adults' eyes drooped. Emily smiled apologetically at Kate.

"They've been like this since Jack's fever." She explains. Kate nodded. "I insisted on staying up with Jack, but Joel and Ivy refused."

"Did his fever break?" Kate asks as she petted Pilot, who came to her while Rose was with Ivy, watching the baby with curious eyes.

"It did. I told them it was nothing to worry about." Emily says matter of fact.

"Maybe to you, mom." Said Joel wearily. Joel opened his eyes to see his wife, child, and Rose. Ivy was letting Rose hold the baby's tiny hand in her small ones.

"You're worse than me when I was raising you." Emily nodded with a smile.

"You weren't battling colic." Ivy looked up, startled.

"Colic!" she squeaked. Emily sighed.

"Why don't you two go out for a few hours?" Kate suggests quickly. "You can have a date night just name the day and I would gladly watch the baby." Joel and Ivy looked at her with relief. "The three of you can see a movie. I'm sure you're tired too, Emily."

"Oh, don't mind me, dearie." Emily says, smiling. "I love to spend time with my grandson."

"But…" Ivy says, thinking over something. "What if Jack gets fussy!? What if he gets a fever again! *Or colic*! or…" she started to hyperventilate. Emily took the baby from Ivy. Joel sighed.

"Thanks for the offer, Kate, but… I'm just as worried about Jack. I've had nightmares of waking up and the baby missing." He shuddered. Kate nodded.

"Just think about it." She says. "until then, there must be something, I could do for you both." In that moment, Ivy's stomach growled so loudly that everyone could hear it. Kate smiled.

336

"I'll go get you something to eat at the diner."

Kate left Rose with Emily as she drove into town, promising to bring enough food for everyone. Kate couldn't help smiling empathetically at the married couple, who were still getting accustomed to the new life they were now raising. Kate parked in the diner's parking lot. Turning off the engine of the car, Kate opened the door and stepped out. The midday was overcast as she walked quietly; passing the parked cars that stood empty without their driver. Kate entered the diner to find it full of the midday patrons; being the weekend lunch crowd, everyone was sitting down talking, laughing, and eating their meals.

Kate walked to the counter where a waitress smiled at her before asking what she wanted. Pulling out a slip of paper that had everyone's orders Kate read out the orders that the waitress took down, asking if she was to take out, to which Kate replies, "Yes."

"Have a seat in the meantime." Said the waitress. Kate obeyed, knowing the food will take time. Kate watched the cooks work in the back of the diner before shifting her gaze to the other patrons: most of the regulars sat chatting amongst themselves while others ate quietly, reading the daily newspaper. No one paying attention to her. A ding made Kate turn her head to see the new customers.

Her eyes widen when she saw a group of women enter the diner all laughing merrily. Before Kate could look away one looked at her. Kate saw the woman's eyes grow wide. She stiffened when she saw the woman nudge her companion before nodding at Kate. All the women stopped their conversation to look at her with wide eyes. Kate looked at them squarely, her face unreadable. It wasn't until the waitress came forth with Kate's meal did, she turn around, breaking their judging stare.

"That will be $82.74." Kate nodded and pulled out her card to pay for her meal. She could feel the eyes of the women on her as she signed the receipt; smiling at the waitress, she thanked her before picking up the large bag and climbing off the stool.

Kate was heading for the door when in her peripheral, she saw the women whisper close to each other, their eyes still on Kate even as she left the restaurant.

C3

Kate parked her van in the supermarket parking lot, killing the engine before she stepped out into the cold late January air with Rose in hand. Kate grabbed a cart and pushed into the fruit aisle, where she placed fresh apples, strawberries, blueberries and…

"Mommy, look!" Kate looked down to see Rose holding a large grapefruit in her two hands.

"You want that too, Rosy?" she asks with a smile. Rose nodded. Kate pulled a bag from the roll before letting Rose place it in the plastic bag. A giggle made Kate look up to see three women whom Kate remembered seeing at the party: one girl met Kate's gaze. Before Kate looked away, she saw the woman look down before her eyes widened with shock. Kate looked down and saw Rose, who was watching the oranges, not a care in the world. Kate looked up and saw the women watching her and… Kate's eyes hardened. She turned her gaze back to her child. She took her daughter's hand and led them away from the fruit aisle.

The rest of the shopping trip was unnerving for Kate. It seemed to her that she was the first human to exist on the planet. That is what it felt as Kate shopped, going from one section of the store to another. It reminded her of when she started shopping after she was released from prison: all eyes full of mocking jeers and snide whispers. But this was different. Instead, she wasn't alone, and the attention she gained was one of wonder, awe, and curiosity, not for Kate. But her child.

All eyes were centered on Rose as the child walked merrily down the aisle, pointing as she helped Kate with the groceries. Kate tried her best to act normal as she picked up food items from their shelves.

"Mommy, I want that." Kate stopped her cart, for they were in the cereal aisle. Kate smiled as she reached for the box of cereal when Rose said.

"I want to get it!" Kate nodded, then lifted Rose, who giggles before reaching for the box. Whispers made Kate turn her head to see two women standing by the sodas, watching her and Rose with amazement. Kate's pulse quickened.

"Come on, Rose," Kate whispered. Before Rose could reply, Kate carried the child to the cart, putting Rose's cereal inside. She placed her down, Rose's hand in hers, before they walked past the woman, head lowered.

"*She looks just like her mother.*" Was the last thing she heard before she left the aisle.

Kate felt trapped. In all the years since she had lived in this town, she had never felt more isolated than she did right now. After being an outcast by the town for the false crime, Kate was resigned to living alone with only her child and her quaint cabin. The town and their gossipy ways had no power over her unless she entered their domain to get her daily bread and sustenance: she had taken their jeering babbles for so long that it became a buzzing that she could tune out once her child was born.

Kate had gotten used to her life of isolation. Instead, she focused on building a sanctuary for her child and herself with the help of ink and paper. It was a welcome distraction from the harshness she had experienced. A wound that hadn't fully healed despite being covered with bandages. The throb of pain still lingered.

But now everything had changed. Kate was once again the center of gossip and scrutiny. The faces that once sneered and laughed were now full of curiosity and…

"Kate?" Kate started looking up to see Emily watching her with concern.

"Oh, I'm sorry, Emily," Kate says apologetically.

"Are you alright, dearie?"

"Yes, I…" Kate trailed off, looking down at her bowl of lobster bisque. Emily watched her quietly as she supported her grandson in his baby carrier.

"Are you not feeling well?" Emily asks.

"No." Kate hunched her shoulders. "I'm not sick. It's just…" she trailed off Emily saw the sad look on Kate's face.

"It was nice of you to invite us to your house." Kate took the distraction. She looked up with a smile.

"It's not a problem, Emi. I know Joel and Ivy needed a break." Emily nodded.

"I'm just glad you let me get to bake something. I haven't been able to make anything in weeks." Emily beamed. Kate chuckled.

"It's nice to have a girl's night," Emily adds.

"Indeed." Kate agrees. She looked down at her full bowl of soup. Her stomach clenched.

"Kate?" she looked at Emily. "What is the matter?" Kate hesitated, then sighs. "You've been so sad since you came back from the diner. Did something happen?" Kate didn't reply. "If something is troubling you, you can tell me anything."

"I know." Kate looked down. Picking up her spoon, she swirled her soup. "It's the town." She finally spoke. Emily's eyes narrowed.

"Were they mean to you?" she says.

"Not... *exactly*," Kate murmured. "That would have been preferable. At least they kept their distance from me." Emily stared in confusion.

"*They know.*" She whispers. Emily's eyes widen.

"They know you're Victoria Starfield!?" Kate looked up glumly.

"I would have preferred they did." Emily looked even more confused. Kate sighed, putting down her spoon as she whispered.

"*They know Nolan is Rose's daughter.*"

"What!?" Emily gasps. Kate nodded weakly, her head down. "B-But how? I-I thought..." she trailed off.

"Nolan told them everything." Kate breathes.

"When?" Kate looked up, eyes shining; she sighed and began her tale, including how the next two weeks, she was the center of gossip once more, hearing the whisperers that plagued her so many years before. But now...
She was not alone.

Tears pool down Kate's eyes as she cried for her daughter, who was included by the gossipy women who were in Camille Roth's clique as they came to

Kate pretending to befriend her when in actuality, wanted a good look at Rose to see if the rumor was true about her real paternity.

"Oh, Kate," Emily spoke when Kate finished. "I'm so sorry this happened to you and Rosy!" Kate sniffed.

"You didn't know," Kate says thickly. "It's just been so hard these past few weeks. I know I can handle the town, but Rose… she's so young. She doesn't deserve this. I don't want her to suffer how I did." Emily got up from her seat and hugged Kate.

"I know, dearie." Emily replies. "None of this is your fault. It's just like I told you years ago, this town is full of gossipy hens who take glee in other people's suffering." Kate half smiles before she looked down.

"All I want is to give Rose a happy life. Not surrounded with gossip because of my past."

"*And you have*." Emily pulled away and looked at Kate, hand on her shoulder.

"But the whole town knows the truth!" Kate whimpered. "They know I never harmed Camille. I should be happy. I'm free." She closed her eyes. "The people in town has been coming to my house to apologize for their actions but…" her breath hitched. "I know they want to see Rose." She let out a shaky breath. "How can I protect my child when everyone is making her look like an oddity to be pointed and gawked? When all they see is Nolan Roth's secret daughter instead of *my child*."

"Nolan Roth was not there when Rose was born," Emily spoke firmly. "He wasn't there for her first steps, her first words or her first birthday. As far as I know, you've been the one who raised Rose, not him. No amount of gossip can ever *change* that."

Kate looked at Emily; her heart lifted as fresh tears brimmed in her brown eyes. Kate wrapped her arms around her carefully.

"*Thank you*." Kate breathes. Emily hugged her back. Brushing Kate's tears after letting her go. Both women jumped when they heard a honk outside the window.

"Oh! How time flies!" Emily says. Kate couldn't help it, she laughed as Rose walked into the kitchen.

"Mommy! Why are you crying?" Kate rubbed her eyes smiling down at her before lifting and sitting Rose on her lap.

"Mommy was sad for a moment, but I'm all better now." Rose nodded; she laid her head on Kate's chest. Emily opened the front door, letting Ivy and Joel enter the house.

"Hey mom." Joel kissed Emily on the cheek as Kate rose from her seat after Rose climbed off to go to Ivy.

"How was the movie?" Kate asks.

"Great." Ivy beamed. "I haven't had a good time at the movies since '*Harry Potter*'."

"This movie was just like it," Joel adds. "But funnier. Thanks for the suggestion, Kate." Kate nodded. "Hey, little man." Joel cooed at the baby who looked at him quietly. Ivy went to Emily who started to pull off the carrier.

"Mommy missed you so much." She croons as Emily handed baby Jack to Ivy's awaiting arms.

"He wasn't too much trouble, was he mom?" Joel asks. Emily shook her head.

"Not at all." She says, eyeing her son. "You both looked refreshed." Joel beamed.

"We have to do this again." He says. Ivy snuggled her son.

"But not too soon." She adds. "I missed my baby too much." Kate and Emily giggled.

"Ready to go, mom?" Joel asks. Emily nodded. "Thanks again for looking after them, Kate."

"It was my pleasure, Joel," Kate spoke. "If you need another movie night, just let me know." Joel smiles as Emily helped Ivy strap baby Jack.

"Oh, you would not believe what I heard tonight," Ivy announced. "You know the Roth's?" Kate stiffened as Emily nodded. "Well, I heard that Camille Roth was in jail a few weeks ago."

"What?!" Kate gasps. Ivy nodded.

"I heard a woman say that." she continues. "Camille and Nolan Roth fought."

"About what?" Emily asks calmly as Kate stared fearfully. Sensing her mother's distress, Rose came to her and hugged her knee.

"I'm not sure, mom. But it must have been something big," Ivy says. "I heard the woman say Camille was so angry that she pushed her husband down the stairs of their mansion."

"What!?" Emily cries. Joel nodded. Kate lifted a hand to her mouth, eyes wide.

"Apparently they were fighting about something during their daughter's birthday party," Joel says.

"*What happened next?*" Kate whispers just as Emily says.

"I hope Mr. Roth is alright."

344

"I heard he's not doing so good," Ivy says conspiratorially.

"He's in a coma."

Chapter Thirty-six

Blizzards, slush roads formed slicks of ice invisible as the end of January and February reigned cold by the breath of old man winter. Days felt like weeks as the seasons called forth its unpredictable charge upon the town, keeping people indoors with mugs of hot cocoa and a good book. It felt that old man winter had won the seasonal race, but it was not to be for mother nature had rose from the depths and kissed the world with her warm lips; casting off the cold, allowing the earth to wake up and sprout forth an earthly paradise for the children of man.

April had finally come upon the Forest-Bend, warm but comfortable as people went on their way preparing for the upcoming holiday. The town was decorated with bright yellows, pinks, and white as Easter preparations were made for the young and old. The town was a buzz with excitement getting ready for the festivities ahead as they greeted one another cheerily whilst the countdown to Easter was soon upon them.

Kate stepped onto the cool mid-day of the town, taking in the sights as she glided quietly, passing by stores that were decorated with Easter fan fairs. Kate smiled as she took in the sun's warmth that beamed over a cloudless day. She turned a corner until she saw the store she was looking for. She entered the quiet Victorian store that sold classical items and clothes.

"I'm here to pick up a dress for Kate Alma," Kate replies politely. "It was made for me a month and a half ago." The clerk nodded before turning toward a desk with a laptop that she perused.

"Yes, we have them ready for you. Just wait here while I get it in back." Kate didn't have to wait long when the woman returns holding two red dresses:

346

one adult and one child. Kate thanked the woman after paying and left with a smile.

I can't wait to see Rosy's face when she sees her play dress. She thought as she made her way through the town. Kate froze when she saw a group of women standing together outside a shop. Kate immediately recognized the women from Camille Roth's group of friends, including Tony's wife and Nicole, who stood at the door of her shop. Kate hesitated. The women seemed deep in conversation as their lips moved fast, their faces excited about their latest gossip. Kate hunched in her shoulders, her head lowered as she walked, her eyes on her feet; people passed Kate as she walked slowly on the smooth black concrete. She had stepped onto the road, for the women blocked the walkway.

"Hey!" Kate didn't stop. It wasn't until she heard her name did, she stopped just a foot from them. Kate lifted her head turning reluctantly toward the voice. Eight pairs of eyes stared back at her; arrangement of emotions, but all had the same face: curiosity. One woman stepped forth; she was the tallest of the group, Kate saw why. She was wearing large wedges that looked too uncomfortable.

"You're Kate, right?" she asks. Kate, her face unreadable saw a few of the women, including Tony's wife, who step forward behind the tall blonde woman. Only Nicole stood by her door.

"Yes." Kate replies. The women looked at one another, almost surprise to hear her speak.

"Oh, that's good." says the blonde. "I know we haven't been properly introduced. I'm Muffy." She gestured to the other girls behind her, introducing them.

347

"I know who you are," Kate's voice was low. "I see you all the time in town."

Silence. Tony's wife cleared her throat.

"Yes." She says. "You came to my house before."

"I did," Kate replies coolly.

"You were a cleaning maid—I mean person." Kate nodded once. "I, uh, I don't see you do that nowadays." She adds awkwardly.

"I left Squeaky Clean," Kate replies.

"Oh! Is that the name of your job?" asks Muffy, her face lit up with excitement. Kate could not help but compare her to a hungry cat.

"Yes."

"You still work there?" a short, squat woman nudged her.

"Did you not hear her say she left the job?!" she hisses.

"Oh." Muffy laughs insincerely.

"What do you do for a living, then?" asks another woman. Kate recognized her as the woman who called her 'Cinder-whora' at the party. Kate squared her shoulders.

"I'm a writer."

"WRITER!" Everyone turned to Nicole, who spoke.

"Uh, what kind of books do you write!?" Muffy squeaked. Kate didn't reply, for Nicole came forward, standing just half a foot from Kate.

"Yes, I am a writer," Kate spoke, unfazed. "Is that a problem?"

"Yes, it is!" says Nicole. "You have a child. Why are you not working a real job?!"

"Writing is my real job," Kate replies calmly.

"Not when you have a child, his child, to take care of." Kate bristled, her eyes narrowed.

"How I take care of my child is my business. How I make my income should not deter me from doing my duty as a mother." Kate replies.

"Your child!" Nicole spoke.

"Yes, she is mine."

"What about Nolan?!"

"Nikki!" the girls cried. She ignored them as she got in Kate's face.

"How can you speak so casually about his child, and you're working a 'job'?" She says job with derision. "That doesn't pay you enough to take care of his daughter. How can you stand here and act so nonchalant while Nolan is fighting for his life!"

Kate watched the woman who had degraded her years before. She stepped forward. Nicole stepped back.

"You have no right to judge my lifestyle," Kate spoke firmly. "I know everything that happened to Mr. Roth, and I don't need you and your friends belittling me. I don't need your input on how to raise my daughter. Especially after how you treated me before and after the truth that your *leader* is not as *perfect* as she appears."

"Camille was saving her daughter!" Nicole raised her chin. "You hurt my best friend!" Kate stared, eyes hard that Nicole and the other women squirmed.

"After all these years, you still accuse me." Kate stepped forward, Nicole stepped back her features shifted show the first traces fear in her arrogant face. "After all your friend has done to ruin my livelihood and the future of my daughter." Kate clenched her free hand.

"*I have worked.*" Kate murmurs solemnly. "Worked hard asking for nothing in return. I have cleaned houses, working ten hours to put food on the table. To build a home from little after all I've done." Her eyes narrowed.

349

"I have entered your homes with your cruel words and sneers on my back." She looked at Troy's wife who paled. "You and Camille have done enough to me. But not anymore." She looked at them firmly.

"You don't hurt me anymore. You can pretend to befriend me, you can hate me all you like." She glared at Nicole, "Your actions and words mean nothing. I am not the same woman you've cast out six years ago. I am no *Cinderwhora*." Kate raised her chin. "Nolan's child or not, you will never—"she stepped forward, close to Nicole who despite being a few inches tall than Kate shrank back. "*EVER*! Dictate how I take care of myself and my Rose!!"

Silence.

The women looked at Kate wide-eyed. Kate took in their stunned faces with grim satisfaction before she turned and walked down the street to go home.

CB

Quiet beeps echoed in the room as the sunlight beamed on the resting figure of Nolan Roth. Nolan lay in the private wing of the hospital ward, machines and tubes attached to his arm and nose bringing life to his being. Thick white gauze lay atop his head as he slept dreamlessly. His only sign of movement was the rise and fall of his bandaged chest. Camille stood beside his bed watching him as he slept, unknown to him that his attacker was just a foot from him.

"Mrs. Roth?" Camille turned slowly to face the man in a lab coat wearing blue scrubs.

"Yes, doctor?" she asks. The doctor looked from her to the patient. "is he going to wake up doctor?" the doctor turned back to her, his face turning grave as he spoke of Nolan's progress, adding how he must pull through himself.

"The accident had done damage, but he was lucky to come out of surgery with no complications. With exception of a broken leg." The doctor's spoke calmly. Camille nodded before looking back at her husband.

"For now, all we can do is wait, talk to him. Hearing a familiar voice might pull him through."

"He won't be happy to hear my voice," Camille murmured. A moment's pause settled into an uncomfortable silence. The doctor cleared his throat.

"Perhaps he would be more responsive if there is more family." Replied the doctor. "Does he have other relations?" Camille shook her head.

"Just me and my daughter." She turned to see the doctor nod once.

"Well, that should be enough. I'm sure he will pull through." Camille nodded before the doctor left the room. She stared back at Nolan, watching his bandaged forehead where he suffered a concussion before the *accident* that left him in this state. Eventually, they would heal and become scars just like… Camille closed her eyes as she thought back to that night, how in her anger pushed her husband after he walked out the room to where she didn't…

Camille opened her eyes as the answer came to her as clear as the noon bells that rang outside the window. Camille looked at her husband before she turned and walked out the door.

ȣ

"Mommy! Look!" Kate looked up at the same time she heard the thrum of a loud engine. Pilot barked where she stood by Rose, who sat on her swing pointing with bright wide eyes at the luxurious car that parked just

10 feet from Kate's cabin. Kate raised her head from the freshly turned earth, where she sowed new seeds that promised to be grown into fresh Rosemary, Fine thyme, Lavender, Basil, and Mint.

Kate and Rose had spent the better part of their Easter Sunday playing in the forest: they had an Easter hunt where Kate woke up early to hide plastic eggs that contained chocolates. Afterward, Kate surprised Rose with an Easter basket containing more sweets, a stuffed bunny, and a drawing set. Before ending the midday with working on the garden plot where Kate started planning seeds that way by summer, they will have a plot of colorful foliage.

Kate got to her feet, dusting soil from her scarlet dress and walking forward. Rose ran to her side and Pilot. Rose hugged her mother's side as a man stepped out of the driver's seat.

"Mommy, who's that?" Rose asks.

"I don't know, Rosy," Kate replies. Without a word, the man walked around the car. Kate and Rose were just by their cabin when the man opened the door and Camille Roth stepped into the bright April sun. Kate froze.

She heard Rose whimper as Pilot growled, but Kate could not react as she saw the woman dressed in expensive attire wearing a large hat with black sunglasses that stared directly at Kate. Both women stared at one another in silence. It wasn't until the other side of the door was open and a child leaped out of the car did the spell break.

"Esme!" Rose squealed. Esme beamed as the driver shut the door. "Mommy, it's Esme!" Kate broke her gaze from the woman and smiles down at her daughter.

"Yes. I see her Rosy." Kate spoke. Camille stepped forward as the driver stood silently by the hood of the car. Esme walked forward, keeping her distance from her mother as she went and hugged Rose.

"Hi Rosy!" says she. "Hi, Ms. Starfield!"

"Hello Esme!" Kate says with a smile. "It's nice to see you again." Esme nodded eagerly.

"Yes." Camille stepped forward; she had removed her sunglasses revealing green eyes that watched Kate with surprise.

"Mrs. Roth," Kate spoke, voice polite.

"K-Kate."

"What brings you to my home, Mrs. Roth?" Camille opened her mouth; she glanced down at the two children and dog that still growled low at her.

"I wish to speak to you… in private." She adds. Kate blinked slowly. Esme and Rose watched the adults quietly, fearfully, especially at Esme's mother. Kate looked at the kids.

"Rosy, why don't you play with Esme, okay." Kate says. "while the grownups talk." Rose looked at Camille Roth, grimaced then nodded, taking Esme's hand she says eagerly.

"Come, Esme!" Esme followed Rose, not looking back at her mother. Kate walked to her door, letting Pilot in first before saying. "Come in." Camille obeyed.

Kate left the door half open in case her daughter decided to come inside; a squeak made her turn to see Camille standing stock still as Pilot sniff her before letting out a low growl.

"Pilot," Kate spoke. The dog didn't respond. Kate sighed, then walked to the kitchen. She petted Pilot, ordering her to lay down, to which the German shepherd obeyed. Camille let out a breath.

"I don't remember you having a dog." She spoke.

"I don't," Kate replies calmly. "I'm dog sitting for someone." Camille stared before she looked around her, from the living room to the small kitchen; each section of the room was cleaned and elegantly decorated with Easter fan fair. Camille marveled at the classical ware and accessories of the house. Noticing her ogling, Kate cleared her throat, calling Camille to attention.

"Is there something you need, Mrs. Roth?" Kate spoke. Camille started.

"What? No, I…" she trailed off.

"You said you wanted to talk," Kate continues after a pause, to which Camille looked down at the shiny floor. "About what, perchance?" Camille looked at her eyes wide, her mouth open to speak, when laughter made her turn her head. Kate followed her gaze and saw the children: Esme was on the chain swing while Rose, her small stature, was pushing her.

"It's been so long since I heard her laugh." Kate looked at her. Camille had lowered her head as she rubbed her arm absently.

"Esme." It wasn't a question. Camille nodded.

"She doesn't do much laughing after…" Camille trailed off.

"Why are you here, Mrs. Roth?" Kate asks. Camille hesitated. She looked at Kate once more, eyes shining.

"I need your help." Kate blinked, surprised.

"Help?" she echoed. Camille nodded meekly. "What help do you want from me?! What can I do to help you after all you've done to me!" Kate's eyes narrowed as her voice hardened. "After what you've said about my daughter! Why should I help someone like you!?" Camille winced.

"**Because Nolan needs you!**" Kate froze.

"N-Nolan?" She whispers.

"He needs you," Camille repeated. "Nolan h-he won't respond to me." She took a step forward; Kate took a step back.

"He won't wake up to my voice. The doctors say they might take him off the machines if he…" Camille trailed off. Kate stared at her in stunned silence, listening, seeing Camille so…

"And what do you want me to do?" Kate asks, voice hard. "What does me going to Nolan…" she trailed off wincing.

"I…" Camille looked at her pleadingly. "Just go to him, talk to him, he won't wake for me, you can—"

"Stop it!" Camille looked up, eyes tear-stained at Kate, who looked at her firmly.

"Why are you telling me this?!" Kate demands. "This should be between you and your husband not…" Kate paused. She looked down, fist clenched at her middle. "Mrs. Roth." She spoke slowly. "I can't help you. What happened between me, and your husband is over, I can't undo… I've moved on. Please don't come to me thinking I can make things right. Because I can't."

"So, you will let him die?!" Kate looked up.

"I never said that." she says.

"But that's what I hear. You don't want to save Nolan—is it money?!" Camille looked at her tearfully. "Just name your price! I'll write a check right now an—!"

"I don't want your money, Mrs. Roth!" Kate says.

355

"**Then it's revenge**?!" Camille cries. Kate started; Pilot barked, going in front of Kate protectively. "You want paybacks for all I've done to you! Say it!! You're doing this because I sent you to jail for something I did to myself. I turned this gossipy town against you, making them believe you were pregnant with another man's baby instead of letting Nolan raise your daughter. Is that what you want!" Kate winced.

"I'm not doing this for revenge," Kate murmured.

"Then what?!" Kate looked at her.

"Because I'm not his wife!" Kate cries. Camille stepped back. "I'm not married to Nolan; you are! You're the one who took the vows. You're the one who had his child. You're not a naïve fling like I am! So, don't come to me thinking I can fix your marriage or your husband. You're his wife and mother to his child. Act like it! Instead of whom you pretend to be!"

"I can't!" Camille cries.

"Why not!?"

"**Because I did this to Nolan**!" Kate froze. She stared at Camille, stunned, as she whimpered, hand in her face. "I caused him to go to the hospital."

"Y-You what!?" Kate spoke. Pilot barked and growled at Camille; Kate stepped forward, saying. "**Down Pilot!**"

"H-How?" The elite looked up glaring at Kate with angry tears.

"I'm sure you of all people heard from this gossipy town." She spat. "You must have heard about how Camille Roth was sent to jail after pushing her husband down the staircase after fighting about his mistress." Kate winced but didn't answer.

"Well, after Nolan fell, he didn't stop to check for injuries. Instead, he was so repulsed by his wife that he ran out of the house before any of the staff could stop him. Nolan had already gotten into his car; to come here probably, if his car didn't collide with a truck!" Camille sobs harder. Kate stared at the woman, stunned. She didn't hear that part of the story. A story unveiled by a woman who weaved lies for her own reputation and enjoyment.

"*So, that's why*." Kate breathes; she took a step back. Camille looked at her piteously.

"Now you know." Camille's voice was horsed. "You know now how I nearly killed my husband, how I spent days in prison; how the town has turned against me for my crimes." Kate didn't answer. "But you can fix everything." Camille looked at her, face wild with desperation. "You can bring Nolan back." She gripped Kate's shoulders tightly.

"We can be a family again," she says, smiling. "Just the three of us."

Kate looked at the woman, stunned.

"Three?" Kate breathes. Camille nodded.

"The doctor says he could have memory loss." Camille explains. "This is the perfect opportunity for me to start over. I get my husband and Esme gets her father. It will be as if nothing happened. We'll be a family again." Kate's hands curled into fists. She didn't hear Pilot beside her and was glad she didn't.

"You will let Nolan believe that all that you've done, never happened." Camille felt Kate's body tremble. "You will let him think you can start over for your fantasy." Kate gripped Camille's left wrist firmly.

"If that means he denies one daughter in the process for your perfect family." She thrust Camille's hands from her.

"Listen Camille," Kate spoke solemnly. "For six long years I have put up with you and your friends torment while you ignored your daughter and antagonized your husband. I have apologized for my actions; never knowing he was married and hurting you as his wife." Kate brown eyes, blazed. Camille stared at her, truly seeing Kate for the first time. She was not the meek, naïve fling she ruined. She was…

"You have no right to say you deserve the title of the *perfect family*." Kate continues firmly. "If that means denying Nolan's right to be a father to Rose, then I won't do it. The town finally sees who you truly are. I won't stand as you play Mother Of The Year for your selfishness!" Camille looked at her with fear on her scarred face.

"Kate, pl-please." Kate looked away.

"Please, leave my home!" Camille opened her mouth, then closed it. She nodded weakly before heading for the open door.

"Nolan is in the downtown hospital," Camille spoke. "He's in a private ward in…" her voice broke. Kate watched as Camille left the house. She heard her call for Esme before she looked through the window to see the driver open the door for his passengers. Kate sat down in her chair, wrapping her arms around herself.

Rose and Pilot entered the house to find Kate crying silently. Rose went to her mother, and Kate hugged her fiercely as Pilot lay by her foot.

Chapter Thirty-seven

Storm clouds loomed ominously with rain as thunder rumbled over the skyscrapers.

Soft beeps sounded automatically as the clicks and whirs of the hospital machines brought oxygen to the sleeping figure. Kate stood outside the door of the small well-decorated room watching with sad eyes at Nolan Roth, her body unable to step forth into the room to visit the man who… Kate closed her eyes.

"Ma'am?" Kate opened her eyes, turning her head to see a male doctor.

"Y-Yes?" Kate spoke.

"Are you here to see Mr. Roth?" Kate hesitated.

"Y-yes." She spoke. The doctor nodded.

"I need to check on my patient." Kate realized she was still standing in the middle of the door. Apologizing, she stepped back, allowing the doctor to go inside. Kate watched as the doctor checked his vitals on the machine.

"I've never seen you before." Kate started; the doctor turned his head to look at her with a kind smile. "Are you a friend of Mr. Roth?" Kate looked down, holding her right arm.

"You can say that." she whispers. She looked at the doctor. "I've known Mr. Roth for many years." The doctor beamed.

"Well, it's nice to meet you. You don't have to be afraid." He adds, seeing Kate's hesitation to enter. "You're the only visitor I've seen…" his lips curled downward. "aside from his wife, of course?" Kate shuddered.

"Am I?" Kate asks. He nodded.

"People sent Mr. Roth flowers." He nodded toward a table full of flowers, baskets, and balloons. "Mr. Roth knows many people in high places." He adds with a smile. She smiled weakly.

Kate took this moment to step inside the room. Her palms felt wet, but she hid it by wrapping her arms around herself as she gazed down at Nolan.

Nolan lay in silent sleep. His chest rose and fell as Kate watched him take air from the breathing tube in his nose. His hair had grown longer than the last time she had seen him; he still looked skinny to her compared to how she remembered him: tall, defiant… scars covered parts of his dark skin from his arms, neck, and head, that was wrapped in hospital gauze. Kate placed her hand on the cool metal railing of the bed.

"How is he doing, doctor?" Kate whispered. The doctor looked at her. Kate had hunched in on herself. Her body spasmed, trying to hold back… he sighed before looking back at his patient.

"It is difficult to estimate," He spoke. "we thought, after his surgery, that Mr. Roth would have awakened, but we can't rush him. Only Mr. Roth has the power to choose. We can't control that. It's a difficult reality that we face each day." Kate looked at him, her face no longer sad as she stared sympathetically at the physician.

"I understand, doctor." She spoke. He looked at her with a small smile. The doctor left soon after, explaining he had other patients to see, leaving Kate alone with Nolan. She walked to the other side of the bed and sat down, watching the still man as the machines clicked and beeped. It was soothing to her as she sat beside Nolan. She looked down.

"I never thought I'd be here again," she whispers. "In this hospital, I mean." She looked up, watching Nolan.

"I'm not really a fan of most hospitals, not since my parents died. I had sworn I would never go back to one." Kate wrapped an arm around her middle.

"But all that changed after I gave birth to Rose." Kate smiles wistfully. "Rose was born here, you know. It was late. I was alone, scared, but all the while, all I could think was about having my baby." Kate's eyes turned glassy as she gazed at Nolan.

"I wished you were there for the birth." She whispers. "I wanted to see you. Even while I was pushing, I kept looking out the door, hoping by some magic you would enter the room and take my hand." Kate lifted her left hand and placed it under Nolan's hand, closest to her.

"I imagined you would be here for me. Telling me everything was all right… that you won't leave me." Kate looked at his hand in hers. A wistful smile crossed her lips.

"Then I had Rose." She continues. "And she was the most beautiful thing I ever laid eyes on. She was so small, so pink—" Kate's smile grew—"And she was mine. I had done it. Me, who thought I deserved nothing, was given this gift. I felt as if I was given a second chance. I wasn't alone anymore. I had a new heart that beat for me. A heart that couldn't be possible without you." Water slid down Kate's cheek as she looked at Nolan.

"You gave me that new heart." She spoke. "That night under the stars where we laid in bed talking about our future, the stories I would tell you under the light of the moon. It was the most magical time I ever had." She squeezed his hand gently.

"Getting to spend time with you, wishing you luck on your job… All I wanted was to be with you, to see you smile, to hold your hand." she winced.

"But you didn't really need my luck, huh?" She whispers thickly. "because you were already powerful. You didn't need some stray penny to make your wish in the fountain." She tried to chuckle, but it came out with a broken gasp as she looked down.

"You were all-powerful, but you hid it from me, but I kind of understand why you did." Kate looked down at her thigh.

"It must be very lonely. Being on top of the world, it's hard to find your equal. Someone whom you can talk to without the money and status. If I were in your shoes, I would have done the same." She smiles sadly.

"I just wished you hadn't hidden who you really were." Kate says. "I wished I hadn't had to find out the truth from your wife. I wish…" she sighs. "But I know there's no point in wishing what you can't get back. I just… when I found out I was pregnant, I was scared how you would react. We've only been together for half a year and with a baby on the way..." Kate looked up to see his hand.

"When I saw your reaction, you looked so… then when Camille came to the inn and told me you didn't want the baby... Your fear, your shock… *You didn't want our baby*, but… *I couldn't give them up*." Kate breathes. "I was happy to become a mother, but Camille… *she got what she wanted*. No one knew you were Rose's father." Kate sighs.

"It hurt at first, being alone, knowing that the whole town hated me for a crime I didn't do, but as the months passed as I worked for Squeaky Clean." She half smiles.

"*I know I did the right thing*. I don't regret my decision about having my child. She's her own person. I wouldn't trade her for anything, not even to take back the pain and suffering. *I've done it*. All on my own, but … I wished

362

you were there. *Just to see her grow.*" Kate paused, swallowed. "She asks about you now, but Rose doesn't fully grasp that you're her father or that Esme is her half-sister." Kate blinked at that, surprised by her own words. She shook her head, before looking at Nolan.

"Camille came to my house." Her hand spasmed in his. "she wanted me to talk to you. she thinks I can wake you from this but, I don't know how I can." Kate closed her eyes.

"She thinks that you three can be a family again." Kate replies. "Camille believes she can be forgiven because…" she shook her head.

"I thought about not coming. To not fall for her trap but…" she hesitated before opening her eyes. "The town's started paying attention to me again." Kate's vision blurred as her breath hitched. "Some who used to talk to me who I worked for…They've apologized for the actions they did from… *You know.*" She smiles sadly.

"It feels odd. After being ignored for so long, I… it's nice to be welcomed, but it's going to take time for me and…" Kate's hand spasmed in his.

"Camille's friends, Nikki, the ones at the party… they watch Rose now," she whispers.

"They don't see Rosy the same as before," Kate says. Her eyes burned as anger boiled her blood. "They see my child as the latest gossip to point and laugh…" she gave his hand a squeeze.

"I'm not afraid of them." She spoke, voice solemn. "I won't let their whispers and jeers keep me from taking care of my child. No matter, how they try to befriend me with their kindness—" Kate says kindness with ire. "I've seen their true colors. I won't let them hurt my child. I'm not a naive fling." She spoke firmly as tears rolled down her cheeks.

"Sometimes I think about leaving the town." She whispers. "Go back to New York or move to another state with Rose, but… This is where it all began. It's where I raised Rose, where I wrote my books, where I started a new chapter of my life…" She smiles.

"It's where I met and fell in love with you," she confessed. "I can't go back. I've met such nice people, people who care for me and Rose. I'm not ready to say goodbye. I..." She squeezed his hand gently as she cries. "I don't know if you can *hea*..." Kate stopped her throat tightened. "*Thank you*," She whimpered. "For setting me free. For finally having Rose know she has a daddy, who did everything to protect her. I… *I forgive you*." Tears, warm and clear, slid down Kate's cheek onto her hand, sliding onto Nolan's. "*We're going to be alright*," she whispers. "Rose, *me*…" Kate lifted his hand and pressed it to her cheek. "*I love you*…I never stopped loving you."

Kate let go of his hand gently before getting to her feet, wiping her eyes as she walked out of the room without looking back.

The machines beeped quietly as the oxygen tubes brought in air to the patient, whose chest rose and fell as his eyes slowly opened.

Chapter Thirty-eight

Sunlight gleamed on panes of cold glass; warming the material as well as magnifying the rays of the sun that cast fractures of rainbows upon the room. Nolan gazed outward at the beauty from the fluffy white clouds that floated over the skyscrapers to the blue sky that hovered over all things.

Nolan stared where he sat upon the hospital bed, marveling at the beautiful world that he had missed while he was under a perpetual sleep, unable to make new memories in the present or future; all he had was the past... Nolan's hand curled into a fist on the bed.

"Nolan?" Nolan turned from the window slowly to see the male doctor that had attended to him the moment he had woken up.

"Yes, doctor?" he spoke slowly. The doctor walked in with a smile.

"How are you feeling today?" he asks. Nolan blinked slowly before he could speak. Fast footsteps came. The men both turned for the door just as Camille stopped in front of the door.

"Nolan!" before the doctor could react, she sped past him and threw her arms around Nolan's neck. "Oh, Nolan!" she sobs.

"Ma'am." The doctor spoke. She ignored him.

"I'm so glad you're awake!"

"Ma'am, please do not be so rough on Mr. Roth; he is still not a hundred percent—"

"Do not tell me what I can and can't do with my husband!" she snaps. "I'm here now—"she looked at her husband. "Don't you worry Nolan; I've hired

365

the best doctor money can buy once you're home; you won't have to be in this ratty hospital!"

"Ma'am, that is uncalled for." Said the doctor, she spun around.

"Who is your supervisor?" she demands. "I will have you fired for talking to me in that manner."

"I am merely trying to tell you that you need to be delicate with Mr. Roth." Said the doctor with strained patients. "He is still weak and disoriented after waking up. He needs time to get his barrens around you." Camille glared. "Now, if you would, let me check on my patient." Camille didn't respond. Instead, she pulled from Nolan, who didn't react to his wife's embrace as the doctor proceeded with his examination: checking his eyes and head that was no longer bandaged to the machines that recorded his vitals.

"Everything looks stable." The doctor concluded after typing his assessment on his tablet.

"How soon would he be able to leave?" Camille demands. The doctor hesitated as he looked down thoughtfully.

"Mr. Roth should be able to come home in two days." Camille nodded as Nolan stared with surprise.

"Home?" he breathes. Camille walked forward as the doctor stepped back.

"Yes, sweetie." She says cheerily. "Back to our mansion, you remember, right? That's where we live, you, me, and Essie." Nolan didn't respond to that; he looked out the window.

   Camille sat down on a nearby chair as the doctor left with a goodbye that Camille ignored, instead she babbled about what he missed while he was away.

"I know the staff misses you." She says. "They've been asking and wishing you a safe return." Nolan nodded once but didn't look at her. "Esme's been asking for you every day when uhm…" Camille trailed off her face flickered. "you know Esme, she's our beautiful daughter that we raised together. She will be so glad to see you. I'm sure you remember your daughter."

"I do." Camille started not because he had finally spoken to her but the tone that he spoke.

"I am well aware of who my daughter is."

A pause.

"Oh, well, th-that's great!" Camille smiles her award-winning smile. "You remember, the doctor said—"

"The doctor told me everything." Nolan spoke. slowly he turned his head to face Camille. "He told me that I could have experienced memory loss after the accident." His face harden as his gray eyes narrowed.

"But I remember everything." He spoke gravely.

Silence.

Camille stared at Nolan warily.

"Did you honestly believe you can take me for a fool?! To make me believe that you are innocent while you try to nurse me back to health?" Silence. "I know what you were trying to do, but your plan failed. I remember everything that night when you pushed me down the stairs."

"Nolan!" Camille cries. "I-I can explain!"

"Explain what?" he asks bitterly. Tears began to water in Camille's eyes. "Honey, I'm so sorry for what I did. I know you're upset with me, but we can move past this—we can go to counseling an—" Nolan pulled free from Camille, who had grasped his arm.

"Fix what, Camille?" he spoke coldly. "Us? This marriage?" he looked down at his bed sheets.

"There was no us. This was never about us. This marriage was doomed from the beginning. We've fought like cats and dogs for years. We've both fought under the same roof as the staff whispered gossip about us and the town…" Nolan felt pain in his head involuntarily he lifted a hand to it.

"Nolan!" Camille cries.

"I'm tired of this." He spoke. "I'm tired of keeping up this charade that we're the perfect family. I have to pretend to be a good man while I let others suffer for my crimes. I'm tired of letting my children suffer something they didn't do. This… This has to stop."

"Nolan." Camille breathes. "Just give me a chance we can work this out, we can fix this, just give it a few months and the town would forget about the accident and we—" Nolan pulled his face from his hand to glare at his wife.

"Is that all you care about!?" He yells. Camille flinched. "At this time, all you can think about is yourself!? Your reputation? Not the welfare of your husband or your daughter!" He shook his head.

"After all these years of trying to work out our marriage. I ignored every fault so I can become a better husband, but I'm not one, just like you've never been a good wife."

Nolan looked down at his hands.

"I'm giving you what you want."

"Wh-what?" Camille says. Nolan raised his head and face his wife, seeing her scar on her cheek.

"I want a divorce."

Chapter Thirty-nine

May flowers sprung up from the warming earth, bringing tidings of good omens for the promise of warm sunny days and cooling nights, where people could take in the beauty of nature from their busy schedules. Kate looked up at the bright orb of light, shielding her eyes to see the sun through the trees that swished lightly in the breeze, soaking in the warmth and getting a dose of vitamin D.

This day is perfect. She thought softly. Laughter and barking made Kate turn to see Rose and Pilot running a race with each other, with Pilot in the lead, barking merrily as Rose landed on the soft grass of early afternoon. Rose laughed as Pilot licked her face as Kate walked toward them. "Mommy!" Rose beamed. Kate smiled. "Is it ready, mommy?! The cake!?" "It sure is birthday, girl!" Kate replies. "Are you having fun with Pilot girl?" Rose nodded, lifting a hand to the German shepherd who sat beside her. Kate walked over to the dog and petted her, scratching her under the chin. Pilot laid down and turned onto her belly to be rubbed, to which Rose and Kate obliged.

"Mommy? When will Pilly have her babies?"

"In a couple of weeks," Kate says, looking down at the dog's swelling belly.

"I wish I could see them," Rose answers.

"You will, honey. You just have to be patient. The puppies need time to grow inside, Pilly." Rose nodded.

"I can't wait to get one." Kate smiles.

"Me too!" Kate agrees. "It was very nice of Emily to give you one of Pilot puppies."

"Emmi said I can pick a girl or a boy."

"Have you decided which one you want?"

"I want a girl puppy. So, I can dress her up in girl stuff." Kate laughs. "I wish Emmi was here." Kate nodded.

"She will be back next weekend with Uncle Joel and aunty Ivy and baby jack."

"Where did they go again, mommy?"

"They went on a boat ride." Rose nodded.

"I wish I could go too!" Kate smiles.

"Someday we will go." Rose nodded, smiling. "Now who's ready to eat confetti cake?"

"Me! Me!" Kate rose to her feet after sitting on the soft grass. Rose got up at the same time as Pilot who shook herself.

Kate walked forward as Rose ran for the house, laughing. All the while, a slight breeze blew Kate's dress as she took in the sunny sky.

"Mommy!" Kate looked from the sky to see Rose standing still by the door. Kate turned her gaze and saw a large luxury SUV park a few yards from the house. Pilot stood beside Rose just as Kate stepped beside her daughter.

"Mommy, who's that?"

"I don't know honey." Kate spoke. They both watched as a large fine dress man stepped out of the driver's seat. He waved to Kate, who wave back, wariness and a creeping fear started to squirm in her. The man opened the back door, and a figure jumped out of the car.

"Hi Esme!" Rose crowed when she saw the blond head walking forward grinning with joy holding a blue box under her arm, Rose ran forward, and the little girls embraced.

"Hi Rosy!" she says. "Hi Ms. Starfield." Kate stepped forward.

"Hello Esme." she replies kindly. Pilot came forward and barked, sniffing at Esme, who she petted.

"What are you doing here?" Rose asked. Esme beamed, before brandishing the box.

"This is for you." She says. Rose's eyes widen.

"For me?" she asks.

"Yes, for your birthday." Rose stared at the box with shock.

"Wow!"

"How did you know it was Rose's birthday?" Kate asks, surprised. Esme smiled as she turned her head.

"From daddy." She replies. Kate and Rose followed her gaze. Kate's eyes widen.

The sound of Pilot barking fell on deaf ears as Kate stared at the tall man who had emerged from the back seat, dressed in black pants and a matching tailored blazer, under a white shirt. One hand gripped a long brown cane while the other held a large bouquet of red roses. The man smiled gently as he stared at the small family that watched him with shocked eyes.

Kate's hand flew to her mouth. Her eyes watered, as she gazed at the face of Nolan Roth. Kate watched with silent awe as the man took his first steps upon the grass. His cane moved with him, supporting his weight as he limped slightly on his left leg. Birds chirped in the still air as mother and child stared at Nolan. Rose gripped her mother's right hand as she watched with timid eyes, pressing close to Kate's thigh. Nolan stopped. The two adults stared. Kate, watching Nolan with wordless amazement as the two children and dog watched quietly.

371

"*Hi.*" Nolan spoke. Kate blinked as lowered her hand from her lips. "*Hi.*" She breathes. Nolan smiled, dark gray eyes bright, shining, in the midday sun. He extended his left arm that held the bouquet.

"*This is for you.*" Kate stared at the flowers with surprise. Involuntarily, she took them from his hand; her eyes shining with unshed tears as she held the roses.

"*Thank you.*" She whispers. Nolan nodded before looking down at the child, who watched her mother quietly.

"*Hi, Rose.*" He spoke gently. Rose watched him before looking down shyly.

"*Hi.*" She says. Nolan kneeled, using his cane for support to look at her. The child met his dark gray with her brown.

"I know you don't know me very well," Nolan spoke. "I have not been a part of your life for many years but…" his eyes glazed over. "*I thought of you every day.*" He breathes thickly. Rose blinked at him.

"Why?" Rose asks. Nolan lifted his hand and took Rose's in his.

"Because you're very special, just like Esme is special to me." He replies. "I have not been there for you and your mother." He glanced at Kate before looking at Rose.

"I have done very unkind things to you and her and I am very sorry." Rose blinked at him with surprise. She looked up at her mother, who was crying silently.

"Mommy? What did Esme's daddy do?" She asks. Kate didn't answer as tears streamed her face.

"I was not here to take care of you, Rosy." Nolan answers. "I wasn't there for you when you needed me. I have kept away from you for many years. I could not see you or your mommy because of my *cowardice.*"

"Oh," Rose spoke.

"You see, Rose, I did something bad to your mommy, and for a long time I felt terrible because I couldn't tell her the truth."

"What truth?" Nolan looked up at Kate, who was weeping silently.

"That I wanted you," he confessed. "I was so happy to know that your mommy was having you." Rose stared at Nolan with puzzlement.

"You wanted me?" Nolan nodded, laying her hand on his cheek.

"I wanted to be a daddy to you just as I was to Esme. I didn't get the chance to before, but I can now." Kate's eyes widen at that. "Will you let me be with you, Rosy? Can Esme and I spend time with you and your mommy? Will you let me be a daddy to you?" Rose stared at him wide-eyed. She looked at Esme, who smiled before looking at Kate, as did Nolan, who watched her quietly.

Kate smiled through her tears. Rose looked at Nolan, her eyes began to water, and tears fell down her soft cheeks.

She nodded.

Tears pooled down Nolan's eyes as a shuddering breath escaped his lips. Involuntarily, he let go of Rose's hand, only to pull her into a one-arm hug. Rose sobbed, not understanding why she was crying when she was so happy. Nolan soothed her as he had never had the chance to do so before.

Kate wiped her eyes, watching father and child be reunited in happy tears; Esme cried. Letting go of his cane, Nolan pulled her in, connecting the two crying little girls.

"Who's ready for birthday cake?!" Kate asks cheerfully.

"Me! Me!" Rose cries. Rose held Esme's hand in her small ones. "Mommy, can Esme stay for my birthday?"

"Of course!" Kate says. "She and your daddy can stay!" Nolan rose unsteadily to his feet with his cane as Kate opened the door. Pilot entered with the two girls walking inside. Nolan motioned to the driver, who stood by the car holding several packages, to bring them into the house. Kate marveled at the parcels before she smiled up at Nolan, who was watching her tenderly. After Nolan told his driver when to return; Kate motioned with a hand for him to enter. Nolan obeyed with a nod before walking inside.

Kate looked out to her woodland home. A soft breeze blew gently, tickling her cheeks, and drying the last of her tears.
She turned her back and entered her cabin...

Shutting the door behind her.

The End

www.ingramcontent.com/pod-product-compliance
Lightning Source LLC
Chambersburg PA
CBHW020837020726
47497CB00005B/1134